I0818005

Causes and Courtships

Causes and Courtships

Zoe van Lingen

This is a work of fiction. Names, characters, places, and incidents either are the product of the author's imagination or are used fictitiously. Any resemblance to actual persons, living or dead, events, or locales is entirely coincidental.

Copyright © 2023 by Zoe van Lingen

All rights reserved. No part of this book may be reproduced or used in any manner without written permission of the copyright owner except for the use of quotations in a book review.

Cover design by

ISBN: 978-1-7776174-8-6 (paperback)

ISBN: 978-1-7776174-6-2 (ebook)

ISBN: 978-1-7776174-7-9 (hardcover)

Also by Zoe van Lingen

The Liberator Duology

The Liberator

The Vanquisher

To Gus. You were the sweetest bunny and my special buddy.

I'll miss and love you always.

July 11, 2012 – February 16, 2023

Note from the author

Causes and Courtships can be read on its own, or before or after The Liberator and The Vanquisher. However, it contains minor spoilers for a side plot in The Liberator Duology. I suggest reading The Liberator Duology first for a spoiler-free experience. If you don't care about spoilers, read on!

Chapter 1

Amelia sat on a stool at the bar of Restaurant Doma in Apartment District 1 and ran her finger over the rim of her glass. Her best friend, Dina Oliveri, was running late to their weekly Saturday meetup. Ever since she'd met and started going on dates with Jack Birch, Dina had been distracted.

The bell on the restaurant's door rang as Dina barged in. She let the door slam behind her, jogged to the bar where Amelia sat and claimed the neighbouring stool.

"I'm sorry, Mellie," Dina said, using the nickname she'd given Amelia when they'd met in the first year of school. Her grass-green eyes sparkled as she pushed a stray lock of hair away from her face. "The bus got stuck in traffic. I got off a few stops early and ran."

Amelia picked up her glass and swallowed a gulp of the water inside it. "You didn't miss much." There wasn't anything to miss. At sixteen, as her parents reminded her daily, Amelia had reached legal age to apply for a Courtship on Clinic Day – the City's legal form of romantic relationship for citizens sixteen or older and unmarried. Courtships were difficult to get, harder to break and always resulted in marriage.

Amelia wanted to make a difference, not get married and play house. The problem was her parents vetoed all her attempts to get involved in anything meaningful. Besides, the boys in her circle were dull, and Amelia didn't like girls that way.

"They still won't let you attend the protest?"

"No." Amelia's parents were adamant that participating in a protest, even one against rising food prices, was too dangerous. Amelia thought issue's importance outweighed the risk. That was a viewpoint her parents didn't share.

Dina waved the bartender over and ordered a glass of lemonade.

Amelia raised an – a silent question about how her friend could afford such a luxury.

Dina smiled as the bartender left to fetch her drink. "I've saved up some money, and I feel like celebrating."

"Jack asked you on another date?"

Dina flung her hands over her mouth to contain her giggles. When they subsided, she beamed. "He asked me to be his Courtship partner, and I said yes."

Marriage suited Dina. Anyone could see that she and Jack were infatuated with each other. "I wish you luck with your Courtship application," Amelia said, clinking her water glass against Dina's lemonade that the bartender had just brought.

Both girls drank and lowered their glasses with a thud. Dina swiped her lips with the back of her hand. "Is it weird that I'm looking forward to Clinic Day this year?"

"Not under present circumstances." Amelia wanted it to be over herself. Then her parents would stop their nagging, at least until after New Year. And she could go another year without worrying over the Government mandated medical tests and the threat of some disease her parents couldn't afford to treat sending her, or one of her parents, to the End Camp where poor, sick people went and never came back.

"Don't worry, your parents won't always be on your case," Dina said, placing her hand on Amelia's. She was wearing a silver ring with a pink gem on her ring finger, which must've been Jack's proposal gift to her. Dina hadn't been wearing it the day before. Amelia wondered how Jack, who was poorer than she and Dina, had saved the money for it, even with a fake stone. No one living in an Apartment District south of 2 bought real gems. Amelia imagined most buyers lived in the four rich Quarters in the north of the City. The farther south someone lived and the higher their Apartment District number was, to the maximum of 12, the poorer they were.

Dina's words weren't reassuring or believable to Amelia. Dina meant well though, so Amelia nodded and drank another sip of water. She and Dina fell into their usual routine, chatting about Jack, school and their parents for as long as they could until the bartender kicked them out for higher paying customers.

After giving Amelia a hug, Dina dashed out to meet Jack before curfew, which the Government set at sundown. Getting caught missing curfew meant being arrested for those too poor to pay the fine, and few people came home from the jail.

Amelia slid off her stool and meandered through the restaurant. Its dim lighting, papered walls and marble tables were more comforting than the beige walls and stark lights in her small apartment. She was grateful her parents rented a two-bedroom apartment. Still, most of their money went to the rent and food.

She smoothed the hem of her shirt to hide its fraying edge. At home, in her closet, she had brand new outfits her parents had bought when she turned sixteen. Her mom forbade her to wear them when she wasn't meeting a potential Courtship partner, and Amelia never did that, so the outfits went unworn. The outfits and her makeup, also reserved for dates and Clinic Day, were expenses her mom had justified by saying Amelia needed to impress whoever she might marry as her everyday pieces were cheap and worn. Amelia didn't think they made her look poorer than anyone else in her Apartment District, but that hadn't stopped her mom from spending a sizeable chunk of their budget.

She was halfway to the door, her mind on the lecture she'd get when she returned home about spending time with Dina instead of dating, when a haughty and shrill voice cut through.

"Malcolm, be serious. Why are you resisting the inevitable? You know we're perfect for each other."

Amelia focused on the table she walked towards. She hadn't meant to impede on this couple's date. Her legs had carried her that direction when she'd been rehearsing excuses to her parents, which were never that effective. She pivoted to change directions when the yellow-blonde, golden skinned boy, Malcolm, the girl had called him, spoke. His emerald green eyes weary.

"I won't marry you, Scarlet. It would be a mistake that we'd both regret. Stop trying to harass me into it."

The girl, Scarlet, flung her ash-blonde ponytail over her shoulder and narrowed her ice-cold, hazel eyes at Malcolm. Her face was red. She shoved her chair back with a screech and enough force to leave grooves in the floor and made Amelia cringe. "I won't give up. You'll change your mind. Someday." She stormed off as Malcolm downed the remnants of his glass.

Amelia had become too engrossed in the couple's fight to move far, and Scarlet, in her haste and fury, slammed into Amelia and shoved her to the side. Amelia screamed as she toppled over and flung her arms up to protect her head from the impact. How could she explain a head injury and hospital bill to her parents? They'd never be able to pay for it.

She closed her eyes, the floor closing in, when strong, warm arms caught her.

"Are you hurt?"

Amelia opened her eyes. Malcolm was in a crouch and holding her up, his brows wrinkled together.

"No." She wasn't injured, only a little sore where Scarlet had collided into her. Her heart was pounding from adrenaline, or maybe because a boy was holding her. Amelia hoped it was the former.

Malcolm helped Amelia to her feet and let her go. Her knees felt weak, and her cheeks warmed. Of all the times to embarrass herself. She'd have to tell Dina they couldn't come back, not after the scene she caused before a rich boy and his girlfriend.

"I'm sorry about Scarlet," Malcolm said, pointing his warm eyes at her. "She's too self-centred to watch where she's going."

Why was he still standing there? "Oh, I should've gotten out of the way. It was my fault."

Malcolm stepped closer to Amelia and pushed his hair back from his forehead, his eyebrows coming together. "You surely don't believe that, Miss…?"

Amelia gulped down the lump in her throat. It shouldn't have been a big deal to tell this boy her name, yet it felt overly intimate. "Amelia Ruby."

He offered his hand. "Malcolm Connor."

Amelia shook his hand. She thought that would be the end of it, but Malcolm walked beside her to the door and held it open.

"Where did you park?" he asked as they stepped onto the sidewalk.

"My bus stop is that way," Amelia said, pointing down the street to her right. Surely this would make Malcolm leave. A boy like him would only have interest in rich girls, ones that lived in houses not cramped apartments.

He stopped mid-step and cocked an eyebrow. "The bus? How long does that take?"

"An hour or so," Amelia said with a shrug, "depending on how many stops it makes."

Malcolm craned his neck back, surveying the late-afternoon sun. "You'll get stranded at curfew. I can drive you."

"No, I can't let you do that." What would the neighbours think? What would her parents think about her arriving at in a stranger's car? She didn't even know this boy.

"Please, it's the least I can do after Scarlet crashed into you. Besides, you did me a favour, and it's only fair that I repay you."

"What favour?" Amelia had done nothing except act as a crash pad for his girlfriend. She didn't see how that was of benefit to him.

Malcolm grinned. "You bolstered my belief that Scarlet isn't the one for me. Please, don't let me send you on a bus to get stranded."

Against her instincts, Amelia gave in. If Dina hadn't been late, or Amelia hadn't dallied, there would've been no risk of Amelia being out after curfew. As it was, her parents would be happy she was home in time if she got a ride. And when Malcolm found out where she lived, he'd never want to see her again.

She walked with Malcolm in the opposite direction from the bus stop. His solar powered car – all vehicles in the City, including buses, ran on solar power – was parked under the Restaurant Doma awning and gleamed like someone had recently polished it. There wasn't a dent or scratch on it. The seat was soft, and the car's interior was spacious, giving her much more legroom than on the bus. And the car didn't smell, not like the mix of grime and sweat that pervaded the bus.

Amelia fastened her seatbelt when Malcolm did his own. If this had been a date, sitting this close to him would have felt personal. As things stood, he was only doing this because he felt bad about what Scarlet had done. It didn't mean anything.

"Where do you live?" Malcolm asked as he started the car and pulled it from the parking space.

"Apartment District 6, Seventh Street."

Malcom turned his car onto the road leading south. "What brings you all the way to Apartment District 1? Surely there are restaurants closer to your home."

And closer to my budget, Amelia added in her head. She assumed that's what he implied. "My friend Dina and I meet here every week and drink water at the bar until they kick us out." It was an escape from parents' prying eyes and the drudgery of their neighbourhood.

He arched an eyebrow. "You've never ordered food?"

"No." If her parents had extra money, she might've. She'd watched diners get their meals and smelled the aromas from the kitchen. Partly why she and Dina had chosen the place was so they could fantasize about being able to eat there, seated at a table under a chandelier, wearing nice clothes and being the envy of all passersby. It was only a dream, one that wasn't possible.

"Someone could take you, one day."

Amelia thought she must've hit her head and been hallucinating. There was no way Malcolm met her eyes in the rear-view mirror when he spoke. He wasn't suggesting– No it was her mind playing tricks on her. "I doubt that. The only people I spend time with are my parents, my friend Dina and her boyfriend Jack. None of them have the budget."

"Someone else then. Like an intended Courtship partner."

Amelia blinked. This time she swore Malcolm made eye contact. "I don't have one, nor do I intend to."

Malcolm turned the car into Amelia's Apartment District, its buildings dingy and crumbling compared to those in Apartment District 1. The dust coating the streets would ruin the shine on his car. "I don't have one either, though I'd like to when I find the right person."

"What about Scarlet? She seemed eager." Amelia didn't recognize the bitter edge in her voice. The other girl's snobby demeanour had unsettled her more than she cared to admit.

Malcolm sighed. "She's after my parents' fortune so she can add it to hers. There are no feelings between us, but I am the only boy at school who isn't outright rude to her."

Amelia kept her opinion that Scarlet would disagree about not having feelings to herself. It was not her business anyway, and they were at her building. She signalled for Malcolm to stop, expecting him to let her off at the curb. Her fingers were on the door handle, ready to make a hasty exit from the boy she expected to never see again, when Malcolm pulled his car alongside the edge of the road and moved the gear shift to park.

He was out of the car and opening her door in the time she needed to unbuckle her seat belt. Amelia slid out of the car and quirked an eyebrow at Malcolm as he shut the door behind her, engaged the lock and pocketed his keys. *What was he doing?* "Thank you for the ride," Amelia said, her manners running on automatic. How many neighbours were seeing her standing on the street with a strange boy? It was best to look friendly, but not too friendly. She didn't want to give any spectators the wrong idea to gossip about or a reason to call a guard, a member of the Government's all-male combination of what the old world called the police and army, with sweeping powers to make arrests and enforce the laws. They wore black uniforms that covered every part of their bodies, making them unidentifiable except by their small nametags. Their helmets had one-way visors, letting the wearers see out and appearing shiny and black to everyone else. The guards looked like clones and were the only citizens allowed to carry and use weapons, and the only people allowed out after curfew. No one wanted a guard called on them; it seldom ended well.

"It was no trouble. Which apartment is yours?" Malcolm asked, his neck craned back as he surveyed her building.

"I can walk to it myself," Amelia said. "You don't need to come with me." Letting him go inside with her would definitely give the neighbours the wrong impression.

"You're not home until you get to your apartment. I'll leave you here, if that's what you want, but I'd like to make sure you get home safely. Scarlet will never apologize, and I feel guilty on her behalf."

Malcolm could've left Amelia at the restaurant, and she wouldn't have minded. He had nothing to be guilty about. Did he have other motivation? Amelia didn't know. The sun was starting its descent, and she didn't want to be caught on the street after curfew if she lingered to argue. Malcolm didn't appear a bit concerned about the time. Why would he when he was rich and could afford to pay a fine? However, there was only so much money could do if a guard found the two of them together on the street. Darkness had a funny way of turning innocent things suspicious. "Alright, you can come inside."

Chapter 2

The elevator was empty, sparing Amelia the embarrassment of explaining Malcolm's presence to a neighbour. And she wouldn't have to climb the stairs. Five flights always tired her legs. She pushed the button for her floor as the doors slid closed.

Her eyes found the floor counter, and she glued them to it as it ticked up: 1, 2, 3… its progress feeling slower than normal. Maybe standing in such a confined space with a strange boy was the reason.

Malcolm cleared his throat, causing Amelia to jump and tear her eyes off the counter. It had just reached floor 4.

"Are your parents nice?" Malcolm asked her, his eyes sparkling in the dim light.

"They will be." They always were around someone they viewed as a potential Courtship partner for her.

"They aren't normally?"

Malcolm was studying Amelia's face. *Why was he so interested in her?* Amelia didn't think of herself as a helpless wretch needing his pity. "They're even more so to someone they think I could marry. They'll *love* you."

Malcolm laughed as the elevator reached Amelia's floor and the doors opened. "Why? Because I'm handsome?"

He was handsome; she couldn't deny that. But it wasn't the sole reason her parents would swarm him. "No. Because you're rich."

Malcolm shrugged as he followed Amelia down the hallway. Thankfully, none of the neighbours were roaming. That didn't mean they weren't watching through the peepholes in their doors. She hoped they'd all exhausted their attention span for that.

"That's a shallow reason to like someone."

"Money has a lot of power. Surely you know that." He must've noticed a difference in the décor of her apartment building compared to the restaurant. The beige paint on the walls was faded, though not yet peeling, and the tiles lining the floor had long ago lost their lustre. There wasn't a single decoration on the walls, just a long stretch of hallway with apartment doors painted the same beige as the walls. The only changes in colour were the steel door numbers and the lit-up exit signs marking the stairways at either end of the hall.

Malcolm gave a curt nod. "Yes, too much power sometimes."

Amelia almost stumbled. Malcolm's statement was akin to things Jack said, a sentiment shared by supporters of the Cause. Amelia had never been to a Cause meeting or a protest, no matter how much she'd yearned to. Maybe if she played along with her parents' requests to go on a date, they'd let her attend one. That was doubtful. Perhaps she could finagle whatever date they set her up with into taking her.

She was still trying to form an answer to Malcolm's statement when the door to her apartment flung open and Amelia's mom shrieked.

"Nathan! Come quick, Amelia brought a boy home!"

No, no, no. "Mom, wait. I didn't—" Amelia stepped forward, stretching her hand out to stop her mom, who was already back in the apartment shouting for Amelia's dad.

Malcolm brushed Amelia's arm with his fingertips as he followed her inside. He stood mere steps away from where she stopped, and her eyes gravitated to him. "Don't worry," he said. "I'll straighten them out."

Amelia swiveled her head back to the door as her mom reappeared.

"This is so exciting," Amelia's mother squealed as she homed in on Malcolm. "Amelia has never brought someone home, other than Dina. Come and sit, I'll fetch something to drink."

Malcolm held his hands up in surrender. "That's kind of you, Mrs. Ruby, but I only offered Amelia a drive after my date knocked her over. I wanted to make sure she got home safe."

Amelia's mom stopped mid-step and plastered a polite smile plastered on her face. Hearing he'd been on a date that wasn't Amelia must've disappointed her. "That was generous of you. I shouldn't have jumped to conclusions. It's too much to hope that my daughter might have interest in someone."

"Mom—" Amelia groaned. She'd hoped her mom wouldn't make an embarrassing scene. Malcolm didn't need another reason to pity her.

Her mom walked off shaking her head, presumably to tell Amelia's dad that she hadn't brought a date home after all.

Amelia offered Malcolm her hand. "Thank you for the ride, and I apologize for my mom. She's overeager for me to get married."

Malcolm lingered by the door, making no move to flee, and clasped her hand. She'd expected him to shake it, not give it a gentle squeeze like he did. "She wants the best for you," he said as he slid his warm hand from hers, leaving it ice cold. He opened the door and stepped over the threshold. "I enjoyed talking to you, Amelia. Maybe we'll meet again."

He was down the hall before she could form a reply.

...

Causes and Courtships

Amelia had let her mom down again. She could tell by the way her mom's hazel eyes, the same shade as Amelia's, dimmed whenever she looked at Amelia. Her mother pursed her lips during supper, and gave repeated shakes of her head, her short brown hair bouncing off her shoulders and making her light skin paler than normal. Amelia played with her own hair, rubbing the light brown strands between her fingers, hoping her own light skin wasn't red from shame.

She hated disappointing her parents, but marriage seemed like a stifling trap. Attaching herself to someone permanently scared her. What if she stopped liking them? The worst thing imaginable to Amelia was being trapped in a Courtship, and later marriage, with someone horrid or boring.

Amelia stabbed her fork into the carrots on her plate. Their meal was simple and small like most nights: carrots, quinoa and bean salad. Oh, what wouldn't she give for seasoning other than salt? There was never any meat, dairy or eggs. Amelia had never tasted those foods as farm animals, alongside pets and wild animals, had gone extinct shortly after the climate crisis that led to the City's formation in the earth's inhabitable land far to the north. If there were any animals left, they were cockroaches in the poorest parts of the City where there was no money, or incentive, to exterminate them.

"Amelia," her dad said from across the table.

She dropped her fork and swung her attention on his face. His blue eyes didn't look angry. *Whatever he had to say couldn't be that bad.*

"Your mom and I want what's best for you. We hate to see you unhappy."

"I know, Dad." Here was the start of the lecture she'd anticipated.

"What your dad means is we've arranged a date for you on Monday. It's time you interacted with someone your age besides Dina."

Amelia froze. She'd expected this nightmare to come to fruition. "With whom?"

"Blake McKelvey is taking you out for supper."

Amelia swallowed back her groan. Blake McKelvey was the son of her mom's friend and one of the dullest people Amelia knew. *At least they'd both been set up by their parents. That would make letting him down easier. Or more awkward.* "What time do I need to be ready?"

"Five o'clock."

…

It came too soon. Amelia spent Sunday night restless, unable to get much sleep. She went to school and ran home from the bus stop on Monday afternoon. It wasn't out of eagerness to see Blake, but because she knew her mom would never let her go out without makeup or while wearing anything other than her reserved date clothes.

As soon as she closed the apartment door behind her, Amelia zoomed to her bedroom, tore off her outfit, pulled a dress out of her closet and pulled the price tag off. It didn't matter to her what dress she wore. If Blake hated the navy-blue colour of this one, that was even better.

In her makeup case, she ripped the packaging off some lip gloss and blush and dabbed some of each on her face. She didn't care if Blake thought she was attractive. The makeup was because she had to show her parents proof of effort on her part.

At the back of her closet, she found a pair of grey, ankle boots with a kitten heel. On her feet they went. They didn't feel uncomfortable, not standing in her room. She threw her usual lace-up, flat soled black boots in her bag anyway think it was better to have something broken in to put on her feet if necessary than to suffer through wearing heels all evening.

At exactly five o'clock, Blake knocked on her apartment door. Amelia grabbed her bag and exited her bedroom. Her mom had opened the door and was hugging Blake, who had spotted Amelia walk up.

"Hello, Amelia," Blake said as he stepped back from her mom and shoved his hands in his denim jacket pockets.

"Hi, Blake."

Amelia's mom put her hand on Amelia's back and steered her to the door. "You two have a good time."

"We will, Mrs. Ruby," Blake said as he grasped Amelia's hand and walked her into the hallway.

Amelia pulled her hand away from his as soon as they were alone, and her apartment door was closed. "I don't want to give you the wrong idea, so I'm going to tell you outright. This date wasn't my idea. My parents arranged it and made me go."

Blake snorted. "I know. So did mine. Let's just get it over with."

"Sure," Amelia said. "Where are we going?"

His brown eyes twinkled bright against his skin. "Catsy's."

"The place on the same street as this building? All they serve are sandwiches and salads."

He shrugged. "It's cheap."

Amelia rolled her eyes. She would've taken that as an insult if this had been a date she wanted to go on. As things were, at least she could afford her share.

...

Catsy's was a small café, with six sets of metal tables and chairs in the middle, on the ground floor of a high-rise apartment building. Along the walls were booths with padded seats covered in old and seldom cleaned vinyl. Amelia preferred the tables and led Blake to a vacant one. He didn't complain. Most patrons had a similar preference.

There was no greeter at Catsy's. Only one server, two cooks, a dish washer and a busser. When Amelia and Blake sat, only two other tables had customers. It didn't take long for their server, a girl with brown skin and bleached hair, to sidle up to them.

"You two on a date?" Her eyes darted between Amelia and Blake as she said this and pulled her note pad and pencil out of her apron pocket.

"Yup," Blake said.

It was technically true and would save them a lot of trouble, so Amelia kept her mouth shut.

The server accepted this and wrote down their orders. It wasn't hard to choose. The short menu was glued to the tabletop .and doubled as a placemat. Five minutes after ordering, their food arrived: a tempeh, lettuce and tomato sandwich for Blake, and a smashed chickpea and arugula sandwich for Amelia.

She knew how it tasted before taking a bite. Like her parents, the cooks at Catsy's didn't use much seasoning. Amelia and Blake talked about school and their moms as they ate. He was as boring as she remembered, and she cleared her throat when the server took their plates. Keeping her voice low, she addressed him when he glanced her way. "Thanks for the meal, Blake. I'm going to head home now."

He frowned. "You can't leave yet."

Amelia closed her eyes and counted to three in her mind. When she finished, she reopened her eyes and gave Blake a closed-lipped smile. "I'll pay my share, don't worry." She was opening her bag to pull money out of her wallet as she said this.

"I know. That isn't what I meant."

"Oh?" He couldn't have other activities in mind when he'd admitted to being roped into this date and to picking a cheap restaurant.

"Both of our moms will get the wrong idea. They'll say we didn't try to make this work."

They weren't trying to make it work, but she understood the benefit of their parents believing they had. "You have a point. And I get to choose our next activity." She had the perfect one in mind.

Chapter 3

Amelia couldn't stop herself from smiling. It wasn't because of Blake's company. He'd told her what a terrible idea hers was and went along with the excuse of keeping an eye on her and knowing he couldn't go home. On the walk to Government office on Fifth Street, Amelia tried to compose herself. She was finally going to attend a protest, or at least she was going to watch a protest. That was all Blake had agreed to let her do. It was enough for her first taste of action.

When they reached Fifth Street, Amelia had to hold herself back from joining the throng of people. Instead, she and Blake found spot a respectable distance away to watch with other spectators that were crowding the street. Amelia dragged Blake by the arm to get a better view near the front.

In the mass of protesters, she was sure she spotted a familiar flash of mousey brown hair. It *was* Dina holding hands with Jack, his chestnut hair a few shades darker than Amelia's and Dina's. They were walking to the front of the protest group, eyeing each other. Dina must've said something funny as Jack laughed.

"We should go." Blake said near Amelia's ear.

"We just go here. If we leave now, we'd still be home too early." She didn't want to leave, not when she was going to get her first experience of a protest. Someday it might be her participating. *It must come with such a thrill.*

"This isn't a good idea."

Amelia rolled her eyes. Blake was dull and dramatic, but she could try to comprise so he wouldn't trash talk her too much to his mom. "If something bad happens we'll leave."

Blake grumbled under his breath, and Amelia ignored him. She turned her attention back to the action where the demonstrators were organizing into lines in the parking lot next to the Government office. The crowd had swallowed up Dina and Jack, so she settled with watching the overall group.

The protesters hoisted handmade signs calling for lower food prices. In unison they swarmed the Government office and started to yell. "People are starving! Lower food prices!"

"Can't eat, can't work! Our City is crumbling!"

Amelia itched to join in and had had to will her feet to stay put. The people around her gave a mix of reactions. Some scoffed and laughed. Others looked pensive, like they agreed with the demands and feared taking a stand.

After a few minutes of shouting, a man in a black suit with slicked back hair strode casually out of the Government office, stood before the crowd and waited for the protestors to quiet. When he spoke, the words carried across the street to the spectators. "You have two minutes to clear the parking lot and the street." With his message delivered, he spun on his heel and retraced his path to the office.

Some of the protesters retreated, but a group of them swarmed the office, their signs clutched tight and held high. They screamed and pounded on the building, the man already inside and the door presumably locked.

As the people around Amelia trickled away, some power beyond her control forced her to stay. She needed to see how this ended. Blake was tugging her arm, which didn't matter or make her move.

She heard marching footsteps coming from down the street, the opposite direction from the one Amelia and Blake had come. They were in sync and rhythmic; uniformed guards were coming to clear the protest.

"Amelia!" Blake yelled. "We have to run!"

He gave one hard yank on her arm, and she snapped out of her daze. There was no way her parents would take her getting shot well. She wasn't sure if that would be better or worse than getting arrested. She sprinted with Blake the way they'd come, clutching her bag tight to her chest. *Of all the times to wear heels.* If Amelia had known she was going to run, she would've changed her shoes. There was no time now.

In less dire circumstances, she would've worried about Dina. Her friend would have to take care of herself and was capable of it.

The crowd thickened as Amelia and Blake sprinted down the street, and they elbowed their way through. The sun was still up, so at least she didn't have to worry about making curfew. Mercifully, the crowd thinned when she and Blake turned the corner to Seventh Street. Amelia bent over, placed her hands on her thighs and panted.

Blake scowled as he wiped sweat from his brow. "I shouldn't have let you talk me into that."

Amelia straightened up and pushed her hair out of her face. "I wanted to go home. *You* said we had to stay out longer!"

"Not so we could run from guards! We could've been arrested. And don't pretend you wouldn't have gone alone!"

"We weren't arrested!" She'd been worried too, but it was over, and they were safe. Did he have to make such a big deal out of it?

Blake crossed his arms, his nostrils flaring. "This was a stupid thing to do. We can't tell our parents."

"Perfect." She didn't intend to tell hers. They'd only be angry. Nor did she still plan to let them believe this date had gone well. "Are you going to let me go home now?" Regardless of the answer, that was where she was headed. She'd meant it when she'd first told him she wanted to go home.

Blake snorted. "Definitely. And I won't agree to a second date. Goodbye, Amelia." He stormed off to the apartment building and waved over his shoulder.

Amelia smoothed down her dress, which somehow had survived her sprint without getting too wrinkled, adjusted her bag and went after him. They lived on different floors of the same building. As a piece of rotten luck, they had to share an elevator as only one was on the ground floor. The other was on floor ten and would take too long to wait for, and her feet were too sore from her sprint in heels to the climb the stairs.

Amelia watched the floor counter to avoid looking at Blake. At least she would be rid of him on the fourth floor. She needed that moment of solitude to collect herself. When the doors opened to her hallway, she erased the frown from her face, ran her fingers through her hair to tame it, adjusted her bag on her shoulder and strode to her apartment door.

Her parents hadn't locked it, knowing she was on her way home. They were sitting on the couch facing the wall screen. The sound of Amelia closing the door and kicking off her shoes made her mom jump.

"Thank goodness you're home." Her mom sprung off the couch, ran to Amelia and wrapped her in a tight hug.

"What's wrong?" Her mom wasn't this jumpy on a normal day. Something must have happened.

"Guards circled and arrested protesters on Fifth Street en masse," her dad said as he rose from the couch. "We worried you might be one of them."

Amelia wriggled from her mom's arms and set down her bag. "Well, I didn't get arrested. Blake and I just went to Catsy's."

Her mom's face softened, like she felt sorry for Amelia, even though she'd arranged the whole event. "He took you there?"

A piece of truth might make them rethink arranging dates for her. Amelia heaved a dramatic sigh and hung her head. "He said it was cheap, like he didn't want to spend money on a better date, even though I paid half."

"I knew this was a bad idea, Sonia," her dad said with a shake of his head. "Meddling in Amelia's love life will only make us all miserable. She'll find her perfect someone when the time is right."

"Yes, you're right, dear," her mom said with a frown. "Amelia, can you forgive me for meddling?"

"Sure, Mom. If you'll stop nagging me about getting a Courtship." Maybe something useful could come out of this disaster of a date.

"That's fair, honey."

Amelia smiled as she walked to her room with her parents off her case, at least for now. The navy dress went in her laundry hamper in exchange for a t-shirt and jeans; she washed the remnants of her makeup off her face and flung her heels back into her closest.

She fell into a deep sleep and woke refreshed the next morning. Dina and Jack came to mind only after she'd gotten dressed, eaten breakfast and was grabbing her school bag. At lunch, she'd find Dina and check on her. They had to be okay.

...

After morning classes in her class group of students with surnames starting from P through R, Amelia went to the cafeteria, coins in her hand to buy lunch. It didn't get her much: an apple, glass of water and a peanut butter sandwich. She sometimes envied the students that could afford some of the warm meal options, or the ones that could buy, juice, dessert and a second helping. That was far from her mind this time as she navigated the room, tray in hand, searching for Dina. Lunch was the only time during the day she saw Dina, as students with surnames M through O, Dina's class group, ate with Amelia's.

At times she wondered what it would've been like to attend a school not separated based on the alphabet, like her parents had. But Amelia's school years occurred within the alphabet system imposed by the City's current Leader. There was no telling how many future Leaders would maintain it. Amelia's dad liked to say the only way to know the City had a new Leader was when there was an administrative change in something trivial like the day stores got deliveries or how schools grouped students. There were no elections or reveals of the Leader's identity, for their protection more than the benefit of citizens.

She'd almost given up on finding her friend, but there, at the back of the room, sat Dina eating a pear. Amelia zoomed to the table and sat across from her friend. "Dina!" Amelia squealed. "I was worried about you."

Dina set her pear down and peered at Amelia, her eyes wide and her lips forming an O. "Why?"

"Weren't you at the protest? A lot of people got arrested."

"Oh that," Dina waved her hand. "Jack and I left before the guards came." She ate another bite of her pear and wiped the juice off her mouth. "And we aren't going to another one. It's not worth risking arrest. Nothing ever comes out of protests."

Amelia's jaw fell. What nonsense was her friend spewing? "I thought you wanted to make things better."

"Public protests where the guards come earlier each time aren't the way."

"Then what is?" Amelia had wanted for so long to participate, and now her only contacts involved in the demonstrations were stopping their involvement. How would she ever make her a difference?

Dina gave an exaggerated shrug. "I wish I knew."

"But— What will I do without you showing me how to get involved? I want to help."

One side of Dina's mouth tipped up and she titled her head to the side. "I know, Mellie. Just, things are complicated right now. Don't give your parents more reasons to worry about you."

Amelia hadn't eaten any of her lunch yet, and now her appetite was gone. Her blood turned to ice, and her fingers gripped the edge of the table. Why was Dina taking the side of Amelia's parents? "More reasons?!"

Dina held her hands up. "Don't get angry. You know they worry about you finding a Courtship partner. You shouldn't add the risk of being arrested to their concerns."

"Actually, they've backed off on pressuring me into a Courtship." She wouldn't mention Blake. Their date was something better left forgotten and never mentioned.

Dina's eyes popped open. "What changed their minds? On Saturday you were stressing over them pressuring you."

Amelia shrugged and bit her sandwich. She'd spent money on the meal and couldn't waste it. There was no extra at home, and she couldn't go all afternoon without eating. "They realized I won't be happy marrying someone they pick out." That was enough of the truth without bringing up her disastrous date.

"How'd that happen?" Dina asked with narrowed eyes as she wiped her hands on a napkin. Her lunch was gone; she'd eaten most of it while Amelia was looking for her.

Amelia groaned. She'd hoped not to admit to this. "They made me go on a date last night."

Understanding dawned in Dina's eyes. "That's why you were so frazzled yesterday. How'd it go?"

"About as bad as it could've," Amelia said. She took a deep breath and dove into a recap of her disastrous date with Blake. There was no more avoiding telling Dina, and Amelia knew her best friend wouldn't tattle to her parents about Amelia roping Blake into attending the protest.

Dina frowned. "It's lucky your mom backed off on setting up dates, but I think you'll be lonely. If you get married, it needs to be someone you chose though."

"Don't you ever worry that someday you'll stop liking Jack? What if he turns out to be the most annoying person in the world, and you're stuck living with him?" Amelia couldn't stand the thought of being stuck with someone horrible for the rest of her life. As difficult as Courtships were to end, marriages were harder. She didn't know what made her this way. It wasn't like her parents hated each other, but she saw how they worried about each other and were codependent. Maybe that was it; she didn't want to get attached to a person only to worry constantly about losing them. Or worse, she could worry about not losing them.

"Everyone is annoying at one point or another. When you're in love, it doesn't matter as much."

In love. Dina did have experience in that subject. Would Amelia ever have some? And did she even want to?

Chapter 4

As the week progressed, Amelia's half expected her parents to change their mind and arrange another date for her. They didn't, nor did they mention Blake. Amelia counted it as a victory and rode the bus to meet Dina for their weekly Restaurant Doma visit on Saturday.

For once, Dina was there first and had reserved their seats at the bar. She hadn't however, ordered water.

"I tried," Dina said with a shrug as Amelia sat and set down her bag. "The bartender was busy."

Amelia surveyed the restaurant. It was as busy as it normally was when they came, yet not as full as it would be during supper. She'd found that out the previous week when Dina had been so late that the end of their visit had overlapped with the start of the supper rush. "We'll have to get his attention. If we don't order anything, he'll kick us out."

"I know."

"Maybe—" Amelia didn't get to finish her sentence as the bartender approached them with a tray laden with two glasses of lemonade and a plate of crostini topped with diced vegetables and onions and drizzled with a deep brown glaze.

The bartender balanced the tray on one hand and used his other to place the glasses and plate in front of Amelia and Dina.

Dina bit her lip.

Amelia was gaping and was powerless to stop it. Why was he bringing them food? "We didn't order this," she squeaked out.

"It's already paid for," the bartender said.

Amelia blinked. "What? Who would do that?" She had no rich friends. Was one of the regular patrons taking pity on her? She didn't think she looked starved or disheveled.

The bartender shrugged. "He didn't give me his name. Only this." He fished a torn piece of note paper out of his apron pocket and offered it to Amelia.

She took the note, flipped it right side up and read.

I thought you should try this. It's one of the best tasting things on the menu.

M.C.

M.C? She racked her brain for recognition of whom she knew with those initials.

"Mellie?" Dina asked, snapping Amelia out of her fog. "Should we eat it?"

Amelia's friend's eyes were on the plate. It did look good, and Amelia's stomach grumbled. "It's already paid for, so we shouldn't waste it." She wasn't about to refuse a loophole around the food laws in her benefit.

She picked up one of the pieces and bit it. The bread crunched then softened in her mouth when mixed with the tomatoes and the tart sauce. The note giver was right; it tasted delicious. She and Dina ate the crostini, three pieces each, and sipped their lemonades.

Amelia's mind was busy trying to puzzle out the buyer's identity, and she let her friend chat away about school and Jack. It wasn't that difficult to contribute responses to the conversation.

As Dina talked and Amelia thought, an ash-blonde girl wearing bright red lipstick sat on a bar stool a few away from Amelia. She leaned forward and snapped her fingers to get the bartender's attention, and he turned to her when she spoke, the words dripping with snobbery. "Are you *sure* no one is waiting for me? I don't get stood up."

"As positive as I am that the sky is blue, Miss Scarlet."

Scarlet. Amelia bolted upright in her seat. She knew who had sent the food as Scarlet huffed and barked her food order at the poor bartender. Amelia waved him over, and he gave her a grateful smile as he left Scarlet, her face red and nostrils flared.

Amelia smiled closed mouth at the man. "Can you take me and my friend to the boy who sent this food? We'd like to say thanks."

"Certainly, Miss...?"

"Amelia," Amelia said as she slid off her seat and beckoned Dina to do the same.

"Right this way, Miss Amelia," the bartender said as he exited through the swinging employee door in the bar and strode across the restaurant.

Amelia sauntered after him with Dina beside her.

"Did you figure out who sent our food?" Dina asked.

"Yeah. The boy I met last week after you left." She'd forgotten to tell Dina about Malcolm in her worry over the protest and her recap of her date with Blake. And she hadn't expected to see Malcolm again, let alone to receive gifts from him.

Dina stopped and squealed. "A boy? You met a boy and didn't tell me?"

"It's no big deal. He took pity on me after his date," she pointed her thumb at Scarlet, "collided with me. I'm sure this is more of that."

Dina chuckled behind her hand.

Amelia put her hands on her hips and turned to her friend. "What's so funny?" She didn't want Dina to lower Malcolm's opinion of her even further.

"Oh nothing," Dina said around giggles as she walked on after the bartender. "I just don't think a boy would send you food out of pity. You don't look that destitute."

Amelia rolled her eyes and stepped into a table as she tried to catch up. She wobbled on her feet and flailed her arms to keep from toppling over, earning her sneers and grumbles from the seated diners as their drink glasses tipped. She muttered an apology and swung her attention on her surroundings as they righted their glasses. Hopefully, Malcolm hadn't noticed her stumble.

To her rotten luck, she'd tripped within a couple metres of his table. He definitely had noticed. Amelia's cheeks warmed, and she was sure they were pink. How humiliating was this?

Malcolm broke into a grin as the bartender deposited Amelia and Dina at his table.

Before he could laugh at her, she stuffed her hands into her pockets and cleared her throat. "Thank you for the food and lemonade. It tasted as good as your note said."

"You're welcome. I thought you and your friend would enjoy it." He looked at Dina then, who was hovering beside Amelia, trying not to laugh. "Your name is Dina, right?"

"Yes," she squeaked.

"It's nice to meet you," Malcolm as he stood and offered her his hand.

Dina shook it, practically bouncing on her heels. "It's nice to meet you too. Amelia didn't even tell me she'd met you until just now."

Malcolm chuckled. "I suppose I didn't make as strong of an impression as I thought."

"Did he, Amelia?" Dina asked with a raised eyebrow. She was enjoying this too much.

"Oh, I don't know," Amelia said, trying to be nonchalant. "We have a bus to catch, Dina. Let's go." She wrapped her fingers around Dina's arm and tried to steer her away from Malcolm.

Dina didn't budge. "It doesn't come for another—"

"We can get better seats if we get to the station early. Come on."

"I can drive you home again if you'd like," Malcolm offered. "I'd like to get to know your friend better."

Before Amelia opened her mouth to launch a protest, Dina squealed. "That would be fantastic!"

"What do you say, Amelia?" Malcolm had fixated his eyes on her. She hadn't thought of herself as interesting or alluring, but he seemed to think so.

"Just promise we won't make a habit out of this. I'd feel guilty."

"You shouldn't," Malcolm said as they started walking to the door. He was keeping close to Amelia, and she made no effort to increase the distance between them. What was wrong with her?

Dina, walking ahead of Amelia and Malcolm, stifled a chuckle, and Amelia rolled her eyes at her friend. "That's nice of you to say," she said to Malcolm.

"I didn't say it to be nice," he replied. "I meant it."

She didn't get a chance to add to their conservation as they passed the bar, and Scarlet leapt to her feet and flung herself at Malcom, making him stop walking. "There you are!" She draped her arms around his neck and licked her lips as she gazed at him.

Amelia stopped walking, not noticing Dina slink out the door. She wanted to shove Scarlet away. It was an alien feeling, which she chalked up to the desire for revenge after Scarlet's collision the week prior.

Malcolm grasped Scarlet's wrists, lowered her arms from his neck and stepped away. "Why were you looking for me?" The tone of his voice portrayed his annoyance and buoyed Amelia's spirits.

She didn't know why she cared whether Malcolm liked Scarlet. It wasn't like he meant anything to her.

"I gave you a week," Scarlet said with a dramatic pout and an eyelash flutter. "Surely you've realized we're a perfect match."

Malcolm huffed. "I was serious when I said I won't marry you."

"Who else could you—" Her eyes bugged open midsentence as she noticed Amelia. "Oh. You're smitten with an Apartment District girl." Her lips twisted into a wicked, toothy grin, and she set her eyes on Amelia. "Good luck fitting into his world and winning his parent's approval. When you fail, and you will, he'll chose me. I can be patient."

What was Scarlet talking about? Amelia wasn't trying to take Malcolm from her. "I don't want—"

"Leave Amelia alone, Scarlet. She's not the reason I won't marry you. I told you that before I even met her."

"I'm not naive," Scarlet said, one hand on her hip and fury blazing in her eyes. "You'd never reject me unless it was for another girl."

Malcolm placed his hand on Amelia's arm and steered her to the door. "You're making a scene. Don't embarrass yourself any further." He grasped Amelia's arm and walked with her out of the restaurant, where they found Dina standing on the street.

"Who was that girl?" Dina asked. "She looked scary."

"Just someone I know," Malcolm said with a wave of his hand as he released Amelia's arm.

Amelia liked that description. It made Scarlet seem unimportant, and she *was* unimportant. What had made her desperate enough to throw herself at a boy clearly uninterested in her?

"I don't think I'd like to know her," Dina said as they all waked to Malcolm's car.

He laughed. "Probably not."

Amelia cleared her throat. She didn't want to discuss Scarlet. "You can take the front seat, Dina. I'll sit in the back."

"If you're sure," Dina said.

"I am." Amelia's hand was already on the rear door handle.

She slid onto the rear seat, glad to have the front seat as a barrier between her and Malcolm. It was necessary so she could clear her thoughts without him eyeing her. Getting rid of Blake had been easy; they'd shared mutual disinterest and meddling parents. Malcolm was different. Would she have to shut herself into her bedroom and stop meeting Dina on Saturdays to avoid seeing him? Did she want that? He was nice and attractive. It couldn't hurt to get to know him, but then he'd leave just as she dropped her guard. Why was it so hard?

Chapter 5

Malcolm dropped Dina off first, her apartment being a couple streets from Amelia's. He insisted on driving Amelia, even after she'd suggested she could walk home from Dina's. She didn't understand the fuss. The sun was still up, and it wouldn't take her that long to walk. She'd done it countless times. At least he didn't follow her inside this time.

When Amelia reached her room, she flopped onto her bed. All week, thoughts of how she could help people consumed Amelia. It felt more important now that Jack and Dina had stepped back from protesting. The problem laid with where to start. Now that her contacts were gone, how would she ever make an impact?

She tossed and turned all night and woke up exhausted. When she got dressed in the morning and left her bedroom, she bumped into her mom.

"Good, you're up early enough that we won't have to fight for the scraps. Come along, Amelia. You can eat on the bus."

Amelia blinked as her mom thrust shopping bags at her and a piece of toast. Her mom was in a hurry for their shopping day. Amelia liked going to the market, which she and her mom did on Sundays, as it meant in the next few days, they'd have to eat some of the food they bought to stop it from spoiling. The Government had worked wonders in getting a variety of grains, legumes and vegetables to grow in greenhouses, but even their technology couldn't stop things from rotting in the heat.

Amelia nibbled her toast while she and her mom rode the bus, having to stand in the aisle as no seats were vacant. She clutched the shopping bags to her chest with one hand and held onto a handle dangling from the bus's ceiling with her other once her toast was gone. Riding the bus to the restaurant to meet Dina was more pleasant than this. Heading to the wealthier Apartment Districts and the rich Quarters usually meant fewer passengers. This bus ride was to a different street in their own Apartment District, and many of the fellow passengers must've had the same idea to do their shopping that day as Amelia spotted plenty of riders with bags in their pockets and hands.

The bus emptied at the stop near the market on the ground floor of a high-rise. The door to the upper floors wasn't visible inside the market, and Amelia knew no one who had ventured to them or was aware of what they contained. Her best guess was that there were offices, storerooms or apartments up there, or some combination of all three.

Amelia rushed after her mom to the market entrance, trying to keep sight of her mom and not get trampled by the crowd. Inside the market was spacious enough that she didn't feel jostled once she got through the door.

On the outside windows, as well as periodically spaced throughout the aisles and at the registers, was a sign advertising the food laws: NO SHARING, NO RESELLING, NO REFUNDS. The laws prohibiting sharing and refunds were universal and punishable with jail time. Restaurants and cafeterias got around the no reselling law with special permits, which were the only exceptions and difficult to get. Smart planning and shopping were vital for citizens as they couldn't ask a family member, neighbour or friend for a needed ingredient. And if you didn't check produce for freshness before you paid, you were out of luck and money if it rotted before you could eat it.

Amelia put her arm through the shopping bags' straps, commissioned a cart and trailed her mom, who had their list. She concentrated on steering the cart wherever her mom went. It was a challenge to move so fast, and she bumped into a few other shoppers along their route. "Sorry," she called over her should each time she or the cart bumped into them. By the time the apology left her lips, she was too far away to hear their reply.

The cart got heavier and harder to push as Amelia and her mom moved through the market. If they'd only been buying food, like most weeks, it wouldn't have been that bad. However, her mom had decided to stock up on their other household necessities this week. Amelia didn't know how they would carry everything home on the bus.

They were in the checkout line, with people both ahead of and behind them, when her mom groaned. Amelia flicked her eyes around, checking to see if anyone was listening, before asking what the matter was.

"I forgot to grab dish soap. Would you run back and grab some? I can stand with the cart, and you are much faster."

"Sure," Amelia placed the shopping bags on top of the cart – there was no need to drag them back through the store – waited for her mom's hands to close around the cart's handle and darted out of line.

The dish soap aisle was along the back wall of the market, almost as far from the check out as possible. There was a man in his thirties leaning against the shelving unit, his hands in his jeans' pockets and his legs crossed at the ankle. Amelia tried to ignore him and searched for the type of dish soap her parents liked. It had to be on one of the higher shelves. She stretched on her tiptoes, her fingers brushing the bottle and unable to grasp it.

The strange man plucked a bottle off the shelf and held it out to Amelia in his large hand. "Dish soap, huh?"

Amelia grabbed the bottle from him. "Yes. My mom sent me to get it."

The man raked Amelia up and down. "Price has gone up. As with most items in this store. You sure you can afford it?"

"We have to." Amelia turned to leave, knowing her mom was waiting. If she dallied, it would make her mom suspicious, and Amelia didn't want that attention.

"That won't last forever. What'll you do after the next prince increase? At some point people will need to make sacrifices or try to change things."

The man's words stopped Amelia in her tracks, and she turned back to face him. "What kind of change?"

He shook his head, his dark hair flying over his ears. "Go back to your mom before she wonders where you went. Come to the corner of Second and Third Street tomorrow at four o'clock and knock twice if you want to learn more."

Amelia swallowed the lump in her throat and willed her pulse to calm. Was this man luring her away to be murdered? "Why should I trust you?"

He shrugged. "Does trust matter when I've given you the chance to help with something important?"

"Yes." How could she take this stranger's word? Even if he'd offered her what she'd wanted for a long time, it felt too good to trust.

The man sighed. "A friend of yours said you were interested in helping people. I can't tell you more than that."

Had Dina? She must've. "How did you know how to find me?"

"You friend told me you'd be here today. Now go, or you'll have too much explaining to do."

...

Amelia jogged to her mom in line, who had moved ahead a couple of places.

She placed the dish soap in the basket and tried to act like a stranger hadn't just tempted her with her strongest desire.

"Did you have a hard time getting the soap?" her mom asked, narrowing her eyes in concern.

"It was on the top shelf, so I had to find an employee to reach it." There was some truth in that. A partial truth was better than an outright lie. At least that's what Amelia told herself. Her mom didn't question it.

They paid for the supplies, the price of which made her mom cringe and dig deeper into her wallet. The stranger had told Amelia the truth; everything had gone up in price. With the cost not displayed on the shelf, people had little choice except to pay for their goods. The alternative was to send items back and suffer that embarrassment as well as annoyance from the others in line for delaying their checkout. People in Amelia's Apartment District, and most others, only added essential items to their carts. They weren't buyers of luxury items.

Amelia hefted half of the bags into her arms and walked with her mom to the bus stop. They didn't have a long wait and were lucky enough to find seats together. Once Amelia sat, she was not going to move until the bus reached their stop. She ignored the longing gazes and glares of passengers that boarded once all the seats were taken. It wasn't her fault she got there first.

...

That night for supper, Amelia and her parents ate stew full of vegetables that wouldn't last long if left uncooked. Amelia's mind wandered through the meal and the hours afterwards. Her curiosity and determination won out. She had to go to the meeting place.

Her parents bought her excuse of needing to stay late after school to discuss an assignment with a teacher. Amelia wasn't a habitual liar, but they would never have let her go if she told them her true plans. It only gave her a mild degree of guilt, not enough to change her mind.

After a restful sleep, Amelia stressed over what to wear. Her normal wardrobe wasn't impressive, and she couldn't wear one of her fancy dresses to school without raising suspicion from her mom. And besides, her parents hadn't given Amelia permission to wear those clothes when they said they'd stop forcing her to date.

She found a clean, not too faded, pair of dark jeans and blue t-shirt with white Swiss dots in the back of her closet. At least the outfit wouldn't make her look too poor, and it was practical. But it was difficult to keep it clean on the bus, so Amelia sat on her backpack.

After school, she rode a City bus to Third Street, and she disembarked with minutes before the assigned meeting time.

With a deep breath, Amelia ran in the direction of Second Street. Dina lived near this part of their Apartment District, so Amelia had a sense of the right direction. It helped that the odd and even numbered streets in each Apartment District ran in a grid, with odd streets parallel to each other and perpendicular to even streets. When she reached the intersection, she wiped the sweat from her brow and approached the building on the corner that looked different from the others.

This had to be the meeting place. It was short, compared to the neighbouring office buildings, and had steps leading up to a small door with a covered window where most buildings in the City had street level entrances. Amelia steeled her resolve, climbed the concrete steps and knocked twice. She'd just lowered her hand when the window cover slid open on the inside of the door.

A pair of eyes, the only thing she could see, peered through the gap.

"Name?"

It was a gruff voice, which didn't intimidate her. "Amelia Ruby."

"Ah. The recruit. You may enter."

Before Amelia could protest that she wasn't a recruit, as she didn't know what she was being recruited for, the door opened. She stepped into the dark void of the building, and as soon as her feet crossed the threshold, the door slammed shut behind her, making her flinch.

She couldn't see anything. Whoever used this space didn't invest in a great lighting system.

"Go downstairs and turn right."

Amelia jumped. The eyes she'd seen through the slit were now centimetres from her. They belonged to a man, she surmised from the tone of the voice. She couldn't make out any of his features apart from his brown eyes.

"Downstairs? In this dark?" Was coming here a mistake? Delivering herself to her own demise was a possibility growing in likelihood, and her heart thumped in her chest.

The man laughed and she saw a flash of his white teeth. His shadowed face wasn't what she wanted as the last image she ever saw.

He clicked on a flashlight and pressed it into her hand. "Don't trust you enough yet to turn the lights on. Use this and be careful where you aim it."

Amelia tightened her grip on the flashlight, pointed it at the floor ahead of her and exhaled at the sight of steps. There was no handrail, so she trod carefully, using the flashlight to illuminate the step ahead of her. It was a long staircase, and there were no sounds except her footsteps, breathing and her racing heart. When she reached the bottom, she gulped and turned right down the hallway.

That was the only instruction that man at the door had given, so Amelia walked on with the dim flashlight displaying little of the surroundings. The floor was made of large stones with footpaths worn into them and making them uneven. It was an uncommon building material, at least in newer City buildings, making her guess at how old this place was.

Amelia was part way down the hallway when a door ahead and to her right opened with a creak of a hinge in need of oil. This had to be her destination.

Chapter 6

Amelia reached the door and staggered on her feet. There was light coming from the other side, and whoever had opened it had left it ajar. With a deep breath, she wrapped her hand around the knob and pushed. The hinge emitted a long and loud creak, making her presence known if it wasn't already.

People in the room laughed. There were more than a couple voices. Amelia turned to look back the way she'd come, tempted to retreat, but the door was open now and light spilled over her. At least one person in the room had spotted her.

A boy with chestnut brown hair, creamy skin and hazel eyes went to the doorway. *Jack.* "I knew you'd come."

Amelia's jaw dropped. "You're the one that gave my name?" She had expected Dina, not her boyfriend. She didn't know Jack that well.

He nodded. "Dina said you wanted to help, so I'm giving you a chance. You need to come out of the hallway though."

On shaky legs, Amelia stepped over the threshold into the unknown. She hovered near Jack, glad to have one acquaintance in this place. The man who'd invited her wasn't in the room. The people present were younger, around Amelia's age. There were three girls on a couch and two other boys, a brunette leaning against the arm of the couch and the other, a dirty-blonde, standing.

"So, Jack," the standing boy said. "This is your recruit?" He appraised Amelia, his eyes giving little away.

"My name is Amelia," she said, putting one hand on her hip. Her pulse had slowed. If someone was going to murder her here, they would've done it in the hallway, and she trusted Jack enough to believe she wasn't in danger.

"She's got spunk," one of the girls, a red head, said.

The standing boy gazed at Amelia. "Spunk or not, we only have Jack's word to base our trust on."

"So, we test her out," the leaning boy said with a shrug.

"Test me?" Amelia still had no idea what she'd gotten involved in, but she wanted to help people. How was meeting in this old, dark building going to accomplish that?

"He means we take you on a mission," Jack said. "See how you do with some action."

"What kind of action?" Were they going to take her to a protest?

The girls on the couch looked at each other, and the one in the middle, with dark skin and black hair, spoke. "We'll take you on a delivery to Apartment District 12."

Amelia had never been that close to the City's wall, or that far south. Her parents hadn't encouraged her to travel to the poorer Apartment Districts. She knew it was the most destitute part of the City, and not much else. "What are you delivering?"

The girls on the couch averted their eyes, as did the leaning boy and the standing one. It was Jack who answered her. "We don't know. We get crates and sacks, drive to the drop off location and unload them."

"You don't know?" Amelia wasn't sure how she felt about transporting mystery, possibly illegal goods. Her parents would never get off her case if she was arrested for smuggling or breaking the food laws.

"The fewer people that know the better in cause the guards interfere," the standing boy said. "They can't dismantle our entire operation if they can't get intel."

"This sounds dangerous," Amelia said, clasping her hands tight to stop them from shaking. She had to be responsible and realistic. She wasn't a hero, only a naïve girl that had gotten in over her head. "I don't know if I can."

"You'll have to decide," the black-haired girl said. "We go in two days."

"Come on, Amelia," Jack said, offering her his hand. "I'll walk you home."

Amelia seized the chance to leave the dark, creepy building, though she didn't relish the idea of traipsing through the pitch-black hallway and up the stairs again with only a flashlight. She needn't have worried as Jack flicked a switch on the hallway wall she never would've found, and small sconces set along the hallway where the walls met the ceiling flicked on.

The hallway was dingy and dirty in the light. At least she could see where she was going as she followed Jack. There was no man at the door when they climbed the stairs, only a doorway jutting off the entrance where Amelia assumed he'd gone. She wasn't too eager to see him anyway and didn't ask Jack about him.

They'd exited the building without speaking, and Amelia broke their silence when they descended the outside stairs. "Dina said you two aren't going to protests anymore."

He sighed. "They don't accomplish anything. The Cause is moving away from visible displays, and the rumour going around is that the Government wants to file them as subversive, and illegal."

"What are you going to do instead?" If Amelia knew one thing about

Jack, it was that his desire to help people was as great as her own, if not greater. That and their mutual like of Dina were the things in common Amelia and Jack had.

"We're going underground," Jack said.

Amelia looked down at the street, imagining a tunnel running under it, or a giant meeting room. "Underground? Won't people see you digging?"

"Not literally under the ground. Just out of sight and secret, so the Government can't find us."

"Oh. And you'll still help people?"

"You're awful curious for someone who doesn't want to go on a mission."

Amelia closed her eyes. "My parents will kill me if I get arrested. They don't want me to get involved with the Cause at all."

"You won't get arrested. It's only a car ride and moving some crates and sacks."

"And if there's food in them?" Amelia had feared the food laws since she could first read the sign. Buying a meal for someone, like Malcolm had at the restaurant, was the only loophole around the no sharing law.

"The food laws keep the poor starving by design. If there is food in the crates, someone took a significant risk to get it for people in the worst Apartment District in the City. I think breaking the food laws is justified when the crime is better than the law."

"You're brave," Amelia said as she and Jack walked. "I'm not sure I am."

"You're letting your fear of your parents reprimanding you stop you from doing what's right. And you know this is right, or you wouldn't have shown up today."

Amelia hadn't known what she was showing up to, but he was right. She was finding excuses not to go when participating in the Cause was all she'd wanted since she saw her first protest on the wall screen as a small child. It had looked so thrilling and exciting. Couldn't she take a risk and help people in need? "Alright, I'll come. Where do I go?"

"The same place at the same time in two days. I'll make sure the lights are on."

...

Jack kept his promise. When Amelia returned, could see light shining through the door slit. Again, she knocked twice and gave her name. The gruff voice belonged to a man with a hardened face. He narrowed his eyes at Amelia as she skirted past him and down the stairs. She didn't try to talk to him, thinking he wasn't the friendly or chatty type.

When Amelia turned the corner at the bottom on the stairs, the meeting room door was open. The boys she'd seen on her first visit were exiting as Amelia neared.

They turned at the sound of her footsteps, and their eyes widened. Jack appeared behind them and swatted the boy nearest to him, the brunette, on the arm. "I told you she'd come, Ethan."

"Heh," the boy, Ethan, said with a shrug. "So, you did."

"Lucas!" One of the girls called from inside the room. "You forgot your keys!"

The dirty-blonde boy, presumably Lucas, grumbled. "Bring them out here, Kylie."

Jack walked over to Amelia as the red-haired girl exited the doorway and thrust the keys at Lucas. "You'll grow to like us."

"I suppose I might." Amelia had liked Jack well enough since Dina had introduced him to her. It wasn't romantic. He and Dina had eyes and feelings only for each other, but Jack had never made Amelia feel awkward or like the friend dragged along out of pity on the occasions the three of them did things together. "Does Dina ever help with deliveries?"

"She used to," Ethan said, answering Amelia's question. "Why don't you tell Amelia why your girlfriend stopped, Jack?"

Jack wiped his hand over his face and groaned. "I'd rather not. Dina would dump me."

"Wait a few months and she won't be able to," Ethan said.

Amelia didn't think Dina would dump Jack no matter how embarrassing or bad the story was. She also knew she had to hear it. Perhaps Ethan would tell her since Jack was too reluctant.

Jack swatted Ethan on the arm again, his eyes narrowed. "Are you saying I'm trapping her?"

"Stop provoking Jack, Ethan," Kylie said. "We all know Dina loves him."

She did. Amelia saw the way her friend's face glowed with every mention of Jack. It almost made Amelia want that for herself, though she still feared being unable to leave a bad Courtship. She didn't even want to imagine the pain of enduring a Courtship review and denial. It was safer and easier to stay on her own.

"We don't have time anyway," Lucas said, twirling his keys in his fingers. "We're running late if we want to make it back before curfew."

Kylie grasped Amelia's hand and pulled her nearer to the meeting room door. "We'll get the stuff. You three," she said to the boys, "go get the truck."

Jack, Lucas and Ethan walked off down the hallway past the meeting room. Amelia had never glanced that way, and she presumed it led to an exterior door. She couldn't assess that assumption at that moment as Kylie yanked her into the meeting room, dropped her arm, picked a hooded jacket off a couch and threw it at Amelia.

"Put that on to cover your hair."

Amelia did as Kylie said while Kylie donned a stretchy hat and tucked her red hair under its brim. The jacket was black denim and a bit big, but the hood stayed up and shielded her hair. "Where are the other girls?" It was only her and Kylie in the room, with some sacks and crates piled on the floor.

Kylie crouched near one of the sacks, tying it closed. She didn't look at Amelia. "Hannah and Brooke will keep watch outside while we're gone. You're taking Brooke's place on the run."

Amelia hadn't wanted to take anyone's spot. "I could stay here."

Kylie straightened up and placed her hands on her hips. Her hardened eyes bored into Amelia. "You're coming with us. You got no choice now."

"But Brooke—"

"Oh, you think she'll be angry," Kylie said, recognition dawning in her eyes. "Don't worry about it. She was happy to stay here with Hannah since we can only take four people plus the driver. And Hannah's been complaining about doing watch duty solo."

"Okay." Amelia didn't want anyone to resent her for taking their place. Kylie seemed convinced Brooke wouldn't mind, and Amelia didn't even know which of the other two girls Brooke was.

Amelia helped Kylie heft the sacks and carry them into the hall. They were heavy, but not any worse than her mom's loaded shopping bags after shopping day. She followed Kylie down the hallway to a propped-open door at the end. When Kylie set her bag on the ground, Amelia did the same. Then she lingered in the door as Kylie turned to fetch the next sack.

The door opened to a small parking lot at the back of the building. Jack and Ethan were at the rear of a pick-up truck lowering its tailgate and taking a fabric cover off the bed. The truck's lights were on, and Amelia saw a male silhouette, Lucas she assumed, in the cab. When Jack and Ethan got the cover clear of the truck bed, they folded it, and Ethan carried it to the doorway where Amelia stood as Jack walked beside him.

Amelia stepped back, hoping they wouldn't be angry she was watching them. On the contrary, Ethan grinned and gave her the folded truck cover. "Bring this to the storeroom for me, won't you, Amelia?"

She took the cover, its fabric sturdy and rough against her skin. "If that's where it goes."

"Don't boss her around, Ethan," Jack said.

Ethan ducked his head and scuffed his right shoe along the asphalt. He peered up at Amelia, and she saw vulnerability on his face. That wasn't an emotion he seemed to show often. "I'm sorry. Will you please carry it?"

"Sure, Ethan," she said. "I don't mind."

He gave her his thanks as she turned and ran back to the storeroom. She was starting to like this sect of the Cause.

Chapter 7

Amelia rode in the backseat of the truck with Jack, Kylie sat up front with Lucas, and Ethan sat on the truck bed with the cargo. It had taken Amelia's and Kylie's combined strength to carry the metal crates from the storeroom. Jack, Ethan and Lucas had loaded them onto the truck.

Amelia was supposed to be keeping a low profile, but she couldn't help looking out the window. The Apartment Districts got dirtier and more run down the closer they got to the wall. She'd never seen the wall or the Gates, and almost wished they could take a detour. That wasn't on the itinerary. Drive to Apartment District 12, find the drop off point on Sixth Street, unload the cargo and go home. No detours, no exceptions. Kylie had drilled that sequence into Amelia's head when she'd asked what they did during a delivery run.

The truck's tires sent up clouds of dust as they drove south. It coated the windows and ruined Amelia's view. Not that it mattered. The grimy buildings were starting to depress her.

On Sixth Street in Apartment District 12, Lucas stopped the truck in front of a dilapidated, four-storey building. It was out of place next to the high-rises that filled the City and this street.

"This the place, Luke?" Jack asked, squinting to try to see through the grime on the window.

"Yup. Same address as on the request."

"Amelia should go with Ethan to the door." Kylie said. "No one will recognize her, so we stand a better chance of keeping our cover if they're unfriendly."

Jack tore his eyes from the window and narrowed them at the back of Kylie's head. "Ky—"

Kylie turned around in her seat and rolled her eyes. "Stop being so protective, Jack. She can pull her weight."

Jack turned to Amelia. "Think you can manage this?"

Amelia curled her fingers around the door handle. "I can knock on a door. It's no big deal." She pulled the handle and opened the door. Jack's rebuttals went unheard as her boots hit the street, and she closed the door behind her.

Amelia walked around the truck to the bed and stood at the end. "Ethan?" She peered up at him and waited for his eyes to land on her. "Kylie said I should go with you to the door."

Ethan climbed over the crates and hopped off the truck bed. Amelia swore there was a grin on his face. "Let's go," he said.

Amelia dipped her head and followed him to the squat building's door. It somehow looked worse in person than through the dust covered truck window. She kept her hood up, as Ethan did, though it felt conspicuous doing so in the sunlight. "Why'd Kylie send us alone to the door?"

"This is a new drop off for us," Ethan explained. "We need instructions on where to unload. Doing it in the street will draw attention."

"So, we need to charm information out of whoever is here. Know anything about them?"

"No. They don't give me those details."

"Who doesn't?" Although Amelia didn't like Ethan the way Dina liked

Jack, or know him that well, she thought he might open up to her if she was friendly. It had to be lonely being the one relegated to riding on the truck bed and sent on menial errands.

"The higher-ups in the Cause. They give Lucas the address and date and tell Kylie when they're giving us cargo. That's all any of us know."

"They're protecting the organization. You can't give the guards any details if you don't know them." Amelia stopped talking. She felt Ethan's eyes on her and didn't know what she'd said wrong.

"Yet it would be nice to know whether we're dealing with hostile people or not. Kylie's sending us as the sacrifice. If someone attacks us, they'll drive off."

"Jack wouldn't do that." There was no way he'd leave Amelia in the middle of a strange Apartment District with no way home. She hadn't brought bus money.

"He isn't driving."

Amelia and Ethan had reached the building while they'd talked, and he knocked on the door with his fist. A wrinkled woman with grey hair and hard eyes opened it. She was short, the top of her head reaching Amelia's chin, and stared up at Amelia and Ethan.

When the woman didn't speak, Amelia bit her lip and looked at Ethan. He blinked. "We have your delivery," he said.

The woman moved her eyes from Ethan to Amelia and to the ground. "Where?"

"In our truck," Amelia said. "We don't know where to unload."

The woman grumbled something unintelligible under her breath. "The back door. On Eighth Street."

Ethan turned to leave. "Come on. Let's go tell Lucas and the others."

Amelia made to follow, but the woman reached out and grabbed her arm, pointed fingernails biting into Amelia's skin and making her cry out. "You stay here, girlie. You can leave when I get my stuff."

Ethan's face darkened, and he balled his hands into fists. "You can't keep her hostage."

"Not hostage," the woman said, her grip strong on Amelia's arm. "Insurance in case you don't deliver my supplies."

"No," Ethan growled. "That's not how it works."

"It does in these parts," The old woman tugged on Amelia's arm. There was more force behind the act than Amelia had expected the woman capable of.

"Go, Ethan. Tell Jack to hurry." Amelia let the old woman pull her inside the building. She didn't look back for Ethan, but she heard his running footsteps. With no reason, she trusted him to come back. She wasn't eager to be this woman's leverage. Desperate people would do desperate things, and Amelia saw no way to fight it.

The interior of the squat building was decrepit. Plaster was crumbling from the walls and laid in piles on the floor. There was a dire need for someone to clean the space, repairs the walls and install updated lighting. The few lights Amelia could see were either dim or flickering.

Broken furniture littered the rooms, and Amelia had to watch her feet to avoid tripping. Every step she took sent up dust. Her parents were going to notice; figuring out what to tell them was a later problem. "Are you worried they'll drive off with your goods?" she asked the old woman.

The woman uncurled her fingers from Amelia's arm when they reached the messiest kitchen imaginable. A pile of dishes filled the sink, each one coated in food and grease. The floor needed sweeping and the walls scrubbing. There was a layer of dust and debris on every surface.

"It happened before."

"Did it?" Amelia's arm was sore from the woman's tight grip, and she rubbed it with her other hand. She didn't know much about the Cause's operations, but she assumed they delivered when and what they promised to.

The woman picked up a broom and thrust the handle into Amelia's hands. "Make yourself useful while we wait, and I might tell you about it."

Amelia swept the broom over the loose dirt and dust on the floor. There was no dustpan, so she just formed a pile at the side of the room.

"They said they'd send supplies, knocked on the door saying they were here and then drove off. Now I demand insurance, and you looked less prone to fight than that boy you were with. He your boyfriend?"

Amelia froze mid-sweep. "No. I don't have a boyfriend. I don't date."

"Heh. Don't limit yourself by being alone. You'll have more of everything with a partner."

More of everything. That included misery, didn't it? "I don't know." She moved the broom again. The repetitive motion kept her hands busy and stopped her from toying with her hair. "I'm fine on my own."

The woman scoffed. She hadn't done anything since handing Amelia the broom. From the middle of the room, the woman peered at Amelia and held a finger to her lips, which Amelia took as her cue to stop sweeping.

They both stood still in the kitchen. The old woman put her hands to her ear and leaned back. "They've come," she croaked. "Follow me and stay behind."

...

The noise the old woman had heard was Jack and Lucas depositing the crates outside the back door. Amelia saw, over the woman's shoulder, there was no parking lot, just a narrow alley between two taller buildings. They must've parked on the street and carried the cargo in.

The old woman hobbled outside when Lucas set the last crate down. "Is this everything?"

"Everything promised," Lucas said, his hands in his jacket pockets, the late afternoon sun making his dirty blonde hair look like ash. "Where's Amelia?"

"Inside," the woman said. She beckoned Amelia to come out, so Amelia did. She squinted as the harsh sunlight hit her eyes. It had been so dark in the house; the sudden brightness was too much.

Lucas turned his face to Jack. "Take her to the truck."

"Luke—"

Lucas's eyes hardened, and he bit out an order. "Take her."

Jack waved Amelia over. She jogged, eager to get away from the strange woman, whose eyes and smirk trailed her. It had been like the old woman saw through Amelia, which felt invasive. She didn't like a stranger being able to read her so well.

"Come on," Jack said, giving Lucas and Kylie a glance over his shoulder as he placed his hand on Amelia's arm and steered her away.

"Where's Ethan?" Amelia asked. She found it strange that he hadn't helped move the crates.

Jack pulled Amelia into the alley and held a finger up. He flattened his back against one building and gestured for Amelia to do the same. She didn't understand at first why they weren't going to the truck, or why Lucas had sent her and Jack away. Then Lucas and Kylie walked up to the old woman.

"We want our payment now," Kylie said, holding her hands on her hips.

"No money," the old woman said with a toss of her head. "I gave you the girl back."

"She wasn't part of our original deal," Lucas said stepping closer to the woman. "Pay up."

Deal? "What deal, Jack?" Amelia whispered.

He held a finger to his lips and shook his head. If he knew, he wasn't going to divulge it in this alley.

"Never cost me money before," the old woman said. "Supposed to be free goods for people in need."

"That's fine in theory," Kylie said with a wave of her hand. "But we're tired of doing all the work and getting nothing for it. Either pay, or we'll take these to someone who will." She kicked the nearest crate with a thunk that made Amelia cringe. It must've hurt.

"I knew it," Jack whispered as he reached for Amelia's arm and pulled her farther down the alley. He didn't run. The sound of their footsteps would've given them away. When they were on Eighth Street, he broke into a sprint and let go of Amelia's arm.

She sped after him, neither of them stopping until they reached the truck parked a few buildings down. Ethan leaned against the tailgate and raised his head, his eyes narrowed, as Jack and Amelia stopped next to him, both panting from exertion.

"What's going on?" Ethan asked widened eyes.

"No time," Jack said with a shake of his head. "We're taking the bus home. It's too far to run. Come on."

Ethan stepped away from the truck, his eyes flicking to Amelia. "Did you get hurt?"

Amelia tossed her head. "I'm fine, but I don't have bus money, Jack."

"I'll pay it," Jack said as he shot a glance down the alley. "You can repay me later. We need to move."

Amelia and Ethan followed Jack as he jogged down the street and turned a corner. Something dire must've been going on for Jack to pay her bus fare. He didn't have extra money, especially not after asking Dina for a Courtship. "Do you know what's going on?" she asked Ethan as they trailed Jack.

Ethan checked their surroundings before speaking. "Jack and I have suspected for awhile that Lucas and Kylie are using delivery runs for their personal gain. Crates have been lighter than they should be, and they show up wearing new clothes and eating more food than they should be able to afford."

"They told the old woman to pay," Amelia said as they caught up to Jack at the bus stop.

Ethan frowned. "Jack, what are we going to do about this?"

"We're going home. We'll tell them they were taking too long, and we were worried about Amelia making curfew."

Ethan crossed his arms over his chest and stared Jack down. "You know that's not what I mean."

"We can discuss it later, after we get Amelia home."

"That's not fair," Amelia cut in. She hadn't consented to being his excuse. "I want to know too."

Jack looked at her with sad eyes. "It's not too late to back out."

Maybe he'd expected this to scare her off and was trying to protect her, but she hadn't fulfilled what she wanted to, and she wasn't afraid. "I'm not backing out."

Chapter 8

The bus was full when they got on, helping Amelia and the boys hide in the crowd. If it had been just her with Jack, or Ethan, Amelia would've been nervous that someone would think they were on a date and watch for physical affection to report to a guard. Only people in Courtships, or married people, with documentation could show affection in public. She and Dina always took separate buses to their Restaurant Doma meet ups to avoid garnering suspicion. There were few worse things than a guard getting the wrong idea about two teenaged friends standing too close. But there was safety in being part of an odd numbered group, so Amelia tried to calm her nerves.

The downside about a crowd on the bus was that they couldn't discuss what had happened, or what to do about it, on route to Amelia's Apartment District. Jack lived in Apartment District 7, and insisted he could walk, or run, if necessary, home once Amelia was safe in her apartment.

Amelia didn't like this. Her protests were to no avail, yet she did get Jack to agree to discuss the situation the following day at Catsy's. There was no avoiding that place it seemed.

…

Amelia ran from the bus to Catsy's after school the next day. She and Jack went to the same school but were in different peer groups on account of their last names, so she never saw him. That he attended the same school hadn't been a surprise when Dina had introduced them. Most people went to the same high school, unless they could afford tuition at the rich Quarter's school.

He beat her to Catsy's and was sitting beside Ethan at a booth. Amelia cringed as she sat on the vacant side. She kept her bare arms from touching the material, not eager to get whatever sticky residue that coated it on her skin.

A server came and delivered glasses of water. Ethan placed a simple order of crackers and hummus, so they could claim their booth by being paying customers without spending a lot. None of them had excess money, and Amelia would pay it to settle her bus fare debt to Jack. When the food arrived, they finally had a semblance of privacy.

"What are we going to do?" Ethan asked as he scooped some hummus onto his plate. "We can't join Lucas and Kylie in exploiting people that need genuine help."

"The Cause isn't the same," Jack said. "It used to be about helping and advocating for people because the Government wouldn't. Now it's scaling back."

"I thought you said it was going underground," Amelia said.

He shook his head. "That's what Hannah told me, but some supporters don't like it. They want credit and reward."

Credit and reward. Amelia wanted neither of those things. There had to be others with the same mindset. "Why did Dina stop doing deliveries?"

Jack looked down at his plate, busying his hands with dipping a cracker in hummus. "She tripped on a sack Kylie left on some stairs and dropped the one she was holding, which ripped and ruined the bedding inside. It wouldn't have been that bad if the recipient hadn't known her parents and called them to complain about the damaged goods."

Poor Dina. It must've been humiliating and embarrassing. If Amelia's parents found out about her involvement, they would force her to quit too.

"So, her parents told her to stop?"

Jack brought the cracker to his mouth. "They didn't have to. She made the decision on her own."

Something about the story didn't sit well with Amelia. She knew Dina better than either of her companions at Catsy's did. Yet, it was a mystery she'd need to unravel herself. "I think Kylie and Lucas are bad news," Amelia said, dipping her own cracker into the hummus and popping it in her mouth. When she chewed and swallowed, she continued her thought. "What about Hannah and Brooke? Did they even show up yesterday?"

"We don't know," Ethan said.

"It doesn't matter. They're close friends with Kylie and Lucas," Jack said as he consumed another hummus-dipped cracker. He looked like he hadn't slept or like he'd lost someone important to him and was going through grief. In a way he had. Although Lucas and Kylie weren't dead, they'd revealed their true intentions. And those didn't align with Jack's.

"Don't you still want to help people?" Amelia asked.

"I don't think it's possible now."

Amelia ate another cracker with a scoop of hummus. "It's always possible. I say we continue. Who needs Lucas and Kylie? We can form a new group."

"They have the truck, the meeting building and the contact for the goods supplier," Ethan said, counting the reasons off on his fingers.

"So, we get our own." It couldn't be that hard. Jack and Ethan must've had connections.

"No," Jack said. "We'll go up the chain of command and try to get back what we already had. The Cause can't be thrilled about what Kylie and Lucas are doing."

"If it doesn't work?" Ethan asked.

This was a valid question. Amelia had her own doubts about it working, though she trusted Jack's judgement. He had more experience with the Cause than her.

Jack sighed. "Then we'll try Amelia's idea."

With a plan settled, they ate the remaining food, and Amelia paid the bill.

…

Amelia assumed Jack would take care of things, with going to higher ups in the Cause being his idea. Yet, the next morning when she walked into the kitchen, her mom, wearing a frown and narrowed eyes, waggled a note in her face.

"Who is Ethan and why is he arranging meetups for you two and Dina's boyfriend? Are you going on double dates?"

This was bad. Terribly bad. What was Ethan doing dropping off notes for her? "Ethan is Jack's friend," Amelia said as she tried to snatch the note.

Her mom held it out of Amelia's reach. "I don't know you anymore. You say you don't want a Courtship, and now you're getting notes from boys. What am I supposed to think?"

Amelia closed her eyes. "Ethan and I aren't like that."

Her mom raised an eyebrow. "Then what are you?"

She held back her sigh. Coming across as inpatient was not the route to take. "We're just friends. I have no plans or interest in dating him."

Amelia felt her mom's eyes on her as she handed Amelia the note. "That had better be true."

Amelia assured her mom it was, grabbed the note, her breakfast and backpack and bolted from the apartment. She held the note with one hand while she shoved her breakfast into her mouth with the other. It wasn't long.

Amelia,

Meet me and Jack on the corner of Ninth and Tenth Street on Saturday at two o'clock.

Signed, Ethan.

Saturday. That was her day to meet up with Dina. She assumed Jack had told his girlfriend about making Amelia miss their weekly tradition, which she could confirm at lunch. That was what a good friend did.

...

At lunch, Amelia beat Dina to the cafeteria. She paid for her sandwich and water and waited. Dina came in minutes later and procured her own meal. Her face brightened when she spotted Amelia leaning against the wall with her tray.

"Mellie! You're here early."

Amelia stood straight and inhaled deep. "I need to talk to you about our meet up."

Dina smirked. "Jack told me you have plans."

Good. That made things less awkward for Amelia. "You aren't upset?"

"Nope," Dina said as she and Amelia walked to their usual table and sat.

Amelia bit into her sandwich, letting the chewing clear her mind. "Jack told me why you stopped helping with deliveries."

Dina froze and lowered her sandwich. She blinked and struggled to compose her face. As Amelia had assumed, the situation must've embarrassed Dina. "What did he say?"

"That you tripped in front of someone that knew your parents. I'm sorry. That must've been embarrassing."

Dina let her shoulders droop. "I did trip, but that's only half the story. Kylie left the sack on the stairs on purpose and gave me one stuffed with items too heavy for it."

Amelia narrowed her eyes. "Why?" What did Kylie have against Dina?

Dina leaned forward and lowered her voice. "She wanted me gone after I walked in on her and Lucas replacing clothes in a supply crate with rags. So, she arranged for me to trip in front of my parents' friend and passed it off as an accident."

"You didn't tell Jack this?"

Dina shook her head. "I wanted to, but Kylie said she'd tell him I was the thief and Lucas would back her up. I wasn't sure he and the others would believe me over them, and I had no proof. It wasn't worth the risk of him dumping me."

Amelia wasn't sure what Hannah and Brooke would think, but she thought Ethan would understand. He shared Jack's suspicions and seemed to be the outcast of the group. If anyone would relate to Dina's story, it would be him and Jack. "Jack won't dump you," Amelia said, laying her hand over Dina's. "Come with us. Jack and Ethan need the truth, as does whoever Jack found to meet."

Dina consented, and that's how Amelia started to feel less anxious about the event. On the day of, she left her apartment with enough time to walk to Ninth Street. She stopped short when she got outside and saw a car parked along the side of the road. Malcolm sat on the driver's seat, one hand on the steering wheel and the other hanging out the driver's window.

Amelia closed her eyes and counted to ten. She never should've told him she went to Restaurant Doma every Saturday. It was tempting to go the long way to her meeting, but she couldn't leave him sitting there. So, she walked to his car and cleared her throat.

Malcolm brightened and sat up straight when he noticed her standing on the road. "I hope you're not angry," he said. "I just wanted to see you."

Amelia clasped her hands at her waist to stop herself from wringing them. "I'm not angry, nor am I going to the Restaurant Doma today. I have other plans." She hoped he wouldn't think it had anything to do with him. Why? Amelia didn't know.

He exhaled. "I shouldn't have assumed you kept the same schedule every weekend."

Amelia would likely regret this, but she didn't want Malcolm to think she was brushing him off, even if they hadn't made plans. And he had hinted at having views that aligned with the Cause. "Come with me."

He blinked. "What?"

"Dina's boyfriend and I do deliveries of goods to people in need, and we've lost our truck. Jack thinks we can get it back. However, if things don't go how he expects, and I imagine they won't, we'll need a new driver."

One corner of Malcolm's mouth tipped up. "You intend to use me to chauffer your friends around?"

Amelia lifted her shoulders. "I thought you might be interested in helping people. If you're not, then I'll go alone."

He settled his sparkling gemstone eyes on her. "And what will your friends say if you show up with me?"

She shrugged. "Dina will tease me. Ethan and Jack, I don't know." In truth, she thought they'd be upset and suspicious. They'd lost Kylie and Lucas, and likely Hannah and Brooke, so Amelia was helping to recruit. Something about Malcolm made her trust him; she just couldn't pinpoint what it was. Her instincts had better not fail her now.

...

Jack and Ethan gaped at Amelia and Malcolm when they walked up to a derelict and dirty office building on the corner of Ninth and Tenth Streets.

"Who is that?" Ethan asked with narrowed eyes.

"Malcolm," Amelia said. "We met a couple weeks ago, and he wants to help."

Jack frowned. "Amelia, you can't just—"

"Malcolm drove us home last week," Dina said. "He's nice. We should give him a chance."

Jack glanced at Ethan who shrugged. "He can stay on watch duty with Ethan."

Amelia looked at Malcolm, and he flashed her a small smile. "I won't cause trouble," he said, holding his hands up in surrender.

"We'll see," Ethan said.

"Come on, Amelia," Jack said, beckoning her over with a wave. "You're coming with me and Dina."

Amelia followed Jack and Dina to the door that was barely staying on its hinges. She wanted to be where the action was, but she wasn't eager to leave Malcolm outside. At least Ethan would be with him. Amelia gave him and Malcolm a closed-lip grin and a nod, and they each nodded in return. She thought she even saw Malcolm give her a tiny smile.

With a deep breath, Amelia turned and went inside the building with Jack and Dina.

Chapter 9

Amelia followed Jack and Dina up a set of stairs made of crumbling cement. She didn't dare touch the handrail out of fear it might break into pieces. Jack got off at the first landing. The hallway on this floor wasn't in any better shape than the stairs. Its walls had peeling paint, and the floor tiles had cracks and missing sections. Amelia made sure to watch where she stepped.

At the last door on the right, Jack knocked. There was no immediate answer. Just when Amelia was about to suggest they leave, a rustling sound came from the other side, and the doorknob creaked as someone turned it.

"Whom are we meeting, Jack?" Amelia whispered as the door crept open, centimetre by centimetre. Whomever it was, they were either trying to build suspense or get a good view of Amelia, Dina and Jack before letting them in.

"The man I asked to recruit you. Arlo Fenn."

The man from the market was behind that door. Amelia thought that had a chance of increasing their chances of getting the truck and meeting place back.

The door was finally open, and Arlo stuck his hand out to wave them in. The inside of the room was dark. Closed, thick curtains covered the window, and the only light came from a single lamp with a dim bulb on the table pushed against the far-right wall. Arlo stood in the centre of the small room with his arms crossed over his chest. Amelia could see the whites of his eyes as he scanned her, Dina and Jack.

"Jack Birch, what's your complaint?" he asked. "New girl not working out?"

Amelia assumed the new girl was her. She was about to interject that she had a name when Jack spoke up.

"No, Amelia isn't the problem. Lucas and Kylie are."

"They're demanding money for deliveries," Amelia added.

"And keeping goods for themselves," Dina added before divulging her story of what she'd witnessed Kylie do.

Jack fixed his eyes on Dina and clenched his hands into fists. He hadn't known the extent Kylie's actions.

Arlo sighed. "Those are serious accusations. Do you have proof?"

Proof. Amelia didn't know how they could. She and Jack weren't supposed to have even heard Lucas and Kylie threatening the old woman.

Jack opened his fists, dug in his pocket and produced a small booklet that fit in the palm of his hand. He passed it to Arlo. "This is what Ethan and I collected. I hope it's enough."

Arlo flipped through the booklet. The room was too dark for Amelia to read his face. She had no idea what Jack and Ethan had found, or what Arlo thought of it.

"They'll no longer be part of the Cause or have our support," Arlo said, as he tucked the book into his pocket. "Unfortunately, the truck and building are not Cause property. I can't help you there. And someone else will take on the deliveries. You don't need to worry about it."

"Won't that add extra work for someone else?" Dina asked.

"It's no longer your concern."

"We can still do deliveries," Amelia piped up. She wasn't about to lose her chance at helping people when she'd barely gotten started. "I know someone with a vehicle."

Amelia saw a flash of white teeth as Arlo grinned. "Do you? It still doesn't solve the question of where to drop off goods."

"Can we pick them up?" Amelia thought this sounded reasonable. Why did they need to rent or buy a building just so Arlo, or someone else, could drop things off there?

Jack made a noise beside Amelia, like a grunt masked with a fake cough. She didn't care too much about whether he trusted Malcolm or hated her idea. What other option did they have?

"I'll look into it and send word when I have an answer," Arlo said. "Now go before someone discovers you're where you shouldn't be."

...

When Amelia had left Malcolm with Ethan, the boys were standing far apart on either side of the doorway. Ethan had been averting his eyes and keeping his distance. When she walked outside, they were grinning and standing beside each other. Amelia blinked. What had happened?

"Any luck?" Ethan asked.

"Not much," Amelia said. She hadn't expected it to go well. At least they had a chance to keep doing deliveries.

"We can't get the truck or building back," Jack said as he stepped outside with Dina after Amelia.

Ethan groaned. "What's the plan then?"

Amelia felt the weight of Malcolm's eyes on her. She kept her gaze straight ahead. "We're waiting for news about whether we can do deliveries if we use our own vehicle and pick them up."

"I think it's a good idea," Dina said.

"I have a vehicle."

Amelia watched the others swivel their necks to look at Malcolm. He didn't flinch. "I assume none of you do. So, I'm offering mine."

"What's the catch?" Jack asked, his mouth pressed into a thin line. "Rich people don't do charity without getting something in return."

Jack was making things hostile, and it was unnecessary. Sure, Amelia had showed up with Malcolm unplanned. What was she supposed to do when he was waiting outside her door?

Malcolm held his hands up. "No catch."

Jack scoffed. "You're saying there's nothing you want?"

"There is, but I won't use bribery to get it." His eyes glittered in the late-afternoon sun, and he glued them on Amelia. She had an idea of what he wanted.

Jack frowned. "I don't trust this. It's too easy."

"Relax, Jack," Ethan said. "A guard came by while you were inside, and *he*," Ethan titled his head in Malcolm's direction, "talked our way out of getting arrested. This place is abandoned and slated for demolishment."

Amelia believed that. She hadn't felt safe inside, and, even on the outside, the building looked like it was on the verge of collapse. Was talking their way out of arrest enough to make Ethan trust Malcolm? It was possible Malcolm had done it for Amelia's sake, not Ethan's at all. She wasn't sure whether to appreciate that.

Jack sighed. "Fine. If we get to continue doing deliveries, we'll use your vehicle. I'll send word through Amelia."

The ghost of a grin appeared on Malcolm's face. "Alright."

"Come on, Dina," Jack said. "Let's go."

Dina moved to Jack's side and gave Amelia a wave as she walked away.

This left Amelia alone with Malcolm and Ethan, neither of whom seemed eager to leave.

"Jack needs to chill out," Ethan said. "He'll come around."

Amelia swiveled her head between Ethan and Malcolm and back again. They weren't friends nor even knew each other. "What happened with you two?"

"A guard threatened to arrest us for loitering," Malcolm explained. "So, I told him my dad is thinking of buying this place and that we were waiting for him. It was no big deal."

Amelia blinked and her jaw fell. "That worked?"

"Yup," Ethan said.

"It might not again," Malcolm said with a glance down the street. "We need to leave before another guard comes."

"You think someone sent a guard here on purpose?" Amelia asked. It was hours from curfew when guards went on patrol. Surely Kylie and Lucas hadn't stooped that low or known about their meeting.

"No doubt someone sent him," Ethan said. "He zeroed in on us like he was on a mission. Malcolm's right; we need to get out of here."

That was how Amelia ended up walking home with Malcolm while Ethan took his own route. They were almost on her street before she decided to break their silence. "So, what do you want?" Amelia's idea needed confirming.

Malcolm exhaled and glanced her way. "Do you really want to know?"

She wouldn't have asked otherwise. "Yes."

"I didn't tell you the complete truth earlier about hoping to just see you. I spent all week working up the courage to ask you on a date. That's what I want."

Amelia gulped, her palms turning sweaty. "A date?" She'd never planned to do that, and the one she'd gone on with Blake hadn't been great.

"Yes," Malcolm said. "Have supper with me tomorrow. I'd like to get to know you."

A small part of Amelia's brain screamed for her to reject the idea and tell Malcolm off. But it was appealing. The meal would be better quality and a bigger portion size than her normal diet. "Alright." She'd likely regret that answer, yet it was out of her mouth before she could second guess it.

Malcolm grinned. That coupled with the sunlight casting his hair in gold made him radiant, like her personal sun on the street. "Really?"

"Yes, I'll go." There was no backing out now. Especially not after Amelia saw the joy on his face. She wasn't a girl who played with a boy's feelings. That was cruel.

"I'll pick you up at six."

"Sounds good," Amelia said. She and Malcolm parted company for the night when they reached his car. Amelia didn't want to lead him on; she actually wanted to go. That was weird. She'd never known anyone that made her want to go on a date. What was it about Malcolm that was different?

It was something to ponder over the next day, and with no school, she'd have free time to dedicate to it. First though, Amelia needed to tell her parents.

…

"A date?" Amelia's mom screeched. "You said you didn't like him that way."

"I hardly knew him then." Not that she knew him much better now. "I couldn't say no when he asked me, and I do want to go." That was the truth, as much as it surprised Amelia to admit it.

"Let her go, Sonia," Amelia's dad said. "She's finally showing interest in going out with someone other than Dina and deserves some fun."

Her mom sighed. "He was nice when he came here. Okay, you can go."

Amelia would've gone even without her mom's permission, but it spared her from explaining why she was wearing one of her fancy dresses, shoes and makeup when she exited her bedroom the next afternoon. Amelia had even tried, with moderate success, to curl her hair. Her hairstyling skills consisted of combing out knots or throwing it in a ponytail, but she'd managed to get it in waves. Without hairspray it wasn't going to last. No matter. She'd at least look nice at the beginning of the date.

Amelia was double checking the contents of her bag to ensure she hadn't forgotten anything when Malcolm knocked. Her mom opened the door before Amelia could react. She heard her mom greet Malcolm, though his reply was too muffled to make out.

Amelia summoned her courage, skipped through the living room, passed her mom with a goodbye and joined Malcolm in the hallway.

He smiled. "You look amazing."

"Thank you," Amelia said. "You look nice too." She hoped that didn't sound awful. It wasn't her fault that she had no experience in these matters and didn't know how to flirt. His indigo jacket and grey chino pants were more attractive than what Blake had worn and made Amelia's body warm and tingly. Spending time selecting her red dress felt less frivolous now.

"Ready?" Malcolm asked. He kept smiling and offered her his hand. She took it. His hand was soft and warm as he gave her hand a squeeze and let go. Malcolm was rich and did little manual labour, which let his hands stay smooth and soft. Amelia's own hands were rougher and had callouses from all the physical effort her market trips and household chores required. It made Amelia feel as poor as she was. What did he see in her? She wasn't about to ask that on a first date.

Chapter 10

Malcolm drove into the rich Quarters. Amelia had never been to them and gawked at the large houses they passed with her eyes fixated on the scenery outside her window. She couldn't imagine living in a space that large. Each house made her apartment seem like a doll's house. Her life centred around her Apartment District, with her school and Restaurant Doma being the exceptions. And Dina had been the one to discover their meet up place.

In Quarter 2, Malcolm turned down a street leading to a retail sector. Wealthy people didn't live amongst their shops and businesses like residents in Apartment Districts did. The restaurant he stopped at had a parking lot it shared with the neighbouring businesses. People that frequented these stores and restaurants didn't take the bus.

When Malcolm shifted his car to park, he got out and walked around to open Amelia's door. This was another difference between him and Blake, who'd done nothing personal for her. Amelia felt like she was floating as she exited the car and walked with Malcolm to the restaurant. *This date might even be fun.*

The restaurant was a single storey building that had a blue and white striped awning hanging over the side with *Sophia's Trattoria* written on it. Only in the rich Quarters, and Apartment District 1, were any buildings single or double storey.

The inside was a much larger and brighter space than Catsy's. Sticky vinyl didn't cover the booths, nor did the place smell weird. The aroma wafting from kitchen made Amelia's mouth water.

The greeter placed Amelia and Malcolm at a booth in the back corner. Amelia rested her hands on the table as the greeter set down the menus. Catsy's used harsh, white lighting that made people want to leave as quickly as possible. Here, the lights were a warmer, yellow hue.

"Order whatever you like," Malcolm said. He wasn't looking at his menu, and Amelia assumed he had it memorized.

Amelia glanced at her menu. There were so many things listed on the multiple pages. She wasn't used to holding a menu, let alone this booklet with multiple laminated pages to flip though. She didn't know how to decide.

"Pages three and four are the supper items," Malcolm said. "Start there."

Amelia felt herself blush. "Thanks." She took his advice and flipped to the third page. The prices made her pause. She and Malcolm hadn't discussed who would pay, yet he had told her to order whatever she wanted, so this was a time to try something different.

When the server came to take their drink order, Amelia asked for a strawberry lemonade, while Malcolm requested a raspberry iced tea. In the minutes between ordering and their server returning, Amelia couldn't come up with anything to say. Being on a date with Blake hadn't been this awkward or sent butterflies to her stomach. She smoothed down her hair, which still held its waves, and reread the menu.

Malcolm's eyes were on her, so she set down the menu.

"This place is nice," Amelia said. "Do you come often?"

"Only when my parents take me every year for my birthday," Malcolm said, not taking his eyes off her.

Amelia fiddled with the edge of her menu. This was a special place to

Malcolm, based on his answer to her question. So, what was she doing here? "I would've been happy to go somewhere else. I don't want to tarnish your opinion of this place."

Malcolm reached across the table and squeezed her hand. "You won't."

"You barely know me," Amelia said. "I could be the worst date imaginable."

Malcolm's eyes sparkled and the corner of his mouth tipped up ass he retracted his hand. "No. You couldn't be worse than Scarlet."

Amelia didn't get a chance to ask what Scarlet had done that was so horrible as the server came with their drinks and took their food order: a lentil tart for Amelia and mushroom risotto for Malcolm. Amelia sipped her lemonade. She drank water almost exclusively, and drinks were a luxury her parents didn't splurge on. The sweetness of the strawberries mixed with the contrasting sourness of the lemons made her wish she could afford juice more often.

When the food came, she tried not to have a physical reaction. The tart was richer and more heavily spiced than her daily diet. The chef here had access to seasoning Amelia could only dream of. She couldn't stifle her moan as she ate the first bite.

Malcolm locked eyes with her, his iced tea glass in his hand. "I'm guessing you like it."

Amelia swallowed the bite of food. "It's delicious. Do you eat like this all the time?"

Malcolm drank a gulp of his iced tea. "My parents do. They eat out almost all the time. At home, I cook for myself."

Amelia couldn't imagine being responsible for feeding herself at sixteen. She knew how to cook, but the chore wasn't her responsibility alone. "That must be difficult."

Malcolm set his glass down. "That's sympathetic of you. I thought you'd scoff."

Amelia looked at him. She didn't presume rich people were immune from difficulties. "Why would I do that?"

Malcolm raised his shoulders in a shrug. "Because I'm wealthy and have no business complaining when so many people are starving."

Amelia's heart sped up, and she clasped her hands together to stop from fidgeting. This sounded like a line he'd told himself often enough that he believed it. "You aren't complaining. I asked."

"Yes, you did."

...

Amelia's nerves settled as the date progressed. She and Malcolm ate their meals and discussed what happened when they went to meet Arlo Fenn. Amelia grew more certain she could trust Malcolm, and she had an idea for how to get Jack to trust him too.

The bill came when they finished eating, and Malcolm paid. Amelia had offered to pay her half, which he'd turned down. She wouldn't deny appreciating this as her meal and lemonade cost four times as much as a sandwich at Catsy's.

On the drive to Amelia's apartment, Malcolm met her eyes in the mirror. "I'd like to see you again."

This date was more enjoyable than the one she'd had with Blake. She could almost understand what Dina meant when she talked about dates with Jack. "How about we double date with Jack and Dina? In my Apartment District."

Malcolm gave her a nod. "That's a good idea. I'll write my address for you when I park, and you can send details there. As well as when you hear about the deliveries."

Amelia wasn't sure why she was so eager for this. Dina would love the idea too, so she'd ask at lunch. "Okay."

Malcolm parked his car outside her building, removed a pen and paper from the glove box and wrote his address. Amelia tucked it in her bag and got out of the car. Malcolm came inside and escorted her to her door. When they were both standing outside it, he settled his eyes on her. "Thank you for joining me."

Amelia felt her cheeks warm. He was much nicer than Blake had been. She didn't even care if the neighbours were watching through their peepholes. So what if they saw her standing with a boy in the hallway? "And thank you for supper. I'll let you know what Dina and Jack say."

"Good," Malcolm said.

Amelia could tell he wasn't eager to leave. His eyes were still on her, and he was beaming like a kid who got what they wished for as a birthday present and hadn't expected it. "I should go inside now before the neighbours start to gossip," she said, reaching into her bag for her key.

Malcolm took a step away. "Good night, Amelia."

She unlocked the door and swung it open. "Good night, Malcolm."

...

It was easy the next day to get Dina agree to a double date. The let down was that Dina hadn't heard anything from Jack about the deliveries. Amelia had hoped to give Malcolm news about that when she sent him a note. Either way, she decided to send it that night.

She must've been smiling without realizing it as Dina was staring at her. Amelia blinked. "Do I have food on my face?"

"You like Malcolm," Dina said in a sing-song voice.

Amelia tossed her head. "We only went on one date."

Dina smirked, and her eyes twinkled. "And you brought him to our meeting and rode home with him twice. And now you're planning another date with him."

"It would've been rude not to," Amelia countered as she tidied her lunch tray. She hadn't invited him to their meeting in advance.

"Sure," Dina said. "But you wouldn't care about that if you didn't like him."

Amelia rolled her eyes. "He's just a nice guy I went to supper with."

"If you really don't like him, tell him. Don't lead him on when he clearly has a crush on you."

Amelia had no intentions of leading anyone on. Nor did she hate being with Malcolm when she'd always expected to hate being with anyone romantically. To her, that made seeing him again worth it. On that note, she wasted no time in sending him a message when she got home.

When the day of their double date came, Amelia dashed around her bedroom. She donned a simple pair of jeans and a t-shirt, with her standard lace up boots and grabbed her bag. Malcolm had met her when she wore an outfit like this and no makeup, so he should like her now.

She'd instructed him to dress casually and not pay for her food. It wouldn't improve the impression Jack had of him if Malcolm paid for more than his share when Jack couldn't do the same.

Amelia felt as light as air as she walked to Darla's Diner. She hadn't wanted to traumatize Malcolm entirely by bringing him to Catsy's. Darla's was a step up in price point and food quality, though still cheap compared to the restaurants Malcolm frequented. If Blake had possessed interest in Amelia, he would've brought her to Darla's. People in her Apartment District went there for special occasions. Like Catsy's, it was on the ground floor of a high-rise, but its building was nicer and cleaner.

Malcolm was waiting outside with Jack and Dina when Amelia walked up.

She hadn't thought she'd be the last one to arrive. "Sorry I'm late."

"Relax, Mellie," Dina said. "We only beat you here by a couple minutes."

Amelia wasn't thrilled Dina was using her nickname in front of Malcolm. It made her seem childish. She plastered on a smile to hide her annoyance. "Let's go inside."

Dina and Jack walked in standing so close to each other their sides almost touched. Amelia and Malcolm followed with more space between them. Amelia could see him smiling at her, and she tried to keep her focus forward and her hands clasped in front. The last thing she wanted was to trip or stumble.

The greeter sat them at a table near a window, which wasn't a private spot. Amelia assumed they looked like a group of friends getting together, not two couples on a double date. It was safer to be visible. That way no one suspected you were up to trouble.

When the greeter gave them menus and walked away, Jack sighed. "I heard from Arlo Fenn this morning." He leaned across the table and kept his voice down when he said this.

Amelia sat up straighter, her interest piqued. "What did he say?"

"He has a delivery for us, but it's different, and riskier."

"Riskier how?" Dina asked, her eyes on her boyfriend.

"We'd have to leave the City overnight."

Amelia didn't understand. Weren't the needy people in the City? She thought only workers without families lived in the Outskirts, and to deliver there wouldn't take an entire day and night. "Where is the delivery to?"

Jack flicked his eyes onto Malcolm, who was running his thumb along the edge of his menu. He didn't trust Malcolm, but he must've decided it was worth chancing. "The Colony."

Chapter 11

"The Colony?" Amelia had never heard of such a place. "Don't you mean the Outskirts?"

Jack shook his head. "The Colony is farther south. It's not City territory."

Father south. Amelia hadn't thought anyone could, or did, live south of the Outskirts. It had to be unbearably hot.

"Who lives there?" Dina asked.

"I don't know," Jack said.

"Anyone that can't or doesn't want to live here," Malcolm said as their server walked up to their table.

Amelia and the others placed their food and drink orders. They waited for the water, which everyone, including Malcolm, had ordered, to come before resuming their conversation. It wasn't something strangers should overhear. There was no way to know who might report to a guard.

When the server set down the glasses and walked away, Jack spoke, keeping his voice down. "I told Arlo I'd let him know, but I doubt we can do it."

"Why not?" Dina asked. She rested her hand, with her Courtship ring on her finger, on Jack's and batted her eyelashes.

Amelia thought this was an odd time to flirt and a poor strategy to use to convince him.

Jack pulled his hand from under Dina's and drank a swig of water.

"There are multiple factors to consider. Plus, we have no way out of the City."

Malcolm sipped his water and set his glass down with a thud. "I have a pass that'll open the Gate."

"You'll have to go without me," Amelia said. "My parents would never let me go, and if I sneak out, they'll report me as a missing person, or runaway."

"Tell them you're staying at my place," Dina said. "Surely they'll agree to that."

Amelia didn't want to lie to her parents again. "I shouldn't."

"Tell them the truth," Malcolm said. "Say you're going regardless of what they think."

Amelia's jaw fell. "I can't. They'll kick me out."

"You can't be scared of them forever," Jack said. "You already decided to help the Cause without their permission. If you need to sneak behind their back to support something you believe in, getting kicked out might be worth it."

Amelia gulped. Where would she go? "I'll think about it."

The server bringing their food stopped their discussion about the Colony. Jack and Dina eyed and smiled at each other over their plates. Amelia ate her stir-fry, aware that her best friend was holding Jack's hand under the table. Amelia and Malcolm were on a date, in the technical sense, except they didn't match Jack and Dina's affection for each other or possess the same bravery. Sitting near them made her feel inferior, which was strange as she'd spent time with Dina and Jack before. Knowing that acting that way with Malcolm was out of her reach had Amelia down, and she didn't understand the feeling. She'd never wanted romantic attention from anyone before.

As Amelia brooded, Malcolm's fingers brushed the back of her arm.

"Don't get too down," he said, his voice too quiet for Jack or Dina to hear, had they been paying attention. "Things will work out."

Amelia set down her fork. "I'll either be homeless or left behind." Neither option was something she wanted.

Malcolm shrugged. "They might surprise you."

Amelia had doubts about that. She cleared her throat and raised the volume of her voice. "When is the delivery, Jack?"

She wasn't sure Jack heard her question until he tore his eyes off Dina and looked at Amelia. "Arlo wants us to leave on Saturday morning."

Saturday. That gave Amelia a few days to figure out how she could get her parents to let her go. It might be possible. She tried to mull it over as she finished her meal.

When the bills came, Amelia was a bit surprised that Malcolm let her pay without offering. She had told him to let her, and she'd expected him to protest.

When their group went outside, Dina smiled at Jack. Amelia knew her friend wanted to do more. Dina liked to kiss Jack and yearned to do it wherever she pleased. It was a big reason she was looking forward to Clinic Day.

Jack turned to Amelia and Malcolm. "This was nice."

Jack was just being polite, so Amelia was in return. "Thanks for agreeing to come."

"I'll take any excuse to eat decent food and see Dina."

That was true enough. Jack's family didn't eat well. He'd taken a weekend job to help make ends meet and have money to spend on dates with Dina and her ring. Helping to pay for a wedding would put even more financial strain on him.

Dina tapped Jack on the arm, which was as much as she could touch him in public. Her cheeks were pink. "Go home before we do something illegal."

Jack waved and walked in the direction of his Apartment District. Dina said goodbye and set off, giving Amelia a knowing look as she went.

Amelia was alone with Malcolm again. "I should go home too."

"Of course," he said. He didn't move, just stood on the street gazing at her.

Amelia went to step around him, and he pivoted. She got a few steps away when he rushed after her. "Wait!"

Amelia blinked. Malcolm kept surprising her. Surely, he couldn't be this interested. "What is it?"

"I know this is sudden, but will you come meet my parents tomorrow? Please?"

The way he looked at her with wide eyes and the edge of his lip between his jaws made her think Malcolm was as nervous as she was. Apparently, he was interested. "Your – your parents?"

He dipped his head. "I want to share my world with you and experience yours."

Amelia stopped walking and spun to face him. "It isn't a good idea. Don't get me wrong. I enjoyed our two dates. It's just that things would never work out between us."

"Amelia—"

"You're rich and used to getting whatever you want," she said before he could finish his sentence. "If your family accepted me, that would be one thing. But you'd find yourself stuck with me, and I can't compete with girls like Scarlet. A relationship would end with both of us miserable."

Malcolm's eyes softened. He didn't walk away or argue. "I don't want a girl like Scarlet. My world is sheltered, predictable and small, and you brought some life into it. I would never be miserable with you."

"You hardly know me. I don't belong in your world."

Malcolm sighed and his shoulders drooped. "You want to know what makes me miserable? Trying to play nice with girls like Scarlet. They're so entitled, snobby and stuck up. It's exhausting trying to reach their standards."

Amelia hung her head. He was so convincing; she was on the verge of caving. "I don't want you to regret liking me."

"I thought it was obvious that I already like you. And I don't regret it."

He liked her? Dina had told her that too. "Alright, I'll meet them. What should I wear?"

"Wear whatever you like. You don't need to pretend to be someone you aren't for me."

Amelia mulled those words over as she left Malcolm and walked home. Without intending or wanting to, she'd gone and found a boy that liked her. The strangest part was that she was starting to like him in return. That was a conundrum she would have to figure out.

…

Amelia's mom was thrilled that she had another date with Malcolm. Meeting his parents, according to her mom, was a sure sign that he'd stick around. With her mom in such a good mood, Amelia decided to bring up her upcoming trip. "I'm going away overnight on Saturday."

The smile on her mom's face and her excited tone disappeared. "No."

Amelia inhaled a deep breath. She was trying to take Malcom's advice. "I'm not asking permission. The Cause needs me."

"Amelia!" her mom screeched. "The Cause?! I raised you to have more sense than to go against the Government."

Amelia's body trembled. She wasn't normally an angry person. However, her mom was trying to stop her from doing something important, and that summoned an unfamiliar rage. "If no one tries to change things, people will always suffer. It's bad enough that we can barely afford food! What are people living in Apartment District 12 supposed to do?"

Amelia's mom's eye had turned to ice and her voice matched it. "Are you saying you've been breaking the food laws?"

"I'm saying people need help, and I'm going to give them some."

"You are not joining a group of subversive criminals! I forbid it."

Amelia crossed her arms and stared her mom down. "As I said before, I'm not asking permission."

"You aren't going anywhere. Not to Malcolm's and not away on the weekend. You'll go to school and come directly home, or I will send a guard to find you."

"I'd rather be homeless than agree to that." Amelia had known this would happen. She shoved past her mom and stormed to her bedroom. Her school bag was on the floor, and she upended it, spilling its contents on the tiles. There were few belongings she couldn't survive without. Into her bag went some changes of clothes, her toothbrush and her essential school supplies on top.

Into her smaller bag, she shoved a hairbrush, a change of shoes and the framed picture of her and Dina as small children that sat on her nightstand. With both bags packed, Amelia hefted them. She was in the living room, passing by her mom, when her dad exited the other bedroom.

He blinked at Amelia. "What's going on?"

"Go fetch a guard, Nathan. Our daughter has lost all sense."

Amelia saw her dad furrow his brows. She could've been on the stairs by now, but something gave her pause. Her dad hadn't moved.

"You'll need to explain it to me better than that, Sonia."

Amelia dropped her bags with a thud. This was an opportunity to sway her dad to her side. "All I did was say I'm going away on the weekend to help the Cause. People are suffering, Dad. I can't do nothing."

Her dad frowned. "Sonia, you want to summon the guards on our daughter for this?"

"We have to, Nathan. The food laws—"

"I'm not breaking them," Amelia said, her voice cracking. That was true to her knowledge. "Although they should be overturned."

Her mom threw her hands up. "You see, Nathan? Our daughter has no respect for the Government or the law. We must do something."

"You're right, dear," Amelia's dad said. Her stomach dropped, and she reached for her bags. Her mom smiled as Amelia's fingers wrapped around the straps.

Our of the corner of her eye, Amelia saw her dad reach into his pocket. He pulled out some bills and thrust them at Amelia. "I assume you aren't going alone. Distribute this amongst your group so you can buy supplies for the journey."

Amelia dropped her bags and gaped at her dad, knowing her parents didn't have excess money and would have to give up something. She traded the bags straps for the money. From a quick glance, it was enough to feed her, Dina, Jack and Ethan – she assumed he was coming – for the day or two they'd be gone. Malcolm could afford his own goods. "I can't take this, Dad."

"Yes, you can, sweetie. Consider it my donation to the Cause."

"Nathan!" Amelia's mom shrieked. "Have you lost your sense too? We shouldn't encourage this."

Amelia's dad tossed his head. "On the contrary. We could easily be worse off and in need of assistance ourselves. I think it's admirable that Amelia wants to make things better."

Amelia saw her mom purse her lips. "I see I'm outnumbered. You had better stay safe."

"I will." No matter what her mom thought, Amelia didn't want to get arrested. She couldn't help anyone from inside prison.

With her mom calmed down for the immediate time, Amelia lugged her stuff back to her room and dumped the bags on her floor. If she hadn't had school that day, she would've left them packed in case she needed to make a hasty exit. Since her mom wasn't summoning the guards on her, she no longer needed to take everything she'd packed to school.

Amelia would've skipped the day's classes if she'd had to move out and find somewhere to stay. Instead, she went and trudged through her day. At lunch she spared Dina the details of her morning and focused on meeting Malcolm's parents.

"I told you he likes you," Dina teased.

"You did," Amelia said as she finished her lunch. "I didn't mean for it to happen, and he'll stop liking me after his parents disapprove tonight."

Dina scoffed. "Why would they disapprove? You're smart, kind and obviously attractive to Malcolm."

"You forgot poor."

Dina waved a hand in dismissal and rolled her eyes. "If Malcolm wanted a rich girl, he'd put up with a snob like Scarlet. It's up to him, not his parents, who he likes. All you need to figure out is if you like him."

Amelia busied her hands with tidying her lunch tray. It gave her something to look at that wasn't Dina's smug face. "I don't know if I do."

Whether she liked Malcolm wasn't something she wanted to dwell on. A couple weeks ago she'd been content to be single forever. The fact that there might be someone she wanted to be with, romantically, unsettled her. It was a life change she wasn't ready to accept. "I like my independence."

Dina laughed. Amelia didn't think it was funny that she wanted control over her own life. "Dating someone doesn't mean you have to give that up. Do you really think I rely on Jack for everything?"

"No, I suppose you don't."

Chapter 12

Amelia thought about her conversation with Dina all afternoon and on the bus ride home. Malcolm hadn't told her otherwise, so home is where she went. Her school clothes would never do for meeting his parents unless she really wanted to turn them off. A couple weeks prior, that would have been tempting.

In her current state, she didn't want to make a horrible impression. Mediocre was realistically the best she could aspire too. With that in mind, Amelia put on a clean pair of black jeans, a flowy long sleeve top and her everyday boots. She went outside and leaned against the wall of her building to wait for Malcolm and eat a sandwich made from scraps of tempeh and vegetables left in her fridge. There was no time to eat a formal supper with her parents.

Amelia was ready to trudge back inside to wait when Malcolm drove up and parked. He hadn't noticed her and was unbuckling his seatbelt. She walked over and grasped the passenger door handle to spare him the effort.

He pushed a button on his door to unlock hers when he spotted her. "I would've come to your apartment."

Amelia sat on the passenger seat, pulled the door closed and fastened her seatbelt. "I know. I wanted to save you the trouble."

"Most girls I know aren't that considerate," he said as he started the engine and pulled away from the building. "It's nice."

Nice. Amelia could think of worse things he might've called her, and better ones. Hopefully, his parents would have half as good of an assessment of her. During the drive to his house in Quarter 3, she tried not to stress. No matter what his parents thought, Malcolm could make up his own mind.

His house was two storeys tall of concrete bricks. The front yard had fresh, green grass and vibrant, colourful flowerbeds against the house. Amelia didn't know the names of the flowers, but they smelled sweet and clean.

Malcolm parked his car on a strip of asphalt that ran up the side of the front yard, perpendicular to the street, while Amelia gaped at the flowers. When he opened her door and she got out, they walked to the front door, and Amelia noticed the curtains hanging in the upstairs windows, which looked thicker, sturdier as well as nicer than the curtains in her and her parents' bedrooms.

Malcolm's front door opened onto the main floor of his house with stairs at the far-left side of the room painted dove grey. At the back of the entryway was a door, and there was a partial wall to separate the entrance from the living room to the right, which had plush couches in front of a coffee table across from the wall screen. Carpet, a couple shades darker than the walls, covered the living room floor while the entry had tiles. A metal shoe rack and coat hooks were against the partial wall.

Amelia hardly had time to remove her shoes and put them in an empty spot when Malcolm's parents walked into the entryway.

"You must be Amelia," a middle-aged woman with yellow hair like Malcolm's said. "Malcolm has told us about you."

"All good things, I assure you," the man that must've been Malcolm's dad said. He shared Malcolm's green eyes and golden skin tone, though his hair was darker blonde, while Malcolm's mom had hazel eyes and a fairer complexion with rosy cheeks.

"He hasn't told me much about you, I'm afraid." Amelia said, making Malcolm blush.

His dad laughed. "Didn't want to bore you with our dull lives, I'm sure."

"Edward, really," Malcolm's mom said with the exasperation of someone used to putting up with their husband's antics.

Edward smiled at Amelia as his wife tapped him on the arm. "Don't worry, dear. I'll behave myself."

Malcolm's mom sighed. "Come in, Amelia. I'll show you where we're sitting. Malcolm, you can help your father."

"Okay, Mom." Malcolm grazed Amelia's arm with his fingers as he followed his dad across the entryway and through the door at the back.

Amelia went with Malcolm's mom. From the front door, she hadn't seen the doorway at the back of the living room, which was where Malcolm's mom led her. On the other side was a dining room with white walls and a rectangular stone table framed with six chairs with red cushioned seats. A matching tablecloth ran down the middle. There was also a closed door on the left wall that Amelia assumed led to the room Malcolm and his dad had gone into. It was a drastically different setup from her kitchen at home that doubled as a dining room.

"You have a lovely home, Mrs. Connor," Amelia said to break the silence.

Malcolm's mom smiled at her. "Thank you, Amelia. And you can call me Rebecca if you'd like."

"Okay," Amelia said. "Where should I sit?"

Rebecca gestured to the chair on the table side farther from the door on the left. "You can sit here if that suits you."

Malcolm's mom was nice, and much more formal than Amelia's mother.

She tried to keep her manners, even though she felt terribly out of place. What was Malcolm doing? "Here is fine."

As Amelia sat, Edward opened the door across from her. She got a peek into their storage room as he and Malcolm walked in with arms loaded with puzzle boxes.

"Sorry it took so long," Malcolm said when he set the boxes down and sat beside her. "They were buried behind some things on a shelf."

It had only been a few minutes, nowhere near long enough to warrant an apology. "That's alright."

Edward and Rebecca sat at their own chairs, across from Malcolm and Amelia. Amelia tried not to fidget. She was under Malcolm's parents' scrutiny and felt a bit guilty that she couldn't invite Malcolm to her house. It wasn't as nice a place and would embarrass them both.

Amelia kept her hands clasped on her lap while Malcolm and his parents chose a puzzle and dumped the pieces. She didn't want the Connors to think she was rude.

Completing the puzzle, a scenic picture of a park that must've been based off one in the rich Quarters, helped Amelia relax and took attention off her. Malcolm's parents asked her questions about things she expected, like what her parents did for livings. Amelia told them the truth: her father worked in an office doing paperwork and her mother was an administrative assistant at one of the elementary schools. Neither job was high paying, but they offered more dignity than the worst jobs in the City.

Between answering questions, Amelia caught Malcolm's eyes on her. She smiled at him, knowing to do more would be too far. There was only so much flirting one could get away with in front of parents.

When the puzzle was complete, Amelia admired it before helping dismantle it. The picture was beautiful, and she'd never seen a real place that resembled it. Amelia imagined being surrounded by that much greenery and fresh air would be calming, especially compared to the grime that pervaded most Apartment Districts.

When the puzzle pieces were back in the box, Rebecca took Edward into the storage room to place it on the shelf it came from.

"Your parents are kind," Amelia said to Malcolm. She had to say something to fill the silence while they were alone.

Malcolm chuckled. "They're happy I brought someone home. My mom fretted all day over what to do that might impress you."

"She didn't have to go to any trouble."

"She did it because I told her I was trying to impress you."

Amelia smirked and made eye contact with him. He didn't need to try hard to do that. "You think I'm shallow enough to be wooed by a fancy house and a beautiful puzzle?"

Malcolm's eyes popped open. "You're not shallow. I just thought—"

Amelia chortled. "I was teasing."

"You really are different from girls that live around here."

Amelia didn't know whether Malcom meant it as a compliment and was spared from replying as Rebecca and Edward re-entered the dining room. In Rebecca's hands was a large photo album with a blue cover.

Amelia perked up when she saw the pictures were of Malcolm when he was younger. She leaned forward to watch as Rebecca flipped through the pages and pointed out her favourite pictures. "He was adorable," Amelia said when they got to his toddler pictures.

Rebecca smiled. "Thank you, Amelia. At least someone appreciates looking at them with me."

Malcolm blushed and ducked his head, grumbling under his breath.

"Malcolm doesn't?" Amelia asked.

Rebecca leaned back in her chair. "Oh no, but I had to get them out. Malcolm never brings anyone to meet us."

Amelia laughed. "My mom would do the same."

It was true, but Amelia had omitted that her parents kept their pictures in a box. The only album they had was one with pictures of their wedding and of their parents. It was smaller than Rebecca's album, and its cover and binder rings were old and worn. Showing it to Malcolm would display how poor her family was.

When Amelia had seen all the pictures, she offered to put the album away, which Rebecca refused. "There's no need. Besides, I don't want to keep you too late. Malcolm needs to make it back for curfew."

"I can take a bus," Amelia said. She didn't want to inconvenience anyone. Malcolm did enough for her already.

"I won't hear of that," Rebecca said. "Malcolm will drive you."

Resigned, Amelia gave her thanks to Rebecca and Edward for having her, and then she left with Malcolm.

"Thank you for coming," he said when they got outside.

"You're welcome," Amelia said as she walked with him to his car. "It was nice meeting your parents. They're lovely." She hadn't expected them to be as nice as they were.

Malcolm unlocked the car and opened the passenger door. "Telling them I was bringing you over got them to stay home. It's only now that I can get a Courtship that they pay me any attention."

Amelia frowned as she and Malcolm climbed into the car and shut their doors. If they'd been dating, she might've rested her hand on his. Instead, she occupied her hands with reaching for her seatbelt. "I'm sorry. I understand the pressure from parents to get a Courtship."

"Did you talk to them?"

Amelia needed a moment to realize what he was referring to, though she'd had that conversation with her parents merely the day before. It was the somewhat ambiguous question that confused her. "My mom tried to summon the guards on me."

Malcolm settled his eyes on her as he started the engine. They were soft, like he sympathized with her. "All because you want to help people?"

Amelia dipped her head. She'd expected her mom's reaction. It was how her dad had handled it that she hadn't anticipated. "My dad talked her out of it. He supports me going."

Malcolm beamed. "Good. You can ride upfront with me."

Amelia shook her head as Malcolm backed his car onto the street. "I don't know where we're going. I'd be a useless navigator."

"You don't need to navigate. We just have to drive south."

Malcolm sounded so confident, and Amelia wanted to be that way. Maybe being near Malcolm would help her do so. "Alright," she said as he drove her home. "I trust your judgement."

Chapter 13

Things between Amelia and her mom would've been tense in the days leading up to Saturday if Amelia had been home much. When she wasn't at school, she was with Dina, Jack and Ethan until curfew getting supplies and setting their plan. None of them had wanted to take her money to buy food, saying they could bring meals from home, but Amelia insisted. It allowed their parents to eat a bit better for a couple days, which her friends appreciated.

Amelia hadn't told Malcolm about the money. It went farther split four ways, and Malcolm didn't need her handout. He probably would've bankrolled their supplies himself if given the opportunity, and that wouldn't improve Jack's view of him.

With food bought for their journey, Amelia spent the remainder of her time doing her homework and packing her bag. Arlo Fenn had told Jack it was warmer south of the Outskirts by a noticeable amount. So, Amelia dug out her lightest pants and a t-shirt to wear and a spare shirt and undergarments to change into. Other than that, she packed her toothbrush and deodorant. That seemed like all she would need for a quick overnight trip.

On Saturday morning, Amelia grabbed a quick breakfast from the kitchen, stuffed her food and bottled drinks for the trip into her bag, hugged her parents goodbye and flew down the stairs. She almost thought Malcolm had backed out as his car wasn't on the street. There was only a bigger, longer, black vehicle. The driver's door opened, and someone got out. A flash of blonde hair peeked over the top of the vehicle, and the figure straightened up. *Malcolm.*

"What happened to your car?" Amelia asked as he walked over.

"I borrowed my dad's van," he said. "We need something bigger. And my car doesn't have the Gate pass."

Amelia wondered at the extent of Malcolm's wealth. There was such a divide between them. How would a relationship ever work out? "Your family has more than one vehicle?"

"My dad didn't buy this or pay for it. It's his work van," Malcolm said. "But yes, we have two cars: mine and my parents'."

Amelia was out of her depth around Malcolm. With his parents' blessing or not, she would never fit into his world. "My parents have to skimp to afford bus money."

Malcolm's eyes softened. "I know. I'm not trying to brag, Amelia. You asked."

Amelia adjusted her grip on her bag for something to occupy herself with. "Yes, I did, and we should go. Before the others worry that we backed out."

Malcolm smirked as he opened the van's passenger side door. Amelia got in and set her bag next to Malcolm's at her feet. She wanted her food and drinks nearby, especially since the drive was going to be long.

In the time before the City was all anyone knew, people had gone even farther than she and her friends were going, and not always out of necessity. She couldn't imagine devoting that much time to traveling. Everything Amelia needed was in the City. She'd never been anywhere else. Citizens didn't go away on vacation; there was nowhere to travel to. That didn't mean she wasn't curious and eager to see the Colony.

Malcolm drove to the pre-arranged pick-up spot for Jack, Dina and Ethan, where they were all waiting on the side of the road with their bags. Amelia hoped Ethan wouldn't feel left out now that she'd been on a couple dates with Malcolm. They weren't an official couple, but Jack had told Ethan she wasn't interested in dating and then she'd gone on a date with Malcolm. It could be awkward.

Amelia exited the van when Malcolm did and waved at her friends. Jack and Ethan had never seen his car, so she didn't bother telling them the van wasn't his typical vehicle. "Have you been waiting long?"

Ethan shook his head.

"Nope," Dina said.

"A couple minutes," Jack added.

"That's not too bad," Amelia said as they all walked to the van and climbed inside with their bags.

The van had a second row of two seats with a gap between them leading to the back row of three seats. Jack and Dina moved to the back row, for a semblance of privacy Amelia assumed, and Ethan sat behind Malcolm.

Amelia turned on her seat as Malcolm started the van and pulled away from the curb. She glanced at Ethan. "How are you?"

"I'm fine," he said, keeping his voice down so no one else would overhear. "Any idea what we're delivering?"

Amelia smirked. "You know they never tell us."

"I thought they might since it's to the Colony," Ethan said, wringing his hands in his lap. "Aren't you wary? Not knowing what to expect has me on edge."

"No. I'm more curious than anything."

"Good. At least one of us should be."

Amelia turned back around on her seat. The road running down the side of the Apartment Districts was dull. Her only view was the sides of buildings and the occasional black guard van parked along the road.

When they entered Apartment District 12, Malcolm steered towards the meeting place Jack had arranged with Arlo Fenn. Outside a dingy, high-rise apartment building with cracks running up its wall stood Arlo. Amelia couldn't see any crates or sacks. Perhaps he hadn't wanted to carry them out himself.

Malcolm parked the van, and Ethan and Jack scrambled out. Dina lingered behind in her seat, seeming unwilling to follow the boys. "You're staying here?" Amelia asked Malcolm.

He nodded. "I should. Come get me if you need help."

Giving a nod of her own, Amelia clamoured out after Ethan and Jack. "Where's our cargo?" Amelia asked as she caught up to them.

"Inside," Arlo Fenn. "It isn't safe out here."

"True enough," Ethan said. "Take us to it."

Arlo turned and held the door open, waiting for Amelia and the boys to enter. The inside of the building was free of dust, though the paint on the walls was faded and the floor tiles had cracks in them. It made her glad she wasn't poor enough to need to live here.

Arlo Fenn led them across the entry to a plain door covered in peeling, white paint. He knocked twice. "Kelsie? You in there?"

The door cracked open, and a teen girl, approximately Amelia's age, with curly brown hair, fair skin and hazel eyes stuck her face in the gap. Her eyes were curious, not the least bit wary. "Where else would I be?"

"Do you have the stuff ready?"

Kelsie dipped her head. Amelia heard her unlatch the look on the inside of the door, and then she swung it open. The tiny room was cramped with items covering every surface. At the far side, someone had made a makeshift bed out of fabrics of varying hues – Amelia couldn't tell if they were clothes, blankets, curtains or random pieces of cloth – just wide enough for a single person to sleep atop on their side.

Between the bed and the door were crates, sacks and furniture buried under dusty stacks of papers, clothes, books and various other things Amelia couldn't identify. On the floor beside the crates and sacks were a duffle bag and backpack. They looked cleaner, or at least less dusty, than the surrounding objects. Amelia wondered why someone would live in this room, as Kelsie obviously was.

"You two can start carrying the crates," Kelsie said, waving a finger over Jack and Ethan. "You," she pointed at Amelia, "can help me."

Amelia blinked as the boys carted off two of the crates. "Help you with what?"

Kelsie titled her head to the side and peered at Amelia. "I have to erase all traces of being here, so I need you to help me dispose of my bed."

"Why?" Surely the crates and sacks were the cargo. Why would she need to disappear? Unless…

"You aren't quick on the uptake," Kelsie said. "You're giving me a ride."

Amelia turned to Arlo. "Our cargo is a person?" She didn't know how she felt about smuggling an entire person.

"You wanted to do deliveries," Arlo said. "This is all I could give you."

"There's no time for this," Kelsie said. She grasped Amelia's arm and pulled her into the room. "Grab an armload and follow me."

Seeing she had no other choice, Amelia scooped up as much of the fabrics as she could, glad there didn't seem to be many in the pile, and followed

Kelsie out the room and down the hall. Kelsie stopped at a metal door, shoved it open with her side and stomped inside. Amelia followed into the small room with black burn marks on the floor and nothing else.

Kelsie dropped her bundle onto the burn marks, so Amelia did the same. As soon as Amelia's hands were empty, Kelsie threw a small lighter at her. "Light the pile. I'll go get the rest."

Amelia didn't have the opportunity to ask questions as Kelsie bolted from the room, so she clicked the lighter and held it to the bundle of fabrics. She had to hold the lighter to a few different spots to get the pile to ignite with a decent flame. Kelsie seemed pleased when she came with the rest of the pieces, and the fire didn't die when she added them.

Kelsie grabbed the lighter from Amelia, pocketed it and yanked Amelia out of the room by her arm. "We need to get my stuff. The fire will die when it's all in ashes." She pulled the door closed with her free hand and speed walked Amelia back to where Jack and Ethan were moving the last of the crates.

In a daze, and wondering how she'd gotten into this situation, Amelia hefted two of the sacks while Kelsie slid her arms through the backpack straps, slung the duffle bag strap over her shoulder and picked up the other two sacks. "Let's go," Kelsie said.

"Are you going to tell me why you're heading to the Colony?"

Kelsie patted the duffle bag. "I have valuables to deliver."

"You're not moving there?" Amelia had no idea there were people that went back and forth. It seemed like a hard and risk-filled life.

"I'm too useful for Arlo for that. He rescued me from the Foster Centre, and I earn my keep, wherever he puts me, by moving goods to the Colony. He can't go himself."

"But—"

"No more questions. I told you too much already."

Amelia sighed as they got outside. Malcolm had exited the van and was helping Ethan and Jack arrange the crates in the trunk. Amelia and Kelsie approached with their sacks, and the three boys stared at the new addition to the group. There was no sign of Dina outside the van.

Malcolm raised an eyebrow in question and looked at Amelia.

"This is Kelsie," she said as she passed Ethan the sacks in her arms. "She's part of our cargo."

Jack swore under his breath. "This is a bad idea."

"We already committed to it, Jack," Ethan said. "Can't really back out now."

"Nope," Kelsie said. "You're stuck with me until we get back tomorrow before curfew."

Malcolm closed the trunk and moved his gaze to Kelsie. "You know where we're going?"

"Yup," Kelsie said with a bob of her head.

Malcolm swung his eyes to Jack. "It was dangerous already."

Jack sighed. "Fine. We'll take you."

Kelsie lifted her chin as she walked to the side door of the van. "I'll let you think you have a choice."

As Amelia walked to the passenger door, she saw Jack shake his head. It was strange seeing him flustered.

When they were all back in the van, with Kelsie sitting behind Amelia and Dina being introduced to Kelsie, Malcolm drove south to the City's wall. In it stood two massive slabs of metal. In front of the slightly smaller one with a vertical split down its middle, stood a lone uniformed guard holding a scanner in his gloved hand with people lined up across from him. This was the Foot Gate for pedestrians that only required ID passes and would've been busier on a weekday with Outskirts workers who lived in the City going to their jobs.

Malcolm drove to the larger piece of metal: the Car Gate. There was no guard, only a built-in scanner that read windshield passes. It flashed red as it processed the one on the van, and the slab of metal rose upward, retracting into the cement wall.

It was an impressive process, and Amelia couldn't help gawking at it. Equally as impressive was the Gate lowering itself behind their vehicle.

"Do you do this often?" she asked Malcolm.

"Not too often. And I've never been the one driving."

So, this was new to him as well. Amelia liked sharing a new experience with Malcolm and smiled as she watched the Outskirts go by outside her window. How unexpected was that?

Chapter 14

The Outskirts were different from what Amelia expected. She'd envisioned apartment buildings with paved roads and shops. The reality was sprawling, short buildings spread out on unpaved roads. There were no high-rises, and few shops. Instead, there were small, single storey, squat houses. Separated from them were the jail and End Camp. Each was short and wide. In the City, buildings went upwards; here, they stretched horizontal. There was so much space.

Kelsie stretched her arm between Malcolm's seat and Amelia's and pointed out to the road running past the End Camp. "Keep going that way."

"Alright," Malcolm said. He kept his eyes on the dirt road, as he had since they exited the Car Gate.

Kelsie retracted her hand, rustled through her backpack and pulled out a small piece of paper. She stretched her hand forward again, leaning on her seat towards Malcolm. "Give the guards this."

"Guards?" Ethan asked, panic creeping into his voice, as Malcolm grabbed the paper and set it on the console between him and Amelia.

Amelia was too distracted by the mention of guards to sneak a read of it. Why did they need to worry about guards out here? Amelia thought they only operated in the City, and perhaps that was naïve.

Kelsie sat back on her seat. "The ones at the checkpoint. Didn't Arlo mention that?"

"No," Jack said from the back of the van. "He didn't."

Kelsie shrugged. "Good thing I have a pass. We'd never get past it otherwise."

"What else didn't Arlo tell us?" Malcolm asked in a deadpan tone.

Amelia saw him tighten his grip on the steering wheel.

Kelsie hugged her torso and gazed at Malcolm with flat eyes. "How would I know?"

"Just keep driving," Ethan said. "We'll figure it out."

Amelia blinked, and in the corner of her eye, she saw Malcolm nod.

...

The guard checkpoint was at the southern edge of the Outskirts. In the distance, to the east and west, Amelia saw outlines of greenhouses and factories that produced the food and supplies that kept the City fed and functioning. A short wall, approximately a metre in height, marked the checkpoint. It stretched to the east and west, with a gap in the middle leading south. Amelia saw a black guard van parked on the Outskirt's side of the wall. In the gap stood two guards facing the van and waving for them to stop.

Malcolm stopped the van in the gap in the wall and lowered the driver's window as one of the guards walked up. Amelia slid the paper from the console between her and Malcolm's seats onto Malcolm's lap.

"What are a bunch of teenagers doing this far south?" the guard asked, the sun reflecting off his black helmet. "Can't let you through without a pass and your ID."

Malcolm picked up the paper, fished his ID pass out of his pocket and held both out to the guard. "Obviously not," he said. "I trust this is sufficient?"

Amelia didn't know how Malcolm stayed so calm. Being this near to a guard and unable to read his expression had her pulse racing and her palms sweating.

The guard lifted the passes, put them in front of his helmet, then lowered them again. Amelia assumed he read them and then glanced back at Malcolm, though his one-way visor made it impossible to know for certain. "You're Edward Connor's son."

"I am."

How did the guard know Malcolm's dad? Surely, Malcolm hadn't expected to run into anyone he knew here.

"He couldn't do the supply run himself, I presume," the guard said as he scanned the checkpoint pass with a portable reader from his pocket.

Malcolm laughed. It sounded a bit forced to Amelia, but she doubted the guard would notice. "He said it's time I helped out, and he has more important things to do than run errands."

The guard grunted and handed back the passes. "I won't delay you any longer. You can go." He signalled to the other guard, and they cleared the gap for Malcolm to drive onward.

A few minutes later, when Malcolm had pocketed his ID pass and Amelia couldn't see the guards in the side mirror, Jack spoke. "What happens if he decides to validate that story?"

"Don't worry. My father will corroborate it. He knows where I went."

"Sent us to get arrested at the checkpoint you mean," Jack scoffed.

"Don't, Jack," Dina said, her tone a warning.

"Amelia," Malcolm said, shooting her a glance. "Open the glove compartment. There's a checkpoint pass in there."

Amelia did as he asked. It required some rifling, but there was a small paper akin to the one Kelsie had pulled from her bag. She plucked it from the stack of documents in the compartment and showed it to Kelsie alongside the one Malcolm had used. "Are these the same?"

Kelsie grabbed both and scanned them. "Why'd I waste mine if you already had one?"

Malcolm shrugged. "How else could I see if I could trust you?"

Kelsie gave Amelia Malcolm's pass back and shoved hers back in her bag. "I suppose you have a point, but giving you a fake wouldn't benefit me."

"Unless you wanted to get us arrested," Jack said.

Amelia twisted on her seat and saw him leaning forward on his. His face was impassive. It was the tension in his shoulders and his clenched hands that gave away his anger.

Kelsie grunted. "Then I'd never get my delivery made. People need what I have in my bag."

"Which is what?" Dina asked. She leaned forward beside Jack and rested her elbows on her thighs.

Kelsie spun in her seat, leaving Amelia unable to read her face. "Trust goes both ways. I don't have enough in you yet to divulge that information."

"Sounds like code for food," Ethan commented.

"Thanks to the City's asinine food laws, it isn't," Kelsie snapped, whirling around to face him. "Food is what the Colony needs most, but buying it in bulk to ship out there garners too much suspicion."

"So, you've tried in the past," Jack said.

Kelsie let out a sound that was a cross between a huff and snort. "Not me personally."

Amelia was getting a headache. They were in the middle of nowhere, in a confined space with nothing other than barren land stretching as far as she could see and no escape from each other. With a deep breath, Amelia gave

Jack her most intimidating glare. "Stop trying to bait her."

Jack scowled, sat back on his chair and crossed his arms loosely across his abdomen. "Fine."

Amelia sighed. Not only was this ride going to be long, but it was also becoming stressful. She went to her bag and took out some food. Munching on her precut apple slices dipped in peanut butter and drinking her water helped work out her frustrations.

With the mood somewhat calmer in the van, and her snack eaten, Amelia resumed watching out the window. As they got farther south, she started to see trees in the distance. She'd never seen a live tree before, only pictures in books of what the world used to look like, and she'd heard the rumours of trees at the northern edge of the City. Only guards and Government officials had permission to go there. If residents of the wealthiest and northernmost housing sector, Quarter 4, could see the coast, they didn't talk about it.

Amelia handed Malcolm food from his bag when he asked. They didn't have time to stop for a break from driving, and his bag sat beside hers at her feet. It didn't bother Amelia to hand him his food, and she didn't snoop through the rest of what he'd packed. She wasn't the naturally suspicious type.

After fetching Malcolm's snack, Amelia nestled against her seat and closed her eyes. There was nothing to do except watch the landscape, and since Jack and Kelsie had stopped snapping at each other, it was peaceful. She could hear Jack and Dina murmuring to each other with words too quiet to decipher. With Malcolm driving and Ethan and Kelsie not speaking, the smooth motion of the ride lulled Amelia into a dreamless nap.

She woke when the sun was low in the sky. They'd been on the road all day, and her stomach growled. Amelia sat up and took a sandwich and carrot sticks from her bag, which, paired with her earlier snack, depleted much of her food. If she was careful, the rest would last her the return trip. "Where are we?" she asked Malcolm as she wiped sleep crust from her eyes. She hadn't intended to sleep as long as she did and hadn't been that tired. It must've been the early start and the monotonous view that put her to sleep.

"Still in the middle of nowhere," Malcolm said. "We should be getting close."

"A few more hours," Kelsie said with a flick of her hand. "It'll be dark when we arrive."

Amelia groaned and bit into her cucumber, spinach and tempeh sandwich. When she swallowed, she wiped her lips with the back of her hand. "Why does it have to be so far away?"

"Any closer and the Government would do something about it," Kelsie said. "Right now, they like to delude themselves into thinking anyone living there will perish."

"People actually survive that far south?" Ethan asked. "Isn't it scorching hot?"

Kelsie raked Ethan up and down with her eyes. "You must know what being hot is like."

Ethan blinked and his cheeks flushed pink; he was unaccustomed to anyone flirting with him. Amelia hid her smile. Ethan deserved someone's attention.

Kelsie smirked. "The Colony is nocturnal to cope with the heat."

"They'll be awake when we arrive," Malcolm said. "Do they know we're coming?"

"I assume so," Kelsie said with a nod. "But I have a question."

"Shoot," Malcolm said. He didn't seem the least bit concerned about what piqued Kelsie's curiosity.

"Why do you have a checkpoint pass? Is your dad involved in the Cause?"

Amelia had been wondering the same thing as Kelsie. Malcolm's dad had been nice when she'd gone to supper, and she hadn't asked him about his thoughts on the Cause. It was a dangerous topic to discuss with people you hardly knew.

"He arranges supplies for the climate scientists stationed south of the Outskirts," Malcolm said. "And he doesn't get upset if some end up at the Colony instead."

Kelsie leaned forward on her seat. "Those supply runs include food, don't they?"

Malcolm glanced at the rear-view mirror. Amelia couldn't tell from her vantage point if his eyes met Kelsie's. "Yes, bought on separate transactions with signed food request lists, permits and money from each of the scientists. It's the only way to do it with the current food laws. Dad says it's a pain."

"Wow," Kelsie said. "Even rich people dislike the food laws."

"The only people that like them are the Government, and possibly the food sellers and producers," Malcolm said.

Amelia saw the need to get rid of the food laws, but she didn't know how to do it. "How do people in the Colony feed themselves?"

"Not well," Kelsie said. "They rely on newcomers to bring food. If someone is desperate enough to move there, they're expected to bring food with them and share it. The Government's laws don't matter to people that stay in the Colony. They're only an issue for people that go back to the City."

Amelia felt for people who were that desperate to flee south of the City. It made her grateful her parents had enough money to keep her fed. "That doesn't sound sustainable."

Kelsie shook her head. "I've heard they grow some stuff, though the heat and soil aren't good for much more than a few select crops, and seeds are difficult to get."

Amelia thought people must've had things terrible in the City to risk the heat and awful food supply of the Colony. She was unequipped to live nocturnally on a few crops and whatever newcomers brought in. No wonder the Government didn't do anything about the Colony. No one could live there long term.

Chapter 15

The sky was black and cloudy when they arrived at a rudimentary wooden fence with platforms under crude roofs built into it at even intervals. Faint moonlight was the only source of illumination. Under the platform they faced was a metal gate with a latch. Amelia had never seen things made from wood, but with all the trees in the area, it made sense for a building material. The Colonists didn't have the capability of making concrete.

Inside the fence, the ground sloped down. Kelsie directed Malcolm to drive down it to two concentric circles of small wooden huts serving as houses. In the middle in the inner circle, there was a stretch of land surrounded with a smaller fence that had an arched entry and a larger gap at the far side. Kelsie pointed at the larger gap, and Malcolm drove and through to the section of dirt marked with previous tire tracks. The arched entry was too narrow to fit a vehicle through.

Amelia was curious about how a group of runaways had constructed the houses and fences without drawing the Government's attention. Surely there hadn't been many skilled crafts people flee the City to come here, or to bring tools and materials with them. Did construction workers in the City even know how to use wood? "How did they build all of this?" she asked as Malcolm parked the car.

"This used to be a research outpost for scientists," Kelsie explained. "They built everything and abandoned it when the weather got too hot this far south. They can't monitor climate and weather at night."

"And no one stopped a bunch of runaways from moving in?" Ethan asked.

"The Government doesn't see the point in stopping them," Malcolm said. "Living conditions are brutal here, and people leaving helps the City's overcrowding problem."

"It's illegal to leave the City without permission," Dina said. "Yet they aren't punishing anyone that makes it here."

"Where do we leave the supplies?" Amelia asked. "I don't see anyone here."

"Someone will come," Kelsie said. She had the door handle in her grasp and slid the door open before scooping up her bags and hopping out of the van.

Amelia scrambled out with Ethan, Jack and Dina. Malcolm hesitated before exiting and pocketing the key.

When her feet hit the ground, warm air enveloped Amelia. She couldn't imagine how hot it would get in daylight. Living in this heat was probably punishment enough for leaving the City in the Government's view.

Amelia heard two sets of footsteps approach from the narrower entrance in the fence. She turned her head in that direction and saw the outlines of two people. One had a flashlight and was using it to illuminate the ground. They must've been Kelsie's contact. Either that or they were Colonists investigating the newcomers.

The incoming people became clearer to Amelia as they neared and got under the patchy moonlight. One was a dark-skinned woman and the other a pale, auburn-haired man, both in their twenties. "Six of you this time, huh?" the woman said as she and the man stopped a couple metres from Amelia and her friends. "Must be a lot of stuff."

"It's never what we need most," the man said with a kick on the ground.

Kelsie hefted her duffle bag off the ground and thrust it at the man. "You'll find this valuable."

He grabbed it and yanked the zipper open. "It'll help some people. You know what we need more."

"Duh," Kelsie said with an eye roll. "Just medicine is easier to get. There are less laws about it."

"Medicine?" Jack asked.

Kelsie swiveled to face him and put her hands on her hips. "You got a problem with it? Lots of people come here when the Government tells them to go to the End Camp."

"No. I don't," Jack said, holding his hands up.

"Hmph," Kelsie said. "There's more stuff in the trunk."

Amelia and her friends unloaded the crates and sacks. When the cargo was out of the van, the Colonist woman walked off. "Follow us," she said over her shoulder. "No use leaving it here."

Amelia held back her sigh as she hefted a sack. It was bulky enough to be cumbersome and to impede her view of the ground. She squished the top down and tried to crane her neck over it to get a glimpse of where she was going. The attempt was in vain. Amelia would have to trust that the ground was somewhat level.

The Colonists led them to a shed across the fenced-in area. Amelia was glad not to have to lug the sack down the street. It was bad enough they had to make two trips to move all the cargo. The woman held the flashlight while the man pried the door open on creaky hinges. Maybe there was lubricant in one of the crates or sacks they could use to grease it.

"Pile it all in here," the man said as he held the door open. "Distribution day is tomorrow."

Amelia waited to put her sack inside. The boys were standing together, speaking in low voices. She saw Malcolm and Ethan nod. Jack stepped into the shed and Ethan passed him one of the crates while Malcolm grabbed the next. Amelia, Dina and Kelsie joined in on passing things to Jack, and the male Colonist stepped inside the shed to place the duffel bag.

When everything sat in neat stacks, the Colonist and Jack exited, and the Colonist shoved the door shut. He pulled a padlock from his pocket and latched the door. "Suppose you'll want somewhere to rest for a few hours before you head back. We'll show you where to go."

Malcolm bit his bottom lip and glanced at where his dad's van was. "I should stay with the van."

"Suit yourself," the male Colonist said.

Amelia and the others returned to the van to grab their personal bags. On that return trip, she spotted plants growing in the centre of this fenced-in area. Amelia had only seen crops in a greenhouse once while on an elementary school field trip when she was younger. She didn't know the names of the plants here in the Colony, but this had to be where they grew their food. It was a wonder they hadn't trampled any when moving the cargo.

When she reached the van, she grabbed her bag from the floor of the passenger seat and snuck a glance at Malcolm. A beam of moonlight shining through the window hit his hair and cast it in soft gold. He gave Amelia a small grin as he settled on his seat and put his hand on the lever to recline it.

"You sure about staying here alone?" Amelia asked.

He dipped his head. "I have to."

The idea of going with Dina and the others wasn't too appealing for

Amelia. She didn't want to leave Malcolm alone. "I could stay with you," she said, keeping her voice to a whisper as the others collected their bags and shut the van's doors.

Malcolm gazed at her with sleepy eyes. "Go sleep in a bed, or at least somewhere more comfortable where you can lie down. We shouldn't give people something to gossip about."

Amelia thought Malcolm would appreciate her company. Instead, it was her worst fear coming true. As soon as she started to let him in, he pushed her away. "Fine." She straightened up and adjusted her hold on her bag. How would she survive the ride home?

Malcolm met her eyes, a spark shining in his through the exhaustion. "Don't be angry. Please, Amelia."

"I'm not. I just thought you might want some company, and that we could get away with it here."

Malcolm's shoulders sagged. "If we were staying here, we could, but we're going home in a few hours. Someone will talk, and there's no telling what trouble it could cause."

He had a point. Kelsie and Jack were the wildcards in their group. Dina and Ethan wouldn't gossip about her and Malcolm. Would Kelsie and Jack keep their mouths shut? "I get it. Goodnight, Malcolm. See you in a few hours."

As Amelia walked with the others down the street, she felt sets of eyes on her from all directions. There were people out and about, and each one she walked by seemed to appraise her to see if she had something they wanted. It was a suspicious and predatory stare that made her hug her bag tight to her chest.

Their two escorts stopped at a small, wooden house. Judging by the exterior, it couldn't have held more than three rooms at the most. "You two," the woman said as she shined her flashlight over Ethan and Jack, "can stay here."

The male Colonist walked to the door, threw it open and gestured for the boys to go in. Ethan went, but Jack hesitated in the doorway and glanced at Dina. Amelia watched as her friend whispered in his ear and gave him a nudge into the house.

"You three are coming with me," the woman with the flashlight said. She started walking down the street, and Kelsie, with a grumble, darted after her.

Amelia fell into step beside Dina. The moon was peeking through the clouds, and her eyes had somewhat adjusted to the darkness, so Amelia didn't feel the need to walk in the flashlight's small arc of illumination. "Do you think Malcolm will be okay by himself at the van?"

"The better question is why you're worried."

"He's our ride home." That fact should've been obvious to Dina and made her worried as well. If something happened to Malcolm, or the van, they'd all be stranded. What if he drove off without them? The idea hadn't come to Amelia before. His dismissal of her offer to stay had shaken her idea of him and reminded her how little she knew him. Maybe this had all been a mistake.

"Are you ever going to admit that liking someone romantically isn't a bad thing?"

"I hadn't planned to," Amelia said. She picked up her pace, taking her chances on Kelsie being a less prying conversationalist. As she reached Kelsie, Amelia thought she saw a grin on the other girl's face.

"So," Kelsie said. "Does Ethan have an intended Courtship partner?"

That was how direct City teens needed to be. Just dating was casual; it wasn't worth the hassle if it wasn't going to lead to a Courtship. There were restrictions on what dating couples could get away with. "I don't think so."

"Huh," Kelsie said. "He's cute, I thought someone would've snatched him up by now."

"I think he's been overlooked and ignored," Amelia said, thinking of how Ethan ended up on watch duty or riding along on a truck bed more often than not. "No one, except Jack, really gives him any attention."

"Pity," Kelsie said. She craned her neck around to glance at the house Ethan and Jack were in. "You think he'd talk to me?"

"I don't know." Amelia said. "I have no experience with guys."

"And yet our driver can't keep his eyes off you."

Amelia didn't want to discuss Malcolm, not after he'd sent her away and when she was worried about him leaving. "Do you know where we're going?" It seemed like the woman with the flashlight was leading them a long way.

Kelsie shrugged and didn't protest the change in topic. "To another vacant house. They're sending us away from the boys on purpose."

"I thought City laws didn't matter here."

Kelsie snorted. "As soon as you, or anyone here, returns to the City, the Government could scrutinize what they did here under a microscope. The permanent Colonists don't care, although they try to help short term stayers break as few laws as possible. You never know who's a Government spy or who'll tattle to a guard for their own gain."

As few as possible. Amelia understood better now why Malcolm hadn't let her stay. Just leaving the City with a fake excuse was one law she'd already broken. Hopefully, it wouldn't impact Dina and Jack's Courtship application. She'd hate for her friends to be forced apart because of it.

Chapter 16

The woman holding the flashlight stopped at a house down the street and around the curve from where Jack and Ethan were. It looked a bit larger than the other house. Amelia just wanted a bed regardless of whether it was in its own bedroom.

The inside had a small kitchen, a bathroom and two bedrooms. The larger bedroom had a bed while the smaller bedroom had bunkbeds. Kelsie insisted on taking the larger room. Amelia assumed this was because she didn't trust her or Dina.

Amelia took Dina by the arm and steered her to the bunkbeds before Dina could protest. Amelia was too tired to argue, so she flopped on the lower bunkbed, threw her bag down beside her, and pressed her face into the pillow.

Amelia heard Dina climb the ladder to the top bunk. "Do you think Jack is okay?" Her voice was soft and quiet. Amelia had never heard her friend so worried.

Amelia rubbed her eyes and rolled over. "Yeah. He can take care of himself, and he has Ethan with him."

"I can't sleep. What if something happens?"

Amelia planted her elbows on the mattress and pushed herself to sitting. She held back a sigh and kept her voice calm. Why was Dina stressing? "I'm sure Jack is fine. What's the worst that could happen?"

Amelia heard Dina shuffle along the mattress and saw her legs swing over the side. She hoped Dina wasn't about to do something rash. Then Dina jumped down from the top bunk and veered to the bedroom door.

"I can't lie here and worry. I have to go check on Jack."

Amelia groaned. This was not a clever idea. It wasn't like Dina and Jack lived together in the City. Surely, she could cope with being away from him. "You shouldn't—" Her friend had darted out of the room before Amelia could finish her sentence. Amelia ran from the bedroom and knocked on Kelsie's door. When there was no answer, Amelia flung it open to find an empty bed and an open window. A quick check of the bathroom confirmed her suspicion that both girls had fled.

Amelia cursed. She'd wasted precious seconds checking for Kelsie, who was also missing. She ran out the front door and turned back the way they'd walked in. It didn't matter to Amelia that people were in the street. She sprinted towards the house Jack and Ethan were in, finding no sign of Dina on route. Amelia hadn't thought her friend was that fast.

Amelia dodged the Colonists in the street and elbowed her away around the ones in her path. She slowed to a walk a few houses away from where Jack and Ethan were, panting and unable to keep up her sprint. In the near distance, she spotted Dina. With a groan, Amelia jogged up to her friend and rested a hand on her shoulder. "Dina, what are you doing?"

"Mellie!" Dina yelped.

Amelia hadn't intended to frighten her, and she moved her hand to Dina's elbow. "Kelsie left too. Come on. We have to find her."

"Not before I check on Jack." Dina wriggled out of Amelia's grip, strode to the door and knocked. "Jack? Are you in there?"

There was no answer. Amelia moved after Dina but was too slow. Her friend was already opening the door and stepping into the house. This was an unwise decision. A pit grew in Amelia's stomach, yet she had no choice except to follow. She couldn't leave Dina alone in there.

The house had Jack's and Ethan's bags thrown on the couch, and the boys were gone. Amelia found Dina standing in front of Jack's bag, wringing her hands and her face drained of colour.

"I knew something happened," Dina said with a shaky voice. There were tears pooling in her eyes.

Amelia grabbed Dina's wrist and rerouted her towards the front door and away from the bags. Getting Dina away from Jack's abandoned bag was imperative. "Don't worry. We'll find him."

Dina clung to Amelia as the two girls made it outside. Amelia stood on the street and turned her face left and right. She heard muffled voices, one male and one female, coming from behind the house. It was on the outer circle, so there was only open land leading to the upward slope behind it. She pulled Dina with her as she went to investigate.

Standing against the rear wall of the house was Ethan. Kelsie stood in front of him, her body centimetres from his and her hands braced on the wall on either side of him and keeping him from moving. Amelia's eyes and mouth popped open. *Well, that's one mystery solved.*

Kelsie was gazing at Ethan and slid one hand closer to his body. Ethan kept his eyes on her face and made no move to push her away.

Amelia cleared her throat, and both Kelsie and Ethan swiveled their heads to her. Ethan's face went red, and he bent his knees to lower his body and duck under Kelsie's arm. Kelsie removed her hands from the wall and stood up straight. There was annoyance in her eyes as she stared at Amelia. "What are you two doing here?"

"Looking for Jack. Right, Dina?" Amelia nudged her friend.

Kelsie rolled her eyes. "He isn't here."

Dina trembled and her face went pale. "Where did you send him?"

Kelsie's jaw dropped open. "He was gone before I got here."

"Jack went to check on Malcolm," Ethan said as his eyes landed on Amelia. "He wanted to make sure our ride was still here."

Amelia should have guessed that Jack was distrustful enough to act on that suspicion. "You didn't talk him out of it?"

Ethan shook his head. "I didn't have a chance. He barely told me where he was going on his way outside."

"Don't get angry at Ethan," Kelsie said as she rested her palm on his chest and stepped in front on him as if to shield him from Amelia. "I arrived just after Jack left and talked Ethan into coming back here with me."

"I'm not angry," Amelia said as she turned to Dina. "Can we please go to sleep now?"

Dina wiped her eyes and raised her chin up. "You know we can't until I make sure Jack is okay."

That was how Amelia found herself jogging back to the garden. There was no changing Dina's mind once she'd made it, and the fastest way to get a few much-needed hours of sleep before they had to leave was to go find Jack. Amelia let Kelsie and Ethan stay behind. Part of her was glad to see someone giving Ethan attention. It had to be awkward for him being the one ignored and not paired up out of their group.

Amelia wasn't sure what she and Malcolm were yet, and had conflicting feelings about his rejection, but she didn't want him getting in a fight with Jack. If things were tense just between the two of them, she would've let them work it out. Since Dina was dating Jack, it wasn't that simple.

Amelia slowed her pace, and Dina's by way of her hand on Dina's arm, as they neared the fence. With no flashlight and clouds obstructing most of the moonlight, she didn't want to damage the Colony's meagre crops.

Amelia led Dina along the edge of the garden beds, using the weak moonlight to find a crop-free route. The van was where they left it. Amelia spotted it before she could see Jack or Malcolm and wasn't sure if the boys were nearby. There was no way Dina would leave before checking.

With the aim of getting this over with so she could sleep for a few hours, Amelia walked with Dina to the van. As she and Dina got closer, Amelia heard voices. They stopped as whoever was speaking heard the crunch of Amelia's and Dina's boots on the dirt.

"Jack?" Amelia called.

A scuffling sound came from inside the van and the passenger door opened. In a beam of moonlight Amelia saw chestnut brown hair and exhaled in relief.

"What are you two doing here?" Jack asked as his boots hit the ground. He closed the van door and headed to the rear, where Amelia and Dina stood.

Dina rushed to him and flung her arms around his middle. "I was worried."

"She insisted on checking on you," Amelia added. "Where's Malcolm?"

Jack was holding Dina tight against him and stroking her back. "In the van."

Amelia inhaled deep and approached the driver's side door as Jack calmed Dina down. She knocked on the window, trampling down the butterflies in her stomach. "Malcolm? Are you awake?"

She couldn't see anyone sitting on the front seats, but Jack had said Malcolm was inside. The tinted back windows made checking for occupants on the rear seats impossible. Amelia didn't want to barge in, especially if

Malcolm wasn't awake. While she debated what to do, the sliding rear door on the driver's side of the van cracked open with fingers gripping the edge.

The door opened all the way, and Amelia spotted blonde hair and tired emerald eyes. It was Malcolm.

"Amelia? Why aren't you sleeping?"

Amelia lifted her shoulders and let them drop. "Dina was worried about Jack. I couldn't let her roam the street alone."

Malcolm sat with his legs hanging over the bottom edge of the van side. His eyes swung towards the back end of the van, approximately where Dina and Jack were. "They seem close."

That was an understatement. "I don't know two people more suited for each other."

Malcolm set his eyes on Amelia and frowned. She hadn't meant to wound him with her remark; it was only the truth as she understood it.

"Yet seeing them happy together hasn't made you want that."

Amelia's jaw dropped, and she snapped it closed. "I never knew anyone worth taking that risk for." She'd taken it earlier, and that hadn't gone well.

Malcolm opened his mouth to reply, but Dina's whisper of "Mellie!" made him close it and scoot back inside the van. "Go get some rest. I'll see you in a few hours."

Amelia walked away as Malcolm shut the van door. Dina was standing behind the van next to Jack and smiling. "We can sleep now."

"You better mean that." If Dina ran off again, Amelia was tempted to let her. She was too tired to be her friend's sitter.

"She does," Jack said. "I calmed her down."

With Jack's reassurance, Amelia led Dina back to their small wooden house. As Dina went to her top bunk, Amelia checked Kelsie's room. The window was closed, and Kelsie's brown curls were peeking out from the top of the blanket. Apparently, her make out session with Ethan, or whatever Amelia had walked in on, was over.

Knowing both Kelsie and Dina were in the house, Amelia flopped down on the bottom bunk and closed her eyes. She woke in a couple hours to Dina shaking her shoulders. With a groan, Amelia sat up. It was pre-dawn, meaning there was little time to waste. They had to make it back home before curfew.

Amelia threw on the change of clothes from her bag and ate more of her packed food. She'd wanted to leave some for the people living in the Colony, but she barely had enough to last the drive home. And who knew which people here reported goings on to the guards in the City? She didn't fear too much for herself, but for Dina and Jack on account of their Courtship application.

With her stomach satisfied, Amelia walked with Kelsie and Dina back to the van. There were people in the street, all heading to their own houses. They gave the girls a wide berth. Amelia didn't blame them. She and her friends were outsiders in this place, there for a night and then gone. It wasn't like she expected to make frequent trips here.

Ethan and Jack were already at the van when the girls arrived. Malcolm was leaning against the trunk, munching on an apple and drinking from a water flask. He flicked his eyes onto Amelia and said nothing. The ride home was going to be tense.

Chapter 17

Amelia glanced at Malcolm as he drove up the slope to the Colony's fence. While they were stopped for Kelsie to get out and open the gate, Amelia cleared her throat. "Malcolm?" she asked. "Are you upset with me?"

"No," he said, flicking his eyes onto her as he drove through the open gate and came to a stop again.

"About last night," Amelia said, keeping her voice down and wringing her hands as Kelsie climbed back onto her seat, having closed the gate. "I – I think you might be worth taking a risk for." It was difficult for her to admit to herself that she was ready to let someone close. She could no longer deny that being with Malcolm felt different than being around the boys she had classes with, or even Jack and Ethan. She wanted to see more of him, and he hadn't rejected her offer to be cruel. The few hours of sleep she'd gotten had given her clarity on that. "Can we just go slow and see where things end up? I don't want to make a huge deal out of it."

One corner of Malcolm's mouth tipped up as he shifted the van back into drive and pressed the gas pedal. "Sure. Whatever you need."

…

The drive to the southern edge of the Outskirts was uneventful and lulled Amelia into a sense of safety and belief they'd make it home well before curfew with no incident. That was until they reached the checkpoint. The guards stationed at it were different from the ones on their journey south.

Malcolm stopped and lowered his window when they flagged him down.

"What are a bunch of teenagers doing this far south?" one of the guards said as he stepped up to the window.

"Making a delivery to the scientists for my father," Malcolm said. He kept his hands on the steering wheel and his eyes on the guard's helmet.

The guard snorted like he didn't buy the story. "I'm going to need a checkpoint pass and the ID passes for everyone in the van." He extended a gloved hand, as if expecting them to hand over the documents that second.

"Certainly," Malcolm said.

Amelia didn't know how his voice stayed so calm. Her hands quaked as she dug her ID pass out of her bag and retrieved Malcolm's from the glove compartment. Sweat beaded on the back of her neck and her hairline, which she left unwiped. Kelsie handed her checkpoint and ID passes, along with Ethan's, Jack's and Dina's ID passes, to Amelia, who added them to the bundle she gave Malcolm. He placed them on the guard's hand, and the guard scanned them one by one.

No one in the van spoke. Amelia kept her eyes on the windshield and her hands, with sweaty palms, clasped in her lap. Showing her nerves would only make the guard more suspicious, but she was powerless to stop her foot from tapping. When the guard finished scanning the documents, he walked over to his partner. Amelia followed him with her eyes. They were too far away and speaking too quietly for her to make out anything they said.

The guard walked back with the stack of documents. "We're calling up the field station to confirm your story," he said to Malcolm. "I might've bought it if you didn't have Apartment District kids with you. This reeks of a contraband run."

Amelia tensed, her foot stilling. She hoped Jack and the others either didn't hear and wouldn't react to the guard's insult.

"Go head and call," Malcolm said with confidence Amelia wouldn't have possessed if she'd been in his position. "They'll validate my story, and maybe next time you'll think twice about stereotyping the vast majority of the City's residents."

The guard walked back to his partner, who pulled out a rectangular black box, pushed some buttons on its front and held it to the side of his helmet.

"Why would you tell him that?" Kelsie hissed. She was scowling and had her arms crossed against her chest as she leaned forward. "They're going to arrest us."

"Arrest us?" Dina asked with rising panic. "Then Jack and I will never get married."

Amelia spun around in her seat to glare at Kelsie. "You aren't helping," she snapped, her heart hammering in her chest.

"We should run for it," Kelsie said.

Ethan glanced out the window at the two guards, his bottom lip between his jaws. "I think I'd rather be in jail than shot."

Jack had curled his hands into fists and was leaning forward with fire is his eyes. "We shouldn't have done this."

Malcolm sat back on the driver's seat, his posture casual. "It's going to be fine."

Jack scoffed. "You say that because you can pay your way out of this mess."

Malcolm's eyes darkened a shade, and he sat up, turned around and glared at Jack. "I don't need to pay my way out of this. As I said, it's going to be fine."

Out Malcolm's window, Amelia saw the guard re-approach their van. He was still holding their ID passes and stuck the pile through Malcolm's window when he reached it. "You're free to go."

Malcolm whirled around to grab the stack of IDs and hand them to Amelia. He gave the guard a single nod, raised his window and drove through the checkpoint. Amelia slid her and Malcolm's IDs into their bags and handed the rest to Kelsie. Her checkpoint pass was now expired, being good for a return trip, and she wouldn't get it back.

"How did you get away with that?" Amelia asked Malcolm. Her heart was starting to slow its pace, though she felt lingering adrenaline rushing through her veins.

Keeping his face pointed forward, he gave her a lopsided smile. "My father has used and lent his truck for Colony supply runs before. He has an agreement with some of the scientists to back up any drivers that are questioned in exchange for extra bottled water."

"They lie to guards just for water?" Amelia wasn't sure she would've done the same. Was it worth the risk of going to jail?

"Definitely," Malcolm said. "The field scientists don't have the option to work at night, and it gets scorching outside."

"Wait," Kelsie said, having just passed Ethan the stack of IDs. "You're really saying your dad helps supply the Colony? Arlo never mentioned any rich members of the Cause."

"No, he wouldn't have," Malcolm said. "The Cause has been fractured for a long time. It's more of a bunch of small groups trying to do things their own way than a unified movement."

"There's truth to that," Ethan said.

He must've been thinking of Kylie and Lucas demanding money from the people they were supposed to help. "It's too bad all the supporters can't find a common ground. They'd accomplish more." Amelia thought there was one issue that might unite a bunch of them, but she didn't dare voice it. Figuring out how to do it wasn't her area of expertise.

"We can brainstorm it," Dina said. "There must be a way."

Dina's optimism did a lot to help dissipate the tense mood in the van. Amelia took to gazing at the barren land at the southern edge of the Outskirts. It was late afternoon and would be close to curfew when they reached their Apartment Districts. The green End Camp and jail, when they passed them, were a welcome sight as they indicated nearness to the City's wall.

Amelia didn't know how much tension she was carrying until Malcolm drove under the giant metal Car Gate and the pressure eased from her shoulders. They'd made it, and the sun was still in the sky.

Malcolm dropped Jack off first, then Dina and Ethan. Once they were gone, there was only Kelsie and Amelia left. She didn't seem in a hurry to leave or tell Malcolm where to take her.

Amelia twisted around on her seat. "Where are you headed?" It couldn't have been the place they'd picked Kelsie up from. Not after she'd burned her makeshift bed.

Kelsie shrugged. "Don't know. Arlo didn't tell me."

Amelia blinked. "What? You can't stay in the van forever."

A flicker of vulnerability flashed across Kelsie's face before she plastered her confident mask back on. "I know. I'll get out when you do and walk somewhere. Arlo always finds me when he wants to."

"No. I'll take you with me," Malcolm said. "You don't want to get arrested for wandering the streets after curfew, do you?"

"You're going to let a Foster Centre escapee live in your mansion?" Kelsie asked.

"It's not a mansion," Malcolm said. "Just a house with a spare room. And my parents can afford to feed you."

Amelia thought the idea of food paid for by someone else was what swayed Kelsie. She saw it in a spark in the girl's eyes.

"I'll go if you swear not to dictate my every minute."

Malcolm laughed. "I wouldn't dream of it." He had the sense to know bossing Kelsie around wouldn't go over well.

...

When Malcolm stopped at Amelia's building, he got out of the car with her. Amelia hefted her bag and gave him a little wave. "Thank you for everything," she said.

Malcolm reached for her hand. He'd stepped closer to her, bringing their bodies so close there were mere centimetres between them. The evening sun heightened his golden hue and sent butterflies flip-flopping in Amelia's stomach. "You're welcome."

Amelia gazed up at Malcolm. Past versions of herself would've pulled her hand from his and stepped away knowing how dangerous it was. Present Amelia wanted to do neither and didn't care about the danger. It didn't matter that Kelsie had moved to the passenger seat, that there were people on the street and neighbours with a view of her standing on the road touching a boy. Amelia went onto her tiptoes, titled her head and pressed her lips onto Malcolm's. She'd never kissed anyone before and wasn't sure she knew how. He responded by tilting his head and moving his lips against hers.

Amelia's knees went weak, her body warmed, and the outside world spun and blurred. The only people in existence in that moment were her and Malcolm. She wanted to stay in that bubble forever.

They came to a mutual, unspoken decision to break the kiss. Malcolm dropped her hand and jammed his into his pocket. He made no move to walk away. Amelia swallowed to calm her nerves and the butterflies in her stomach, certain her cheeks were pink. "I should go inside. Try not to let Kelsie pester you too much."

"I'll be fine," Malcom said. "I hope I can see you soon though."

Amelia adjusted her bag and stepped towards her building. "Me too."

…

She must've been grinning like someone that had inherited a fortune when she walked into her apartment as her parents both turned and stared at her from their places on the couch. Amelia gave them a small wave as she traipsed down the hall to her bedroom and dumped her bag on her bed, spilling the contents over her comforter.

Amelia was still surprised she'd kissed Malcolm. It wasn't that he'd kissed her and she'd reciprocated out of obligation. Kissing him had been her idea and her decision. She'd enjoyed it and thought he did too. As she'd walked into her building, she'd seen the hunger in his eyes and his lopsided smile.

This changed things in ways Amelia didn't want to admit to herself. Now Malcolm might expect something from her. Why did one kiss, done on a whim, have so much power?

Amelia had eaten all the food she'd packed, so there was only the previous day's outfit and her toiletries to put away. The menial tasks helped clear her mind. It didn't matter that she'd kissed Malcolm. Amelia refused to let things become awkward over it. Surely, he wouldn't presume too much over one moment. If he did, that would be his problem. They weren't anything official, and she wasn't sure whether she wanted to be.

Chapter 18

Amelia found it difficult to return to her daily routine. She hadn't told her parents anything about her kiss, only given them the condensed, drama free version of the trip. It wasn't something she wanted to discuss. She almost got away with telling no one about her moment with Malcolm, but she'd forgotten about the one person that knew her better than anyone.

As Amelia sat to lunch with Dina, her friend's eyes widened, and she beamed. "What are you hiding? I know it's something. You've got a dreamy, faraway look in your eyes."

"Nothing." Telling Dina what had happened would only give it more power to change things. She wasn't lucky enough for her best friend to let it go though.

"Tell me. You know I'll pester you until you do." Dina was leaning across the lunch table and pouting. She'd even clasped her hands to bolster her begging.

Amelia sighed. "I kissed Malcolm."

Dina screamed so loud Amelia had to cover her ears. The students at other tables stopped what they were doing to stare, making Amelia shrink in her seat. She felt heat flush to her cheeks and was sure they were red from embarrassment. "Dina, please."

Dina beamed. "This is so exciting. I knew you'd see that liking someone isn't a terrible thing."

"We aren't anything serious," Amelia said, ducking her head. "It was just a kiss."

"Do you want it to be serious?"

Amelia closed her eyes. She wished she'd skipped lunch today or eaten it somewhere else. This was too much of a scene, even if the other students had mostly resumed eating their own lunches. Amelia's love life wasn't interesting enough to keep their attention. "I don't know."

"Malcolm asked Jack about you," Dina said. "In the Colony."

Amelia's jaw dropped. This was news to her, as it wasn't something either boy would've announced to the van, and she hadn't seen them since. "What?"

"Jack told me." Dina said. "He said when he went to check on Malcolm that Malcolm asked him if he knew what you were looking for. Jack said he didn't know."

Amelia was desperate to get away from the topic of her feelings. "Kelsie moved in with Malcolm," she blurted. That did the trick. Dina burst out laughing and moved on from Malcolm's conversation with Jack.

Amelia was curious herself how Kelsie's move in was going. Malcolm's parents seemed like the lax and laidback type, but she hadn't any idea how they would react to him bringing a stranger home to stay. She hoped they weren't treating Kelsie like a charity case; she would not respond well to that.

Amelia would have to ask Malcolm by mailing him a note as her parents weren't wealthy enough to own a phone. She supposed she could show up unannounced and risk him not being home when she made a spontaneous visit, though it seemed the more considerate thing would be to send a note, which is what she decided to do.

When Amelia got home that afternoon, she grabbed a piece of paper and penned Malcolm a message. She didn't ask and give him the option to say no, just told him when she was coming.

...

On Sunday, after shopping with her mom, Amelia boarded the bus heading for the rich Quarters. Thankfully, the bus took her most of the way. It didn't go down Malcolm's street, but she was used to walking. The only tricky part was trying to remember the directions from when Malcolm had driven her.

Amelia got turned around a few times before eventually finding Malcolm's house and knocking on the front door. He was the one who opened it, and he gave her a small grin.

"Hello," Malcolm said. He was standing in the doorway, clutching the door jamb with one hand. His other was hanging at his side.

Amelia gave him a nod. "Hi. Where's Kelsie?"

"In the living room," Malcolm said. He stepped away from the door frame and beckoned Amelia in. "You've come to see her then? Not me?"

The twinkle in Malcolm's eye told Amelia he was teasing. "Well, both of you. I have an idea."

"An idea about what?" Kelsie asked, sticking her head through the doorway leading to the Connors' living room.

"Later," Amelia said as she kicked off her shoes, walked into the living room and sat on the couch. "First, I want to know how you've been doing. Have you heard from Arlo?"

Kelsie sat on an armchair across from the couch and wrinkled her eyebrows. "Why do you care? Are you scared I'm going to steal your boyfriend, and you want me gone?"

Amelia's eyes widened. She'd always tried to show interest in Dina's life. That was her idea of what friends did, and she'd only intended to be nice to

Kelsie.

Malcolm sighed. "Kelsie, I told you Amelia and I aren't dating."

That answered Amelia's question about whether he expected anything from their kiss. What if this was her nightmare come true and she meant nothing to him? She could process that later. At the moment, the important topic was Kelsie. "I don't want you to leave. I was trying to be friendly."

Kelsie huffed. "I told Arlo I'm here, and he wanted to send me on another assignment. I said no."

Amelia hadn't expected the bitterness in Kelsie's voice. She'd assumed the other girl had liked her life before, but she didn't know much about it. "I'm sorry," Amelia said, for lack of anything better to say.

"I'm not. I'm sick of being a nobody." She held up three fingers and counted off a list: "No home, no legal ID, no food."

Amelia had all those things. She didn't realize there were people in the City that didn't have at least the first two. The third did tie into one of the reasons she came here though. "We need to go after the food laws." She blurted it without context or lead-in while she had her courage. "It should be a cause a lot of people can get behind."

Kelsie was staring at her like she'd sprouted a second head. But Malcolm was regarding her with an upturned tilt to one side of his mouth.

"It could work," Malcolm said. "If executed well. If not, we'll end up in jail."

Amelia appreciated how he'd made himself part of it by using 'we' when they didn't even have a plan yet, and he could afford to pay his way out of a jail sentence. "It's worth it," she said. "I have nothing to lose."

"Me neither," said Kelsie. "I'm in."

Amelia assumed Ethan would be on board without hesitation, but Jack and Dina had one important thing to lose. She wanted their help, even if it would take some convincing. They'd have to do as much legally as they could. That was a detail she could work out when they had a solid plan. It was still only an idea.

Malcolm offered to drive Amelia home. She didn't want to accept, but he insisted, and it saved her the cost of return bus fare. Her parents needed every coin they could save to pay for groceries. Prices had gone up again, which furthered Amelia's belief that the food laws needed to go.

"You're inspiring," Malcolm said as he drove toward her apartment building.

Amelia blushed and averted her eyes. She wasn't trying to be anyone's inspiration. "Thanks. I'm only trying to find a solution to a problem before it gets even worse."

"You have the courage to try. A lot of people don't."

"Courage or not, it doesn't matter if we can't solve the issue."

Malcolm met her eyes in the rear-view mirror. "How good are you at sucking up?"

"What?" Amelia was picturing protests like the one she'd gone to with Blake. The kind of activism she was aware of didn't involve flattering or sucking up to people.

"Nothing will change unless rich people demand it. That's how the Government works. Scarlet's father has shares in the greenhouses in the Outskirts. If he lobbies for changes, the Government will listen."

A pit settled in Amelia's stomach. This wasn't going to be as comfortable for her as she dreamt. "You're saying we need to suck up to Scarlet, aren't you?"

"It wouldn't hurt. I doubt her father will listen to us without her backing."

Schmoozing Scarlet wasn't Amelia's idea of an enjoyable time. Yet, circumstances warranted it. "I guess I can try to ply her with flattery."

"I'll set up a meeting with her and be in touch," Malcolm said as he pulled up to Amelia's building.

"I'll be waiting," Amelia said as she scrambled out of Malcolm's car and headed to the door of her building. She would wait for Malcolm's message, but that didn't mean she'd be idle. There were Jack, Dina and Ethan to tell in the meantime.

...

The next day, Amelia walked with Dina, Jack and Ethan to their old meeting place. Jack wanted to find out what side his former Castmates and friends were on and stake a claim on the building to have a safe place to discuss Amelia's idea. The trouble started when the door guard refused to let them enter.

Jack was ready to force his way inside when Dina touched him on the arm and the anger drained from his body.

Ethan stood behind Jack with his head hung. "I didn't think Kylie would stoop to this."

Amelia only heard him because she was standing next to him. He'd spoken quietly enough that Jack and Dina had no reaction. "Maybe it was Lucas," Amelia said to comfort him. It didn't matter to her who had arranged this.

Ethan sighed. "Jack," he said, loud enough for the others to hear. "Let's try around back."

"Worth a try," Jack said, and their group descended the stairs and rounded the building to the back lot.

It looked bigger to Amelia with no trucks or crates crowding it, and the door was unlocked, causing the back of Amelia's neck to tingle. "This isn't a good idea," she said.

Dina eyes opened wide. "Mellie's right. It could be a trap."

"Doesn't matter," Jack said. "I have to know for sure where we stand with Lucas and the girls."

"Exactly," Ethan said. "We need to do this."

Amelia could see Kylie and Lucas weren't on anyone's side except their own. And Arlo Fenn had warned them about losing the building, no matter how much Jack and Ethan hadn't wanted to believe it.

Yet there was no deterring the boys from this idea, and Amelia wanted to discuss her plan with Kylie and Lucas anyway as their help would be of benefit. So, Amelia and Dina took up the rear as the boys walked in and down the hallway. They didn't get far when Brooke and Hannah stopped them. Amelia still didn't know which girl was which.

"What are you doing here?" the first girl, with black hair and skin, asked. She had her arms crossed while her companion had her hands on her hips. Both girls were scowling.

"Where are Kylie and Lucas?" Ethan asked.

The second girl, with hazel eyes and brown skin, laughed. "There's no reason we'd tell you that, Ethan. Lucas gave us strict orders to keep all interferences away."

"What are they doing that's so important it can't be interrupted?" Amelia asked.

Hannah and Brooke looked at each other. "Business stuff," the first said.

"This is silly," Dina said. She'd pushed her away past Ethan and Jack to stand across from the girls. "We just want to talk to them."

Both girls' eyes bugged open. "Wow, I can't believe you showed up here, Dina. Kylie will love to hear this," the second girl said.

"Definitely," the first said. "Go tell her, Hannah."

The Brooke and Hannah mystery was finally solved.

Dina had formed fists at her sides and set her jaw. "I'm not scared of Kylie."

Brooke laughed. "Whatever you say, Dina."

Jack tensed, and Amelia bit her lip. Brooke was obviously trying to bait them and saw Dina as the easy target. Amelia didn't get a chance to defuse Jack as Hannah returned with Kylie.

Kylie's face gave away none of her emotions until her eyes landed on Ethan a flicker of remorse flashed in them. "What do you want?"

"Only to talk," Ethan said. "Amelia has an idea you'll want to hear."

Amelia's idea became the excuse for their visit now that Brooke, Hannah and Kylie showed hostility. She didn't correct Ethan's story; this was what she wanted, even if it wasn't what Jack had intended.

"An idea, huh?" Kylie's eyes swung onto Amelia. "Seems like you've grown some confidence. Come this way, and we'll discuss it."

She turned on her heel and walked away with Hannah and Brooke. Amelia and her friends followed to the meeting room where Amelia had first met the girls, Lucas and Ethan. When they reached the door, Kylie shooed Brooke and Hannah away.

Inside, Kylie went to the couch and sat beside Lucas. He reached for her hand and rubbed the back of it with his thumb.

"You got nerve showing up here," Lucas said. "This is our turf now."

Amelia saw Jack clench his teeth. She had to intervene before the hostility crossed into a fight. "Fine. We don't want or need the building." She ignored

Ethan's, Jack's and Dina's stares. It was only a building, no matter how sentimental Jack was over it.

"Then why are you here?"

Amelia looked Lucas in the eye. He wasn't going to intimidate her. "I thought you might be interested in a deal."

Chapter 19

Amelia explained her intentions to Lucas and Kylie. It was also the first time she'd outlined them in detail to Jack, Ethan and Dina. She'd expected Kylie and Lucas to brush her off, dismiss her, tell her the plan would never work, something along those lines. Instead, they stared.

"What makes you think you can overthrow the food laws?" Lucas asked.

"I know someone with connections," Amelia said. She wasn't about to give him Malcolm's name. Scarlet's, however, she might drop under the right circumstances.

"We aren't interested," Kylie said with a flick of her hand. "This is just another cause a bunch of rebels will get behind to thwart the Government in the name of helping the unfortunate. There's no benefit for those of us devout to the Government."

"Mellie," Dina said with a tug on Amelia's elbow. "Let's go before they make it worse."

"That's right, Dina," Kylie goaded. "Run away again. Your little rebel cause won't get anywhere with cowards backing it, Amelia."

Amelia saw Jack bristle at Kylie calling Dina a coward, so she flung her arm out to hold him back. Now wasn't the time to escalate things. "You like money, right?" she asked Kylie.

"Duh. Who doesn't?" Kylie rolled her eyes while Lucas chuckled.

"Think about how much you could make if you could sell excess food. I imagine you'd earn a healthy profit."

"No way the Government would let us do that," Lucas said with a scoff. "They'd sell it themselves."

Amelia didn't know why she was helping them figure out how to make money, other than she wanted as much support as possible. It would require some sacrifices and concessions. "They'd let it rot before doing that. Just give them a percentage of the profits and keep the rest. If you're as devout to the Government as you said, it shouldn't be a problem."

Kylie and Lucas shared a look, and Kylie nodded. "We'll help," Lucas said. "If you swear that we don't have to sign up for your rebellious cause."

Amelia tuned out the grumblings of her friends. They needed this. "Deal."

Kylie flashed a predatory grin and shooed Amelia and her friends away. "Good. Now get out and send word when you have news."

Amelia couldn't help smiling as she followed Dina and Jack back out into the hallway. This was a victory, no matter how small of one. Ethan lagged behind, so Amelia waved Dina and Jack ahead and peeked through the gap made by the door left ajar. She needed to know what this was about. Was Ethan going to turn on her?

Ethan had stepped closer to Kylie. "Kylie, are you really that obsessed with money now? You didn't use to be like this."

"Things are more complicated now. You know that."

Amelia blinked. Kylie's usual cold and detached tone was gone from her voice. She sounded almost tired.

"I have to think about money," Kylie continued as Lucas picked up her hand and held it.

"This isn't going to bring your dad back," Ethan said.

Kylie snorted. "It will help my mom, and someday my child, when I have one."

"Kylie—"

"Look, Ethan," Kylie said, some of her usual coldness returning to her voice as she leaned into Lucas's side. "We've chosen our sides. I'll help you with this, and then we'll go our separate ways. Sometimes our goals will align; sometimes they won't. And we can still be friends if you'd like."

Amelia heard Ethan sigh and saw him nod. "You know I would."

"Sentimental fools, both of you," Lucas jibed.

Kylie's face twisted, and she sat up, pulled her hand away and glared in Lucas's direction. "Butt out, Lucas. This doesn't concern you."

"See if I care when this backfires," Lucas said as he crossed his arms and leaned back against the couch cushions.

"It won't," Ethan said. "I'll see you, Kylie. I need to go before Jack and the others wonder what's taking me so long."

Amelia sprung away from the door and bolted down the hall, adrenaline boosting her speed. She didn't want to risk having her face pressed into the gap, or him seeing her, when he left. Ethan catching her eavesdropping would destroy whatever trust he had in her. She burst outside and tried to control her breathing and slow her heart rate while Dina and Jack gaped.

Amelia pushed her hair back and stood tall. "Ethan's coming."

When Ethan came outside, he was expressionless, leaving Amelia to wonder how he felt. There was history between him and Kylie, enough to make them stay friends. And Kylie had said she'd help him, not Amelia or her other friends.

"Amelia, why did you tell them we don't want the building?" Jack asked as their group walked around the building.

"Because we don't," Amelia said. "What we need is their help." She didn't understand Jack's fuss over a building. It was just cement made into walls and floors.

Jack sighed. "It had better be worth it."

"Go easy on her, Jack," Ethan said. "We can find somewhere else to meet."

"It's already worth it," Amelia said. "We need a name for our movement, and they gave me an idea."

Dina and the boys were silent except for the sound of their footsteps. Amelia wanted to scream but held herself back. Malcolm at least would want to hear her idea.

It was Dina who broke the silence. "You mean what Kylie said about our 'little rebel cause'," she said with air quotes.

Amelia liked that her best friend had picked up on the same idea. "We need a name to unite people that want to help. And what we're trying to do is rebellious in the eyes of the Government."

"It's just the food laws," Ethan said.

For now. "There will always be things to fight for and people that need help."

"Amelia's right," Jack said. "A name is what we need. That and a new meeting place."

Amelia had one in mind, but she had to ask Malcolm first. And Jack would dislike it.

"We can't go around advertising that we're rebelling against the Government," Dina said.

"Obviously, we can only tell certain people," Amelia said. "No putting it on banners or building signs. It'll be our own underground network to help people."

...

As Amelia expected, Malcolm liked the new name of their cause. They imagined at first it would be small, but there was no telling what it would someday become. Malcolm was also receptive to using his house as their new meeting place. His parents were rarely there, and they had connections and sympathies to removing the food laws. He was also the only one of their group who lived in a house without neighbours on the other side of thin walls. Amelia and the others could speak freely at Malcolm's.

Amelia would've felt tempted to hug or kiss Malcolm at receiving this news if they'd corresponded in person instead of mailed notes. Postage was cheaper than bus fare, and Amelia hadn't wanted to make him come to her. That would've required a mailed note anyway.

Jack offered no resistance to meeting at Malcolm's house. Amelia thought something must've happened to lessen his distrust of Malcolm, or Jack just realized there were no other options.

Whatever the reason, he didn't complain or protest as Amelia, Ethan and Dina rode the bus to Malcolm's with him. Amelia sat with Ethan and tried not to watch Jack and Dina sit close to each other. They could get away with touching sides on a crowded bus. Most people sharing seats couldn't help it; the seats were narrow. Amelia clasped her hands on her lap and gave Ethan a small smile as she adjusted her position to make a gap between their sides. "Are you excited to see Kelsie?"

Ethan's eyes bugged open, and Amelia thought she saw his cheeks blush. "I suppose."

Amelia bit back her laugh. "I think she likes you." It had been obvious to Amelia from what she'd witnessed in the Colony and heard Kelsie say.

He tossed his head. "She doesn't know me."

Malcolm hadn't known much about Amelia either when she'd found him parked outside her apartment building, and he'd done that anyway. Amelia looked him in the eye. "Do you want her to?"

Ethan's eyes dulled, and he turned to look out the window. Amelia wondered what her question had triggered.

"What made you let Malcolm get close?" Ethan asked, his eyes still on the bus window.

There wasn't a simple and straightforward answer to his question. "I don't know. It happened gradually and so slowly that I didn't realize it until it had already happened."

"Kelsie is so confident; I don't think she'd have any interest in me."

Amelia swatted Ethan on the arm. He couldn't be that oblivious. "Don't talk like that. And besides, no one is confident all the time." Kelsie sure hadn't seemed it when Amelia had last seen her. She'd appeared more exhausted, vulnerable and frustrated. It seemed to Amelia that Kelsie's confidence was a forced coping mechanism from Arlo Fenn moving her around so often.

"I guess I'll see what happens."

Amelia didn't get to say anything else as the bus reached their stop. At least this time she knew the direction to take on foot.

When they arrived at Malcolm's house, Amelia saw Kelsie try to hide her grin at seeing Ethan. It wasn't that Amelia wanted their group to split into couples, but Ethan and Kelsie each deserved to be someone's number one.

Her mind wandered from Ethan and Kelsie when she saw Malcolm. Then she tried to figure out whether Jack would make a scene. Things previously had been tense between Jack and Malcolm, and the last thing Amelia wanted was for them to argue.

Everyone gathered in the living room and Amelia sat beside Dina on the couch. She needed to stay as distraction free as possible, which required a bit of physical distance from Malcolm. They all looked at her and expected her to recap their visit to Lucas and Kylie, so Amelia told it. She wasn't eager to be a leader. It meant shouldering all the focus and pressure, and she wasn't sure she could handle it or even wanted to.

"I'll send word to Arlo," Kelsie said when Amelia finished. She was sitting on a chair across the room, as near to Ethan without touching him as she could get. "He has connections."

That he did. Amelia didn't know much about Arlo Fenn, having only met him in the market, in the dilapidated building and when they picked up Kelsie. Yet, she realized enough to know he oversaw some level of the former Cause. "You think he'll help us?"

Kelsie shrugged. "He might."

Whether Arlo Fenn would help them was of little importance to Amelia during that meeting. She was more concerned about having to play nice with Scarlet. Malcolm presented his plan and delivered news even to Amelia. Scarlet had agreed to meet her and Malcolm on the weekend.

No one protested or told Malcolm it was a bad idea. Amelia had already agreed to it, but now that it was happening, a pit formed in her stomach. Her previous encounters with Scarlet hadn't exactly been fun or pleasant. However, Amelia would be on her best behaviour. She'd do whatever it took to sway Scarlet.

Amelia left with her friends and tried to prepare over the following days. Malcolm had instructed her to wear something nice, so Amelia turned to the section of her closet reserved for dates. Surely this had to count. She hadn't told her parents anything more than she had a date with Malcolm, which was technically true. Even though Amelia's dad had supported her going to the Colony, she was unsure how he'd react to this. Her mom would take it badly, so Amelia wasn't keen to tell them too much too early.

On the day of, she donned a blue dress and her pair of low heels, twisted her hair up and brushed some makeup on her face. Dressing up would go a long way to impressing Scarlet. With her outfit done, Amelia grabbed her bag and set out to meet Malcolm. This had to go well; there was no other option.

Chapter 20

Malcolm drove Amelia to a restaurant different from the one he'd taken her to on their date. This one was large and had tables set with white napkins, matching tablecloths and silverware. There were chandeliers hanging from the ceiling, casting a warm golden glow over everything. Behind the greeter's desk was a display of glassware; each sparking cup perched on metal shelves.

The greeter, wearing a black suit and crisp, white shirt, led Amelia and Malcolm to a table in the back corner. When they reached it, the greeter pulled out Amelia's chair. Scarlet was already sitting and watched with a critical eye as Amelia sat and the greeter pushed her chair in.

Amelia tried not to embarrass herself or Malcolm as the greeter placed a menu on her placemat. She picked it up as they departed; it was one page with a limited selection of high-priced dishes. If Amelia had had to pay for this herself, she would've made an excuse not to eat. In an effort to blend in, she scanned the menu like someone used to dining in high-priced places.

"I hope we didn't keep you waiting too long, Scarlet," Malcolm said with forced politeness.

He sat between Amelia and Scarlet on their four-sided table. Amelia tried not to be upset at having to face Scarlet and let her be in touching distance of Malcolm.

Scarlet pushed a stray lock of hair out of her face. "I wanted to see you arrive. You always look so handsome when you think no one is watching you."

"Scarlet—"

"You should've come alone," Scarlet said, resting her hands on Malcolm's arm and batting her eyelashes. "We don't need a third wheel on our date."

Amelia clutched her menu and willed her face to stay impassive. Where did Scarlet get the idea that this was a date between her and Malcolm?

"You know this isn't a date," Malcolm said, as he shifted his arm out from under her hand. "Amelia and I are here to discuss business."

Scarlet huffed and pouted as she clasped her hands in her lap. "I suppose you did mention that. Pity, I thought you might've come to your senses."

Amelia shared a nervous glance with Malcolm. The server for their table came with glasses of water and took their orders. Amelia picked a dish at random and hoped it sounded like she knew what she was doing. When the server was gone, she gulped some water to soothe the knot in her stomach and her racing pulse.

While they waited for their food, Malcolm launched into his spiel. Amelia joined in where she felt she could contribute. It was hard to charm Scarlet into wanting to help anyone other than herself.

"Why should I care that the Apartment Districts can't afford food?" Scarlet asked once Malcolm and Amelia finished their pitch and the food arrived. "Starving them off would only help the overcrowding problem."

Amelia wasn't surprised that she was so heartless. Everything in her life she'd gotten with no effort. "You don't have to care about that," Amelia said. Trying to make Scarlet empathetic to less fortunate people was a futile exercise, even though Apartment District citizens provided many services to the rich. The only way through to her was to make her think she was gaining something. "Imagine how much more money your family could have if it was legal to resell food."

Scarlet covered her mouth with her hand and giggled. "That argument might work with my father, but there's only one thing I want, and it's my condition to setting up a meeting with him."

"Name it."

Scarlet reached for Malcolm's hand, and he pulled it away. "I want an equal shot at becoming your Courtship partner. For each date you go on with *her*," she titled her head in Amelia's direction. "You go on one with me, and no moping or mentioning *her* on our dates."

Amelia closed her eyes and counted to ten in her head. When she opened her eyes, she saw Malcolm fixing an icy stare on Scarlet. His body had gone tense. "Absolutely not."

Scarlet tsked. "Don't be hasty. If you refuse, I'll tell my father to lobby for keeping the food laws and driving prices up. It won't matter what you do, you'll never win against that."

Malcolm clenched his teeth and his nostrils flared. "Go ahead and be heartless. You won't threaten me into marrying you."

Scarlet patted his arm. "You'll have the final choice as to whom you propose to. I only want my chance."

Malcolm's body tensed and fire sparked in his eyes.

Amelia knew he was about to ruin their chances of overturning the food laws due to pride and stubbornness. "Do it," she said. "We can't lose this chance."

The anger drained from Malcolm, and he deflated, his shoulders sagging.

"Seems your little pity crush has some sense," Scarlet said as she lifted a bite of her meal to her mouth.

"Fine," Malcolm said, stabbing his fork into his food.

Scarlet's eyes gleamed. She assumed she'd won, which had Amelia on edge. Malcolm was always going to see her as unworthy, and this was only precipitating that realization. But she liked Malcolm, and she'd do anything in her power to be around him.

Amelia ate her meal as she couldn't flee without lessening Scarlet's opinion of her even farther. This situation was her fault, so she had no right to complain about it. She couldn't be guilty or jealous whenever she saw Malcolm. Not when she'd told him to agree to Scarlet's deal.

Scarlet, between bites of food, babbled on about making a schedule and how Malcolm owed her the next date as he'd taken Amelia this time. Amelia only half listened. Scarlet saw her as so little a threat, she didn't spare Amelia a second of attention.

Scarlet had turned her chair to face Malcolm and inched closer to him. Malcolm, for his part, agreed to whatever Scarlet said but kept flicking his eyes onto Amelia. She tried to give him a reassuring smile. Whether it worked or not, there was no way to tell.

...

Malcolm paid for his and Amelia's meals and led Amelia out of the restaurant. He didn't say anything until they were in the car and out of the rich Quarters.

"I hope roping me into dates with Scarlet is worth it."

"I'm sorry," Amelia said. She was sorry, though that didn't change anything. "I couldn't let her become an obstacle."

Malcolm huffed. "Sometimes I think all you care about is the plight of strangers."

Amelia froze on her seat. Did he really think that? "We come from different worlds, Malcolm. It might be unimaginable to you that my family isn't far from being moneyless and starving. I think it's a reason my mom wants me to get married so badly. With me out of the house, they could eat better."

"I get it," Malcom said. "I just wish I didn't have to be nice to Scarlet."

Amelia took a chance and rested her hand on his leg, knowing there were no witnesses to this bit of touch. He didn't brush off her hand. "It's only a couple months until Clinic Day. Certainly, you can put up with her that long, and it won't be daily."

Malcolm glanced Amelia's way and met her eyes. His were vivid and sparkled like she imagined real gemstones would when held up to a light. "And then what? I can't marry her."

"Then don't." Amelia wasn't about to beg him for a proposal. She wasn't ready for that nor sure she wanted it, yet she didn't want him to marry Scarlet.

Malcolm gave her a small nod, his eyes now back on the road.

It was the start of a change in their relationship. Amelia saw him at the meetings held at his house, but their dates were few and far between. She sensed this was his way of avoiding taking Scarlet out.

...

It turned out that Kelsie and Ethan were good at working out organizational details. Together, with Amelia, they listed out the main goals of their Rebel Cause and the types of activities and duties that needed fulfilling.

There was also the matter of the Colony. It was already a place people escaped to when they couldn't stay in the City, but it had such little support and wasn't sustainable. What it needed was regular supply runs and a better food source, which would be easier without the food laws. Jack showed interest in helping supply the Colony, though there was nothing he, or any one in their group, could do without money, a vehicle of their own and a pass for the Car Gate and guard checkpoint. Amelia shelved the idea for the time being. Tackling the food laws was her priority.

There were numerous details they needed to figure out, and no money to use to do it. Amelia was starting to think this was a cause too big and expensive for her and her friends to tackle. They were only teenagers, after all.

"There's a solution to this," Malcolm said.

He was sitting on a chair next to the couch where Amelia sat with Dina and Kelsie. Scarlet hadn't insisted on reciprocal time with Malcolm based on group meetings, if she knew about them, but on time Malcolm and Amelia spent alone, so they relished these meetings as an excuse to see each other. These instances never led to kissing, and Amelia and Malcolm didn't discuss his dates with Scarlet.

Amelia turned her face in his direction and raised an eyebrow.

"We need to fundraise," he said.

Everyone else in the room turned to look at Malcolm. He drank a sip of water from his nearby glass. "There are wealthy people who want to make themselves look good by doing charity. We just have to tell them they're supporting small causes, like giving clothes to the poor, and not mention anything about rebelling against the Government. And we *can* use their money for what we tell them it's for, at least partly."

"It's worth a try," Dina said.

The others gave their assent, effectively adding another item to Amelia's list of things to plan. Fortunately, Malcolm did most of the work. He went to his parents' contacts and set up an event. On the day of, Amelia donned one of her fancier dresses and shoes and applied makeup to her face. This would definitely count as a date in Scarlet's mind, so Amelia had to try to enjoy it as much as she could, even though there was work to be done and her friends were attending too. Dina and Jack were going as a couple, as were Ethan and

Kelsie after Kelsie had charmed him into agreeing.

Amelia rode the bus with Dina, Jack and Ethan to the rich Quarter holding the event. There were no spaces large and extravagant enough to impress wealthy might-be donors in the Apartment Districts, if they would even travel into that part of the City. Dina and the boys had put on their best clothes, which weren't that lavish compared to what the people they needed to impress would be wearing. Amelia thought this might be a good thing. She wasn't above letting them pity her if it earned the Rebel Cause money.

When Amelia, Dina and the boys approached the venue, Malcolm was waiting for her. He offered her his arm, so she rested her hand on it and walked with him inside.

"Are you ready?" Malcolm asked. His green eyes were sparkling and soft as he gazed at her.

"I hope so," Amelia said. In truth, she wasn't sure how to prepare for this, having only been around a handful of wealthy people in her life. What if she made an embarrassment of herself? The Rebel Cause desperately needed money and influential people on their side.

Malcolm rested his free hand atop hers. "You'll be great. Just use your charm on them."

Amelia didn't consider herself charming, so this wasn't reassuring. She and Malcolm were inside the doors now, and she tried not to gape or stare at the crowd of people. Her heart sped up and her palms sweated. There were women wearing sparkling dresses with elaborate hairdos and men wearing tailored suits. A sizeable percentage of the people were dancing to the music a small string band played, while many others were standing around chatting and holding drinking glasses. Beverages, excluding water, came under the food laws, but exceptions were possible for parties if you had enough money to bribe the right official. Amelia guessed someone had done that today as the chances of water being in those glasses were slim.

Amelia and Malcolm had just gotten to the edge of the dance floor when she saw a familiar flash of ash-blonde hair and painted, red lips striding in their direction.

"Malcolm," Scarlet cooed. "It's about time you got here."

Chapter 21

Amelia forced herself to smile. "Hello, Scarlet."

Scarlet flicked her eyes to Amelia's hand resting on Malcolm's arm. A flash of annoyance moved through them. "Don't worry. I'm not infringing on your date. My father is here. I intend to make introductions."

Malcolm slid his arm from under Amelia's hand and stepped back. "Go on, Amelia. I have something to discuss with Jack."

He walked away in the direction of Dina and Jack, leaving Amelia alone with Scarlet, who scowled at her.

"You think you've charmed him, don't you?"

Amelia's mouth formed an O. "I never claimed that."

Scarlet snorted and beckoned Amelia to follow her with a wave of her hand. She walked around the dancefloor to a beverage table where a middle-aged couple stood in conversation. The woman had Scarlet's face shape and hazel, though her hair was light brown, and her skin tone was paler. The man had Scarlet's hair and skin tone. These were her parents.

Amelia relaxed her face. Regardless of whether Scarlet intended to humiliate or help her, she didn't need to make a bad impression through her own actions.

"Mother, Father," Scarlet said. "This is Amelia."

Scarlet's parents gazed at Amelia with cold expressions. She wasn't on their list of favourite people.

"You're Malcolm's friend, aren't you?" the man asked.

"Yes, I am," Amelia said. "It's nice to make your acquaintance, Mr....?"

"Everbee," Scarlet's father said. "It is nice to make your acquaintance as well, though I was under the impression Malcolm would be here too."

"He'll be along," Scarlet said. She jutted her bottom lip out, giving an exaggerated pout. "It's such a bother getting alone time away from him; I wanted a moment to get to know his new friend."

That was ridiculous to Amelia, who had an idea of how little time Malcolm spent with Scarlet. She wanted to correct Scarlet and couldn't as they were standing in front of Scarlet's parents, who Amelia needed to impress. However, there was a subtle way she could let Scarlet know she was on to her tricks. "Spending so much time with Malcolm must be exhausting for you. How do you manage it?" Amelia kept her voice innocent and gazed at Scarlet with wide eyes, which she hoped would make the Everbees think her question was genuine.

"You would know exhaustion, what with your circumstances," Scarlet said. Her pout disappeared, and she raised her chin and straightened her posture. "I have an abundance of energy."

Mrs. Everbee chuckled behind her hand. "Oh, to be young and invigorated."

Amelia stole a look around the room while Mrs. Everbee spoke. It took her a few moments to spot Malcolm standing before Jack, with Dina nowhere in sight. He was gesturing with his hands as he spoke, and Jack nodded along. When Malcolm finished, Jack said something in return, and then Malcolm turned and walked Amelia and Scarlet's way. *What was all that about?*

Scarlet zoomed to Malcolm's side as he reached where she, her parents and Amelia stood. She wiggled under his arm, nestled against his side and rested her palm on his chest. Malcolm made no move to brush her off, but he didn't reciprocate Scarlet's overdose of affection or hold her tight.

"Mr. and Mrs. Everbee," Malcolm said. "It's nice to see you again."

The Everbees had brightened and perked up when Malcolm walked over, and their attention was entirely on him.

"That's kind of you, dear," Mrs. Everbee said. "It's always a pleasure to see you."

With the arrival of Malcolm, they forgot about Amelia. She could've walked away and none of the Everbees would've noticed. She assumed Scarlet had led her over here to endure the humiliation of Scarlet's parents fawning over Malcolm. That didn't matter. She gave Malcolm a subtle tap on his side unclaimed by Scarlet. They had business to attend to.

Malcolm grasped Scarlet's wrist and removed her palm from his chest. "Mr. Everbee," he said. "Scarlet said you agreed to meet with me and Amelia. Is there somewhere private we can go to discuss business?"

Recognition lit in Mr. Everbee's eyes. "Yes, Scarlet did mention that. I'm sure there's an office around here somewhere."

"Go along, darling," Mrs. Everbee said. "I'll keep Scarlet company."

Scarlet pouted as Malcolm pried himself from her and walked away with Amelia. As Amelia left, Scarlet leaned in and whispered. "Enjoy his company while you can still have it."

"You sound jealous," Amelia said. "Are you worried you haven't convinced him he's wrong about you?"

Scarlet scoffed. "You're awful confident for a charity case. He pities you, while he understands me. I'm from his world."

Malcolm would be wondering what was taking Amelia so long and why she wasn't walking with him, but she couldn't let Scarlet have the last word.

And she no longer believed Malcolm only felt pity for her. "You're delusional. He tolerates you because I told him to. You gave us no other choice."

She rushed after Malcolm before Scarlet could reply or knock her over again. Maybe she should've stuck around for that to happen, not because she wanted bruises but because it might've revealed Scarlet as different the image her parents had of her.

...

Mr. Everbee knew the layout of the building well, no matter how much he tried to pretend otherwise. Amelia could tell as she and Malcolm followed him across the dancing room to a door that led to a hallway. Once in it, Mr. Everbee turned right with the assurance of someone who knew where he was going. His intended destination was a distance from the dancing room, giving Amelia time to talk to Malcolm.

"Scarlet seems confident she's won you over," Amelia said. She and Malcolm trailed Mr. Everbee far enough behind that he wouldn't overhear if they kept their voices down.

Malcolm groaned. "I've been polite to her, as she told me I had to."

Amelia believed Malcolm. Why would he lie? "Since she set this meeting up, does that mean you don't need to take her out anymore?"

Malcolm's stuck his hands in his pockets and lowered his gaze to the floor. "Not quite. Our arrangement is until I pick a Courtship partner, or Clinic Day, whichever comes first."

Clinic Day was still a couple months away. Amelia gazed at Malcolm. She felt a bit bad for getting him in this situation, just not bad enough that she wouldn't have done it again. It was worth this chance to sway Mr. Everbee. That was assuming they could sway him. If he didn't agree to lobby for overturning the food laws, then she'd feel guilty. "I'm sorry you have to put up with her for that long."

Malcolm studied her. She couldn't read his face as he'd wiped his emotions from it. "Good."

Amelia wanted to ask him what was so good about it, except she didn't have the chance. Mr. Everbee had reached his intended room and was holding the door open.

…

The room was an office decorated with expensive pictures on the walls and a plush rug on the floor, and there were intricately carved legs on the stone coffee table, couch and chairs. It was nothing like Amelia's dad's office with its drab, bare walls, metal desk and office chair.

Mr. Everbee reclined on the couch and rested his feet, legs crossed at the ankle, on the table. "Make yourselves comfortable," he said, gesturing to the chairs.

Malcolm and Amelia each sat on one. Amelia's wasn't comfortable with its rigid back and firm cushion. She clasped her hands in her lap and sat up straight. Something about this room and the fancy dress she wore gave etiquette an extra importance, and slouching made her back sore by touching the hard chair back.

"What is it you wanted to discuss? Scarlet gave me no details," Mr. Everbee said.

Malcolm leaned forward and rested his forearms on his thighs. "How are profits from the greenhouses?"

Money was the way to get the wealthy's attention, and Amelia let Malcolm take the lead in this conversation. He could take a natural interest in profits without coming across as greedy and overreaching as she would.

Mr. Everbee removed his feet from the coffee table and sat back against the couch cushions. "I suppose I should be flattered that you're taking an interest in my business. Scarlet will be pleased."

Amelia spotted Malcolm wrinkle his eyebrows. Obviously, Mr. Everbee thought Malcolm was dating his daughter. An idea Scarlet had no doubt fed him.

"But, to answer your question," Mr. Everbee continued. "They are lower than I'd like even with the sale price increase."

Malcolm sat up and glanced at Amelia. She gave him a small nod.

"Do you have an idea why?"

"I know why," Mr. Everbee said. "Food rots in the greenhouses. The shops only order so much because people can only afford and go through so much."

"Mr. Everbee," Amelia said. It was time to take a chance, albeit not a huge one. "Do you think that's because of the food laws?"

Mr. Everbee swung his eyes onto Amelia, as if just noticing she was there. "You're cunning. If you're saying they're a problem, I agree with you."

It was Malcolm and Amelia's turn to smile. "We want to overturn the food laws," Malcolm said. "With your connections, Mr. Everbee, you'd be of great assistance."

Mr. Everbee crossed his arms loosely over his abdomen. "That's a treasonous sentence. Getting the Government to change their laws is difficult and delicate work. It'll end with jail time if not done right. I'll need a plan for a replacement before I can be of any help."

"A replacement?" Amelia asked. She'd never thought of replacing the laws with something else, only of removing them, which she was now realizing wasn't enough.

"You can't just wipe the law out and let it be a free for all," Mr. Everbee said. "Prices will either skyrocket or plummet, and if they plummet, supply won't keep up. People will hoard food either way. The Government likes control, not chaos. There needs to be a replacement."

"So, you'll help us once we have an alternative?" Malcolm asked.

Mr. Everbee grunted. "If it's a good alternative."

That was as much support from him as they could hope for that day. They thanked Mr. Everbee, promised to be in touch, and walked back to the dancing room.

Amelia wasn't eager to see Scarlet throw herself at Malcolm again, so she kept her pace slow. There was also something on her mind she needed to ask Malcolm while she was alone with him. "What were you discussing with Jack?"

"Nothing important," Malcolm said. His answer was too fast and too easy. It made her think it had definitely been important.

"Really?" Amelia arched an eyebrow.

Malcolm held his hands up, palms facing her, in surrender. "Don't worry about it. It's nothing bad, I promise."

Amelia scowled. "What are you hiding from me?"

Malcolm turned his head to look at Amelia, his expression giving little away. "I asked him for a favour and told him who to talk to. That's all I'll say about it."

"Fine," Amelia said. If Malcolm wouldn't give her details, Jack or Dina might.

...

Amelia spent the next couple hours trying to charm the wealthy attendees into donating money. The cause she and her friends were supporting that day was officially clothes and shoes for the poor. It was something those people needed and was a test run for future fundraising efforts.

It was also where Amelia and the others were supposed to scope out potential future allies. That's why Amelia shouldn't have been surprised to see Kylie, Lucas, Hannah and Brooke grouped together on the edge of the dance floor.

Chapter 22

Amelia steeled her nerves and walked over to Kylie's group. She could be nice.

Kylie spotted Amelia and gave her a wave with her hand that wasn't hooked on Lucas's arm.

Amelia waved in return.

"Enjoying yourself?" Hannah asked while Brooke smirked from her side. They were standing so close to each other that they were almost touching at their sides.

"Where's your rich boy?" Kylie asked.

"This isn't about enjoyment," Amelia said. She chose to ignore Kylie's question about Malcolm meant to bait her. "I've been in a meeting."

"Did it lead anywhere productive?" Lucas asked.

Amelia inhaled a deep breath. Kylie and Lucas were low on her list of people she trusted. "Are you just here to get information out of me?"

The three girls burst into giggles. It was almost eerie how they all laughed at the same time when Amelia hadn't tried to make a joke.

"That's a big bonus," Kyle said when her laughter had subsided. "But Ethan invited us. Well, me. Luke and the girls," she swept her hand over Hannah and Brooke, "come with."

Ethan. Amelia would get into that later. "Well, I hope you *enjoy* yourselves." She took a step to move around then when Brooke spoke.

"We've been busy getting a list of potential supporters for our movement. This isn't fun for us any more than it is for you."

Amelia had intended to find Jack and ask him what Malcolm had wanted. It was Brooke's words and the smug way she said them made Amelia change plans to find Ethan. She was ready to throttle him.

...

Amelia found Ethan at the edge of the dance floor in conversation with an older man in a pinstripe suit. *At least it looks like he's working.* She waited until the man walked away before approaching Ethan.

Ethan frowned. "What's wrong?"

Amelia hadn't tried to show her annoyance, but she must've been scowling. "Why did you invite Kylie? She's here with Lucas, Hannah and Brooke recruiting supporters to her side."

Ethan's eyes bugged open. "Because you wanted her to help us. Why does it matter whether the support comes direct to us or through her?"

Amelia pressed her lips into a thin line. Did he really not see the problem? "Because someday her interests and ours won't be the same. We barely have one issue in common now."

He sighed and ran a hand through his hair. "I think you're making this into a bigger issue than it is. We can make a deal with Kylie. She's not entirely unreasonable if she gets something in return."

Amelia closed her eyes and counted to ten. She needed those moments of clarity to clear her head. "You better hope that's true."

Ethan nodded. "It is. I know her well enough to trust her."

"I believe you." Ethan and Kylie had history Amelia could only guess at, and there was definitely trust between them. Now that she'd gotten her frustrations out about Kyle, she switched tactics. "Have you seen Jack?" Ethan might know where he went.

"Not since he and Dina danced."

"Thanks anyway," Amelia said. She was back to the beginning of her search and turned and walked away to do a perimeter of the room. Jack had to be here somewhere.

...

Amelia found Jack with Dina on the far side of the room. They were alone yet concealed behind a crowd of people. People they were supposed to be talking to. Amelia might've been annoyed under other circumstances that her best friend and her boyfriend weren't doing what they came here to do. Under current circumstances, Amelia was glad to have a semblance of privacy.

"Hi!" Dina squealed as Amelia walked up. She was beaming, and Jack was trying to conceal a grin.

Amelia stopped short and furrowed her brows. "What made you two so happy?"

The smile on Dina's face shrunk. She couldn't quite manage to erase in entirely. "I'm just glad to see you. Today has been long."

Amelia didn't buy this. They'd only been here a couple hours, not long enough for Dina to have missed her that much. "Dina, I need to ask Jack something. Can I steal him for a moment?"

"Sure," Dina said with a smile that did not look natural. She shot Jack what looked to be a nervous glance as Amelia grasped his arm and led him a few steps away.

Jack offered no resistance and stayed put when Amelia dropped his arm. He'd done a better job of vanishing his grin than Dina. "What is it?"

"I saw Malcolm talking to you, and he wouldn't tell me what about. What did he want?"

"He was just explaining who I should talk to that might help us."

Amelia crossed her arms. He and Malcolm had both said the same thing, but it was a flimsy excuse when they were here to talk to everyone. "That can't be whole truth. Did he say he's going to ask Scarlet to be his Courtship partner and swore you to secrecy?" It had to be something that awful for Malcolm and for Jack to agree on a cover up.

"No. Definitely not."

Amelia exhaled all the air in her lungs. She'd wished that had been the explanation, though it would've meant Malcolm had lied to her. She would've understood Malcolm wanting to marry someone he could relate to and had history with, and Scarlet had shown up here acting like she was on a date with Malcolm. The idea that he didn't want Scarlet or Amelia was what she couldn't cope with.

Malcolm had said he liked being with Amelia, then their dates had gotten less frequent, and now he was getting her friends to keep secrets from her. She'd assumed it was something to do with Scarlet; now she knew it was something worse. Malcolm was going to break up with her and intended to do it here. "Thanks," she said. "If you see Malcolm, tell him goodbye for me."

Jack's eyes popped open, and his jaw lowered. "Wait! What do you mean by goodbye?"

Amelia spun around to face Jack. She had walked a few steps away. "I'm going home."

Jack blinked. "So not goodbye as in you never want to see him again?"

"Even if that were true, it isn't possible. I have to see him. We use his house as our meeting place."

Jack visibly swallowed. "Okay, I'll tell him you went home. Are you leaving now?"

Amelia wanted to, but there was still work to do here. "No. But you can tell Malcolm I did. I don't want to see him anymore today." She walked away before Jack could stop her.

Amelia had come here with a date and was now avoiding him. The issue was she didn't see what explanation there was for Malcolm keeping a secret from her other than he intended to break things off. Even if he had sworn it was nothing bad. Ending whatever fling they had might've been for the best, but she still wanted to avoid a scene in public. Let him work for the chance to tell her. She wasn't going to make it easy.

...

She spent the next hour charming donations out of the wealthy attendees. It was almost too easy, like they wanted to empty their pockets to show off how generous they were. Amelia assumed her demeanour might have contributed. An unshakable gloominess had settled on her and made her look like a poor wretch in need of assistance.

Amelia had just compiled her list of supporters when she saw Malcolm with Scarlet. Scarlet was clinging to him and speaking with her mouth close to his. Malcolm said something back, but Amelia was too far away to hear the words. She could see, however, that Malcolm placed his hand on Scarlet's, and that he didn't try to move away. Scarlet smiling at Malcolm was the last part of this display Amelia could take. He *had* lied to her about not wanting Scarlet.

Amelia turned and ran to the exit, tears forming in the corners of her eyes and blurring her vision. Jack must've been wrong about Malcolm's intentions with Scarlet or trying to shelter Amelia from them. Malcolm was flirting with Scarlet and touching her in public and didn't care who saw. Amelia tried to tell herself that it didn't matter. She didn't fit into Malcolm's life and didn't want to get married anyway. Those were lies she'd told herself and started to believe. How was she going to face him at their next meeting when they needed to brainstorm a replacement for the food laws?

Amelia fled the event without alerting any of her friends. It hadn't crossed her mind as she bolted outside. Now that she was outside, she sat on the ground at the edge of the parking lot and hung her head.

"What are you doing?"

Kelsie. Amelia didn't want to explain what happened to the girl living with her soon-to-be former fling. She wiped her tears and sniffled. "Trying to remember when the next bus comes."

"Why? We still have a couple hours before we should leave."

Amelia fished her list of potential donors out of her pocket, stood up and thrust it at Kelsie. "Go ahead and add to this. I'm going home."

Kelsie's face softened and she made her voice small. "Did something happen?"

Amelia swallowed the lump in her throat. Kelsie was living with Malcolm and maybe knew what his intentions were. "Did Malcolm tell you he's going to ask Scarlet to marry him?"

Kelsie gaped. "No. Did he tell you that?"

Amelia kicked at a piece of gravel on the parking lot. "I saw him talking to Jack, and neither of them will tell me what they talked about. And then I saw Malcolm holding Scarlet's hand while she snuggled up against him. He didn't need to tell me."

"That's why you ran out."

Amelia closed her eyes. Seeing Scarlet draped over Malcolm was still too painful and fresh. "I couldn't stay there and give him a chance to reject me in public."

Kelsie flung herself at Amelia and wrapped her in a hug while Amelia still had her eyes closed. "He can't marry Scarlet; she's horrible."

Amelia buried her face in Kelsie's shoulder. "I know."

"The last time they had a date, he paced the hallway for three hours before it because he was so stressed. And he came home even more worked up. I can't imagine what changed."

Amelia wriggled out of Kelsie's arms and took a step away. "Scarlet fits in with his family, his upbringing and his lifestyle. I don't. He's just realized how inadequate I am."

Kelsie burst into laughter and doubled over. Amelia didn't think what she'd said was funny, especially not humorous enough to warrant laughter that made Kelsie breathless. Surely the bus would come soon. She took a couple steps, and Kelsie called after her.

Amelia stopped and spun on her heel.

"You're assuming Malcolm wants the life his parents have," Kelsie said. She'd closed the space between herself and Amelia and had calmed her breathing. "Yet you have no clue how much he hates that idea."

Amelia felt her brows move together. "He— he hates it? Why wouldn't he tell me?"

"I didn't think you were that naïve," Kelsie said with an eye roll. "He didn't tell you because he doesn't want you to think of him as a spoiled rich kid that complains about his privilege."

"Then why'd he tell you?"

Kelsie stared at Amelia. "He didn't. I can't help noticing. His parents are rarely home, and it tears him up to be alone in that big house all the time. I also see a spark in his eyes whenever someone mentions you, and it's never present when someone mentions Scarlet. He grimaces at her name when she's not around."

Amelia crossed her arms and stared back at Kelsie. "If that's true, then why are he and Jack conspiring to keep a secret from me?" she asked with a breaking voice. "And why is he in there flirting with Scarlet?"

"All I'll say is not all secrets are bad," Kelsie said. "And I'm sure he's not flirting with Scarlet, though she's definitely flirting with him. Scarlet would love to know it upset you so much. That's her number two goal."

"Thanks for trying to cheer me up," Amelia said. She wasn't cheered up, only confused. "I'm still going home. I need to think, and I need to be alone to do it. Collect the donor lists when you're done."

...

Amelia spent the next few days avoiding Dina at lunch and trying to come up with a replacement for the food laws. There had to be a way to ensure everyone got what they needed and could afford to do so.

Amelia was in history class, a mandatory subject she usually tuned out, when the teacher presented a possible solution to her. It was unintentional on her teacher's part. They were studying the history of the City unit, dolled out to every grade in increasing levels of detail. That was why Amelia, and her classmates, generally tuned out history class; it was repetitive. However, this time, the teacher, thirty-something Mrs. Duffy in a simple, belted, blue dress, was delivering the script about the beginning of the food laws. Even the teachers found this repetitive after saying it so many times, made obvious by their monotone voice and defeated posture.

"The food laws came into being as a result of the disastrous ration system our early Government implemented," Mrs. Duffy said, causing Amelia sit up and pay attention.

Amelia even took notes, something she hadn't done in City founding history lessons in years.

Mrs. Duffy, as per her usual method, was scribbling keywords on the whiteboard as she droned on. Amelia assumed this was an excuse to use her hands and not stand still. No students cared what was on the whiteboard or so much as glanced at it. "The ration system failed because the shop keepers couldn't validate ration tickets. They were easy to counterfeit, and everyone participated in their forgery. Supply plummeted and shop keepers complained about the poor compensation. The current food laws are fair for everyone."

Amelia tuned out once more as Mrs. Duffy delved into the so-called benefits of the food laws a teacher paid by the Government was expected to cover. Amelia wasn't sure whether Mrs. Duffy believed the script she had to stick to, and it didn't matter much. She'd inadvertently given Amelia a solution.

Chapter 23

Amelia spent that school night in her bedroom working out her idea. It had to be better than the Government's desultory attempt. There could be no loopholes for people to exploit, meaning ration passes weren't an option. It took Amelia a few hours, interrupted by a brief supper with her parents, to realize the obvious answer.

The Government already had records of everyone and how many people lived in each dwelling. There was no need for Citizens to carry ration tickets when they had their ID cards.

Amelia shoved all her notes on her idea that was starting to take shape into her bag. Tomorrow at lunch, she'd discuss it with Dina.

She spent the night too wired to sleep. Her good mood lasted through her morning classes, and she jogged, as fast as she could get away with, to the cafeteria to claim her lunch and usual table.

Dina jumped when she walked up and saw Amelia sitting there. Amelia watched as Dina righted the food on her tray that had tipped over. "Where have you been?" Dina asked as she set the tray down and took her seat.

"Around," Amelia said. "I had stuff to think about." In truth, she hadn't devoted energy to Malcolm, nor had he contacted her. She'd been so absorbed in a solution to the food laws that she hadn't let her mind wander to Malcolm and what he might be doing with Scarlet, or what Kelsie might've told him.

"Jack told me you're worried about where you stand with Malcolm."

Amelia frowned. Why was her best friend stuck on that topic? "That isn't important. I found a solution to our—" She leaned forward and lowered her voice. Even in a crowded and noisy cafeteria, there was no way to know who might be listening in. "—dilemma."

Amelia dug out her notes and slid them face down across the table.

Dina grabbed the stack, turned it over and flicked through the pages, a smile blooming on her face. "This is smart. How'd you come up with it?"

"From Mrs. Duffy of all people," Amelia said. "During one of her history of the City lectures. There was a ration system before the food laws, but it stunk."

"There's only one problem," Dina said. "The rich will hate getting the same amount as everyone else. They'll never support this."

"They'll love getting some for free, and they have money and can pay for more. It'll be another way to show off how much they can afford and to bolster their superiority complexes."

"This means you'll have to face Malcolm again," Dina said, her eyes locked on Amelia. "And the others."

Amelia shrugged. She hoped the gesture made her seem like she was unbothered. "I can handle it."

…

Before the fundraiser, Amelia and her friends had agreed on their next meeting date. As she hadn't heard news of it changing, Amelia got ready on the day of and headed to the bus, her notes packed into her bag.

Amelia had expected to be the first of her group at the bus stop, but when she walked up, there was Ethan leaning against the wall of a nearby building. He stood up straight when he spotted her, and the corner of his mouth tipped up. "Hi, Amelia."

Amelia gave Ethan a small wave. "Hi, Ethan."

"Are you okay?"

Amelia hadn't positioned herself to face Ethan, preferring to watch the street for signs of the bus, and she still felt his eyes on her. "Yup."

Ethan came closer; she could tell by the sound of his footsteps. "If something is bothering you, you can tell me."

Amelia turned to Ethan and heaved a sigh. "I'm anxious about seeing Malcolm, especially since I'm sure he's asked Scarlet to marry him by now."

By being so close to Ethan, Amelia could see his throat move as he swallowed. Something was making him nervous. "You can tell me too, you know." Ever since Kylie had volunteered Amelia and Ethan to knock on the door during her first delivery run, Amelia had felt a fondness for him. They were the hangers-on of the group, her as a newcomer and him as Jack's, now possibly Kylie's, tagalong friend.

Ethan's eyes focused on something over Amelia's shoulder. "I shouldn't."

"Why—" What had caught his attention?

"Mellie!" Dina squealed, ran up from behind and flung her arms around Amelia.

That was why Ethan hadn't told her what was on his mind. Dina and Jack were here, and Ethan didn't want to tell them. Amelia would need to ask him again later.

"Hi, Dina and Jack," Amelia said. She didn't return her friend's hug.

Dina stepped away and grabbed Jack's hand. There were other people at the bus station, so this was a bold choice on Dina's part. Jack gave Dina's hand a squeeze and pulled his free.

Amelia thought it was unfortunate that couples couldn't show affection in public without paperwork making it legal, but that was a law she didn't dream of overturning. The wealthy already paid their way out of consequences related to breaking it, and the poor didn't complain too much. Besides, there was no real enforcement for brief displays that a guard didn't witness, such as when Amelia had kissed Malcolm. It was too easy to deny and too difficult to prove unless someone took a picture, or a guard saw it happen. Still, it was obvious Dina and Jack were counting the weeks until Clinic Day.

Amelia was dreading it, not because she was worried about her health but because it was when Malcolm and Scarlet would become official, assuming her suspicions about him marrying her were correct. She didn't want to think about that and tried to distract herself on the bus once it came and everyone got on.

Ethan was sitting beside Amelia, which proved to be her best chance at a distraction. He had the window seat, so she turned her body in his direction to give them a measure of privacy. "Are you going to tell me what's on your mind now?"

Ethan's eyes darted around the bus, looking for anyone that might overhear. Dina and Jack were in conversation across the aisle, which seemed to put Ethan at ease, and he reclined against his seat. "I want to ask Kelsie on a date, and I'm scared she'll say no. Our first was to that fundraiser, which was more by default that anything else."

"Do it today," Amelia said. "Delaying will only make you fret more. And I know she'll say yes."

Ethan lifted his eyebrows. "How?"

"Because she likes you." He should have figured that out by now.

"I don't know," he groaned. "You don't think she just danced with me out of pity?"

Amelia swatted Ethan's arm. "Kelsie won't turn you down, and she didn't do anything out of pity." *Unlike Malcolm.* He must've felt sorry for Amelia, both for being ran into by Scarlet and for her poor living conditions. Once he'd taken her on a few dates, his conscience was satisfied. How was Amelia ever going to handle seeing him?

She was about to find out as the bus reached their stop. Amelia hoisted her bag and followed Jack and Dina off with Ethan trailing behind. They walked as a group to Malcolm's house, and it was Kelsie this time who opened the door and ushered everyone inside.

Maybe Amelia had lucked out and Malcolm wasn't here. She'd almost convinced herself of that when he appeared in the door across from his entry, and his eyes landed on her. Amelia's heart sped up as she tore her eyes off him. She was desperate to focus on something else. Once she got her shoes off, there was nothing. She couldn't walk into the living room and act like he wasn't there in his own house.

"Amelia," Malcolm said, causing the others to give him and Amelia a wide berth. No one wanted to get in the middle.

"Let's go this way," Kelsie said to Dina, Jack and Ethan, who's side she'd attached herself to, and darted into the living room. "And give them some space."

Amelia tried not to wince as her friends muttered greetings and apologies to Malcolm and dashed after Kelsie. She heard someone open the dining room door, her friends' footsteps head that way and the door close after them.
"You're not with Scarlet?"

Malcolm's lips turned down at the edges, despite his attempts to keep his face neutral. He walked in her direction, stopping short a few steps away. Amelia hadn't gotten much farther than the entry. "Why would I be with

Scarlet?"

Amelia affixed her eyes on a spot on the wall. Why was he making her say this out loud? She wasn't naïve enough to not know what was going on. "Because you're going to marry her."

Malcolm closed the distance between them and reached for her hand. "Is that what you want me to do, or what you think I'm going to do?"

Amelia let him clasp her hand in the safety of his house, free from prying eyes. She wanted this chance to touch him and enjoy the tingle of his skin on hers. "You are, aren't you? I saw you flirting with each other at the fundraiser. I wish you'd just admit to it. I don't want your pity."

Malcolm held tight to her hand and exhaled a deep breath. "Kelsie told me. And I don't pity you. I thought you trusted me more than this. I said I wasn't keeping anything bad from you."

"Then what were you talking to Jack about?" Maybe this time he'd tell her the entire truth. "And why were you letting Scarlet drape herself all over you?"

"Scarlet has wanted to marry me for years. Now that we're old enough, she thinks she can force me into it. I told her I didn't want that attention from her, that I was on a date with you. Then I turned around and you were gone. I found out from Kelsie and Jack that you left."

Amelia inhaled a shaky breath. She still couldn't bring herself to look at him. "And Jack?"

Malcolm squeezed her hand. "I told him who he should talk to and asked him for a favour. You have to trust me that I can't tell you what it is yet."

"I'll try," Amelia said. He'd given her the same story as he had at the fundraiser. She wanted to trust Malcolm, secrets or not. Trusting him, and her friends, was easier than believing they were all conspiring against her. The warmth of his hand encasing hers had her body tingling. She'd missed him, even though it hadn't been long since she'd seen him. "And I'm sorry I left without telling you. It's just that you're going to realize that we're not right for each other, and I thought Scarlet had expedited it."

Malcolm bent his head down to look in Amelia's eyes, forcing her to see him. His forehead was almost touching hers; it was so close. "It doesn't matter how poor your family is or where you live. When I'm with you, I know the future I want. Scarlet only reminds me of what I don't want and have been trying to avoid. I won't trap myself in a Courtship with her, and I would never hurt you that way."

Tears pooled in the corners of Amelia's eyes. She wiped them with her free hand and blinked away the remnants. "I believe you."

The smile that crept onto Malcom's face lit it up like Amelia's personal golden sun. She went onto her tiptoes and kissed him. She kept it brief, not giving him time to reciprocate or react. "Let's go. Everyone's waited long enough, and I have news."

Chapter 24

Amelia laid out her plan. Only Dina, unless she'd told Jack, knew about it earlier. Amelia had worried that no one would like it and that Dina had placated her, but the others grinned, and Ethan and Kelsie dove into the numbers.

Kelsie, from spending so much time around Arlo Fenn – who she'd given the list of clothing donors to, had an idea of how much food a person needed. Amelia she was happy to delegate the part she hadn't known how to calculate to Ethan and Kelsie.

She was also glad to see them so close to each other. Ethan was holding one of the papers in his left hand, and Kelsie extended her arm over his to point to a place on the page. He didn't brush her off. It made Amelia wonder if Ethan had asked her on a date while Amelia and Malcolm were in the hall.

"This was a good idea," Malcolm said. He was sitting beside Amelia on the couch, his fingers mere millimetres to the side of hers. She could feel warmth radiating off his hand without touching it.

"Thank you, but I can't take all the credit. My history teacher gave me the idea without meaning to. It was the first time I paid attention to the class in years."

Malcolm chuckled. "They shouldn't make history a mandatory subject every year when they recycle so much material."

Amelia clasped her hands in her lap and swallowed. "Do you think Mr.

Everbee will go for it?"

Malcolm exhaled. "I don't think he expects us to come back with a solution, so I'm not sure."

"Does Scarlet know what we're trying to do?"

"On a basic level. She hates when I try to talk about it, and she's too self centred to care about anyone other than herself."

It was Amelia's fault he spent so much time with Scarlet, and for talking herself into believing Malcolm would marry Scarlet. "I'm sorry I got you into all this." If she'd never invited him along to meet Arlo Fenn, things might've been different. She'd still be the girl going through the days wishing she could help people. "And I'm also glad I did."

Malcolm shifted on his seat to better face her. "You shouldn't be sorry. I know why you agreed to Scarlet's terms."

"You're not upset I got you involved before that? I could've gone alone to meet Arlo Fenn."

"No. I want to help. You remember when we were coming back from the Colony and the guard stopped us?"

How could she forget? They'd almost been arrested that night, and she had no desire to repeat the experience. "What does that have to do with anything?"

Malcolm flashed her a conspiratorial grin. "While you were sleeping, I drove to the scientist's outpost, paid them their wages and dropped off some hardware they'd requested."

Amelia gawked. "So, you lied to Kelsie about them backing you up for water?"

"My dad does have that deal, and did send more water, but I was actually there."

"Why though, if you knew they'd lie for you anyway?"

Malcolm lifted his shoulders. "We needed a solid alibi, especially for Jack and Dina's Courtship."

He'd gone out of his way to protect her friends. Amelia tucked her feet underneath her, so she was kneeling. She placed both hands on the couch to raise herself up and planted a kiss on Malcolm's cheek. "That was kind of you, especially with how unfriendly Jack was."

Malcolm blushed and opened his mouth to speak when Kelsie squealed.

She got to her feet and waved a piece of paper. "We got it!"

"Enough to present the idea anyway," Ethan said with a spark in his eye.

Dina stood up, walked to Kelsie and snatched the paper. Jack was a step behind and leaned over her shoulder to scan it.

"This is pretty good," Jack said.

Amelia got off the couch and offered Malcolm her hand. "Coming?"

Malcolm slid his hand along hers, their fingers interlacing. "Instead of sitting here alone? Definitely."

…

Kelsie's work had impressed Amelia enough that she wanted to bring Kelsie to the next meeting with Mr. Everbee. Maybe he'd consider them more credible with another person. It couldn't make their chances worse.

Amelia whispered her idea in Malcolm's ear, and he nodded. "Kelsie," Amelia said, getting her attention. "You should come when we see Mr. Everbee again."

A wicked grin blossomed on Kelsie's face. "To help? Or to tell him what I think of Scarlet? Because I'd love to do both."

Malcolm laughed. "Unfortunately, only to help."

Kelsie stuck her bottom lip out in an exaggerated pout. "Fine. Can I at least tell Scarlet? Someone needs to deflate her ego."

"That's true," Dina said with a shudder. "She's horrible."

Amelia agreed with her friends, but she wasn't on board with telling Scarlet. At least not with so much at stake that Scarlet could ruin if put in a bad or vengeful mood. "We have to wait, and Malcolm should be the one to tell her off anyway."

"Heh," Malcolm said. "I think you deserve to tell Scarlet how you feel too, Amelia. She's put you through a lot."

Amelia would relish the opportunity to tell off Scarlet, but that wasn't the point of the meeting. "Thanks. Can we get back on topic now? We need to figure out when we're going to see Mr. Everbee again and what we're going to tell him."

...

It was late afternoon by the time Amelia and her friends finished polishing the plan and needed to leave. Kelsie walked Ethan to the door with Dina, leaving Malcolm alone with Amelia and Jack. Amelia found this a bit odd. Why hadn't Jack gone with Dina?

Malcolm was standing a few steps away from her with his hands thrust into his pants pockets. The sun shining through the window cast a gold hue over his head, making Amelia's heart race and butterflies flip in her stomach. She'd never imagined anyone could've done to her what Malcolm gazing at her with glittering emerald eyes did.

"I'll let you know when I arrange another meeting with Scarlet's father," Malcolm said.

"Thanks." Amelia hesitated about saying more with Jack in the room, even though he was standing at the window with his back to her.

Amelia grabbed her bag and retreated from the room before she could embarrass herself. Malcolm made her want things she thought she'd never wanted to share with anyone. Like a future. It scared her, and there was no way she could tell him, especially when they weren't alone.

Dina and Ethan were waiting in the entry for her. Amelia hoped she didn't appear too flustered and that she wasn't blushing. She was about to suggest they leave without Jack when she heard his voice. It was muffled, like he was in the dining room, so she couldn't make out his words. Then footsteps came her direction, and by the time she got her shoes on, Jack was standing in the entry.

Jack whisked Dina out of the house before Amelia could ask him what he and Malcolm had talked about. She had an idea it was about the favour Malcolm wanted. Yet, Amelia didn't think they were friends. What had made Jack's opinion of Malcolm change?

"Are you coming, Amelia?"

Amelia blinked and snapped herself out of her daze. Ethan was standing in the doorway, holding it open for her and gazing at her with a question in his eyes.

"Yeah," Amelia said as she grabbed her bag and darted outside with Ethan. Jack and Dina were so far ahead she couldn't make out their features anymore. Amelia had stood frozen longer than she'd thought, or Dina and Jack had ran away from her. She preferred to believe it was the first option.

"You didn't have to wait for me," Amelia told Ethan as they stepped onto the road.

Ethan inhaled a deep breath. "I asked Kelsie on a date."

Amelia turned her face to him. "And? What did she say?"

"She said yes, as long as it's not a double date."

Amelia squealed and hugged Ethan, the impact making him wobble on his feet. "I told you she wouldn't reject you."

"You know anywhere cheap?" Ethan asked as he wiggled out of Amelia's arms.

"Cheap?" Amelia gave his arm a playful swat. "That's a great way to impress her."

Ethan started walking again, making Amelia rush after him. "Kelsie has no money. Arlo Fenn used to pay all her expenses, but he's cut her off since she won't go back to working for him. She doesn't want to use the Connors' money for it, and I don't have a ton."

"There's always Catsy's, except it's, well… you know."

"Awful."

Amelia laughed. Kelsie would agree with that statement. "Take her to Darla's. It's not much pricier."

"Good idea," Ethan said. "Thanks."

Helping Malcolm plan his date with Kelsie made Amelia long for one with Malcolm. She'd missed being with him, and, armed with the knowledge he wasn't going to marry Scarlet, she had hope he'd take her out again. Amelia hadn't asked him about it, and now she'd have to mail him a note to do so.

She spent the bus ride home pondering it and forgot to ask Jack what he'd said to Malcolm. It was when she got to her stop and disembarked from the bus that Amelia cursed herself for not cornering him. No matter. Amelia would ask Dina at lunch.

…

Amelia sprung her question on Dina the next day in the cafeteria. She didn't get a response she wanted or hoped for.

Dina drank some of her water and gave Amelia a shrug. "Jack didn't mention it. He only told me he had to get home because he had stuff to do."

That sounded like a sketchy excuse for running from Malcolm's house to Amelia. Especially since they'd all ridden the same bus home. "And you didn't ask him what stuff?"

Dina shook her head, sending her hair flying. "I assumed he meant he had chores, homework, or work. His job stresses him out."

There was truth to this. Jack's parents were poorer than hers and Dina's. He needed as much extra money as he could get to pay for his wedding to Dina, assuming their Courtship application was successful. "Are you still looking forward to Clinic day?"

Dina dipped her head and wrung her shaky hands on the table. "I'm getting nervous. There's a chance we'll get a rejection, and I don't know what I'd do without Jack."

Amelia stretched her arm cross the cafeteria table gave Dina's hands a pat. She didn't want her best friend to entertain those doubts. Their friend group had enough to go around. "Don't think like that. You and Jack are perfect together, and you're going to get married."

Dina wiped the tears forming in her eyes and gave a weak smile. "Thanks. I needed that bit of affirmation."

"That's what best friends are for, isn't it?"

Chapter 25

Amelia decided to let whatever Jack and Malcolm were keeping a secret go. Neither of them, nor Dina, was going to tell her anyway, and finalizing the details for meeting Mr. Everbee again brought enough stress.

Amelia was in her room, going through her closet to plan her outfit for whenever the meeting, was when her mom cleared her throat. Amelia jumped and turned around, having not heard her mom walk in.

"You've been awfully busy recently," her mom said. She had her hands in her pockets, her elbows bent and her eyes narrowed. "Your dad and I are worried. We hope you aren't neglecting your studies."

"I'm not." Academics had always been a strong suit of Amelia's and she always tried her best, which still wasn't enough to land her an impressive career. Only people with a list of established connections seemed to land high paying jobs in the Government or fields like medicine. People like Malcolm and Scarlet. Amelia didn't have the necessary connections or the budget to study at the university in the rich Quarters to even give herself a chance. Still, school was one thing she could control regarding how well she did.

"It seems to me," her mom said, like Amelia hadn't spoken. "That you're more concerned with impressing your new friends and going against the Government than your future."

Amelia let her shoulders droop. She *had* started to think about her future, one with Malcolm. She wasn't ready to admit that to herself and definitely not to her mom. "And what future is that?"

"Someday you'll want to live elsewhere, might even have to," her mom said. "How will you support yourself without either a high paying job or a spouse?"

Amelia pressed her lips together and crossed her arms tight over her chest. Her vision tinted red. "I thought you said you'd stop meddling and trying to force me to get married. If it happens, it'll be with someone I choose when I'm ready."

Her mom huffed. "I don't want you to miss out on opportunities for a brief period of enjoyment with friends your dad and I don't even know."

Amelia groaned. Why was her mom questioning her judgement? "You know Dina and Jack. Do you really think Ethan, Kelsie and Malcolm are terrible people?"

Her mom pressed her lips into a thin line. Amelia hadn't seen her mom this firm about something since she'd set Amelia up on the date with Blake. "I spoke to your dad about it, and we've agreed that you cannot continue seeing that group until you bring them here to meet us. I'm not asking for anything unreasonable."

Amelia froze. She didn't dare ask what would happen if her mom still didn't approve after meeting them. What Amelia would do was clear, and no one would talk her out of it this time. "Fine. I'll arrange it."

She would have to do it fast. Malcolm hadn't contacted yet her with a date to meet Mr. Everbee again, and there was no way she was sending a reply, when his message came, saying she couldn't go. She'd sneak out if she must, though she preferred not to. Things were so much easier when done with her parents' knowledge and consent.

...

Amelia was jumpy while waiting for her friends' replies. She spent her free time pacing the floor or her bedroom and twirling her hair around her fingers. It was imperative that they all came and made a favourable impression on her mom. Her dad wasn't the one pushing for this. He preferred to let Amelia make her own choices, provided she didn't get into trouble with a guard.

Dina and Jack had no issues with or worries about meeting Amelia's parents. Jack had even promised to vouch for Ethan. It was Kelsie and Malcolm that Amelia fretted over. Her mom would have to take her word, and their actions, as evidence they weren't trouble.

Amelia had instructed everyone to wear something nice but not overly flashy; the last part was specifically for Malcolm. She, herself, turned to the regular section of her closet to find an outfit that would appease her mom. She wanted to show she could be responsible and not only a reckless, and fun-loving teenager like her mom thought she was.

Amelia moved her pacing and hair twirling to her living room on the day her friends had agreed to come. Dina arrived first and shook Amelia by the shoulders, stopping Amelia's lap across the room. She'd spent every lunch hour all week trying to calm Amelia down.

"Stop worrying," Dina said, making eye contact with Amelia. "It's going to be fine."

Amelia sighed. "I hope you're right. My mom can be difficult."

Dina rolled her eyes. "All moms can be difficult. Fretting isn't going to help."

"I know."

Dina turned Amelia around and walked her to the couch. When they reached it, Dina dropped her hands from Amelia's shoulders. "Sit and try to relax."

Amelia did as her friend said. Working herself up wasn't going to help or make it less important that her mom didn't stand in the way of her making a difference or seeing her friends.

Her mom came out of her bedroom and chatted with Dina. The ease of their conversation helped settle Amelia's nerves. Her parents had always approved of Dina, which was what made her mom's ultimatum so confusing. Hadn't Amelia proven herself a good judge of character?

The boys and Kelsie arrived minutes before their agreed upon time. Malcolm had followed Amelia's instructions and wore khaki-coloured pants and a simple grey button-up shirt that no one would look at and think was super expensive. He gave her a small, closed-lipped smile as he walked to the couch, and he brushed her fingers with his own.

Amelia tried not to react to the tingle of electricity in her hand from his brief contact. "Mom," she said, getting her mom's attention away from Dina. "You remember Malcolm and Jack. And these are Ethan and Kelsie," Amelia said with a sweep of her arm.

"It's nice to meet you, Mrs. Ruby," Ethan said, extending his hand for Amelia's mom to shake.

Amelia swore she saw her mom fight back a smile at Ethan's politeness.

"Your home is lovely," Kelsie said, with a big, charming smile that at first glance didn't look forced.

If anyone could charm Amelia's mom, it was her friends. Amelia led them to the couch and kitchen chairs she'd helped her mom move over, while her mom called for her dad.

Once everyone had a seat, Amelia's mom eyed Ethan and Kelsie. "Tell me, how did you meet my Amelia?"

Amelia folded her hands in her lap to stop from wringing them. Were her friends going to tell her mom the truth? Amelia wasn't sure that would go over well. It would end with Amelia locked in the apartment.

"Jack introduced us," Ethan said.

Kelsie shifted on her seat, tucking her feet under her. "I met Amelia when she came to pick up cargo for the Colony from where I was staying."

"And where was that?" Amelia's mom asked.

"A building in Apartment District 12," Kelsie said with a shrug and a tone that made it seem like no big deal when Amelia knew how much Kelsie never wanted to return to that life.

"Kelsie lives in my house now," Malcolm said. He was sitting beside Amelia with a respectable distance between their bodies, and he moved his hand over to brush hers.

Amelia thought Kelsie and Malcolm's admissions had ruined their chances of her mom's approval. She wasn't going to like knowing a different girl had moved in with the boy Amelia sometimes went on dates with and had narrowed her eyes at Malcolm's statement.

"Your parents don't mind?" Amelia's dad asked.

Kelsie shook her head. "They can't. They're dead."

"Amelia," her mom gasped, her eyes now wider. "Why did you never mention this?"

It was Kelsie's secret to share, not Amelia's. "It's not my business to tell."

"You could've," Kelsie said, causing everyone to look at her. "I don't care who knows."

"So brave," Amelia's mom tutted. "You poor thing."

Amelia saw Kelsie blanch. She clearly hadn't expected or wanted this attention.

"Amelia," her mom continued. "You should invite Kelsie over more often. I'd like to take her under my wing."

"That really isn't necessary, Mrs. Ruby," Kelsie said, her lips turned down at the corners. "I have everything I need."

Amelia stood up. She wasn't about to let Kelsie turn her mother back to distant and judgmental. "Come with me, Kelsie." She walked to the hallway before Kelsie could protest.

When Amelia was out of sight of the living room, she waited for Kelsie's footsteps. When Kelsie reached her, Amelia took her by the wrist, led her into her bedroom and closed the door.

"I don't want your mom's pity," Kelsie said, her eyes blazing.

Amelia dropped Kelsie's wrist. "She doesn't pity you. She just wants to help."

Kelsie turned her face away, her mouth a hard line.

"Look," Amelia said. "If you want to never see me or my mom again, go out there and tell her off. Then she'll tell me she was right about my friends being bad influences."

Kelsie huffed, and Amelia could see tears glistening in the corners of her eyes. "Before you showed up at Arlo's, he was the only person that ever did anything for me. It was reciprocal; he always wanted something in return. Now I'm Malcolm's charity case, at least to his parents. I stay because it's better than going back to Arlo, moving around all the time and pretending I don't exist. At least now I have a legal ID card."

"You're unformattable accepting help, aren't you?" Amelia asked.

Kelsie barked out a humourless laugh. "You would be too if it came with conditions and pity."

Amelia grasped Kelsie by the shoulders and shook her. "My mom's trying to be nice. There's no pity or conditions. I, for one, am happy that she didn't scoff at you and kick you out."

Kelsie locked her eyes on Amelia's, understanding lighting in them through the tears. "You really want me to accept her help."

Amelia dropped her hands and handed Kelsie a napkin from the bedside table to wipe her eyes. "I'd like you to not tick her off. It's important to me that she accepts you and Ethan and Malcolm."

"Fine. I'll be nice to her because Ethan would be angry at me for ruining our group."

This was close enough. "Whatever works."

...

Amelia's mom went into hosting mode when Kelsie came back and accepted her offer. Amelia watched her mom usher her dad into the kitchen to fetch water and cups that could pass for matching. If it had been legal, and she'd had enough money, Amelia was sure her mom would've set out a spread of food and other beverages.

"I told you not to worry," Dina said. "Your mom isn't that bad."

"At least you see her," Malcolm said. "Mine only appears when we have company she wants to impress."

Amelia lifted her shoulders. Her friends made valid points. "We just disagree on so much stuff."

Malcolm took her hand and ran his thumb along the back. He could make small physical touches in the privacy and safety of Amelia's apartment, so Amelia didn't yank her hand away. Why should she deny herself this bit of comfort and support Malcolm wanted to give her? Besides, Dina and Jack were holding hands and had done so in front of Amelia's parents without reprimand.

"That's typical of parents," Jack said. "Mine want me to get an office job, but it sounds like drudgery to me."

"My parents want me to become a teacher," Dina said with a shudder. "I don't like kids or school that much."

Kelsie grunted.

Amelia swiveled her head in Kelsie's direction. She had her arms crossed and wore a scowl. "I think all of you should be glad you have parents at all."

Ethan hovered his hand above Kelsie's shoulder, like he was deciding whether to touch her, before resting it on her. "Do you remember anything about yours?"

Amelia saw her lean into Ethan's touch and some of the tension ease from her body. Her scowl disappeared. "No. Arlo got me when I was five. I remember nothing from that time or before."

"Do you miss Arlo?" Dina asked.

Kelsie shook her head. "We were never family. He was more like my boss, or my keeper. I only saw him when he needed or wanted something."

Amelia, from her three experiences with him, had found Arlo serious and imposing. He wasn't the nurturing or comforting type.

"And my parents aren't the hands-on type either," Malcolm said.

"They're nice to me when they are home," Kelsie said. "I kind of prefer hands-off. I don't need someone hovering over me all the time."

Amelia envied Kelsie for that. She would take her mom being less involved in every part of her business if given the chance. At least her mom had come around to seeing her friends as decent people.

Amelia thought she was lucky, as her parents came out of the kitchen and distributed glasses of water to her friends. She had both parents, food for every meal, and a decent, though small, apartment with her own bedroom. It was more than a lot of people in the City had.

Chapter 26

After Amelia's friends left, she helped her parents clear the glasses and clean them. Her mom rinsed and scrubbed, her dad dried, and Amelia put them away.

"So, Mom," Amelia said as she placed one of the glasses in the cabinet. "What do you think of Kelsie and Ethan?"

"I'll admit," her mom said, keeping her eyes and attention on the glass she was scrubbing, "they aren't bad kids."

Amelia saw her dad smirk. This had turns out better than Amelia hoped, thanks to her mom's affection for Kelsie. "I knew you wouldn't hate them."

Her mom sighed as she passed the glass to Amelia's dad. "Things have changed so much and so fast for you. I want to stay part of your life."

"I get that," Amelia said as she took the next glass from her dad. She did understand it. Not too long ago, Amelia's only friend had been Dina, and she'd been home much more. "Just, it feels like you're fighting me on everything."

"I think you two could find a compromise," Amelia's dad said.

Her mom passed another glass to her dad. "I suppose I could have more trust in you."

"And I'll try to share more stuff with you," Amelia said and hugged her mom in agreement. She didn't specify how much stuff, or what kind, as she wanted to reserve the right to keep somethings to herself.

Still, the compromise with her mom lessened the tension around their apartment. And Amelia's mom beamed when a note came a few days later from Kelsie asking to go clothes shopping for a dress she could wear on a date with Ethan.

Amelia liked that Kelsie and Ethan were hitting things off, but she didn't relish the idea of helping Kelsie get ready for a date. It was a reminder that she hadn't heard from Malcolm since he'd come to her apartment. Regardless, Amelia pushed that from her mind as she rode the bus with her mom to the store Kelsie had asked to meet at in Apartment District 1. This was about Kelsie and Ethan, not her and Malcolm.

Amelia and her mom got off the bus and walked down the street to the boutiques. Amelia felt out of place in this posh Apartment District with its clean, polished buildings and walking paths on the sides of the street dotted with trees growing in pots. It was nothing like home, and she felt underdressed. If she'd thought about it, she would've convinced her mom to let her dip into her makeup and date clothes. Alas, she was wearing one of her standard jeans and fraying t-shirt outfits. She ran her hands through her hair, trying to smooth it. That was the only part of her appearance she could alter in such a brief amount of time.

Kelsie was waiting outside one of the stores, standing in the shade of a potted tree along the spotless curb. She brightened and gave a little wave when she saw Amelia and her mom. "You made it!"

"We promised we would, dear," Amelia's mom said, smiling and giving Kelsie's shoulder a pat.

Kelsie grabbed Amelia by the wrist. "Come on. Malcolm suggested a place to take Ethan dancing, and I need a dress that'll catch the light. Malcolm said it has a mirrored floor and chandeliers."

"How does he know?" Amelia asked as dodged the door swinging closed behind Kelsie. "He never told me he dances." Amelia couldn't picture him in a place like that. Their dates had solely been to restaurants where they could talk in relative privacy.

Kelsie snorted. "Scarlet dragged him there to show him off."

Malcolm never told Amelia what he and Scarlet did on dates. Evidently, they did activities other than eat. She took a deep breath to calm herself. Today's outing was about helping Kelsie, not comparing herself to Scarlet, regardless of whether Scarlet's dates with Malcolm seemed more extravagant and public than Amelia's.

"Don't worry," her mom said, giving her back a pat. "I saw Malcolm's face when you weren't looking. He's smitten."

Kelsie dropped Amelia's wrist and darted over to a rack with glittering dresses. Amelia had never seen clothing so sparkly. Where did people wear such things? Kelsie grabbed a sapphire blue dress with short, puffy sleeves, a sweetheart neckline, fitted bodice and knee-length, A-line skirt off the rack and thrust it at Amelia before Amelia could process her mom's words. "You have to try this on."

"What?" Amelia blinked as her arms adjusted to the weight of the dress. She didn't dare glance at the price or size tags. What use did she have for a dress like this? She would look overdressed even wearing it to a restaurant with Malcolm. "I can't afford it, nor do I need a new dress."

"Go try it on. I can't be the only one," Kelsie said as she steered Amelia to the fitting room sign at the back of the store.

The fitting room attendant perked up when she saw Amelia holding the blue dress. "Right this way," she said as she turned and strutted down the small hallway of fitting rooms, her heels clacking on the floor. The attendant stopped at a vacant room and gestured to its open door. "Let me know if you need a different size." With her instructions given, the employee returned to the desk at the fitting room entrance.

"Get in there," Kelsie said.

"I thought we were here to find you a dress."

"We are," Kelsie said as she brushed a stray curl over her shoulder. "But you deserve something nice, and Malcolm's mom gave me more than enough money. Rich people don't really know how much anything costs."

Amelia groaned. "Fine. I'm only trying on this one dress." She stepped inside, closed the door and latched it as Kelsie walked away giggling.

Amelia hung the dress on the hook on the left-hand wall and sat on the padded stool. She got a glimpse of herself, and the dress, in the mirror that took up the entire rear wall of the small room. It was a stunning dress. Amelia had to admit that, but she had nowhere to wear it. If Malcolm took her dancing someday, she'd find a use for it. That wouldn't do. Amelia didn't have the money to plan things on possibilities. Nor was she eager to copy Scarlet's dates. Yet, Kelsie had said Mrs. Connor gave her extra money.

Amelia grasped her hair with her hands and hoped yanking on it would put some sense into her head. Just because Malcolm's parents were rich didn't mean she could take advantage.

Her scalp was sore, and she was ready to flee the fitting room, leaving the dress behind, when she heard multiple pairs of footsteps and the attendant's heels. The footsteps stopped at the room next to Amelia's and she heard muffled voices followed by the fading sound of heels.

A pair of feet appeared under Amelia's door, and someone knocked.

With a sigh, Amelia stood, unlatched the door and swung it open. Kelsie was standing on the other side, and her face fell. "It didn't fit?"

Amelia shrugged. "I don't know. I couldn't try it on."

Kelsie placed her hands on her hips and peered at Amelia. "Why not?"

Amelia crossed her ankles and leaned against the door frame. "I can't take advantage of your extra money."

"Malcolm's mom told me to spend it on whatever I want. Take advantage."

"Kelsie has a point," Amelia's mom from where she sat on a cushioned bench behind Kelsie said. "It's not a bad thing to accept a gift."

Amelia huffed. "Fine. I'll try it on."

Kelsie beamed and darted into the fitting room next door. "Great. Come out when you have it on, and we can give each other opinions."

Amelia hadn't realized how starved for friendship Kelsie was. If Amelia had paid better attention, she would've known that from the moment she met Kelsie. Having Dina had blinded Amelia to the fact that others might need a friend, and it was a good thing that Kelsie wanted her friendship. "Okay."

Amelia stripped off her outfit and unzipped the back of the blue dress. She stepped into it and pulled it up, sliding her arms into the sleeves. Contorting her arms, she got the zipper most of the way up.

The tulle skirt had glittering sequins sewn on that sparkled in the mirror when Amelia turned. She stifled a gasp at her reflection. If she'd done her hair and put on some makeup, Amelia wouldn't have recognized herself. She would've looked like a girl that belonged with Malcolm. As it was, she looked like a poor girl who'd spent her family's yearly budget on a fancy dress. Still, for a moment she felt light, like she was floating on a cloud.

She heard Kelsie opening her door, so she unlatched her own and stepped out. The first thing she saw was Kelsie posing in a glittering, gold, bodycon dress. Then, before she could form words, Kelsie grabbed her by the wrist and pulled her in front of the mirror.

"Don't you like it?" Kelsie asked as she dropped Amelia's hand.

"Yes," Amelia said, feeling a strong urge to twirl. "It's the best-looking thing I've ever worn."

"So is mine, except I don't love it," Kelsie said. "I'm going to try the next one. Stay here."

Amelia walked over to her mom and sat beside her on the bench. Reality hit her like a wave. No matter how pretty the dress was and made her feel, she couldn't have it. "I know you said I should accept this, but I have nowhere to wear it."

Amelia's mom patted her on the knee. "You never know when you'll need a nice dress. Malcolm might take you somewhere with a formal dress code."

Amelia didn't think that would happen. The fanciest place Malcolm had ever taken her was the restaurant his parents liked to frequent. Everywhere they went seemed to be sentimental to him on some level or a part of her world. "I suppose."

Amelia was ready to get up and return to her fitting room to take off her dress when Kelsie reappeared. This time she wore a knee-length, V-neck gown with wide shoulder straps and a flowy, A-line skirt. It was bright pink with an encrusted, sparkling bodice, and she looked radiant.

Kelsie ran to the spot in the hallway that faced the mirror and twirled, sending the skirt out to her sides. "Oh my gosh," she said when she stopped and brushed her curls back. "I think this is the one. Amelia, do you know if Ethan likes pink?"

"I have no clue. Jack might know."

"Heh. That's not helpful."

"If you like it, that's all that matters," Amelia's mom said.

Kelsie nibbled on her bottom lip. "What if he hates pink, and it makes him sick to look at it?"

Amelia got off the bench and grasped Kelsie by the shoulders. She wasn't sure how Kelsie and Ethan ever got anything planned when they were both so overpowered by their worries. "Calm down. You look exquisite, and Ethan isn't going to hate anything you wear."

"If a boy is turned off by the colour of what you're wearing, he isn't the right one," Amelia's mom said. "I'm saying that to both of you."

"Yeah," Kelsie said, lifting her chin and squaring her shoulders. "If Ethan hates pink, too bad. I'm buying this one."

With Kelsie's decision made, both girls returned to their fitting rooms and put their normal clothes back on. Amelia draped the blue dress over her arm. Even if Malcolm wouldn't take her somewhere fancy, she'd find an occasion to wear it. There was no reason, Amelia convinced herself, that she couldn't let Kelsie buy it. Maybe Dina would even let her wear it to her wedding to Jack.

Amelia was behind her mom and Kelsie as they exited the fitting rooms, so she didn't see at first what made Kelsie stop and tense up. It was when she sidestepped Kelsie to move around her that Amelia saw familiar ash-blonde hair. *What was Scarlet doing here?*

Scarlet had her side to Amelia and Kelsie and was gesturing animatedly to a salesperson who was nodding along.

"If we go this way, she won't see us," Amelia muttered as she took a step to her side, away from Scarlet's line of sight.

"Possibly," Kelsie grumbled.

"Who is that you're trying to avoid?" her mom asked, keeping her voice down.

"Scarlet," Amelia said. "The girl that wants to marry Malcolm."

Her mom put hand on Amelia's arm, stopping her from retreating to the side. "Running away and hiding is letting her win."

"I shouldn't—"

"Come on, Amelia," Kelsie said, with an eerie calm. "Let's go say hi."

Amelia thought Kelsie must've been up to something as she strode over to Scarlet. With a sigh, Amelia followed.

"Hello, Scarlet," Kelsie said, with a wide and fake grin. "You shop here too?"

Scarlet wheeled around and fixed Kelsie with an icy glare and an upturned nose. "Obviously not anymore if they've lowered their standards to let the poor in."

"We can afford to shop here as much as you can," Kelsie said, lifting her own chin.

Scarlet scoffed. "Amelia is Malcolm's charity case, and you're his parents' pity project."

"Hey!" Amelia said, fury bubbling in her veins and making her body vibrate. Why did Scarlet have such an effect on her? She knew exactly how to get under Amelia's skin. "That's not true."

Scarlet stepped closer, like a murderer cornering their next victim. "Why else would he spend so much time with you and only take you places to eat? You're a nobody that he feels sorry for and thinks he has to feed so you don't starve."

Amelia didn't flinch or back up. Her mom was right, running away would make Scarlet feel like she won, and Amelia didn't want to give her that satisfaction. "Malcolm likes me. He tolerates you because we need access to your dad. You're just a cold, cruel, selfish witch."

"You know nothing," Scarlet spat. "Keep believing your delusions. They'll comfort you when Malcolm marries me."

"Amelia doesn't have delusions," Kelsie said. "Feel free to cling to yours."

Scarlet whirled around, her nostrils flared and her jaw set. "Why, you little—"

"Let's go buy our stuff, Amelia," Kelsie said. "Bye, Scarlet." She gave a little wave, turned on her heel and walked off to the cashier.

Amelia didn't bother saying goodbye to Scarlet. She just walked away with Kelsie. It had felt good telling Scarlet off a little bit, though she hadn't said everything she would've liked to say. They were in public, and she needed Scarlet not to block access to Mr. Everbee. Still, she was in a good mood. "Good idea."

Chapter 27

Amelia placed her dress on the checkout counter beside Kelsie's. She still hadn't checked the price tag and averted her eyes as the cashier scanned it. It was better to be oblivious to her dress's exact cost.

The cashier bent and brought out a cloth drawstring bag.

"We'll take two bags, please," Kelsie said.

The cashier dropped the first bag on the counter and reached for a second before placing each dress in its own bag and telling Kelsie the price. Amelia winced at the number. Her parents could've paid the rent and bought a month's worth of food for the same amount.

Amelia watched Kelsie take a small money purse out of her pocket, open it and count out the price in bills. When she got her change and receipt, she grabbed the bags and thrust one at Amelia.

"We should walk past Scarlet to rub it in that we bought stuff."

Amelia took her bag and stepped away from the cashier with Kelsie. "You're bold. I think we should get out of here before she spots us again."

Kelsie gave Amelia's side a playful nudge with her elbow. "You lost your nerve after telling her she was a witch, huh?"

Amelia had plenty of nerve, but making a scene with Scarlet would do little good. "You know we need her and can't make her too angry."

"Yup," Kelsie said. "We can go."

Having avoided a confrontation with Scarlet, whom Amelia didn't spot on her way outside, the two girls exited the boutique and found Amelia's mom outside.

"Thank you for the help, Mrs. Ruby," Kelsie said as she gave Amelia's mom a hug.

"You're welcome, dear."

"Thanks for the dress, Kelsie," Amelia said.

Kelsie, having stepped away from Amelia's mom, grinned. "You're welcome."

...

Amelia and her mom walked back to their bus while Kelsie headed to the one that would take her into Malcolm's Quarter.

"I'm proud of you," her mom said.

Amelia wrinkled her brows. "For what?"

"Standing up to Scarlet," her mom said. "You shouldn't worry. She's trying to bully Malcolm into marrying her. It won't work. Desperation shouldn't be the basis of any relationship."

"Thanks, Mom." Amelia couldn't see Scarlet succeeding. Malcolm wouldn't fall for her cunning, threatening and calculating tactics. They only made her less appealing to him. Still, if Scarlet was insulted enough, she could cancel her dad's meeting. That was what worried Amelia.

She spent the next few days pacing and wringing her hands as she waited for news from Malcolm. Amelia was sure she'd arrive home from school to a note from him about their meeting's cancelation, but days went by with nothing.

Finally, when Amelia had given up on hearing anything, she walked into her bedroom after school and saw a piece of note paper addressed to her on her nightstand. She grabbed it as she flopped onto her bed, her hair splayed out.

Friday afternoon. I'll pick you up at school.

Amelia groaned and sat up, dropping the note on her blanket. She would need to wear a nicer outfit to school, which would start her classmates gossiping. That was never what Amelia wanted. Things were much better when she blended in and was anonymous. At least now her worries were on what to wear and what she'd say to convince Mr. Everbee instead of whether she would get the chance.

Amelia decided on a simple, flowy blouse and jeans. It wouldn't draw too much attention at school to make her classmates gossip, yet it was nice enough to show Mr. Everbee that she was serious.

Her bag was heavy that Friday, packed as it was with her school notes, homework and the ration system plan to present afterwards. Amelia was glad to hand in her assignments throughout the day, just to create space in her bag. She'd never loved her locker, located on the ground floor of the school with every other student's, but that day she was thankful it existed. Its door had dents, the hinges creaked, and the lock was sticky, but it stored her extra stuff and saved her shoulder and back from the increased weight going up and down stairs all day between classrooms and the cafeteria on the upper floors.

At lunch, Amelia gobbled her food to have more time to discuss the plan with Dina, who, along with Jack and Ethan, wasn't participating in the meeting; they'd all agreed that too many people would crowd the space and overcomplicate matters.

"Calm down," Dina said after Amelia ran through her spiel again. "You must have it memorized by now."

Amelia gulped the remnants of the water in her cup, held in a shaky hand. "I'm not usually this nervous. There's so much pressure."

Dina rolled her eyes. "What pressure? If he says no, things stay the same. No one is any worse off."

Amelia chewed on her bottom lip. "It would be letting you and the others down. I convinced Jack to let Malcolm help and that we could change things. I'll be a huge failure if it doesn't work out, and Kylie and Lucas and their Devout movement will win, which'll make things worse."

"You should take Kylie to your meeting," Dina said.

Amelia blinked. She was certain she hadn't heard correctly. "What?"

"Isn't it better to have her on our side?"

"Not if we're giving her ways to undermine us."

"I thought you wanted her to work with us. She won't if she feels excluded."

Amelia huffed. "I get that, but it's a bit late to invite her." She didn't even know how she'd contact Kylie.

"Get Lucas to ask her," Dina said with a casual flick of her hand. "He's in your classes."

Amelia didn't have the energy for arguing with Dina. Besides, it wasn't a terrible idea. "This better not ruin things."

"I think on a deeper level Kylie wants similar things. It'll be fine."

Amelia would find out later that day whether that was true or not. She went through her afternoon classes, trying to focus on them and absorb what her teachers were saying, but her anxiety grew as the end of the school day neared.

When classes were finally over, Amelia grabbed her backpack – stuffed again with the weekend's homework, and cornered Lucas in the hallway. He huffed and tried to sidestep her, but Amelia mirrored his movements.

"What do you want?"

"I need you to get a message to Kylie." Amelia dug in her pocket for the note she'd scribbled between classes and thrust it at Lucas. "Tell her to meet me at this address."

Lucas took the note without giving it a glance and shoved it in his pocket. "Another fundraiser?"

"No. A meeting to propose a replacement to our problem. And she can't bring anyone." Amelia would have to hope Lucas knew what she meant by problem.

"I'll try."

"Good." Amelia turned and sped down the stairs. After exchanging her workbooks for her notes for the meeting at her locker, she went outside and stopped short at the sight of a crowd gathered on the edge of the lot. What was everyone doing? There wasn't enough space in the City for the school to have much to its grounds, other than a parking lot for the buses and faculty, and the crowd wasn't anywhere near the bus spot.

Amelia pushed her way through, keeping her head down and swatting arms and legs away as she walked. She ignored the grumbles and complaints of the other students. Somewhere past them was the road where Malcolm would be.

"Amelia!" Kelsie called. "Hurry up."

Amelia lifted her head, having gotten to the edge of the crowd. It was Malcolm's car that everyone had gathered around to gawk at. Most of her classmate had never been this close to a fancy car, let alone ridden in one. Everyone around her mumbled and swiveled their attention onto her as she darted forward. Kelsie's shout had marked her as someone noteworthy.

Malcolm had his forearm sticking out the open driver's window, his face angled away from the crowd. Kelsie sat on the passenger seat, the side facing the school, her head and shoulders out the window. She was waving Amelia onward.

Amelia opened the rear passenger door and climbed in before her classmates could pepper her with questions. They could gossip about her over the weekend. By Monday, the focus would be on something else.

Malcolm had just pulled away from the school when Kelsie turned around in her seat. "Do you have classes with Ethan?"

Malcolm and Kelsie's school in the rich Quarters required tuition and didn't group students in the same way. From the few details Malcolm had told her, it was based on student specializations. Many pupils there went onto the university and needed different subjects as entry requirements depending on the program. Amelia's school taught everyone the same general subjects.

"No. You'll have to ask Jack if you want school gossip on Ethan. They separate us alphabetically by surname into three letter's worth per group. I have classes with Lucas."

"Pity," Kelsie said. "Lucas was dreadful the time Ethan and I doubled dated with him and Kylie."

Amelia could believe that. At least she and Malcolm didn't have to double date with Kylie and Lucas. She wasn't sure she could endure it. "Dina told me to invite Kylie to our meeting, so I got Lucas to send her a message. I have no idea whether she'll come."

"It's not a terrible idea," Malcolm said. "She might be helpful."

"Or she might sabotage everything," Kelsie grumbled as she turned back around.

Amelia hoped it was the former. She decided not to worry until they knew whether Kylie would show. Instead of using her energy to dwell on Kylie, Amelia mentally rehearsed her pitch.

Mr. Everbee had elected to meet at his business office in a sleek, high-rise in a commercial sector of northernmost and wealthiest, Quarter 4. As typical of important and affluent people in the City, his office was on a higher floor: the twenty-fourth out of twenty-six.

When Malcolm parked in the lot, Amelia tried not to gape as she got out of the car with her bag. There were people in suits and tailored dresses darting between parked vehicles and the building, their arms loaded with satchels and papers, seemingly employees on errands for their bosses. Amelia didn't want to garner attention or suspicion.

"Let's get inside," Amelia said. "We can check for Kyle in there."

Kelsie nodded and walked off to the building. Malcolm stood in place and extended his hand in offering to Amelia. She raised an eyebrow at the risk, slid her palm against Malcolm's and intertwined her fingers with his because she liked holding his hand.

Malcolm lifted their clasped hands to his mouth, planted a peck on the back of Amelia's and then pulled his away. "I wish—"

Amelia didn't get to find out what Malcolm wished, though she had an idea.

"Are you two coming?" Kelsie asked, having doubled back. She was standing a couple metres away with her hands shoved into her pants' pockets.

"Yep," Amelia said as she walked with Kelsie to the office building. Her moment with Malcolm was over, and she couldn't ask him what he'd wanted to say with so many ears around. It didn't appear though that anyone had seen their hand holding. If someone had, they weren't saying.

…

The building's large, glass, automatic double door opened when Amelia, Kelsie and Malcolm got within a couple steps. She felt underdressed and out of place compared to the employees scurrying around them.

The white painted lobby was bright, thanks to numerous glass windows. On the left was a staircase door, and on the right were bathrooms and utility closets. People crowded the space, making up for the lack of decorations and furniture. It took Amelia a moment to spot the elevator diagonally behind the charcoal reception desk.

"Can we just walk up to the elevator?" Kelsie asked. "I don't want to climb twenty-four flights of stairs."

"I think we—" Malcolm started.

The doors opened behind their group and footsteps approached. Amelia stepped to her right to let whoever it was move by as they sounded in a hurry.

"You're actually here," Kylie said.

Amelia whirled around. Where else would they be? "You thought I asked Lucas to send you here as some kind of joke?"

Kylie shrugged. "I haven't decided whether I trust you. And I don't know either of your friends here."

Kelsie extended her hand. "I'm Ethan's girlfriend, Kelsie. He talks about you often."

"Oh," Understanding dawned in Kylie's eyes as she shook Kelsie's hand. "You're his mystery girl. Brooke and Hannah wanted to pester him about who he found to spend so much time with. I'll have to report back. Their relationship is so calm, they love to feed off other people's drama."

Kelsie's face fell, and she retracted her hand. "Great. I love being the source of gossip."

Malcolm rested his hand on Kelsie's arm for a moment before offering it to Kylie to shake. "I'm Malcolm Connor, Amelia's friend and the one who got us this meeting. Maybe your friends will be more interested in that than

Kelsie."

Kylie grasped his hand and stepped closer to him. She titled her face up to look him in the eye. "What's a rich boy like you doing spending time with a couple pieces of Apartment District scum? Is it to show off how charitable you are?"

Amelia's jaw dropped, and she saw Kelsie freeze. What had made Kylie think she could insult Amelia and Kelsie in front of them? Amelia's vision reddened, and she wanted to tell Kylie off, but there were too many potential witnesses to get away with that.

"Are you seriously going to call us names when we're standing right here?" Kelsie asked. Her hands were in fists at her sides, her nostrils flared, and her body shuddered.

Kylie dropped Malcolm's hand and turned to look at Kelsie. She didn't step away from Malcolm. "Touchy, aren't you? It's not like I'm not one too."

Malcolm backed up. "I spend time with Amelia because I like her. And Kelsie's right. You shouldn't call people things like that."

Kylie flicked her hair over her shoulder. There would be no apology. "So, did you invite me here to just stand in the lobby or what?"

"We were debating whether we can just walk up to the elevator or not," Amelia said, choosing to let Kylie's remark go. Ruminating on it would only impair her pitch.

"Ha," Kylie said. "In a place this fancy, I doubt that. Let's go ask the person behind the desk." She walked off to the reception desk before Amelia or the others could offer an opinion.

Amelia rolled her eyes and darted after her. This was going to be a tense meeting.

Chapter 28

The person behind the desk was a woman in her late twenties wearing pink lipstick and eyeshadow that matched the print on her belted dress, and her brown hair pulled into a bun. She didn't look up from the papers she was scribbling on when Kylie and Amelia reached the desk.

"Excuse me?" Amelia said, getting no reaction from the woman.

Kylie leaned over the desk and waved a hand in the receptionist's face. "Hello?"

The woman dropped her pen and swiveled her eyes onto Amelia and Kylie, now joined by Malcolm and Kelsie. "We don't employ teenagers here. You'll want the building next door."

"We aren't here for jobs," Kelsie said.

"You also can't shadow your parents here," she said in a bored monotone, like this was a well-rehearsed script. "There is too much confidential and important business taking place to have uncontracted eyes snooping around."

"No, none of that," Malcolm said. "We have an appointment to meet Mr. Everbee. It's probably listed under Malcolm Connor."

The woman sighed and grabbed a thick spiral bound book with a tab marking every page off her desk. All that was missing to signify her annoyance at teenagers wasting her time was an eye roll. She flipped through pages until she found the tab she wanted and skimmed the page, running her finger down it. When she reached a line mid way down the page, she snapped the book shut. "My apologies." She reached under the desk and pulled out a key that she offered to Malcolm. "You can head to the elevator."

"Thanks," Kylie snatched the key from the receptionist's hand and marched around the side of the desk nearest the elevator.

"Heh," Malcolm said. "This'll be interesting."

...

They didn't have to share the elevator with anyone else, giving Amelia necessary space from employees crowding the lobby and parking lot to clear her head, not that it worked when she had to fill Kylie in on their plan.

"That all sounds great for you and your Rebel Cause," Kylie said when Amelia finished the shortened version. "I don't see how it'll make me money."

Was money all Kylie cared about, other than Lucas?

"Buy the excess that doesn't get allotted to rations and resell it," Malcolm said. "Or sell part of your own rations. Whichever. Don't expect Amelia to solve your selfish problems."

Kelsie laughed from the corner of the elevator beside Amelia. "Seriously, all you seem to do is complain and try to insult people. You need to chill."

"Hmph," Kylie snorted and crossed her arms, scowling.

"It makes me wonder why Ethan likes you so much," Kelsie continued.

Amelia thought this was a step too far and backed away from Kelsie as the scowl on Kylie's face intensified.

"You hardly know Ethan," Kylie spat, eyes blazing. "I've known him forever. Our parents are friends, as Ethan and I will always be. Your novelty will wear off eventually. I just hope it's not after he gets stuck with you."

Fire sparked in Kelsie's eyes as she stepped closer to Kylie. Amelia braced herself to duck if the other girls decided to lunge at each other. Before that could happen, the elevator pinged and opened its doors. Amelia grabbed Malcolm's wrist, sprinted out of the confined space and pulled him down the hall. Witnessing a fight between Kelsie and Kylie wasn't high on her to-do list.

"You can let go now," Malcolm said when he and Amelia had passed a few doors.

"Sorry," Amelia said as she dropped his wrist. "I wanted to get away in case they got physical."

"I understand," Malcolm said as he shoved his hands in his jacket pockets. "But I don't think they went there."

Malcolm was facing the way they'd came from, so Amelia turned around to see what he did. Kylie and Kelsie were standing in the hall near the elevator door. There were no signs of a physical alteration. Their hairstyles were too neat, and their clothes too rumple-free.

"You're probably right," Amelia said. "Did I at least lead us the right way?" It would've been great to call Kelsie and Kylie over and not have to deal with the embarrassment of doubling back.

Malcolm turned in a slow circle and read the room numbers on the nearby doors. "You got lucky. We need to go farther this way."

"Great," Amelia said as she waved Kylie and Kelsie over.

"Ready?" Malcolm asked as the other girls approached him and Amelia. "We can still back out if you've changed your mind."

She swatted his arm. "You're not getting out of this that easily."

Malcolm laughed, and his eyes lit up. Past versions of Amelia would've thought she'd lost her sanity and her focus, letting herself tease a boy. Present Amelia liked to tease him. She also knew Malcolm's support was invaluable, and no one could be serious all the time. She needed moments of levity to ease her stress, or she'd crumble. Then she'd be of no help to anyone.

Their moment ended when Kelsie and Kylie walked up. Amelia stepped away from Malcolm to put a respectable distance between their bodies. "You two look less angry," she said.

Kylie smirked and Kelsie shrugged.

"We came to a mutual understanding to tolerate each other since we both care about Ethan," Kelsie said.

This seemed fast, making Amelia wonder about what had happened. "Seriously? A couple minutes ago I thought you were going to hit each other."

Kylie snorted. "We almost did."

"But—"

"We'll have to continue this later," Malcolm said as he walked down the hall, reading the room numbers. "We're going to be late."

"I apologized for what I said to Kelsie," Kylie said as she, Amelia and Kelsie followed Malcolm. "It was too far, and I know how much Ethan likes her."

"It was as I said," Kelsie added. "You need to chill. Amelia isn't your problem solver."

Amelia, standing between the other girls, braced herself for their fight to resume.

"Nope, she definitely isn't," Kylie said.

Amelia frowned. The way Kylie had spoken felt like she was taunting Amelia. Apparently, anything involving Ethan was too far, and calling Amelia and Kelsie names wasn't. She hadn't invited Kylie here to cause trouble and throw insults. She would've spoken up, but Malcolm had stopped at a door, and the girls had caught up to him.

"This is it," Malcolm said.

Kelsie inhaled and rapped on the door with her fist. "There's no use in delaying further."

Amelia's heart sped up, and her palms sweated. She closed her eyes and tried to force her nerves, and annoyance towards Kylie, to settle.

"Come in," Mr. Everbee called from the other side of the door.

It was time. There were no more opportunities to back out. Whatever the result of this meeting, Amelia promised herself she'd be satisfied.

Kelsie, having been the one to knock and still the closest to the door, grasped the knob and turned it.

...

Mr. Everbee was sitting on an armchair when Amelia and the others entered. He inclined his head at Malcolm and gestured to the chairs across the coffee table from him. "Please, sit."

As Amelia walked to a chair, she wondered why Mr. Everbee wasn't sitting behind his desk at the end of the office. She also was curious about whether he'd read all the books on the shelves next to his armchair that covered the entire wall. Amelia had only seen more books in one place in the school library. Neither question was pertinent to this meeting, however, so she didn't voice them.

"I see you've brought new faces this time, Malcolm," Mr. Everbee said once everyone had claimed a seat.

"Actually, I invited Kelsie and Kylie," Amelia said, gesturing to each girl in turn.

"Amelia's idea is why I asked you for this meeting," Malcolm said. "She's more important to this than I am."

Mr. Everbee sat up straighter on his chair and inclined his head in the direction of Amelia. "You're good at problem solving then?"

"I suppose," Amelia said. She didn't want to inflate her own ego, but disagreeing with the man who held the power to shut down her idea was a bad move.

He rested his forearms on his thighs, his attention zeroed in on Amelia. "Pitch me your solution."

Amelia reached for her bag and pulled out her notes. She laid them on the coffee table and delved into her speech, with Kelsie piping in when they got to the numbers.

Mr. Everbee made noncommittal noises throughout Amelia's and Kelsie's presentation. When they finished, he picked up a couple pages of Amelia's notes and scanned them. "It's a clever and thorough idea," he said. "After some tweaking, I may be able to do something with it. The issue remains about what to do with the excess in surplus times. Production is not always steady, even with all our technology, and getting produce to last outside of the greenhouses is an issue."

From the corner of her eye, Amelia saw a wide grin bloom on Kylie's face.

"Mr. Everbee," she said, in a tone Amelia assumed was meant to be placating and charming. "As a businessman, you surely see the need for profit."

Amelia forced herself not to groan. If Kylie scooped this deal out from under her, she would have words with Dina about her bad advice.

Malcolm reached over and squeezed her hand while Mr. Everbee's focus was on Kylie. "Don't worry," he whispered.

Amelia swallowed and gave him a nod as she turned her attention onto Kylie and Malcolm retracted his hand.

"Yes, of course," Mr. Everbee had said.

"As do I," Kyle said. "My friends and I aren't part of Amelia's… group. We're profit focused more than charity. We support this idea, if we can have rights to sell the excess goods to whomever we please."

Mr. Everbee raised an eyebrow. "And why should I ask the Government to let your group earn money from that?"

"We're willing to give the Government a cut. They can call it a permit fee, or whatever they'd like. We'll buy directly from suppliers, and the Government won't have to do a thing."

Amelia should have known that Kylie would come prepared.

"Hmm," Mr. Everbee muttered. "We'll need to determine specifics, but this might work."

"Does this mean you'll submit our proposal?" Malcolm asked.

"Yes, after I finalize some details."

"Thank you, sir," Amelia said, shaking his hand.

"You shouldn't thank me yet," he said as he leaned back on his chair. "I give no guarantee that it'll be approved."

Amelia knew this and remained hopeful regardless. Mr. Everbee advocating for her cause would add credibility to it if he didn't just trash her notes and do nothing. If he did do nothing, Amelia would never know.

When Amelia got back outside to the parking lot, she exhaled and let her shoulders slouch. Her bag was lighter thanks to Mr. Everbee keeping her notes, but that wasn't the only weight gone from her frame. Amelia hadn't realized how much her anxiety about this meeting had pressed down on her.

"Amelia?"

Malcolm saying her name brought her mind back to the present, and she blinked. He was standing nearby, his head titled to the side, and his soft eyes on her face.

"Sorry. I zoned out."

"We all noticed," Kelsie said. "You just stepped outside and stopped moving."

Amelia looked around. She hadn't noticed that she'd frozen in place as soon as she exited the building. "Weird."

Kylie snorted. "Yeah, you are. And I'm out. Lucas and I have a double date with Hannah and Brooke." She walked off, giving Amelia, Kelsie and Malcolm a salute over her shoulder as she went.

Amelia didn't think Kylie could leave insults out of conversations. It seemed like a barrier she'd erected to keep everyone, excepting a select few, away. And she directed them specifically at Amelia as of late. What had made Kylie protect herself that way? Losing her dad was the only cause Amelia could think of.

"That was interesting," Kelsie said as she, Malcolm and Amelia walked to Malcolm's car. "Do you think he'll actually make the proposal?"

Malcolm dug his key out of his pocket and inserted it into the driver's door. "Scarlet hinted that her parents are having money troubles. I got the idea that food sits in the greenhouses because the shop owners aren't ordering that much."

"If prices were lower, shops would sell more," Kelsie said, as she opened the passenger door.

Amelia walked to the rear passenger door and got in. She wasn't going to fight Kelsie for the front seat. "People like to buy foods with a long shelf life, which is one reason why stores don't order more often." When Amelia and her mom went shopping, most people bought similar things: root vegetables, canned goods and dried beans and grains, all meant to last a long while without rotting. There were other foods available, but the space things like lettuces and fruits took up on the shelves was smaller. They were items people bought to use up right away, making them irregular purchases. Rationing would resolve the slow turnover issue as everyone would get an allocation of every available, non luxury, food.

"Yeah," Malcolm said as he started the car and drove out of the lot. "He should have personal motivation to push it through."

Kelsie sighed. "Why are rich people so concerned about themselves and no one else?"

"Not all of them are," Malcolm said, with a glance at Kelsie. "The ones that are think that if they don't protect their own interests, they'll end up poor, and that's their worst fear."

"It's not so different from people in Apartment Districts," Amelia said. "Those living in 1 and 2 don't want to end up living in 11 or 12." Her own parents, while they had sympathy for those living farther south, did all they could to maintain their lifestyle.

"Arlo had no problem moving me to different Apartment Districts."

"That must've been difficult," Malcolm said.

"The worst part was getting a new ID card with every move. Arlo stopped doing that a few years ago."

ID cards required a current address. Changing Kelsie's address all the time would've drawn suspicion Arlo Fenn didn't want, especially since he wasn't her father, though Amelia suspected he'd taken her from the Foster Centre under the pretense of making her his foster child.

"It could've been worse," Kelsie continued. "At least I had somewhere to live."

Amelia didn't think the place she'd met Kelsie had been a decent environment to live in. The only alternative was the Colony, which might've been a better option. At least it had houses with beds. There were no homeless people in the City, not because everyone could afford a home but because the guards arrested anyone they found trying to live on the streets. No one risked it with the City-wide, Government imposed curfew and nightly guard patrols of the streets.

That left many unhappy people, especially children, living in unfortunate situations like the Foster Centre. Amelia had never seen that building, as it was in a section of the City she didn't frequent, but the tales she'd heard of the place didn't make her eager for a visit.

"Hopefully, my house is better than that," Malcolm teased, nudging Kelsie in the side with his elbow.

"Yeah, it is," Kelsie said. "Except I can't live there forever. Someday you won't and your parents aren't going to want an unpaying boarder around."

"They won't kick you out," Malcolm said.

"If they do, my mom will let you move in with us," Amelia said. Her mom's change of attitude when she'd learned Kelsie was an orphan had gone a long way to smoothing things over between them. It would be more cramped than Malcolm's house, with worse meals, yet better than sending Kelsie back to Arlo.

"Thanks," Kelsie said.

Chapter 29

Amelia didn't bring up the possibility of Kelsie moving in to her parents when she got home. Ethan would offer a different solution if the need came, and it was possible. She'd planned to delve into her homework before helping make supper, but she'd barely stashed her things in her room when she found her dad standing outside her door.

"How'd it go?" he asked.

Amelia leaned against her door frame. Her parents knew where she went and what she did that afternoon. "Mr. Everbee said he'd submit our proposal after some tweaking. I hope that doesn't mean he's going to change the entire thing."

"Whether he does or doesn't, it's out of your control now," her dad said. "There's nothing to gain from worrying about it."

"You sound like Dina. She said if Mr. Everbee doesn't help us, no one will be worse off."

"It's true."

Amelia closed her eyes and let her body sag. When she spoke, her voice broke. "I want to help so badly. You and Mom can barely afford food. What are people worse off supposed to do?"

Her dad wrapped his arms around her and stroked her hair. She let herself flop onto his chest. "You have such a giving heart. Helping doesn't always require huge gestures and law changes. It can come in small, personal ways."

Amelia kept her cheek pressed to his shirt. "Thanks." He was right; she didn't need to exert all her energy in making radical changes that would face resistance and pushback. There were small ways to help people.

She started with cooking supper with her mom. It wasn't that this was a rare thing Amelia did, but she usually put minimal effort into it. This time, she chopped vegetables, stirred pots and salted the sauce.

"What's gotten into you?" her mom asked. "You usually come in, dump some cans into a pot, stir a couple times and call it supper."

Amelia gave a one shoulder shrug as she mixed boiled rice into the stir-fry pan. "I'm just trying to help."

"Sure," her mom said. "I'll appreciate this while it lasts."

Amelia wanted to roll her eyes. Instead, she angled her face at the stir-fry pan and sprinkled in some dried herbs.

Growing food in the City was illegal as was owning, buying or selling seeds without extremely had to get permits. Someone had obviously stolen and smuggled some to the Colony. Only greenhouses in the Outskirts, where the engineers could control the temperature, grew produce and had unhindered access to seeds, soils and other supplies. Amelia knew it wasn't worth trying to overturn that law as nothing would grow on people's fire escape balconies in the City's heat, and the wealthy weren't about to put gardens or greenhouses on their manicured lawns.

And Amelia was sure fresh herbs couldn't taste that different from the dried ones her parents had bought months ago. It was becoming a luxury in their pantry, after the most recent price surge, and their supply was running out, so Amelia restrained herself from dumping in the amount she wanted to. She added just enough to taste. It would be days before she or her parents used herbs again. Salt was cheaper and flavoured most of their dishes.

With the herbs mixed in, Amelia dumped in a can of pre-cooked beans and her sauce. The aroma wafting from the pan as she scooped out portions made Amelia's mouth water. Her simple cooking wouldn't impress Malcolm, not that she would ever cook for him. Amelia held back a sigh. Why was Malcolm creeping into her thoughts?

"It's ready," Amelia told her parents as she set down the filled bowls and claimed her seat. She needed the distraction of conversation to get ideas of cooking for Malcolm out of her mind.

Her parents walked in and sat. Amelia's dad gave her a grin. "It smells wonderful."

"Yes," her mom said as she lifted her fork. "I'm impressed. It didn't all come out of a can."

Amelia knew her mom was half-joking, though canned foods were easy to use, cheap and a common item in her family's pantry. She shouldn't eat canned foods forever though. "I tried to broaden my range," she said before eating her first bite. It was good, albeit nothing like the restaurant food she'd eaten with Malcolm.

With Clinic Day now a few weeks away, Amelia feared her days with him were numbered. Following Clinic Day, it would be illegal for her to see him alone without a Courtship until after New Years. That made Amelia vow to enjoy the times she did get to see him in the coming weeks. Those occasions would be precious.

...

Her weekly shopping trip with her mom went faster than usual because there had been another price hike, not because they didn't need an extensive list of items. Amelia trailed her mom with a basket on each arm as her mom crossed items off her list with a pencil and shake of her head.

Amelia's mom stopped in the cleaning aisle in front of the discount, all-purpose soap display. Amelia had doubts it would work as well at the label claimed, but it was in a giant jug and advertised as for dishes, laundry and household cleaning. So, in a basket it went. Amelia tilted to her left as her arm adjusted to its weight. She preferred shopping with a cart, but they didn't buy enough stuff to fill one anymore.

"I hope it smells good at least," Amelia muttered as she followed her mom out of the aisle.

"For that price, I wouldn't bet on it," her mom said.

Amelia would've loved something with a nice scent, but she was fortunate that her parents could still afford soap without watering it down more than the discount soap already way. The prices of cleaning goods and household products hadn't increased at the same rate as food, yet they'd become luxuries to many people who'd decided eating was more of a priority.

Malcolm's family, and Scarlet's, didn't need to buy all-purpose soap. It made Amelia feel inadequate, knowing the differences between her family and theirs.

Amelia followed her mom through the rest of the store, getting the last few items not crossed off their list. It was painful watching the tally go up with every item at the checkout and her mom having to remove items. Her mom spent relatively the same amount each week but got fewer items for it as the weeks progressed.

Something had to change. Amelia's family couldn't survive like this in the immediate future. Whether or not Mr. Everbee submitted the proposal, and the Government passed it or dismissed it, her family was on the verge of starving.

Amelia and her mom walked home from the market, each carrying half of the bags. When they'd first walked, to save money from bus fare, Amelia had found it exhausting lugging the heavy bags home. They'd gotten lighter each trip.

"We're going to have to make this last two weeks," her mom said. "Your dad I decided we don't have the budget to shop weekly anymore."

Spreading a meagre trip's worth of food over two weeks must've been depressing for her parents to agree was necessary. "The problem is we don't have enough money," Amelia said. She felt like an added expense, piled onto her parents' list of bills. No wonder her mom had wanted her to get married so badly.

"I know. And your dad and I can't get more hours at work."

Amelia understood Jack's situation more now and knew what she had to do to help her parents. "I'll get a job."

"We'd hoped you could wait until you were out of school for that," her mom said. "It looks like you have little choice now. You have to promise me you'll keep up with your schoolwork."

"I will," Amelia said. Jack did it, so she could. If he and Dina got their Courtship, he would leave school to work fulltime, both to help pay for the wedding and to support himself and Dina. With no Courtship, Amelia would have two more years of mandatory schooling.

Amelia would need to ask Jack how he handled work and study while she had the opportunity. He might even have advice about what job she could get. She certainly didn't feel qualified to do much of anything.

"I'm sorry you need to take on extra responsibility," her mom said as they stepped onto their street.

Amelia could see their building now and picked up her pace. Even with the bags being lighter than they used to be, her arms still felt their weight. Depositing them on the kitchen counter was always a relief. Even more so was that her dad did the putting away.

"It's fine," Amelia said. "I'm almost an adult anyway." That was a scary thought to Amelia. She would be a legal adult after Clinic Day if she got an approved Courtship. Without one, she wouldn't age into automatic adulthood until her eighteenth birthday, which was less than two years away. Part of her wanted to slow time down and appreciate her remaining childhood, but there were privileges adults had that she didn't, making her eager for the future.

Her mom adjusted her grip on one of the bags she carried and gave Amelia a pat on her arm. "Yes, you are."

…

At the end of the next school day, Amelia darted through the hallway, pushing and shoving her way through the sea of students at their lockers, until she reached the section for students with surnames starting with A through C.

Amelia slowed her pace and scanned the crowd for a head of chestnut brown hair. She wasn't intimately familiar with the back of Jack's head, and there were a lot of brown-haired people. Amelia walked on, scanning the crowd and keeping an ear out in case Jack said something she could overhear. She had no luck, and was about to leave, when she heard her name.

Amelia spun in the direction of the voice and found Ethan staring at her with wide eyes. "Ethan!" she cried as she darted over to him. "Thank goodness."

He closed his locker door and looked at her. "What are you doing here? You look lost."

Amelia titled her head back to gaze up at him. "Trying to find Jack. I need his advice about getting a job."

"His locker's that way," Ethan said, pointing further down the hall. "I'll take you."

Amelia launched herself at Ethan and hugged him. "Thanks."

She heard whispers and snickers from nearby students who turned their heads away as Amelia let Ethan go and stepped back. Ethan paid them no mind, making Amelia wonder if they gossiped about him often, and about what. Her hug had been a friendly gesture, nothing more.

"A job huh?" Ethan asked as he led Amelia down the hall to another batch of lockers. "I thought your parents were doing okay."

"We can't sit around anymore and hope things get better," Amelia said as she delved into what her mom had said about making their meagre weekly trip last twice as long. "I said I'd help out by getting a job."

"I'm sorry," Ethan said. "It must make you feel even further from Malcolm." He likely thought the same about Kelsie since she was living with Malcolm.

"I know that soon I'll never see him again, so it doesn't matter. I'm sure he'll get over it if I have to cancel a couple dates." Saying what she assumed to be true didn't make her feel better about it.

Ethan stopped walking and whirled around in front of Amelia, making her stumble mid-step as she bumped into him. "What does that mean? Are you dumping him?"

This conversation was happening whether Amelia wanted it to or not in a crowded school hallway, and the only way out of it was through. "I know he likes me, but it's only short-term infatuation. He won't tie himself to me on Clinic Day."

"I thought Kelsie and I had enough self-doubt for our group."

"I'm being realistic, Ethan. I can't live in a fantasy land where a rich boy who took an interest in me is going to always want me."

Ethan studied her face and remained an obstacle blocking her path. "You want him to."

This was something she didn't want to admit. To do so would raise her hopes, and she couldn't have that. Reality would never meet them.

Chapter 30

"Will you please just help me find Jack?" Amelia asked. She hoped that would help Ethan drop the subject of Malcolm.

Ethan turned around and resumed walking. "I said I would."

Jack's locker was nearby, and he had his hand on its door as he closed it. Amelia saw him sigh and turn around. The stress and weariness in his eyes vanished as they widened, and his mouth opened when he spotted Amelia and Ethan.

Jack shut his mouth and blinked. "Amelia? If you're looking for Dina, she isn't here."

"I'm not," Amelia said, already knowing this. Dina's locker was much closer to Amelia's. "I want your advice."

Jack flicked his eyes back and forth over Amelia and Ethan and shifted his backpack. "About what?"

"Nothing to do with me," Ethan said, holding his hands up. "I just saved Amelia from wandering the hall looking for you. I'll leave you two to discuss."

"Thanks, Ethan," Amelia said as he walked off with a wave over his shoulder.

"If you want to talk, you'll have to do it walking. I need to get home."

Amelia's eyebrows shot up. "You walk home?" Dina had never mentioned that. She imagined it wasn't something Jack was secure about.

He gave one nod and averted his eyes from Amelia's face. "Planning for a wedding that might never happen is expensive. I had to cut expenses where I could."

"Don't be embarrassed. I understand more than you think. And it's why I want to talk to you." She understood the need to cut expenses, even without planning for a possible wedding.

Jack walked away from his locker, and Amelia fell into step beside him. He headed to an exit she'd never used, it being in a different part of the school than she frequented. "Oh?"

"I told my parents I'd get a job to help out. We can't really afford food anymore, or to wait for things to improve. I can be your walk home buddy too if you want." She wasn't looking forward to the idea of walking home. If Jack could do it daily, Amelia could try, at least after school. She couldn't imagine making it on time in the morning if she went by foot. At least one bus fare a day could go into her parents' food budget. She intended to do her part.

"So, you want my help finding a job?"

They were outside on the school lot now, and Jack veered along the side of the building to the street. Amelia was going to be sore when she got home, but there was no turning back now, and she could hear the buses departing. If walking was too much effort, she could wait for a City bus at the nearest stop, though that would defeat the purpose of saving her bus money.

"I don't know where to look. I'm not exactly qualified to do anything."

"You're too young to have qualifications. Any place that hires someone our age doesn't want experience, only cheap labour to do menial tasks no one else will do."

"Is that what you do?" It seemed like a huge hit to one's self-worth to willingly do grunt work no one else would.

"I wash dishes at a café," Jack said. "Like Catsy's, but closer to my apartment."

Amelia grimaced at the mention of Catsy's. She had a feeling about where this was going. "Please don't suggest I work there." Too many people she recognized frequented the place. It would be awkward getting pitying looks in the hallway of her apartment building and at school.

"When you're in the back, no one can see you. They won't make you a server to start. If you're set against it, apply at the market. You might even get a discount on household stuff."

Amelia supposed there was no way around finding a job someone she recognized would go to. "I guess I'll try."

"You might need to apply to more places. Spend a day going from business to business and see who's hiring."

If Amelia didn't tire herself out from walking home, she would by walking around her Apartment District. She'd have to go on foot. Spending money on the bus wasn't an option. "Thanks for the advice."

...

Amelia's legs were weak and unsteady when she finally staggered up the stairs and down the hall to her apartment. Walking home from the market was easier than this. She pressed her back against her living room wall to prop herself up as she kicked her shoes off. With one hand, she wiped the sweat from her forehead.

Someone had started cooking. Amelia could see steam rising from the pot on the stove, though it wasn't aromatic enough to waft a scent her way.

"Where have you been?" her mom asked as she walked into the room from the master bedroom.

"I walked home with Jack so I could ask him about getting a job. I told him I'd do every day to help save money." Amelia was regretting it that now that her entire body ached.

Her mom tutted. "We're not destitute yet."

"I know," Amelia said as she straightened up and took off her backpack. "But it'll all help. And I can get used to the exercise. I'll still ride the bus in the morning."

"You shouldn't have to sacrifice for us. Paying the bills is your dad's and my job."

Why was her mom so against her help? Amelia could see her mom being too proud to accept it from the neighbours or Malcolm's family, but she wanted to do her part for her own family. "I'm going to help, one way or another. If you don't want to spend my bus fare on our shopping trips, I'll spend it on my lunches."

She brushed past her mom and went into her bedroom. There was little time before supper, and she had homework to start. It was something she wanted to get out of the way to free up her evening for making a plan to find a job.

Amelia scarfed down her meagre evening meal when her parents called her. They acted like nothing was out of the ordinary; Amelia assumed this was for her benefit, though they could've been in denial. Whatever the reason, she wasn't naïve enough to believe everything was fine.

Their dire financial situation wasn't something her parents would appreciate discussing, and it fueled Amelia's desire to be part of the solution. That resulted in her bringing her list and pencils to her weekly Saturday meeting with Dina. They'd decided to resume the tradition after the meeting with Mr. Everbee as there was no immediate need to gather at Malcolm's house anymore.

That was a let down. Her new Rebel Cause was petering out before it ever got a good start. Groups were hard when they had to be secretive, and she couldn't advertise they were looking for members. Amelia sighed and diverted her attention back to her list. She always got to Restaurant Doma before Dina, and this time she promised herself she would finalize her job-hunting plan. After she ordered a glass of water from the bartender.

Amelia was deep into her list, hunched over her stool. She was so absorbed in her task that she didn't hear the door open and close or Dina walk over. It was the sound of the stool next to hers scraping against the floor that snapped Amelia out of her trance. She dropped her pencil on the counter and sat up.

"Sorry to frighten you," Dina said with an impish grin. "I didn't realize how focused you were."

Amelia smoothed down her shirt, which had started to crease from her bad posture. "It's fine."

"Jack said you're looking for a job. Is that what you're working on?"

Amelia should've known Jack had told Dina. He'd probably told Ethan too, and that source would lead to Malcolm through Kelsie. "I'm planning out my route for tomorrow when I go apply to places. It's a bit overwhelming."

"You'll be fine. You're intelligent and polite. Someone will hire you."

"Easy for you to say," Amelia grumbled. "You're not the one that needs a job."

Dina waved the bartender over. Once he'd come and taken her water order, she huffed. "I will soon enough. It's not fair of me to expect Jack to pay for everything once we're married. Unlike you. Malcolm could pay all your expenses if he married you."

Amelia slouched on her stool and drank a big gulp of her water. Why was everyone fixated on her and Malcolm? "He won't marry me. What we have is a short-term fling, for fun."

Dina fixed her with a serious-eyed stare. "Is that what both of you think? Or just what you're telling yourself so you don't get disappointed?"

Amelia grabbed her bag and shoved her paper and pencil inside it. "I'm tired of talking about Malcolm. Why does no one believe me when I say we aren't getting married? I'll never marry anyone. I've said that forever. What made you think it's changed now?"

Dina's mouth had opened, and her eyes were popping out of her head. She snapped her jaw shut. "I think you're lying to yourself because you're scared, and you feel inadequate."

Amelia pursed her lips. "What's there to be scared of? Malcolm and I are too different to marry. I'd feel useless and isolated in a giant house."

"You think Jack and I don't have differences? If you love someone, you find a way to bridge them."

That might be possible for some, yet there was a larger gap between her and Malcolm, one that felt insurmountable. "Whether that's true or not, I still need a job. My parents wouldn't take Malcolm's help if he offered it."

"You're looking for a job?"

Amelia almost toppled off her stool. She hadn't realized the bartender was listening from a couple seats away with his face angled in her direction. "Yes, but I don't see how that's your concern."

He gave her a bored glance as he set a glass down in front of a patron. "Just thought, since you used to be here every week, you might be interested in a job. Comes with a free meal per shift."

"A job here?" Amelia hadn't seen a sign advertising an open position.

He shrugged. "Since as it's not my concern, I'll offer it to someone else."

He made a show of turning and walking away. Amelia groaned and set down her bag. She slid off the stool and walked along the row of stools in the direction the bartender went. Her trailing of him lasted the entire length of the counter before he finally set eyes on her.

He polished the glass in his hands with a cloth, his face giving nothing away. "I take it you're interested."

"I suppose," Amelia said. "What's the job?"

"Clearing and setting tables. Sunday afternoons and evenings."

"That doesn't sound too bad," Amelia said. She had no aspirations of working tons of hours with her school schedule. "Why you're offering it to me when there's no sign advertising a job?"

The bartender flicked his eyes left and right, scanning their surroundings. He leaned in, under the guise of grabbing something under the counter, and kept his voice low. "Arlo Fenn told me you're trying to change things. I thought I'd do you a favour. There is an opening, but the manager doesn't want a sign in the window deterring the rich regulars. Lucky for you, there's been no other applicants."

Amelia bit down on her bottom lip. It would take her all day to walk here if she took the job. And she'd never make it home by foot in time for curfew. "The bus fare—"

He waved a hand as he straightened up. "You'll make more here than in whatever Apartment District you come from, plus a share of the tips. Don't worry about bus fare. Wear something simple and black and show up at noon tomorrow if you're serious about my offer." He turned around and retreated behind the swinging door that gave Amelia a glimpse of the back kitchen. Overhead was a small sign saying: Employees Only.

Amelia stared at it for more seconds than necessary. She'd imagined spending Sunday on her feet, going business to business in her Apartment District. This seemed too convenient, but hearing Arlo Fenn's name also gave her hope that her Rebel Cause wasn't as dead as she feared.

Chapter 31

Dina was bouncing on her seat when Amelia returned. "Did you really get a job?"

Amelia sat on her stool and drank the remnants of her water glass. "If I decide to take it. I'll have to discuss it with my parents."

Dina sprung off her stool and almost knocked Amelia over with the force of her hug. "That's great."

"Great?" Amelia leaned back to look at Dina. "Minutes ago, you were telling me to let Malcolm pay for everything."

Dina let Amelia go and sat back down on her own stool. "I was trying to get through to you that you're lucky, and that you're too scared and down on yourself to see it."

"Unless Malcolm tells me otherwise, we aren't getting married. We've only known each other for a couple months." How long would it take for her friend to realize this? Amelia wasn't living in a fantasy.

"Whatever you say."

Amelia didn't want to discuss Malcolm and hoped this was the end of it. She hefted her bag on top her lap and crossed her arms over it. "Are you still excited about Clinic Day?"

Dina twirled a lock of her hair between her fingers. "Now that it's getting closer, I'm nervous."

"Worried you'll get denied?" That's what would've given Amelia anxiety if she'd been in Dina's place.

Dina tossed her head. "A bit, but I'm more nervous about after, when we move in together, and the wedding. It'll be small, thank goodness, but I still don't like being the centre of attention. What if I trip or mess up my words?"

Jack would think Dina was perfect whether any of that happened or not. "You'll be fine."

Dina reached over and rested her hand on Amelia's arm. "You'll be my attendant, won't you? I can't make it through without you by my side."

City weddings allowed each person getting married to have one attendant that stood at their side for the ceremony and carried their intended's ring, if the couple could afford rings. "If that's what you want, then you know I will." Amelia had expected Dina to ask her, though she wouldn't have blamed her friend for waiting until after Clinic Day. "Is Jack going to ask Ethan?"

Dina retracted her arm and gulped some of her water. "Yeah. And you'll have to dance with him."

"I don't mind," Amelia said. Ethan was her friend. Sharing the attendants' dance couldn't be that awkward. They'd also walk down the aisle together, as attendants did in City wedding ceremonies.

"Great."

With Dina now distracted from the topic of Malcolm, she started babbling about the ideas and plans she had for her wedding. Amelia half-listened and agreed when she needed to. After a while, long after their water glasses were empty and tables started to fill for the early supper rush, Amelia and Dina exited Restaurant Doma and headed for the bus. The sun was starting its descent, leaving them a couple hours before curfew. That relieved Amelia, who was unsure how they'd spent all afternoon at the counter without someone kicking them out, especially since they hadn't ordered refills on their water.

Maybe the bartender that had offered her a job had something to do with it. Amelia didn't know his name, but that was easy to rectify if she took him up on his offer. As she rode the bus home and then walked back to her apartment, she realized this had been the last time she and Dina could go and sit at the counter, ending their tradition. She didn't see a way to justify two bus trips a week to their meeting place.

Amelia tried to shove aside that disappointment as she unlocked her apartment door and went inside.

"Did you have fun?" her dad asked as Amelia removed her shoes.

"Yeah. Dina asked me to be her wedding attendant, and the bartender offered me a job."

Her dad's eyebrows shot up. "A job? Did you take it?"

"I didn't really give him an answer. He said to show up tomorrow at noon if I wanted it and walked away before I said whether I did."

"Noon, huh? That'll give you all morning to prepare."

"I don't know, Dad," Amelia said with a sigh. "Wouldn't it make more sense to find a job closer to home that I could walk to?"

"Don't waste time on that for less pay when you already have an offer."

"An offer for what?" Amelia's mom asked as she walked into the living room.

That was a downside of living in such a small space. Everyone could overhear conversations unless you had them behind closed doors and whispered. Amelia told her mom about the job offer, seeing as her dad would've if she'd tried to stay quiet about it.

Her list and mapped route of the businesses near her apartment felt like a waste of time and effort now, and Amelia dropped it in the recycle bin. It wasn't a waste of paper, as the City collected and repurposed every scrap. New paper was hard to come by as trees only grew on the north coast, which were illegal to cut down, and on the edges of the Outskirts. Amelia had also seen some in the distance on the way to the Colony, though she imagined those were harder to access and bring back.

After supper that night, Amelia rummaged through her closet for black pants and a top that were a similar shade. She didn't want to show up in a clashing outfit that labelled her as the poor girl they took pity on when hiring. It took a while for her to find a pair of black linen pants and a flowy top. Jeans and a t-shirt felt appropriate for Catsy's, which she was relieved not to have to apply at, but not for an upscale restaurant. Next week's outfit was next Saturday's problem, if Amelia didn't just wear the same one.

She laid her selection on top of her dresser and went through her few pairs of shoes. The only pair in black she owned were her boots. It was an easy decision. She wore them every day, even on some dates with Malcolm.

Amelia felt lost in her relationship, if she could even call what they had a relationship. If she'd never pressured him to accept Scarlet's deal, she would've seen him more and know what they were. As things stood, he'd only called her his friend. Would knowing have been better though? Wasn't it preferable to hardly see him? This way, after Clinic Day, moving on would be less devasting. Amelia tried to rationalise that with herself as she went to bed. It wasn't convincing. When she was alone with her thoughts and nothing to do, she missed Malcolm, his smile and the twinkle in his eye when he looked at her.

Amelia rolled onto her stomach, pressed her face into her pillow and groaned. When that didn't relieve her frustration, she climbed out of bed, walked down the short hall to her parents' room and knocked. "Mom?" she called as she waited for an answer. "Can I talk to you?"

Amelia was about to give up and go out on the fire escape balcony to stare at the neighbouring buildings. It always made her feel small and insignificant, like her problems didn't matter, which was comforting in its own way. Then the door opened to show her mom in rumpled pajamas with bedraggled hair. "What's wrong?"

Amelia led her mom to the living room and sat on the couch. She wasn't ready to admit any of this to Dina or Kelsie and especially not to Malcolm. "I never wanted to like someone romantically," she said as her mom settled on the couch beside her, her body angled towards Amelia. "Now the less I see Malcolm, the more I want to. He's never going to marry me, so why is being away from him so hard?" Amelia's voice broke, and her eyes watered.

Her mom wrapped her in a hug. "You don't have much control over liking him or not liking him," she said. "As for being separated from him driving you to despair, you have two options. You can throw yourself into other things as a distraction and hope your feelings go away, or you can talk to him about it."

Amelia sniffled and let out a sob. "What if he says he doesn't want to see me anymore?"

Her mom stroked her back, and Amelia closed her eyes. "I doubt he'll say that. But if he does, then you'll know where you stand, and you can stop torturing yourself by wondering about it."

"H – how did you know Dad liked you?"

Her mom smiled. "He was never subtle about it. He was constantly doing things for me and trailing me in the school hallway. I asked him on a date when we were fourteen just to put him out of his misery since he was too shy to ask me. It wasn't long before we were smitten with each other and an official couple."

Amelia sniffled again and wiped away her tears. "You never had to worry about fitting into Dad's world. Malcolm and I can't relate to each other's lives."

"Oh, Amelia," her mom cooed. "Telling yourself excuses isn't making you happier, is it?"

"No." No matter how many times Amelia told herself there was no future between her and Malcolm, is didn't make anything easier. It only made her feel worse about herself and more inadequate.

"All that should matter is whether you both like each other and want to spend time in each other's company. You can figure out the rest together. Don't distance yourself because you're afraid."

"I am scared." Amelia hadn't feared talking to Mr. Everbee or fleeing the guards with Blake McKelvey. It was Malcolm throwing her aside like a worn-out plaything while Scarlet watched on and gloated that terrified her. Every time she saw him or got a note from him, Amelia was certain he'd say he'd had his fill of her.

"That's because he's important to you," her mom said. "I know you can be brave, and you'll feel so much better afterwards."

Amelia swiped the last of her tears away. "I'll try."

…

Amelia got some much-needed sleep after her mom's advice. She woke in the morning, showered and threw on her pre-picked outfit. Her nerves tumbled in her stomach as she ate a breakfast of oatmeal. In the past she would've stirred in sugar, cinnamon or fruit. Her family had none of those things now. So, her breakfast was just oats cooked in hot water. On another day, she might've mourned the lack of flavour, but her job and the note she wanted to send Malcolm were the bigger issues on her mind.

Amelia shoved Malcolm to the back of her mind. After work, she would write him a note asking to meet up. There was no way she'd let it distract her on the first day of a job she was desperate for.

Her parents wished her luck as she grabbed her bag, with her ID card and bus fare inside, and zoomed out the door. Her feet flew down the stairs. One glance at the elevator floor counter told her the stairs would be quicker. Outside, the street was busy with people doing their Sunday shopping as for many this was their one day off. Amelia's parents had unsuccessfully tried to increase their workday. Neither could get more than five days a week.

Amelia dodged the shoppers as she jogged to the bus stop. She had a few minutes to spare, as had been her plan. Showing up disheveled because she had to stand on the bus with people bumping into her was not the first impression she wanted to make with whomever her boss was.

The bus came, and Amelia snagged a seat. As it traveled north and the Apartment Districts got nicer, more people boarded it. These people were the Sunday brunch type and had some pocket money to spare. It made Amelia wonder how long they could sustain their spending habits. Surely the price hikes weren't affecting only the poorer Apartment Districts.

When she got off at her stop and walked to work, few of her fellow bus riders went in the same direction. At five minutes before noon, Amelia stopped short outside Restaurant Doma's door. The bartender who'd offered her the job was leaning against a section of wall that held no window. He lit up when he spotted Amelia.

"You came."

Chapter 32

Had he been waiting for her? "You didn't give the job to someone else, did you?"

"Nope, it's still yours," he said as he stood upright. "Come with me, and I'll show you the back entrance and where to put your stuff."

Amelia followed him down the alley beside the building to a metal door with a sign saying: Employees Only. She inhaled deep and followed him inside. There was nothing to be nervous about. She almost believed herself.

A middle-aged man with thinning hair, wearing suit pants and a grey collared shirt with the sleeves rolled up, was standing in the kitchen doorway leading from the small storage room the metal door opened to. There were coats on hooks on the storage room's lefthand wall atop cubbies with bags and other items shoved in. The righthand wall had shelves covered in cleaning supplies and boxes with labels like Cutlery or Plates.

The man squinted at Amelia. "This the girl you told me about, Caleb?"

Caleb. Amelia finally had a name for the man.

"Yup, boss."

The boss grunted. "Show her where to put her stuff and send her to my office." He turned and walked into the kitchen, the door swinging closed behind him.

Caleb gestured to the wall of hooks and cubbies. "Pick one that isn't labelled."

Amelia approached the wall and scanned it for a vacant spot. The hanging coats covered most of the labels, making it obvious that those spots were taken. Second from the right end, there was a vacant hook and empty cubby. On the wall under the hook was a worn spot on the paint where someone had taken off the label. Amelia bent and deposited her bag in the cubby. "I'm ready," she said as she straightened up.

Caleb flashed her a grin. "This way."

Through the swinging door, they went into the kitchen. Cooks were at the stations preparing dishes with ingredients Amelia's family couldn't afford. She dodged out of the way just in time as the dish washer, a girl about her age with brown skin and tied up, straight, black hair, wearing a wet apron, veered to the sink with a pile of dirty dishes in her arms.

Caleb laughed. "Best to stop gawking and pay attention. Vera will run you over. She's laser focused, especially when the plates pile up."

"Noted." Amelia turned and darted after Caleb to the boss's office on the back wall between the break room and walk-in cooler. Its door had a little plaque on it that said: Mr. Polman.

The office door was open, and the boss, who she assumed was Mr. Polman, waved her inside. "Shut the door and sit."

Amelia did as she was told. The seat he'd referred to was metal with a thin cushion on it, which did nothing to make the seat comfortable when she sat.

"Seeing as we're desperate and Caleb vouches for you, I'll spare you the interview. The owner will be pleased we finally have someone after the last busser quit."

Amelia forced her mouth to stay closed. Gaping at her knew boss might make him reverse his decision. "Thank you, sir." She wasn't about to ask the man who had power to fire her why they had such trouble filling the position.

"Mr. Polman to you. Read this and sign at the bottom," he said as she shoved a paper across his desk to her.

Amelia flipped it around and read it. There wasn't much to the document, only the hours, description of her duties and pay. It was the amount listed that made Amelia's eyes bug out. She scribbled her name on the signature line before he could lower the number. Surely it was a mistake.

Mr. Polman laughed. "You're an Apartment District kid. I was wondering how Caleb convinced a customer to take a job here. It never worked before."

If they'd been trying to recruit their rich patrons, no wonder they'd had trouble filling the position. "I wouldn't call myself a great customer, Mr. Polman," Amelia said, focusing on that part of his statement. There was no reason to let him have a false impression of her.

He took back the paper, opened a desk drawer, rifled through until he found the file he wanted and slid in the paper. "Only bad customers are the ones that make a mess or a scene. Or put an order in and refuse to pay. You any of those?"

"No." Amelia would've been kicked out long ago for doing any of that.

"There you go," he said. "You'll shadow Vera until you get the hang of things. She'll show you where to get an apron."

"Thank you," Amelia said, earning a nod in response. She took this as her cue to leave and exited the office, closing the door behind her at the boss's command.

With a deep breath, Amelia veered to the sink where Vera was scrubbing dishes. Amelia cleared her throat and kept her hands in her pants pockets. Washing dishes hadn't been on the list of duties on the paper she'd signed.

Vera dropped her scrub brush in the sink and turned around, her face expressionless. "You the new hire?"

"Yes, and you're supposed to show me what to do." Amelia didn't want to come across as rude, but standing by the sink wasn't how she was going to learn her job. "The sooner you show me, the quicker I'll leave you alone."

Vera laughed, her eyes lighting up. "Nope. Your job is to bring me the stuff to wash. But once you can do it alone, things will go quicker."

"You've been collecting it and washing it?"

Vera rolled her eyes. "There was no one else to do it. The last busser quit. His parents wanted him to learn responsibility, and they let him quit when he complained about having to wear an apron and touch used plates. Rich kids are such snobs."

Amelia didn't think this was a fair statement when made universally. Before she could say that, Vera walked past and beckoned her to the storage closet at the far end of the kitchen. "Aprons are in here," she said as she opened the door.

Amelia grabbed one off the hook on the storage room's wall and put in on. It was black, a shade not too dissimilar to her outfit.

"What's your name anyway?" Vera was standing outside the storage room, her brown eyes on Amelia.

"Amelia."

Vera grinned. "You're the girl Caleb's kept going on about. The one Arlo Fenn told him about."

Amelia hadn't expected to have a reputation or be well known. Why was Arlo Fenn talking about her? "Does everyone here know Arlo? I've only met him a few times."

Vera shook her head, her tied up hair swinging side to side. "Caleb and I used to do deliveries for him."

"Oh." Amelia filed this tidbit of information away for later. Did they know about her work to overthrow the food laws?

"We've talked enough," Vera said as she walked away from the storage room. "The plates won't collect themselves." She grabbed a deep, rectangular, metal bin off a shelf in the kitchen and thrust it at Amelia. "You'll need this." She walked off through the employees only door that opened at the side of the bar before Amelia answered.

Caleb flashed Amelia a small smile when she emerged behind Vera, who was so quick Amelia had to speed walk to keep up with her. Vera headed to a vacant table along the back side of the restaurant and waited.

When Amelia got there, Vera pointed to the tabletop. "Find an empty spot, if there is one, to put the bin. It's easier to load if you have both hands. And don't worry about cleaning the table. The greeter does that."

Amelia scanned the table with her eyes and set the bin down in the least-crowded section. She started stacking the plates, cutlery and cups inside, Vera's watchful eyes on her the entire time.

Vera grabbed Amelia's wrist and stilled it. "You're going to break it all. Stack from largest to smallest, plates under bowls, and tuck the cups and cutlery around it."

Amelia emptied the bin and restarted. She hadn't thought her first attempt was that wobbly until she restacked. With a nod from Vera, Amelia hefted the bin once it was loaded. She'd only done one table. It seemed like a waste to go back into the kitchen now, but Amelia took a step in that direction.

"Wrong way," Vera said, grabbing Amelia's elbow to stop her and turn her around. "You can fit three normal tables' worth in there."

Amelia followed the other girl to two more tables and slid their plates into the stacks. When she'd collected and stacked all three tables' dishes, the bin was so heavy Amelia grimaced when she hefted it. It weighed much more than the groceries she carried home with her mom, though those trips had been good practice.

"You'll get used to it," Vera said as she led Amelia back to the kitchen.

When they got to the sink, Vera transferred the stacks to the counter beside it. "Think you can get the next tables? When you get back, I'll have these done and show you how to reset the places."

"Okay," Amelia said. She hadn't expected to work solo this soon, but Vera did have her own workload to complete. Amelia also wasn't sure she needed someone to tell her how to set plates out. It couldn't be that different from what she did at home, an opinion she kept to herself as she re-entered the restaurant floor with her bin.

Amelia was on the third table – they seemed to turn over a bunch at once – when the door opened and closed. She wouldn't have paid any attention to it if a familiar, high-pitched, entitled voice hadn't carried from the entrance.

"I always sit at the same table, and I expect to do so today."

Amelia winced and ducked her head. What was Scarlet doing here? She didn't want Malcolm to find out about her job through his wannabee girlfriend, if Kelsie hadn't told him. Amelia zeroed in on her task and hoped Scarlet wouldn't walk by or notice her.

"Yes, Miss," the greeter said. "Right this way."

Amelia's shoulders sagged in relief as she heard footsteps and the click of heels fade towards the other side of the restaurant. When she retraced her route to the employee door, she stole a glance at Scarlet.

She was sitting with her mom, whom Amelia recognised from the fundraiser. Amelia hoped they'd leave quickly, before she had to start on that side of the restaurant. Having to be polite to them was low on her list of things she wanted to do. However, telling them off would get her fired.

Back in the kitchen, once Amelia's bin was empty, Vera snatched it from Amelia and deposited it on the counter. Next to the sink was a fully loaded bin with clean dishes and cutlery wrapped in napkins. "Grab it and let's go."

Amelia did as instructed, biting back her groan from the weight of another full bin. She was glad, at least, that Vera went in the direction opposite from Scarlet's table. The table Vera took Amelia to wasn't one she'd cleared earlier. Someone else really was cleaning them.

The necessity of that became clearer to Amelia throughout the afternoon. After the first three tables Vera showed her how to set up, which was like her table at home, though with more pieces, Amelia was on her own.

She kept an eye on Scarlet's table as she cleared the opposite half of the restaurant, hoping she and her mom would leave before Amelia would need to work that side. With every bin she brought back to Vera, the likelihood of having to get closer to Scarlet grew. It seemed that Scarlet intended to say until closing.

"It's break time," Vera said after a couple hours. "It should be quiet enough out there that we can eat. Come on."

"What about those?" Amelia said, gesturing to the bin she'd just brought Vera and the one waiting for her to take.

Vera waved a hand. "They can wait. Aren't you hungry?"

In truth, Amelia had been too busy and worried about running into Scarlet to notice her hunger. Her stomach grumbled now that Vera was talking about food. "Yeah, a bit."

"Then come on before the cooks get busy again."

"I'm coming," Amelia said. She'd spent the past couple hours walking by the cooking stations and never had a chance to see what they were making.

Her curiosity grew as Vera led her over to the stoves.

"The usual again, Vera?" one of the cooks, a woman with dark skin and black hair in a bun asked without looking up from her cutting board.

"You know it."

The cook slid a plate of a sandwich on toasted bread to Vera. "Someday you need to try something different, kid."

Vera grabbed the plate. "I eat different at home."

"What about you, new girl?" The cook looked at Amelia when she asked this and set her knife on the cutting board.

"Oh, um," Amelia said. "I don't know." She'd only ever had the crostini that Malcolm had paid for. "I haven't eaten here much."

The cook snapped her fingers. "Lentil and potato stew. You need some fuel to keep up with all the lugging and running back and forth."

Before Amelia could say whether she liked stew, the cook plucked a bowl from a shelf, walked to another station and ladled a thick, hot and steamy stew from a large pot into it. She came back, pressed the bowl into Amelia's hands and added a spoon. "Tell me what you think later. I'll let Kurt know. He cooks it, not me."

"Thanks, Iris," Vera said as she hooked her hand on Amelia's elbow.

"Yes, thanks," Amelia said as Vera pulled her away.

"In here," Vera said, indicating the break room door between the storage closet and Mr. Polman's office. "I'll get us drinks."

Chapter 33

Amelia walked into the breakroom and sat at the small metal table. There was nothing in the room besides the table, six chairs around it and a row of cabinets along the back wall. She didn't go investigate what, if anything, was in them.

Once she pulled her chair in, Amelia tucked into the stew. Kurt had access to better ingredients and more spices than her parents. Amelia hadn't tasted as much flavour in a dish since the last time Malcolm had taken her out for a meal. And she was never full at home. Nor was she constantly starving. It was more of a constant desire and a faded, ever-present pang calling out for more food. She had grown so accustomed to it that whenever she ate a larger portion and it went away, its absence was strange.

"You're acting like you're either in a hurry or have eaten in days," Vera said as she came into the break room with two glasses of water and set one down in front of Amelia.

"Do you have lots of food at home?" Amelia asked between spoonfuls as she reached for the water.

"Enough," Vera said as she sat and placed her sandwich plate on the table. "I've been working for a year and pay for some of my own food."

Amelia swallowed a gulp of water. "I got a job to help my parents pay for food too."

"Heh," Vera said. "It's not all bad. I'd rather be here than at home most of the time anyway. My mom's been so cold and closed off since my dad died."

Amelia frowned. "I'm sorry. That must be tough."

"It's reality, and I'm dealing with it," Vera said as she bit into her sandwich. Once she swallowed, she wiped her mouth with the back of her hand. "I don't need anyone's pity over it."

"You sound like my friend Kelsie. She hates people trying to show her sympathy too."

Vera closed her eyes and breathed in deep. "When you're used to relying on yourself, it's hard to take sympathy. Sympathy doesn't fix problems or change anything. If you ever lose people important to you, who you relied on, you'll understand."

Amelia gulped down some of her water. "Got it. No trying to relate to your personal life."

Vera gave Amelia a lobsided smirk as she chewed another bite of her sandwich. "You're smart. No wonder Caleb thought you could handle this job."

"Apparently Mr. Polman doesn't, or he wouldn't have assigned you as my chaperone." She hadn't expected Vera to usher her through her break, and it didn't feel necessary.

"Someone has to teach you how we do things. Would you have rather me sent you out there alone to be scolded for being too slow or doing it wrong?"

That was definitely not preferable. "No. I'm grateful you showed me what to do."

"Like I said, smart. You ready to get back out there?"

Amelia bit the corner of her bottom lip. Was Scarlet's long meal over yet? There was no way to know until she went back onto the restaurant floor. "I suppose."

"What's got you nervous now?" Vera leaned across the table with her eyes narrowed.

There was nothing to do other than tell her. "A girl that hates me was eating with her mom. I swear they must've ordered the entire menu to come one dish at a time."

"Why's she hate you?"

There was no going back now, no matter how much Amelia wished she'd never brought up this topic. "She wants to marry the boy I like."

Vera gaped at Amelia. "You're competing with a rich girl over a boy?"

"It's not really a competition," Amelia said. "He doesn't like or want her and is too different from me. He won't choose either of us in the end."

"Boys are more trouble than their worth," Vera said. "I'm never going to get married."

"Not to a girl even?"

Vera pushed her chair back and got up. "Nah. I don't like anyone that way. Besides, no courtship means more school, so I can get a degree and support myself."

Amelia rose from her own seat and followed Vera across the break room. "I used to think I'd never like anyone that way either and that keeping my independence was more important."

"Until you met a certain boy, right?"

Amelia dipped her head. She liked Malcolm. A lot. Admitting it to her friend group was too awkward and scary. Vera was only her co-worker.

"You should tell him that."

Amelia and Vera were back in the kitchen now, and Vera zoomed to the sink. Amelia passed her the stew bowl and grabbed the bin full of clean dishes. It was late afternoon now; surely Scarlet was gone.

That proved too optimistic. Amelia walked through the employee door, turned to approach a section of empty tables that needed setting and heard Scarlet's laugh.

"Mom, look. Won't Malcolm find this hilarious?"

"I'm not certain he shares your sense of humour, dear. He'll probably find it embarrassing."

Amelia ducked her head and darted to the table, setting the dishes as fast as her hands could move without breaking anything. They were having fun at her expense, and she could do nothing about it without risking her job.

"I'll bring him next week, so he can see for himself," Scarlet said. "That'll snap his delusions about *her*."

"If it doesn't, nothing will."

Amelia tensed as she heard Scarlet and her mom giggle their way out the door. Scarlet would be back next week to humiliate her in front of Malcolm. And she'd come weekly as her twisted form of entertainment. That made Amelia's need to send Malcolm a note urgent. In the few hours between the end of a school day and curfew, there was enough time to meet him and talk things out. No matter what, she wasn't going to be degraded by Scarlet in front of Malcolm.

Amelia set every table in the restaurant during the lull before supper service. When the rush came, she hid out in the kitchen with Vera, gulping down glasses of water. Neither of them had anything to do until the first batch of patrons was finished eating.

"You look stressed," Iris said as Amelia grabbed another glass of water.

"I'm alright," Amelia said. "This girl I know and her mom were laughing at me on their way out earlier, and the girl said she'd come back next week."

Iris stopped cutting the vegetables on her cutting board and fixed her eyes on Amelia. "If she's a friend of yours, you have bad taste."

"She's not." There was no scenario where Amelia and Scarlet would be friends. Amelia was certain there never would be, and she didn't want to.

"Then ignore her. Cruel people switch their attention to someone else when they get no reaction."

That was a logical way to deal with Scarlet, but it wasn't easy to execute. Amelia would handle Scarlet her way, through Malcolm. For the rest of her shift, she finalized her plan. While she ran dishes to Vera and set tables, she went over details in her mind.

Amelia had all the tables set for the next day, except for the one occupied by a couple that came in an hour before closing. She watched them from the cracked-open employee door and kept track of the time.

"Watching them won't make them eat any faster," Caleb said from the other side of the door where he was standing, back against the wall, behind the bar.

Amelia sighed. "I have nothing else to do." Nothing except stress over the note she needed to write Malcolm and mail in the morning.

Caleb smirked "Enjoy it. You've been running all shift."

That was true enough, but Amelia didn't feel worn out, which said something for the comfort of her cheap yet rugged boots. Walking home with Jack would be easier now that she'd proven to herself that she had some endurance. "Being busy was nice."

"I'm glad you're not second guessing taking the job," Caleb said as the couple finally rose from their chairs and started walking out.

Amelia waited until they were out of the door before picking up the empty dirty dishes bin and darting to the table. They'd ordered enough food that the plates, bowls and cutlery took up as much space as two normal tables' worth. It only paled in comparison to Scarlet's table that had taken two trips for her to clear. Both tables still had bites of food left on the plates, a waste Amelia could never bring herself to replicate. What was with rich people and ordering excess of everything? Did they need to show off their wealth that much?

Caleb was already in the kitchen when Amelia handed her bin over to Vera who grumbled and turned the faucet on.

While Vera scrapped off leftover food and scrubbed the dishes, the greeter came out of Mr. Polman's office with stacks of money in his hands. He veered to Amelia and thrust a wad at her. "Your share of the tip and weekly wages. Count it if you like."

Amelia grasped the stack and flicked through it, mentally adding up the bill amount. The number was a lot higher than she'd expected. "Is this all mine?"

"I told you the tip was worth it," Caleb said as the greeter doled out the next employee's wages.

"I didn't expect it to be this much." She clutched it tight and knew she'd hold her bag close to her body on the bus. No one was going to get between her and this precious money.

"Someday it might not be such a surprise," Caleb said. "Or seem as excessive as it does today."

Amelia had a hard time picturing that. The staff that had received their wages were starting to leave, and she had a bus to catch. She got halfway across the kitchen when Mr. Polman called her name.

Amelia stopped midstride and turned. "Yes, sir?"

"Good job today. Keep it up, and you might get a raise. Note I said might. The final decision is up to the owner."

"Thank you," Amelia said, earning her a nod and a grunt. She took this as her dismissal and jogged to the employee entrance where her coat and bag were. At the start of her shift, she hadn't known what to expect. It hadn't gone amiss, aside from Scarlet. She tucked her money into a zipped pocket in her bag, tugged the zipper closed and hugged her bag to her chest. Until she got home, there was nothing that could make her let it go.

The people she rode the bus home with were fellow workers. It was also obvious by their hunched shoulders and worn faces. There were plenty like her, keeping a tight hold on bags as if the contents were too valuable to set down for a second.

Amelia sat by herself midway to the back of the bus. No one paid her any attention, which was fine. She didn't need looks or conversations. The sun started to dip in the sky as the bus crawled closer to her stop. Amelia tapped her foot and stared out the window, her bottom lip between her jaws. The bus needing to stop so many times to let people off hadn't occurred to her.

When it finally neared her stop, Amelia jammed the stop request button. She was up out of her seat while the driver slowed, and she almost lost her balance as she sped down the aisle. Once on the street, Amelia ran to her building, never having been so glad to see it. She climbed the stairs, not wanting to wait for the elevator, and panted when she reached her door. With a quick turn of the key, she was inside.

Chapter 34

Amelia's parents insisted that she keep some of her money. She didn't protest too much as she would use it to buy lunch for the week and to mail her note to Malcolm. Her parents left her alone after supper, during which she gave them a recap, minus running into Scarlet, of her day.

In her room, Amelia rummaged through her desk drawer for a piece of paper and cut it in half. What she had to say to Malcolm wouldn't need a whole page, and the envelope she found in her drawer would fit her half piece without folding. She wrote her note, telling him that she needed to speak to him. It wasn't meant to come across as an order or a confrontation. She needed him to realize its urgency.

In the morning on her way to the school bus stop, Amelia dropped the note into the postage box. All that was left to do was wait for his reply.

Amelia forced herself to concentrate during her morning classes. Whatever Malcolm said or did because of her note was out of her control. Plus, she'd promised her mom she would devout energy to school.

At lunch, Amelia splurged on some apple juice. She was at her usual table sipping it when Dina set her tray down and sat across from her.

"You took the job?"

Amelia set down her juice cartoon. "Yup."

Dina eyed the juice. "It must pay well if you're already buying luxuries."

"I needed something to calm my nerves," she said. "I told Malcolm we need to talk."

Dina frowned and her eyes softened. "He's going to think you're dumping him."

Amelia and Malcolm weren't even a couple. How could she dump him? "It doesn't matter. I need to talk to him."

"I hope it goes how you want it to," Dina said.

So did Amelia. She wanted to come out of her conversation with Malcolm in a better place, not a worse one. Regardless, her mom was right. After it was over, she could stop torturing herself with the wondering.

She didn't bring it up with Jack on their walk home, but she did tell him about her first day at her new job, including the part about Scarlet, and especially about Caleb and Vera's connection to Arlo Fenn.

Jack turned his face to Amelia and raised his eyebrows when she mentioned that Caleb used to do deliveries for Arlo. "Did she say why they stopped doing them?"

"No, and I didn't think to ask. I can next week. She might tell me."

"It's no big deal," Jack said as he and Amelia reached the road into her Apartment District. "I was just curious is all."

Amelia filed it as an issue she'd bring up with Caleb or Vera when the opportunity was right. They didn't need to see her as a nosey snoop trying to dig up their personal business, so it required delicate handling. That was next weekend's problem, not what she needed to mull over as she parted from Jack with a wave and turned down her street.

She was planning how she would tackle the night's homework and letting her feet carry her down the route she'd taken countless times. It wasn't something Amelia usually needed to pay attention too closely, so she didn't spot the expensive car parked on the street or the boy with pricey clothes standing against the wall of her building, twirling keys around his finger.

Amelia walked to the door of her apartment building and placed her hand on the bar to open it.

"Amelia!"

She, jumped, dropped her hand and took a shaky step back to turn around. "Malcolm? What are you doing here?"

His eyes glistened like emeralds as he set them on her and stuffed his keys in his jacket pocket. "You told me you want to talk."

"I didn't think you'd come so fast." He must've gotten her note right after school and driven immediately over.

Malcolm groaned, his lips pulled into a frown. "You thought I'd drag this out? I—"

Amelia grabbed his wrist. "We aren't doing this here. There are too many eyes and ears."

She opened the door to her building with one hand and pulled Malcolm after her, dropping his wrist as soon as they were inside. Per her usual routine, she headed for the stairs and started to climb.

"Will you at least tell me what this is about?" Malcolm asked.

To his credit, he kept pace with her on the stairs and wasn't out of breath when they reached her landing.

"When we get in my apartment," Amelia said. Surely, he could wait to get down the hall and for her to unlock the door.

"Alright," he said as he trailed after her.

Amelia knew she could've been less aggressive in her note, and he might not have rushed to her building the same day. However, she'd written what she felt compelled to before she'd lost her nerve.

Amelia swung her apartment door open and beckoned Malcolm inside.

Her parents' voices were coming from their bedroom, giving her and Malcolm a modicum of privacy. She kicked her shoes off and set down her bag. "Come on," she said as she headed to the hall. "We can talk on the fire escape."

Malcolm pulled off his shoes and followed her. Amelia held up a hand as they neared her parents' room. "Mom? Dad? I'm going on the fire escape to talk to Malcolm. I'll help with supper when we're finished."

As they voiced their consent, Amelia waved Malcolm after her. Getting to the fire escape meant going through her parents' room or her own, a situation that was a smidge awkward. There was no way around it. The fire escape balcony was the only place they could go to have their much-needed conversation without her parents hovering or the neighbours listening.

So, Amelia led Malcolm through her room and opened the window. She saw his eyes dart around, but his face didn't give away what he thought of her personal place. Amelia didn't own enough stuff for it to be messy at least, and she had pulled her blankets up that morning.

When Malcolm climbed out the window behind her, Amelia shut it, turned around and grasped the metal bar of the railing. She stood beside the vertical ladder, giving her a view of the street behind her apartment building. Standing there and breathing the fresh air had a calming effect on her nerves.

Malcolm moved to her side, deciding to stand in the corner instead of the other side of the ladder. He didn't touch her, though his body was close enough that she could've kissed him if this had been romantic.

"Now will you tell me what you want to talk about?"

While Malcolm's went to her, Amelia's eyes went to the street. She couldn't bear the pain in his. Nor could she waste this opportunity. "I can't stand it anymore."

His eyebrows furrowed. "Can't stand what? You're going to have to be more specific."

Amelia inhaled deep. She couldn't cower her way out of this. It was better to know the truth, and if that meant ending whatever she and Malcolm had, she could survive it. "I know you said you like being with me, but I'm not naïve enough to believe we could have any type of future that doesn't end in us hating each other."

Amelia tightened her grips on the railing and braced herself for him to say she was right that they had no future and that he did like her as a short-term fling or a friend. She didn't expect him to suck in a breath and to place his warm hand over hers.

"I'll never hate you, Amelia. You've brought such light and life into my world; all I want is to be with you all the time. But I can't."

Amelia pulled her hand away, sliding it along the railing. Her eyes threatened to water, and she refused to cry. "I'd rather never see you than only the few times you think you can fit me in."

Malcolm's face fell and his eyebrows moved apart. "That isn't what I meant."

Amelia took a half-step back, let go of the railing and shoved her hands into her pants pockets. She needed space between her body and his. "Then what did you mean?"

"There's nothing I'd like more than to you see every day. But we go to different schools and live in different parts of the City. And Scarlet keeps track of how many times I see you."

Amelia felt a frown form on her face. "I'm sorry. That was my fault."

Malcolm stepped closer to her, and Amelia let him. "She gave us no alternative. I don't blame you for it, nor can I stand being nice to Scarlet. That's why I've limited the number of times I see you."

"Don't."

He wrinkled his eyebrows again. "Don't?"

Amelia swallowed the lump in her throat. "Don't be nice to her. She doesn't deserve it."

"Our agreement—"

"Was that you wouldn't mope or mention me. She didn't make you agree to be nice." Not unless she'd changed it when Amelia wasn't present.

Malcolm gave Amelia a dip of his head.

"The more you're nice to her, the more she's convinced you'll marry her. She came to my job and said she's going to bring you next time to laugh at me. Is that what you want, Malcolm? To play nice to a snobby rich girl that enjoys making fun of me?"

Amelia had unloaded a lot of details onto Malcolm. Blurting about her job could be the final deterrent. It might've been the last piece of her average, struggling existence that convinced him that she was wrong for him.

"Scarlet feels threatened by you," Malcolm said. He was now the one gazing at the street and not making eye contact.

Amelia stepped back on wobbly legs. That couldn't have been what he'd said. "What?"

"She's jealous. Whenever I see her, she whines about not understanding why I like you. I'm not allowed to say your name in her presence. It doesn't stop her. I think she enjoys torturing and dragging compliments out of me that way."

"What are you going to do on Sunday when she brings you to my work?" Amelia removed her hands from her pocked and clasped them tight. What would she do if he answered that he'd play along or do nothing? How many more confirmations did she need that Malcolm didn't care about her feelings?

"Why did you get a job at the place Scarlet goes to every weekend?"

How could Amelia have known Scarlet's schedule? And Malcolm hadn't answered her question. She should've realized he'd know where she was talking about as Scarlet would've divulged her schedule. Or Kelsie had told him about her job. "The bartender offered it to me, and my family needs the money. I had no idea Scarlet was going to be there until she walked in."

Malcolm swiveled his head to Amelia again, and there was a twinkle in his eyes. "Don't worry about Sunday. I'm not going anywhere with her to make fun of you or anyone else."

Amelia turned away and placed her hands back on the railing. "She'll come alone, or with her mom again." Every Sunday she would, Amelia was sure.

Malcolm stepped closer to Amelia and covered her hand with his again. "I'll tell her tonight that I won't marry her. And I'll make it clear that she needs to leave you alone."

"Thank you," Amelia said. It did nothing to reassure her of her own standing with Malcolm, and there was no guarantee Scarlet would listen to him.

"I'm sorry I've let things get this bad. I never wanted you to think I'm avoiding you or leaving you to fend for yourself against Scarlet."

Amelia swallowed the lump in her throat. "I can handle Scarlet. It's not knowing what you want from me that is tearing me apart."

Malcolm reached for her other hand and gently pried both off the railing. He turned Amelia to face him and titled his head down to rest his forehead on hers. "You don't need to give me anything. Being yourself is enough. And after tonight, I'll be around more. I promise."

Tears pooled in Amelia's eyes and her nerves tumbled in her stomach.

She did nothing to wipe the tears; Malcolm holding her hands was too nice to ruin. And it might've been the last time he touched her. "Mr. Everbee—"

"We made our pitch. He'll do what he wants with it regardless of whether I marry Scarlet. She said I had final say in that."

It sounded too easy. Amelia tried not to think of the ramifications this could lead to. Yet, it was like Dina said. If Mr. Everbee did nothing, things stayed the same. The issue was that the current state of things was terrible. And how could Amelia force Malcolm to play nice to Scarlet when it made them both miserable? "You've made your decision then?"

Malcolm gave her hands a squeeze. "I won't marry Scarlet. That was true before I ever met you."

Amelia didn't dare ask about his intentions with her. Where they ended, and when were clear to her: on Clinic Day. "Good. You shouldn't marry someone that selfish and snobby."

Malcolm pulled his head back so he could look in Amelia's eyes. "What about you? Jack told me you never want to marry anyone. Has that changed? You said I might be worth taking a risk for."

Amelia bit on her bottom lip. She could be truthful and tell him yes, she wanted to be with him. That meant being vulnerable, and that was hard. "I meant it when I said it. My views on getting married might've changed."

Amelia saw a corner of Malcolm's mouth quirk up, as much of a smile as he seemed to allow himself.

"You deserve to be happy and loved," he said. "Don't deny yourself that because you're afraid."

Chapter 35

Malcom kept surprising Amelia. She'd expected their conversation to have ended already with heartbreak, at least for her. Yet, he was still grasping her hands. There was nothing more she wanted in that moment than to close the distance between them, so she made no move to pull away. Why should she deny herself this? It was one of a finite number of times she'd be alone with him before Clinic Day when her life returned to how it used to be.

With all the courage she had, Amelia yanked Malcolm to her. This was her chance to tell him the truth. Time was running out before her parents would call her for supper and Malcolm would leave to see Scarlet. Yet, saying it out loud would mean admitting it to herself. Amelia closed her eyes. To keep denying what her heart knew was going to destroy her.

"I am afraid," she told Malcolm, standing on her tiptoes with her mouth almost brushing his. "Because I've found the person I love, but we're so different that the future for us seems impossible."

"No two people are the exact same," Malcolm said. "Differences can be overcome if both people want to try hard enough."

Amelia swallowed. Her body was trembling, and she didn't want to cry. She lowered herself so her heels were on the floor again. "I want to try, Malcolm. Every day I don't see you or hear from you is torture, and I'm tired of denying myself what I want."

Malcolm's eyes and mouth had bugged open. "Wait. Amelia, are you saying—"

"I love you, Malcolm." There was no taking back those words. Amelia steeled herself for him to say he liked her, only liked, as one liked a colour or certain food.

She didn't expect him to beam, yet an enormous grin broke out on his face and his eyes lit up. "You're serious?"

"I wouldn't lie about that," Amelia said. Even if he still rebuffed her, telling him had lifted a weight from her.

Malcolm sucked in a breath. "I thought you were going to tell me to stop seeing you when I read your note. I told myself to accept whatever you wanted, but the truth is I love you, and being with you whenever I can makes me happy."

Malcolm was starting to babble, and Amelia didn't want to waste however many minutes, or seconds, of privacy they had left on her fire escape balcony. She went on her tiptoes again to reach his face. With nerves making her shaky, Amelia took her hands from his and cupped his face, tilting it down as she kissed him with all the pent-up longing that she'd denied herself for too long. The world around her spun, and her knees wobbled. That didn't matter, not when Malcolm's lips responded to hers and his hands found her waist.

The sound of her parents moving around in her apartment broke them apart. Amelia cringed; her parents' noise was an obvious sign for her to come inside. She opened her window and climbed back into her room with Malcolm at her heels. Not wanting to see him leave, but knowing she had to, Amelia walked him to the door, past her parents who pretended to be busy with making and plating supper, and brushed his fingers as she opened it. "Goodbye, Malcolm."

"I'll see you soon, Amelia. I promise."

Amelia blinked back tears as he went down the hall. He'd said he loved her and that he was going to Scarlet's to break things off. Yet, Amelia had no idea what the future held for her and Malcolm. They'd made no plans or promises, other than that he'd be around more. Clinic Day was approaching, and Amelia had a new dread for it. How could she survive not seeing the boy she loved again?

She gave her parents the simplified version of their conversation, telling them that she'd see Malcolm more and that he was trying to break things off with Scarlet. Admitting her love to Malcolm had been one thing, but she wasn't ready to announce it to her parents at the supper table.

There was no avoiding telling Dina at lunch the next day. As soon as Amelia sat down, Dina leaned in with wide eyes. "So? Did you hear from Malcolm?"

Amelia nodded. She tried to give Dina the condensed version, that he'd been at her building waiting for her and promised to see her more often. Her friend would have none of it.

"That can't be the whole story, or why you've got a dreamy, faraway look in your eye. What happened? You *have* to tell me."

Amelia sipped her water. She hadn't splurged on juice again. "He thought I was going to tell him to stop seeing me, like you said. And he told me he would go to Scarlet's to dump her and get her to leave me alone," which Amelia still doubted would work. "And we both admitted we love each other." She kept her voice down for the last part, which didn't prevent Dina from screeching and causing the students at nearby tables to turn and stare.

Amelia slunk down on her seat and ducked her head. Having the cafeteria's attention on her was something she didn't want. It put too much focus on her relationship with Malcolm that still wasn't guaranteed to go anywhere. "Calm down," she said as Dina stopped squealing. "We aren't getting married, and I don't think Scarlet's going to give up."

"Forget about Scarlet," Dina said with a flick of her hand.

"She could ruin everything if she tells her dad to not support our idea." Amelia couldn't get the vision of a scorned Scarlet destroying the change Amelia had worked so hard for out of her mind. Scarlet was selfish and vindictive enough to do it without a second thought of the damage it would bring.

"You can't control what she does, so stop stressing over it. Be happy that Malcolm said he loves you."

Amelia wanted to do that, but turning the panicking part of her brain off proved too much of a challenge. So, she threw herself into her lessons. After her afternoon classes, she met Jack at school's rear door, and didn't bring up Malcolm at all as Jack opened the door and she followed him outside.

Amelia was getting used to hearing the buses leave without her and starting to enjoy the fresh air, as fresh as air could be amidst dusty streets and dirty buildings. The part of walking home she didn't like was that it cut into her homework time before supper, leaving her feeling rushed.

"Did Dina tell you the news?" Jack asked as he and Amelia turned around the side of the school.

"What news?" Dina hadn't mentioned anything to her at lunch; she'd only asked Amelia about Malcolm.

"Ethan wants to propose to Kelsie."

Amelia stumbled and tripped over her feet. Her arms flailed to her sides as she tried to right her balance. "Really? They only met a couple months ago!"

"I know, but it's either now or no going on dates after Clinic Day until next year. He said he couldn't stand that."

Citizens under sixteen didn't have to abide by the dating ban from Clinic Day until New Years. However, for citizens sixteen or older who didn't apply a Courtship with the person they loved, the law forbade meeting up alone until the start of the following year. Couples that got a rejection on their Courtship application were permanently banned from dating each other. The laws were meant to ensure only those with Courtship papers were going on dates, or those that were underage, and there was a hefty fine for breaking them, or jail time for those too poor to pay. That was why Amelia had extra dread for Clinic Day; it was the expiration date for her and Malcolm. By next year, he would like someone else.

"I hope it works out for them," Amelia said. "And that they're both sure of each other."

"Ethan seems certain. I'm going shopping with him this weekend to pick out a gift for her."

Months ago, Amelia wouldn't have cared that her friend group was pairing up and applying for Courtships. Jack and Dina dating had never bothered her. Yet, soon she'd be the single one who'd had a short-term fling with a boy she loved yet couldn't marry. Regardless, Ethan and Kelsie were perfect for each other, so Amelia wasn't going to deny them their happiness. "Good," she told Jack. "Make sure he gets something nice."

...

When Amelia got to her apartment, there was a note from Malcolm waiting for her on table. She scooped it up and took it to her bedroom, where she dropped her bag, sat on her bed and tore open the envelope. His brief message made Amelia shriek with joy.

I have good news that I can't write here. I'll drive you to school tomorrow and tell you then.

He ended his message with a heart. Amelia pressed her thumb over it and almost didn't notice her mom sticking her head into Amelia's room.

"Is everything okay?" her mom asked.

Amelia got off her bed, bounced over to her mom and gave her a hug. She broke away and showed her mom the note she was still clutching. There was a huge grin on her face; she could feel it in her cheeks. "He must mean Mr. Everbee decided to help us."

Her mom rested a hand on her shoulder. "Don't get too ahead of yourself. You'll risk getting your hopes dashed if it's something else."

"I'll be fine," Amelia said. She wasn't some delicate creature that would crumble if Malcolm told her some other piece of good news, but she did have a tough time focusing on her homework. When she finally completed it, the sun was down, and the streets were devoid of activity except for the guards on patrol that walked and swept their flashlight beams left and right.

Amelia usually paid them no mind, but that night she stood at her window and let the rhythmic arc of the nearest guard's flashlight beam soothe her nerves. It felt hypnotic and calmed her mind. She was still giddy from the idea that she might've accomplished what she wanted most, though her buzzing energy faded by the time the guard moved out of her range of vision.

Amelia rifled through her dresser and closet for a simple, cute outfit that Malcolm hadn't seen her wear and that none of her classmates would think was out of place. It was a harder task than she'd imagined. Most of her pieces were either fancy date clothes or simple and well worn.

In the end, she settled on jeans and a top. Why should she care too much about impressing Malcolm? It was like her mom had told Kelsie; if her outfit turned him off, he wasn't the right person for her. Also, Amelia thought she could wear her most faded and fraying clothes and he wouldn't care.

Amelia woke before her alarm the next morning, giving her time to style her hair and dot a miniscule amount of blush on her cheeks. This wasn't a date; she couldn't wear a full face of makeup. It would've been wasted anyway when she was going to sit in school all day.

When she was ready, and had eaten her meagre breakfast of toast, Amelia said goodbye to her parents and walked down the stairs. Outside on the street, Malcolm was leaning against the passenger side of his car. He walked to her with his hand extended when she exited her building.

Amelia met him halfway to his car and took his offered hand. She didn't care that this was an intimate gesture they couldn't get away with in public for long. Amelia would take any physical contact Malcolm was willing to give.

He didn't drop her hand until they reached his car, and he opened the passenger door. Amelia's heart hammered from the risk they took. She got in and closed it as he rounded to the driver's side. When he pulled away and drove to her school, Amelia turned to look at him.

"So, what's the good news?"

Malcolm didn't take his eyes off the road. "Scarlet was surprised to see me unannounced last night, and furious when I told her I won't go on anymore dates or marry her. I said I didn't care; our deal should've ended when we made our case to her father anyway."

Amelia had expected Scarlet to be angry. How was this good news? "And then what?"

"She clenched her hands, got in my face and said: 'You're lucky my father already presented your case, or I'd tell him to lobby against it.'"

Amelia gaped as her heart continued to pound. "He supported us?"

Malcolm nodded. "I pushed past Scarlet and asked him in his office. He said the Government told him it was a passable solution to the slow turnover of food, after some tweaks to the numbers. You can't spread this publicly yet. The food laws are still in effect while they work out details."

Amelia bounced on her seat. "How long? Do you know?"

"Should be by next week."

That was both soon and far away. At lunch, she would tell Dina, and Jack after school. They understood how important it was to keep the secret.

Chapter 36

"We'll throw a party. Everyone can bring something," Dina said at lunch with a look that indicated she meant food. "And we can all dress up."

"If you think everyone will go for that and can afford to bring something," Amelia said.

"We'll make it work," Dina said. "Don't you think it's nice to have something to celebrate?"

"Yeah, it is." But a party meant dates, one of the last few Amelia would have with Malcolm, and that was a depressing thought. She drank some of her water and fixed her gaze on Dina. "Jack told me that Ethan's going to propose to Kelsie."

"Yeah, he plans to this weekend. I would've told you, but I thought it might be awkward."

As Amelia had known Dina since the first year of school, she appreciated her best friend trying to accommodate her feelings. "I'm happy for them. It's not awkward and has nothing to do with me and Malcolm. I can't expect other people to stay single because I am."

Dina cocked her head and looked at Amelia from an angle. "Isn't it going to be difficult for you after Clinic Day?"

Yes. It would be, and Amelia imagined she'd spend days crying over it, especially if her friends all got approved Courtships and started to plan their weddings. "It'll be better than trying and getting a rejection letter. And I'll be able to see him again, just not on a date or alone." Maybe saying those words often enough would make her believe them.

Dina frowned. "You know that won't be the same."

It wouldn't. Yet what choice was there? "Next year it can be." While Clinic Day was fast approaching, New Years remained months away. To district herself from that agony, Amelia threw herself into helping Dina party plan, which was a difficult task when they didn't know when their news would come.

After school that day, Amelia told Jack the news. It was easier to give him the few details she had as they were free from numerous ears that could turn into gossiping mouths.

"This is only the beginning," Jack said. "The Rebel Cause will get a lot more supporters."

This wasn't unexpected. People tended to support safe and sure issues. "We still need to be careful though. I don't imagine the Government will be open to changing things they don't see as issues."

"I know. We'll be an underground movement for a while yet."

Jack had such confidence that Amelia dreamed about and never possessed. "Under your leadership it won't be for too long."

Jack scoffed. "I'm not a leader, and I don't want to be. I just want to do my part and what I need to for Dina."

"The Rebel Cause needs a leader, and it's not going to be me," Amelia said. Without one, it would never last. Then who would stop Kylie and Lucas from taking advantage of desperate people or the Government from doing as they pleased? Amelia wanted to help without having the overwhelming pressure of the spotlight and responsibility on her shoulders. She was more of a behind the scenes supporter.

"Arlo Fenn will take over," Jack said. "He's used to recruiting and coordinating."

As true as this might be, Arlo Fenn hadn't helped change the food laws. Amelia assumed he wouldn't accomplish much in terms of change. Yet there was value in helping people at a personal level within the current and existing laws. Arlo had proven he could do that, and he had the lists of potential donors from the fundraiser. Besides, what other option was there? People weren't going to follow a movement for long when teenagers were in charge.

It was also weight lifted from Amelia. She wanted to be involved in the Rebel Cause she'd help form and name without having everyone rely on her. Finishing school was her priority. While her friends would all leave it if they had approved Courtships, Amelia could have her education.

Her homework and studying provided distractions while she waited to hear news from Malcolm. He started sending her notes every day; when she walked in her apartment door after school, there was usually one waiting for her. They didn't give news, only messages saying he missed her and was thinking of her.

With her smaller budget, Amelia only sent replies to a couple. She would wait until she saw him in person to tell him how much she missed him. And it still felt like they were playing a reckless game. Why was she letting herself get attached to a boy she'd soon be barred from dating?

In truth, Amelia felt powerless to stop it. Every time the rational part of her tried to assert some sense, her heart won out. She was like metal drawn to a magnet; forces beyond her control were urging her to him.

She didn't see Malcolm the rest of the school week. If she'd told him she'd been walking home, he would've been there daily to drive her, but Amelia didn't want him turning into her chauffer. Her independence was important.

On Saturday, Amelia did the shopping with her mom. It replaced their Sunday trips due to Amelia's work schedule. This trip was yet another biweekly one diminished in size. Her mom had refused to use Amelia's money until she had to relinquish and accept a portion of it when their standard budget didn't cover everything they needed. Amelia and her parents had long ago given up any forms of luxuries or wants. what they bought now was purely things they needed, and even that was starting to leave Amelia hungry.

On Sunday, Amelia used her remaining money for the bus fare to work. She would need to use that week's paycheque to cover her ride home.

At work that day, Amelia didn't shadow Vera. Her training had lasted the one day, and she was thrown into tasks at full speed. It was only at break time that Amelia had the opportunity to ask Vera why she and Caleb stopped doing deliveries for Arlo Fenn.

"I stopped when my dad died, and I needed to get a job," Vera said. "Caleb didn't last much longer. Neither of us has the time anymore."

"Do you miss it?" Amelia asked. She had only done two deliveries herself and hadn't heard from Arlo about another one. Planning to replace the food laws had kept her mind off them.

"A bit, I suppose," Vera said as she finished the water in her glass and picked up her empty plate. "Honestly, I'm too busy to notice these days. Caleb keeps in touch with Arlo Fenn though. That's how he got your name."

Amelia gathered her own plate and empty water glass, and she walked with Vera out of the break room. "Yeah, he mentioned that." She would need to tell Jack that the next time they walked home.

…

She was setting a table when Scarlet and her mom walked in. Amelia pressed her lips together and kept her eyes on her task. It was the last table she had to set before switching to the dirty dishes bin. Not that it helped when she'd just started, and Scarlet was headed her way.

Luck was not on her side. She heard three sets of footsteps move from the door, and only two moved past her. Amelia hoped it was the greeter who'd stopped, but an 'ahem' shattered that hope.

Amelia set down the glass she was holding and turned around. There was Scarlet with venom-filled eyes and predatory scowl locked on Amelia. She stepped closer to Amelia, who had nowhere to go as the back of her legs were brushing the table.

"You ruined everything," Scarlet hissed. "I hope you're happy."

Amelia didn't lower her face or avert her eyes. She stood tall, braced her hands on the tabletop and lifted her chin. "He was never going to marry you, whether he met me or not."

Scarlet tittered. "And he's not going to marry you. You're a worthless nobody."

"No, I'm not," Amelia said. "You're selfish and cruel. That's what drove him away." She took her hands off the tabletop, turned back around and finished setting the table, her hands flying.

Scarlet growled and fumed. Amelia ignored her. She had work to do, and getting into a fight with Scarlet would end with Amelia fired. As she grabbed the empty bin and whirled around to retreat to the kitchen, she caught a glimpse of murder in Scarlet's eyes.

When Amelia exited the kitchen with the dirty dishes bin, Scarlet was seated with her mom, and her eyes tracked Amelia. It was going to be a long shift.

Amelia thought Scarlet would never leave. She and her mom ordered more than they had the previous week, and Scarlet kept her focus on Amelia whenever Amelia was nearby.

Amelia lingered in the break room when she could and took her time switching her bins. When she was clearing and setting tables, her hands moved at record pace. If every week was going to be like this, she'd never last.

"You okay, kid?" Iris asked as Amelia gulped a glass of water.

Amelia swiped water off her lips and gave a nod. "I'm just hoping Scarlet leaves soon. She's angry at me because she got dumped."

"Is she the girl that was here last week? The one you said hates you?"

"Yeah," Amelia said. "She's been watching me and glaring all afternoon."

"That's why you've been running back here so fast?" Vera asked, wagging her scrub brush at Amelia. "And making me wash dishes at breakneck speed?"

Iris shook her head. "Letting her see she's affected you is letting her win. Go out there and slow down. You'll only win this if you stay calm."

Amelia tried. Yet going at her previous week's pace was too slow and left her squirming under Scarlet's venomous gaze. She ended up going at a pace somewhere in between. The mid-afternoon lull was a relief for her, as she hid out in the kitchen with nothing to do until Scarlet left or the first supper table came and left. Mr. Polman didn't like to disturb diners by having Amelia take their plates while they were still at the table.

At least she thought she had no work to do until one of the servers approached her. Amelia didn't know the girl's name.

"I need you to clear some of the dishes. We're running out of room, and it's threatening the tip. Mr. Polman okayed it."

Amelia held back her sigh and grabbed her dirty dish bin. She wasn't about to question the boss. "I'm on it."

"Good." The server bobbed her head and walked to the outgoing food counter to collect Scarlet's next course. Amelia followed through the employee door and across the restaurant, a knot twisting in her stomach. It was like walking into a killer's lair where one wrong move or word could lead to certain demise.

As the server set down the plates of food, Amelia stepped to the side of the table farthest from Scarlet where the previous dishes sat. Many of them had half-eaten, or untouched, food on them. She tried not to cringe as she piled as much as would fit into her bin that she cradled between her torso and one arm. There was no space to set it down. The server retreated to the kitchen when she'd deposited the plates, leaving Amelia alone.

"I don't see why Malcolm likes her so much," Scarlet said to her mom. "She's so poor."

Amelia kept her mind blank, and her hand and eyes focused on the stacks of dirty plates. Their words wouldn't wound her.

"He obviously has bad taste. You shouldn't fixate so much on him."

"I fixate," Scarlet snapped as she picked at the food on her plate, "because I've wanted to marry him since the first day of school when he was the only boy to say hello to me. He's played hard to get since, but I will become Mrs. Connor."

Amelia placed one last dish in her overflowing bin, turned and retreated from the table as fast as she could walk. She should've known Scarlet had such a shallow reason to pursue Malcolm.

As soon as Amelia gave the bin to Vera, the dish washer thrust another one into her hands. "Go get the rest. No use in waiting; you'll need it to reset tables."

Amelia sighed and trudged her way back to Scarlet's table. There was no avoiding it.

"I'll say one good thing about you," Scarlet said, leaving the remnants of the food on her plate untouched.

"What's that?" Amelia asked. She didn't bother to look at Scarlet. Stacking dishes with one hand required her focus.

"You're efficient. You darted around all afternoon getting things done. It would be impressive if it wasn't so pitiful."

"Thank you for the compliment," Amelia mumbled. It was the closest to one Scarlet was ever going to give her, even if it was meant to be an insult.

"I do wish I could've convinced Malcolm to come," Scarlet cooed. "Seeing you in this element would break whatever idyllic fantasy he has."

Amelia squeezed the glass in her hand so hard it would've shattered if it had been one of the cheap ones from her house. She set it in the bin before she did damage it and have to pay out of her paycheque.

Scarlet snickered. "That bothers you? Having Malcolm see you in everyday life, away from the luxury he pays for?"

Amelia breathed deep and tried to tune Scarlet out as she stacked the last few dishes in her bin. It was once again overflowing and impeded Amelia's view. The route to the kitchen had been clear when she walked to the table, so Amelia trusted it was the same this time. She'd walked it numerous times by now.

She got a couple steps before tripping over Scarlet's outstretched foot that she didn't see until she was falling to the floor. The bin upended with a crash, sending dishes and glasses tumbling and shattering. Food crumbs mixed with the shards spilled in a wide radius, and some landed on Scarlet's clothing.

"You clumsy fool," Scarlet seethed as she stood up and glared at Amelia. "You're going to pay to clean my outfit."

Amelia had landed on her stomach with her face atop her hands, which had braced her impact. She pushed herself up to sitting and clamored to her feet. A quick glance at her limbs showed she hadn't cut herself, but she was shaking. "I'm not paying for anything. You tripped me."

Scarlet rolled her eyes, walked over and got in Amelia's face. "So naïve. You ruined my life, and now I'm going to ruin yours. You're a lowly busser, easily replaced."

"And you're about to get banned from stepping foot in here again," Caleb said from behind Scarlet. He was standing with his arms crossed. "You can't trip employees and threaten them."

"I'm a paying customer," Scarlet said as she spun around with her hands on her hips and her chin jutted up. Caleb towered over her, which didn't seem to have an effect. "You don't have the authority to ban me."

"Oh no, not me personally," Caleb said with a sly grin. "Mr. Polman will ensure it happens when he watches the security tape."

Amelia saw Scarlet's face turn red as she pounced on Caleb, using her nails as claws on his shirt. He didn't back down or flinch. Amelia wished she had his nerve.

"Scarlet," Mrs. Everbee said. She was still sitting and set down her napkin on the tabletop. "We should go. You don't want to cause any more of a scene."

"No, no, no!" the greeter said, blocking Mrs. Everbee's escape from the table. "Neither of you are leaving until you pay for your food and whatever dishes broke and clean up the mess."

Chapter 37

Caleb ushered Amelia into Mr. Polman's office while the greeter collected Scarlet and her mom's bill. "Tell him what happened," Caleb said as he nudged Amelia towards a chair and sat on the other one.

Mr. Polman harumphed. "Yes. Tell me what you two are doing in my office."

Amelia gulped and delved into her recap. Once she started, the words flowed in a steady stream. She was powerless to stop herself and was thankful it was a short tale, after she left out most of the details about Malcolm.

"This girl blonde and always wearing red lipstick?" Mr. Polman asked. He'd leaned back in his seat, rested his elbows on his desk and tented his fingers. "She undertips and insults the staff. You're not the first one, but you are the first one she's tripped and caused to break property."

He believed her? Amelia blinked and snapped her mouth shut. "You're just going to take my word for it?"

"Nope. I have proof." He opened a drawer on his desk and pulled out a flat, rectangular metal object with a shiny screen and rounded corners. It was as large as a school notebook. "I saw it on here," he said, waving the device. "All the security footage gets sent here, and I watch it live at times. You're lucky this was one of them. I was out of paperwork."

"I suppose I am," Amelia said, having not known portable screens that could show non-Governmental programming existed. Did Malcolm have one?

Or was it exclusive to higher ups in business? And she didn't feel lucky that her hair and outfit were a mess, or that she'd bruised at least one part of her body.

Mr. Polman got to his feet. "Time to go kick her out. Go decompress in the break room for a few minutes. The rush hasn't started yet." He exited his office, leaving the door open and Amelia and Caleb sitting.

Caleb stood and offered Amelia his hand. "You could do that, but watching her throw a fit would be more fun, don't you think?"

Amelia accepted his help, sliding her hand from his when she was standing. "Definitely."

Amelia and Caleb weren't the only ones to peek through the employee door to watch Scarlet. The server who'd overseen Scarlet's table stuck her head in the gap, and Vera crouched to peek below Amelia.

"Is that the same girl that spilled her drink all over the bar and you, Caleb?" Vera asked.

"I'm surprised you remember that," he said. "She was angry her ice cubes had melted and insisted I make her another one. This was after she left the drink on the counter for twenty minutes untouched."

"She sends back so many dishes," the server said with a groan. "I got assigned her table because no one else will deal with her. At least once per visit, she orders something, changes her mind and sends it back, and then demands she doesn't have to pay for it. Her mom enables the bad behaviour."

"That sounds about right," Amelia said. She cracked the door open a bit more to better hear the conversation.

Mr. Polman was standing across from Scarlet and her mom. Mrs. Everbee huffed and fidgeted with the rings on her fingers, her attention not on her daughter.

Scarlet was scowling and threw the mop she was holding to the ground. The unbroken dishes and cutlery were stacked in Amelia's bin and the broken pieces were in a garbage can someone had placed nearby. There were still food crumbs and smears on the floor. "I don't see why I have to clean this," Scarlet fumed. "I didn't spill it! That clumsy busser tripped on her own feet."

"I have a witness and video evidence proving the opposite," Mr. Polman said. "Mop this up, and you can go. And you won't be welcome back."

Scarlet's nostril's flared, and she squeezed her lips together so tight the top one disappeared. "I wouldn't dream of coming back to a place that treats me so horribly and has such terrible service."

Amelia muffled her giggles with her hand. She, Caleb, Vera and the server had to stand up and back out of the way as the greeter came with the bin full of unbroken dishes.

He thrust it at Vera. "Shouldn't take too long. A bunch of items broke, and it'll be a while before we have replacements."

Vera accepted the bin. "Is the boss making her pay for that?" she asked, cocking her head at the door to indicate Scarlet.

"He's going to try."

This was relief to Amelia as her paycheque wasn't big enough to pay for broken dishes. It would've taken weeks, or months, and her family needed her money.

When the greeter went back into the restaurant to take his position at the door, Amelia stole a last glance. Scarlet and her mom were walking out with their noses thrust to the ceiling. No doubt, Scarlet would try and get further revenge. Amelia wasn't worried. There was little Scarlet had left to threaten her with.

The rest of Amelia's shift was busy, and she was ready to collapse when she pocketed her pay and grabbed her bag. Her feet took her on autopilot around the side of the building to the street. Getting to the bus fast so she could snag a seat was her priority.

When she stepped on the street, Amelia stopped. Parked at the alley entrance was Malcolm's car, and his gold hair was shining in the evening sun. What was he doing here?

Amelia inhaled and approached his car. He must've heard her footsteps as he lifted his face, turned it to Amelia and smiled.

"I thought you might like a ride home. I'll go if you'd rather ride the bus."

Amelia grinned. The bus was always stuffy, crowded and slow. "Thanks for this. You didn't have to."

"I know," he said, as he pushed the unlock button so Amelia could open the passenger door. "I wanted to."

When Amelia was in the car with her seatbelt fastened, she told Malcolm about Scarlet's scene and resulting ban. It was better to hear it from her than from Scarlet, who would turn herself into the victim.

"It's about time she had consequences," Malcolm said, "especially after I made it clear that she needed to leave you alone."

Amelia lifted her shoulders. "I knew she wouldn't, but I'm not afraid of her. What does she have left to do to me?"

"Nothing," Malcolm said. He took one hand off the steering wheel, thrust it in his pocket and pulled out a large, folded paper. He stretched his arm out, offering it to Amelia. "I couldn't wait to show you this."

Amelia plucked it from his hand and unfolded it. She didn't try to contain her squeal when she read the text on it. "When did you get this?"

"Today. The Government distributed news of the new ration system to the Rich Quarters to appease them before they hear it on the wall screen tomorrow with everyone else."

Amelia bounced on her seat. In less than a day, her biggest goal was going to be accomplished. Mr. Everbee had successfully lobbied the Government to throw out the food laws. "Tomorrow? That's fantastic!"

"At curfew when everyone's home. The new system comes into effect officially on Tuesday morning."

"I can tell Dina we can have a party on Saturday then?" Amelia's best friend would be thrilled.

"Sure."

...

The first people Amelia told were her parents. Dina would have to forgive her. The news was too exciting to keep to herself when she got home, and there was no time to make it to Dina's and back.

Her parents hugged her. Amelia thought she might burst from the giddiness in her veins. She was still wired at lunch the next day and needed all her of self control not to tap her foot while she waited for Dina.

As Dina sat, Amelia pushed the paper from Malcolm across the table. "You can have our party this weekend."

Dina flung her hand over her mouth to muffle her squeal when her eyes landed on it. "I'll come over before to help you get ready," she said. "We can go together and meet the boys. Jack told me he has plans with Malcolm in the morning."

Malcolm hadn't mentioned that, and she'd seen him just the night before. When had he found time to make plans with Jack? "What plans?"

Dina lowered her eyes and picked up her sandwich. "I don't know." She bit the sandwich and chewed slower than Amelia had ever seen someone chew.

What was Dina hiding? "Dina—"

Dina gave a small shake of her head and tilted it in the direction behind Amelia. There were footsteps approaching, which Amelia had assumed belonged to someone heading to another table. With a sigh, she spun around and saw Lucas walking her way. Pulling secrets out of Dina would have to wait.

Amelia raised an eyebrow and waited for Lucas to stop before her. "What are you doing here?"

"Kylie heard from Ethan that you might have news."

Of course she had. Amelia turned back around, plucked the paper off the table and held it up to show Lucas without displaying it to the entire room. "You can tell her it'll be on the screen this evening."

Lucas came closer and bent forward to peer at the paper. If he was happy, he didn't show it. "It actually worked?"

"Yes." Amelia knew why others doubted. She'd done the same.

"I'll tell her to watch," Lucas said.

The Government mandated that everyone watch their wall screens when they came on as they only turned on to show news or Government announcements. Kylie shouldn't need to be told. Amelia rolled her eyes as Lucas walked away. He wasn't a person Amelia talked to often, though they shared classes. She hadn't even recognized him at the first meeting Jack had taken her too. And he always seemed cold and calculating.

Lucas had ruined her opportunity to get Dina's secret from her. As soon as Amelia faced Dina again and ate some of her lunch, her friend dived into her party-planning ideas. She gave Amelia no chance to change the subject.

After school, Amelia told Jack what Vera had said about stopping deliveries with Caleb and asked what Jack's plans were with Malcolm. She assumed someone, either Dina or Ethan, had told him about their victory over the food laws.

Jack waved a hand. "He said he needs my opinion on something he wants to buy. Before you ask, no, I don't know what it is."

Since when were Jack and Malcolm friends that went shopping together? Whatever Malcolm was shopping for had to be something boring, or he might've asked Amelia or at least mentioned it to her when he drove her home. She tried to forget about it as she walked to her apartment, which proved a difficult task.

Later that night, a few minutes after curfew, the wall screen in Amelia's apartment came on. She and her parents sat on the couch, her mom and dad holding hands, and read the screen when the announcement of the new ration system came.

"Citizens," the voiceover said. It was always a voiceover, never an image of a person speaking. "Effective at eight AM tomorrow, the food laws will be replaced with a ration system. Scan your ID cards at market entrances to see how much your household qualifies for. This amount will be confirmed at checkout. Everyone is entitled to buy more, or non-rationed foods, at cost. Food may also now be shared. Refunds and reselling without a permit are still prohibited."

Amelia had never dreamed she'd hear those words. She chased a goal, knowing it was possible yet fearing she would never achieve it.

On Tuesday morning when Amelia opened her apartment door to leave for school, she stepped on a piece of paper. There was one at every door stretching down the hallway. She retrieved it from under her foot. Printed on it was the list of foods falling under the ration system. It listed basics like vegetables, bread, beans and fats. Salt and pepper were the only seasonings listed, and tomatoes, apples, pears and bananas the sole fruits. The amounts differed per age group and between sexes and were lower, though not by a huge margin, than the numbers Kelsie and Ethan had come up with. *This was the tweaking Mr. Everbee talked about.* Regardless, this was a better system than the old.

Chapter 38

Amelia put the paper on the table in her apartment for her parents to read. They would still need to spend money on food, but hopefully to a lesser extent. It all depended on what the prices were for luxury goods, which was the label for everything not on the ration list.

Amelia also needed to decide on what she would bring to the party on Saturday. Dina was insisting everyone bring a snack as it would be cheaper than going to a restaurant and was the first time that they could share food. She was also keeping the location secret from Amelia and wouldn't divulge any details, no matter how hard Amelia tried to pry them from her. Amelia stopped asking on Wednesday.

She spent the rest of the school week, when she was home, analysing the food in her apartment and deciding what to bring. After a lot of deliberation, Amelia settled on a layered dip and carrot sticks. Her friends, apart from Malcolm, would be happy to eat anything they didn't have to make, and its varying hues would look appetizing if nothing else.

On Friday evening, after her homework and supper, Amelia got to work. Her mom had approved the ingredients Amelia wanted to use and offered to help. So, Amelia and her mom chopped and mashed canned beans and vegetables.

"How are you feeling about tomorrow?" her mom asked.

Amelia kept her focus on the beans she was mashing with a fork. "I don't know. A mix of excited and confused. I wish Dina would've given me some details other than to wear something nice and bring a snack."

"You've done enough planning over the past few weeks," her mom said. "Let Dina worry about the details. Sometimes just showing up to an event is enough."

Amelia tried to take her mom's advice as they finished the prep for her dip and assembled the layers. When it was finished, Amelia pressed the lid on the container and nestled it in the fridge. She could be a party guest this time with no input on planning, but it felt like Dina was either hiding something or doing a poor job of trying to take responsibility off Amelia.

Amelia struggled to turn her thoughts off and spent the night tossing and turning. In the morning, she dragged herself out of bed and ate a breakfast of toast. She was still in her pajamas, though she'd brushed her hair, when Dina showed up wearing a purple dress and her hair pinned up.

"It's a good thing I got here a few minutes early," Dina said as she set down her bag.

Amelia groaned. "I didn't know what to wear."

"You must have something in your closet," Dina said. She reached for and grabbed Amelia's wrist. "Let's go dig through it."

"Show Dina the dress Kelsie picked out for you," Amelia's mom piped up as Dina dragged Amelia across the living room.

"Yes! Show me!"

Dina dropped Amelia's wrist as they stepped into Amelia's room. Amelia rubbed it with her other hand as she walked to her closet to flick through the hangers. "It's in here somewhere."

Amelia had buried it at the back. The sparkly blue dress was gorgeous, but there were no occasions in her life to wear it. She found the hanger and pulled it out.

Dina squealed and jumped. "You have to wear it!"

Amelia held it up to her torso and looked in her mirror. "It isn't too fancy?"

"No. It's perfect. Put it on."

Amelia shooed Dina out of her room. Some things required privacy, even from best friends. She re-opened her door when she had the dress on, though she couldn't zip the back all the way up. Amelia lifted her hair and turned. "Can you zip it?"

She felt Dina's hand brush her back, heard the zipper move and felt the dress close. "Done," Dina said.

"You really don't think it's too much?"

"Nope. You look exquisite. But your hair and makeup need doing. I'll help."

There was little Amelia could do to stop Dina. And she did like the excuse to dip into her small makeup supply. When Dina finished pinning her hair, Amelia gathered her cosmetics. It had been a while since she'd put on a full face. Thankfully, her skills weren't too rusty, and she only had to redo the mascara once.

With her makeup on and hair pinned, Amelia glanced at her reflection. She was still there, but she almost didn't recognize herself. The girl in the mirror looked like she could pass for wealthy and have an address in one the rich Quarters.

Dina clasped her hands and hopped up and down. "It's perfect! Bring a jacket to sit on when we ride the bus."

Amelia followed Dina across the living room and snatched her jacket off the hook on the wall. "Bye, Mom. Bye, Dad," she said as she retrieved her dip from the fridge and stuck it in her bag.

She hardly heard her parents' reply, telling her to have fun, as Dina ushered her into the hall and to the elevator.

"The stairs would be faster," Amelia said. She watched the floor tracker tick slowly. "And more private."

"It's easier to lug stuff in the elevator."

Amelia pressed her lips together and kept her eyes from rolling. There was no changing Dina's mind, and Dina had already pressed the call button. So, Amelia waited for the elevator and rode it down with her friend and the neighbours from higher floors.

When they reached the ground floor and got outside, Amelia followed Dina to the bus stop. It wasn't a surprise that Dina led her to the route heading north. There were few party venues in the Apartment Districts, and none that weren't decrepit.

Amelia watched Dina, who sat between her and the aisle, for a sign of when they were getting off. The scenery out the window grew less and less familiar as the ride stretched on. The bus passed through Quarter 3's main commercial street and turned onto a road lined with patches of grass and flowers with concrete paths running through the beds. It pulled into a depot at the edge of the greenery with a paved road that looped back the way they'd come.

"Come on," Dina said as she stood and lifted her bag. "This is our stop."

Amelia got up and grabbed her jacket. She'd sat on it on Dina's request and now a layer of grime and dust coated it. Amelia held it with one hand, as far from her dress as her arm reached. When she and Dina got off the bus, Amelia shook her jacket, sending dust flying into the air. The breeze blew it away from Amelia, and she waited for it to dissipate before shoving her jacket in her bag. With that done, she looked around. "Where are we?"

"In the entrance to a park," Dina said. "It was Kelsie's idea to have the party here. It's just a couple minutes walk."

"Show the way," Amelia said. She'd never thought to ask Kelsie about the party location.

As she and Dina walked, Amelia gazed around and took a deep breath of the crisp, fresh air. She wasn't used to seeing so many flowers and plants. On a typical day, people must've filled the space, but this day it was empty and quiet.

"Did you pay to reserve this?" Amelia asked. It seemed irresponsible for Dina to have done that.

"No. Malcolm's dad got it for us for free," Dina said as she and Amelia rounded a corner and an enormous metal fence with an arch entry came into view.

"This way," Dina said as she veered to the arch. "We're almost there."

...

The arch opened into a lush, manicured park. There was a massive gazebo in the distance and a fountain in the centre where the paved path led. Ethan, Kelsie and Jack were standing near a table someone had set up next to the fountain. Amelia didn't see Malcolm anywhere.

Dina pulled Amelia over to their friends and deposited her in front of Kelsie. Amelia gave Kelsie a wave and handed Dina her dip as Dina walked to the table.

"You're wearing the dress I picked out!" Kelsie squealed.

"And you're wearing yours." Kelsie's pink gown was glittering in the sunlight, and it made Amelia feel a bit less overdressed. She looked radiant, and Ethan's gaze was glued to her as he approached.

"This dress is lucky," Kelsie said. She raised her wrist and thrust it out to Amelia. "See what Ethan gave me?"

Amelia leaned in. On Kelsie's wrist was a thin band of silver studded with small, blue gemstones. "You said yes?"

Ethan beamed. "I didn't get the complete question out before she did."

"Congrats you two," Amelia said. "And good luck." It was poor form to congratulate an engagement without wishing luck. The most expensive engagement gifts and elaborate proposals weren't guarantees of accepted Courtship applications.

"Thanks," Kelsie said. "Come get some food with me. I'll be right back, Ethan."

Once again, one of Amelia's friends was leading her somewhere. Amelia let Kelsie hook her arm and walk her to the table laden with food. Dina had added Amelia's dip as well as whatever she'd brought before finding Jack's side.

Kelsie said picked a strawberry off a fruit tray. "I thought you'd be happy with the news, but you look down. What's wrong?"

Amelia eyed the fruit tray. Either Kelsie or Malcolm, or both, must've brought it, considering the price of fruit. She plucked some grapes off the stem and cradled the bunch in her hand as she munched one. "It's weird now that you and Ethan are engaged. I feel like the odd one out. And Malcolm isn't even here."

Kelsie patted Amelia on the arm and popped her strawberry into her mouth. Amelia stuck another grape in her own mouth and chewed. It had been a long time since she'd had fresh fruit, and she'd forgotten how sweet it could be.

"First of all," Kelsie said when she'd swallowed. "Ethan and I have no idea if we'll get to have a wedding. We're just enjoying the possibility. Not everyone is as optimistic as Dina and Jack. Second, Malcolm is here. He told me to send you to the gazebo."

"Why?" Amelia asked. Surely, he could've greeted her with the others.

Kelsie gave Amelia a shrug. "You'll have to go find out."

Amelia could've ignored Kelsie's instructions and waited for Malcolm to come and find her. But she wasn't that stubborn or petty, and her curiosity fueled her to take the path to the gazebo.

It was even more massive up close, and the dais in its centre was higher than Amelia was tall. She climbed the steps. There was no way around the structure as shrubs and bushes stretched outward from its sides. Fighting a path through them would ruin her dress and the greenery.

When she reached the top and crossed it was when she finally spotted Malcolm. He was getting to his feet and turning around from where he'd been sitting on the steps going down the other side. His hair shone like polished gold in the sunlight.

"You're here," he said, giving her a wide grin and climbing up the stairs to offer her his hand.

Chapter 39

Amelia took Malcolm's hand and descended the steps at his side. "Kelsie told me to meet you here." The stairs they climbed down opened to another half of the park with a winding path through colourful flowerbeds dotted with benches.

He dipped his head. "Sorry for making her the messenger. I wanted some alone time with you, and I didn't want to make a big deal to get it."

Malcolm was holding tight to her hand. On another day, or in a more public space, Amelia would've pulled away, but there were no witnesses here. Why shouldn't she enjoy it while she could? "I get it. Things are different now that Kelsie and Ethan are engaged. Doesn't it make you feel left out?"

Malcolm steered her down the path to one of the benches around a turn and turned his head to look at her. "Seeing our friends have a chance to get married is awkward for you?"

Our friends. Amelia hadn't noticed when Malcolm became so integrated into their group. That was another complication they'd have to navigate after Clinic Day. She'd assumed that without her Malcolm's ties to her friends would dissolve. What if she'd been wrong? Kelsie lived with him, after all, and he and Jack seemed to have grown close.

Amelia sighed. "If they get approved, I'll be the single friend. They'll get wrapped up in building their own lives, and you'll return to the life you had before we met. We must face it, Malcolm. Whatever we have has an expiration date."

"You mean Clinic Day."

"It's coming, and I'm dreading it," Amelia's voice broke, and her body trembled. She couldn't look at him. "It might be best if we end things now."

"Have a seat, and let's talk about this," Malcolm said.

They'd reached the bench around a turn in the path. A geometric topiary bush blocked the view of the gazebo. They were alone.

Amelia lowered herself onto the bench, and Malcolm perched beside her. He ran his thumb over the back of her hand and made eye contact. "Do you want to stop seeing each other?"

"No." There was nothing Amelia wanted less. "But—"

The corners of Malcolm's mouth tipped up, and he removed his hand from hers as he got off the bench and dropped to one knee before her. "Good. I don't want to lose you."

Amelia's heart thumped in her chest, and she clasped her hands in her lap to still them. What was he doing? She didn't need him to beg for her to stay. If it was possible, she would do it. Yet the world they lived in had countless barriers, and she couldn't fight them. "We don't have much of a choice."

Malcolm ducked his head and reached into his pocket. He pulled something out and concealed it between his hands, shielding it from Amelia's view. "There's always a choice," he said, bringing his gaze back onto her face.

Amelia saw Malcolm swallow. He was clutching the object in his hands with enough force to break something more delicate, and he was chewing on his bottom lip.

"I don't want to rush you into anything you're not ready for, but…"

Amelia blinked to keep her tears at bay. She knew he was about to say but next year they could try dating again. He didn't need to make such a show out of it or give her any promises he wouldn't or couldn't keep. "But what?"

Amelia watched him close his eyes and inhale a deep breath. His hairline was sweating, and he stopped chewing on his lip. When he opened his eyes, there was a certainty in them, like he'd made up his mind and gathered his courage.

"I'm going to ask you something important. There's no pressure for you to give a specific answer."

Her heart continued to pound in her chest. Her palms were sweating, so she separated her hands and rested each on the bench, trying to wipe off the moisture without obviously rubbing. "Ask me."

Malcolm shifted his right hand, giving Amelia a glimpse of a black velvet box as his fingers found the latch and he flicked it open.

Amelia stared. Inside the box, nestled in the lining, was a gold ring with a large, red centre stone circled by smaller, clear ones. Framing the ring was a matching bracelet, with small, alternating red and clear stones covering its length, minus the clasp.

"You haven't necessarily changed your mind," Malcolm said. "Still, I need to take my chance. Amelia, will you be my Courtship partner?"

Amelia flung her hands over her mouth, though no noise escaped her lips. Her eyes watered, and she made no move to wipe them. Had he really asked her what she thought she heard?

Amelia could tell Malcolm was trying to keep his face neutral as he waited for her answer. Yet there was a furrow to his brow and a downward turn to the corners of his mouth. Did he expect her to say no? Amelia closed her eyes and inhaled. She couldn't leave him kneeling without an answer. The fear and repulsion she'd always imagined having if faced with this situation was absent. Her brain screamed at her to hurry up and say something.

Amelia lowered her hands from her face and rested one on Malcolm's knee. Regardless of whatever answer he expected, she could, and would, only give a truthful one. "Yes."

The tension on Malcolm's face disappeared, and he beamed. The afternoon sun shone on his hair, casting him in gold. Amelia wanted to run her fingers through it, to see if it was as soft as it appeared.

"Truly?"

Amelia grinned. "Yes, I'll apply for a Courtship with you."

She placed her hands on the bench to brace herself, leaned down to bring her face to his and kissed him.

"Wait a minute," he said in between kisses.

Amelia pulled back, sat upright on the bench and cocked an eyebrow. Was he wishing he hadn't asked her?

Malcolm picked up the ring in the still-open box. "Give me your hand."

Amelia lifted her left hand and held it out. Malcolm slid the ring on her finger, and the gemstone sparkled in the sunlight. He fastened the bracelet around her wrist, and she gazed, mesmerized, at the glittering gems. "They're beautiful."

"Jack helped me pick the set out this morning. That's why I didn't meet you at your apartment."

Dina's insistence on helping her get ready made a lot more sense now. "Did you send Dina to help me?"

Malcolm laughed. "I didn't have to. It was her idea."

"One more question," Amelia said, running her right-hand thumb over her bracelet. "What are the stones?" Most people in Apartment Districts that bought Courtship proposal presents bought stainless steel or silver jewelry with manufactured stones. Real gemstones and gold were rare and expensive. The Government kept a vault full, collected from citizens for various, not always voluntary, reasons, usually to pay fines or debts. The jewellers repurposed them into new pieces.

"Rubies and diamonds. I hope that's not weird for you."

Rubies, like her last name that she might not have for much longer. "It's perfect."

...

Amelia and Malcolm returned to the party. Their friends had eaten most of the food and were sitting together by the fountain. It was Dina who rose first and ran to Amelia. "What did you say?"

Amelia lifted her hand to display her glittering gems. "I said yes."

Dina screamed and flung her arms around Amelia. "I'm so excited. We'll get to wedding plan together."

Amelia didn't want to ruin her best friend's excitement, even though she wasn't ready to dive into wedding planning, and their budgets would be different. "That's assuming we get a Courtship."

"You worry too much," Dina said as she broke the hug and grabbed Amelia's wrist. "This is supposed to be a happy day."

Amelia got the feeling, as Dina thrust her into the attention of her other friends, that this party was more of an opportunity for Malcolm to propose and her friends to celebrate it than for them to revel in the end of the food laws. None of them were surprised when Amelia showed off her gems. They'd all been in on it and had kept it secret from her. Amelia wasn't sure whether to be impressed or annoyed.

When the party was over, and the food gone, Malcolm insisted on driving Amelia home. She still had to work the next day, but she wondered for how much longer. What would life married to a wealthy man be like?

Amelia resolved to focus on one thing at a time. First was telling her parents, and next was readying the Courtship application. Only when she had the verdict on that would she devout energy to the future.

Malcolm insisted on going to her apartment with her. Until Clinic Day, her jewelry was protection enough from prying eyes. However, they still couldn't get away with much affection in public. Holding hands in the elevator and walking down her hallway was as much as they could risk.

Amelia's parents were sitting on the couch when she walked in with Malcolm. Her dad's eyes widened, and her mom wrinkled her eyebrows. If they'd known about Malcolm's proposal, they were adept at feigning surprise.

Amelia let go of Malcolm's hand to take her shoes off and put down her bag. "Mom, Dad," she said as she came up to them. "We have something to tell you."

Amelia saw her dad glance at her mom, and in the corner of her eye, she spotted Malcolm move to stand beside her, and she felt his hand brushing hers.

"What is it?" her mom asked.

Malcolm gave Amelia's hand a squeeze. She inhaled deep. "Malcolm and I are going to apply for a Courtship."

"Is that what you both want?" her dad asked.

Amelia knew he had reason to be hesitant. She'd been vocal about never marrying. "Yes."

"I'd never force Amelia into anything she didn't want," Malcolm said. "This is her choice as much as mine."

Amelia's mom got off the couch and hugged Malcolm. "I wish you both luck and happiness."

Amelia tried not to laugh at Malcolm's awkward attempt to hug her mom. His parents were out often and didn't seem overly affectionate. It made Amelia wonder what Malcolm would be like as a parent if they had a child.

"Thanks," Amelia said.

Her mom broke away from Malcolm and came over to hug Amelia. If she had a kid, Amelia wanted them to know love and affection. She'd do whatever she could to ensure that.

...

Amelia left her jewelry at home when she went to work the next day. It wasn't that she was going to keep Malcolm's proposal a secret, but the ring and bracelet were too expensive and delicate to wear when she had to do labour with her hands.

She told Caleb, Vera and Iris the news during the lull between lunch and supper. Getting their congratulations and wishes of luck was different than when her friends had done the same. Her coworkers hadn't known ahead of time, and they shared in her surprise and excitement about it, which was a nice change.

Her shift went by without much incident, and without a Scarlet sighting. It was the last calm day Amelia would have for a long time.

Malcolm was waiting to drive her home again. When Amelia got in his car, she told him she left her jewelry at home before he could notice and ask.

"I'm not upset," he said. "You should keep it safe."

"Soon I won't have to worry about it anymore. If we get married, I won't need this job." The idea of leaving her parents to fend for themselves while she lived off Malcolm's money saddened her. Could she really give up her independence like that and rely completely on Malcolm? Regardless of the answer to that question, she didn't want to.

"I know I have rich parents, but we'll need our own money. It wouldn't hurt for you to keep working if you want to."

Amelia wanted to contribute as much as Malcolm to whatever life they got to have together. The fact that Malcolm didn't expect her to stay at home eased some of her nerves. She knew his mother worked, yet many rich citizens had a reputation of living off family fortunes. Amelia hadn't wanted to join their ranks. Spending all her time idle in a house would plummet her mood.

"I suppose if I leave school, I can ask for more shifts," she said. That's what she would've done if she were marrying someone like Blake McKelvey who had little money, and why it was legal to leave school with a Courtship acceptance.

"We can finish school," Malcolm said. "There's no law saying we have to leave early."

School without Dina at lunch? Amelia had assumed she'd have to endure that anyway. She hadn't imagined being in a Courtship and still a student. Few, if any, Apartment District citizens did that. Changing her last name in marriage would get her reassigned to a different class group, the one Ethan and Jack would be leaving; it would be akin to being a new student. Or she'd switch to Malcolm's school where the standards were higher, the classes smaller, and there was tuition to pay. "It'll just be different if I stay." As many things would be.

Chapter 40

Amelia's life became busier after that work shift. When she wasn't doing homework, she devoted her evenings to gathering medical documents on her and her family, as far back as she could get records. She spent many hours after school in the local Government office filling in forms and requests for documents.

It would've been easier if Courtship applicants could keep their own records, but the Government only loaned them out for a few days at a time. It meant Amelia had to make handwritten lists of details relevant to the Courtship application. Her parents were at least helpful in that regard as they knew what information the form would ask for.

On the Saturday afternoons between Malcolm's proposal and Clinic Day, Amelia and Malcolm met up, sometimes at Darla's, other times in his Quarter, with paper and pens, making lists of information they needed about the other for the application.

Those occasions brought stress for Amelia and served as the only time she got to see Malcolm. They always felt too short as Saturday mornings remained her shopping time with her mom. It was one such Saturday, at Darla's, when Amelia was sipping on water, wondering whether she was ever going to finish her family tree so she could compare it to Malcolm's. Having a common ancestor in the past five generations would disqualify them.

Malcolm sat across from her, having just arrived. "Not making any headway?"

"It's slow. There should be a faster way."

Malcolm reached across the table and patted her hand. "I bet someday they'll automate it or run names through a database instead of making applicants collect it."

"I wish they'd done it already," Amelia groaned. "It's so hard to get records."

"I'm sorry. I didn't think you'd have to go through all this stress."

Malcom had completed his family tree long before. The Government offices in the rich Quarters worked at a much quicker and more efficient pace. Amelia also suspected their records were better organised and detailed.

Amelia had gotten records of her great-great-grandparents and was working on their parents' generation, the final one she needed. The problem was she had to go through a thick stack of papers to find all the names from birth documents or marriage ones, a job made more difficult when some of the papers only listed first initials.

Malcolm got up and walked around the table to sit beside Amelia. He took half of the papers from the stack and pulled a highlighter out of the stash spread out on the table. "It'll go faster if we both look."

Amelia picked up the other half, and together they went through the papers and filled in names on the chart. It took up that Saturday afternoon and a couple more, and Amelia had to file extension requests on the documents, and use part of her paycheque to fund them, but the process wasn't as daunting as doing it by herself.

While she and Malcolm poured over the documents, Amelia learned more about her family history, and Malcolm told her some of his. It made her eager for the future; she wanted to share more with Malcolm and have experiences with him.

When they finished her family tree, and swapped information they both needed for the Courtship application, Amelia focused on her standard Clinic Day preparations. Every year, during the few weeks leading up to it, her parents splurged on fruits and vitamins. This year, with the ration system, they used the money that in the past would've gone to their groceries for the week. Amelia ate meals stocked with fruits and vegetables and swallowed vitamins on her way out the door every morning. She didn't know whether it made a difference in the results, but her parents swore by it.

Amelia was also in the best shape of her life from walking home with Jack every day and lugging bins of dishes at work. There was little possibility of the Government rejecting her application based on her fitness.

At lunch during the week, Dina babbled about her excitement over Clinic Day, a sentiment few shared.

"How are you so optimistic?" Amelia asked one day as Dina retold her wedding plans for what felt like the hundredth time.

Dina set down her sandwich. She was eating her normal diet, not trying to nutrient load as Amelia's family did. "If I let myself think I might not marry Jack, I'll spiral into depression, and that helps nothing."

Amelia wished she could replicate her best friend's positive outlook. Yet every night when she went to bed, the worst-case scenario ran through her mind, and she tossed and turned in bed. If her Courtship application came back with a rejection, she'd never see Malcolm again. It would be worse than them parting ways with their own volition.

Still, Amelia tried to distract herself from the negative thoughts. Keeping busy with schoolwork and finalizing details with Malcolm helped, as did her job. Running back and forth carrying heavy bins left her too tired to dwell.

This new busyness was an exhausting routine, and Amelia didn't put on as much weight as she did in previous years when her parents splurged on food. She'd still look like a starved-thin Apartment District kid on Clinic Day, yet there was nothing to prevent it. At least her clothes would still fit comfortably.

When the day arrived, Amelia threw on her best pair of jeans and a blouse. She dipped into her makeup supply for some blush to colour her cheeks and tied her hair up. Her family didn't have their appointments until the afternoon as they were in alphabetical order, so Amelia had no need to rush. She almost envied Ethan, Jack and Malcolm. They'd be long done with their appointments before her family even arrived at the clinic. Still, Amelia and her parents left well in advance of their appointment. Being early had no consequences, but being late would bring a hefty fine.

...

Amelia stood tall and still beside her parents as they checked in. It was important to give the staff no indications of poor condition or nerves. She followed the nurse and her parents down the hall, where she and her parents each stepped into a separate room. When she'd been little, the nurse had sent her and her mom in together. For the past few years, Amelia had gone alone.

Amelia went through the tests and answered the questions from the nurse that entered her room. It was always tiring being poked and examined, but she maintained her posture and kept her mouth closed when she could to prevent yawning.

When the nurse finished her assessments, she set down her clipboard and looked at Amelia. "I'm going to ask what I ask every sixteen-year-old. Are you interested in applying for a Courtship?"

"Yes." This was the part she was more nervous about than her medical tests.

The nurse removed a form off a tear-away notepad and handed it to Amelia. It was double sided and covered in boxes requesting information. "Fill this in and slide it in the box by the nurses' station. Results will come within a few days. Best of luck." That message delivered, she exited the room, leaving the door open for Amelia.

In the hallway, Amelia sat on one of the vacant chairs and joined other teenagers and young adults in filling in Courtship forms. She grabbed a pamphlet off a nearby table to use as a solid writing surface.

The form was long and detailed. Amelia had to use her notes she'd compiled with Malcolm and slid into her bag the night prior to complete all the boxes. By the time she finished and slid the form into the labelled box, her hand was cramped.

Her parents were waiting for her outside. They weren't a family that discussed the events of Clinic Day after it was over, which Amelia didn't mind. Rehashing it wasn't high on her list of necessary activities. There was always a fear that one of her parents would get a letter describing negative results and an order to go to the End Camp. So far, they'd been lucky.

Instead of going home, Amelia made excuses to her parents and headed to Catsy's. Jack had mentioned on one of their walks home that he and Ethan would be there, and Amelia had no desire to worry in her apartment. Nor was Dina's optimism bearable in Amelia's current state, and she couldn't go see Malcolm.

Ethan and Jack were sitting at a table with glasses of water. Amelia took a chair and flagged a server over to order a glass of lemonade. It was a justified splurge considering her nerves.

"I'm so glad it's over," Amelia said as the server left to get her drink.

Ethan gave her a nod as he gulped his water.

"Sure, the appointment is over, but the waiting's just started," Jack said.

He had the beginnings of dark circles under his eyes and was wringing his hands that had raw cuticles. It looked to Amelia like he hadn't slept the night before. "You're worried about your application?" He and Dina had been certain their application would be approved. Now that the day had come, it was easy to be scared. Amelia had her own apprehension.

"Aren't you two worried?"

Jack meant her and Ethan. "Sure," Amelia said, while Ethan dipped his head again. "Malcolm and I might be worse off than if he'd never asked me."

"Kelsie and I don't have high expectations, with her being a foster kid," Ethan said. "We did all the prep, and we'll see what happens."

Amelia guzzled her lemonade when it came. Maybe she could rid herself of anxiety by getting a sugar rush. Unfortunately, Catsy's lemonade didn't have much sugar in it. "I'm trying not to stress over it."

"It's hard not to," Jack said. "If bad news comes, I won't blame you for choosing Dina over me."

Amelia set down her glass. Jack had directed this at her, as she was Dina's best friend. Ethan had no ties to Dina. "Who says I'd have to choose?"

"Could be awkward is all."

Amelia had hoped that wouldn't be the case, but maybe Jack had a point. She had joined her friends to have something to focus on other than her own worries, and now they were multiplied, and the mood of the group dampened. "All this gloom is making me more stressed. Let's get some food."

Jack waved the server over, and they placed orders for sandwiches. The meal increased everyone's spirits, even though there were people missing. Malcolm and Kelsie had gone to a clinic in the rich Quarter they lived in and were likely at his house. And Dina had gone home to worry with her parents, as the law forbade her from seeing Jack until their Courtship was approved, if it was, as it forbade Amelia from seeing Malcolm and Ethan from seeing Kelsie.

Jack deflated and tensed his shoulders. Amelia imagined she looked similar. The fact that she might receive a letter saying she couldn't see Malcolm again did not help her mood. Ethan must've been feeling the same as he flashed Amelia a smile that didn't reach his eyes.

When the food was gone and paid for, Jack left for home.

Amelia lingered with Ethan on the street outside Catsy's. "If one, or both, of us gets bad news, we'll stay friends, won't we?" she asked.

Her question got a genuine smile from Ethan. "Definitely."

Amelia wouldn't be friendless. Dina and Ethan, at minimum, would help her through her heartbreak if it came. And she'd do the same for them, Kelsie and Jack. She and Ethan walked away from Catsy's to get out of the foot traffic. "Is it bugging you that you can't see Kelsie?"

"It is," Ethan said. "But we told each other what we needed to yesterday. She said if we get a rejection, she'll go back to Arlo Fenn and help him run the Rebel Cause."

Amelia hadn't done the same with Malcolm. The day before Clinic Day, she'd spent at work and then preparing. If she was being honest, she didn't want to give Malcolm a goodbye speech; doing that would've meant facing the possibility of a rejection, and avoiding it was easier on her psyche. "At least she has a plan." Even if it wasn't what Kelsie would've chosen for herself. "That's more than I have."

Chapter 41

Amelia ate supper with her parents that evening and retreated to her room afterwards. She got out paper, an envelope and a pen. She wrote Malcolm everything she hadn't been brave enough to say in person. If the worst came, he'd have her letter to remember her by. If the best came, she wouldn't send it.

There was no news on her Courtship application the next day, though her and her parents' medical tests came back clear. That was always a relief; they didn't have enough money to treat any serious disease, and no one sent to the End Camp ever left alive.

Amelia tried to go about her life as normal and kept up her walks home with Jack. He and Dina hadn't heard news either that day, and Amelia knew at lunch that not being able to see Jack was eating at Dina from her frazzled appearance and lack of usual optimism. It was the same with Jack, though he tried to hide his anxiety and did a better job than Dina.

Being in a constant cycle of school, walking home and then doing her homework started to suffocate Amelia. Her apartment felt tiny, and she had nothing to do during the week and couldn't see Malcolm. The food laws were gone, and Clinic Day was in the past; waiting in limbo threatened to drain her sanity. At least when the news came, good or bad, she could move on.

The first piece came three days after Clinic Day. Amelia, feeling like a lifeless machine walking through the motions, grabbed her lunch tray, walked to her and Dina's table and sat. Her eyes weren't focused enough to see Dina's exuberant expression.

"Mellie!"

Amelia blinked and looked up. Dina must've called her name multiple times, but only the last had sunk in.

"Jack and I are getting married!" Dina slid a creased letter with an official Government letterhead and a small card – what the Government called Courtship papers – across the table. "When I opened my door this morning, these were there in an envelope, and so was Jack."

Amelia plastered on a fake smile she hoped looked genuine. "Congrats."

Dina snatched the papers back, tucked them into her pocket and patted Amelia's hand. "Yours will come soon."

Amelia had no high hopes for that. It felt like the Government was toying with her by delaying sending her a letter. She didn't know whether to think the long response time was an indication they were reviewing it for an excuse to reject it.

After school that day, Amelia let Jack tell her his news. She didn't want to spoil it by mentioning she'd already heard it from Dina, though he likely knew. And Amelia offered him her congratulations. He was glowing and looked more rested than he had on Clinic Day and the days following. Good news tended to lift invisible weights from people.

The fourth day after Clinic Day, Amelia still had no news. But Kylie was at Lucas's locker with her hands on his chest. She and Lucas each held Courtship papers, which evaded Amelia. Of course those two got an acceptance; they were a perfect match.

Amelia skirted around them on her way to class. Lucas rarely spoke to her, but Kylie often had something she felt needed said. This day was no different. Kylie stepped away from Lucas and beelined into Amelia's path.

"You heard any news about you and rich boy yet?"

Amelia tried to step around Kylie, who mirrored her movements.

"Too bad," Kylie said with an exaggerated, fake pout, taking Amelia's silence as the no it was. "If it's taking this long, it'll be a rejection."

"Leave her alone, Kylie," Lucas said. "The waiting is stressful enough."

Amelia glanced at Lucas and flashed him a small smile. That was the kindest thing he'd done for her, and she hadn't thought him capable.

Kylie rolled her eyes and leaned closer to Amelia. "It's just a pity that you're the last of your friends to find out, don't you think?"

Amelia stumbled as she stepped back. "You mean Ethan heard?" Was it good news or bad?

"He told me this morning."

Amelia pushed past Kylie, ignored her complaints and ran. She didn't have a clear memory of his locker's exact location, so she slowed her pace to a walk when she got to his section of the school. There were few minutes left before classes started, and the halls were busy with students on route to classrooms. Amelia saw no sign of Ethan and assumed he was already in his first-period class.

She turned to run back to her own classroom while she was early enough not to sprint. That's when she saw Ethan straightening up from collecting an object that had fallen to the floor. His back was to Amelia, and he held a book in his right hand and used his left to brush dust off it before jamming it into his bag. He turned around and jumped. "What are you doing here?"

"Kylie told me you got news, and I had to ask you."

"Heh," he flashed a lopsided grin. "Sorry. I didn't think she'd try to rub it in."

Amelia closed her eyes and mentally counted to five. She didn't have time for Ethan's apologies. "Forget it. Was the news good or bad?"

Ethan reached into his pocket and produced a small card and Government letter like the papers Kylie and Lucas had been carrying, and the ones Jack and Dina had shown her. "I haven't seen Kelsie yet."

Amelia hugged Ethan. She'd been happy for Dina and Jack, but their documents had seemed like more of a formality. Ethan and Kelsie had such doubts and low hopes that their good news made Amelia's heart leap. "Aren't you pleased?"

"Yeah, and overwhelmed. I want to make her happy, and I'm not sure how I'll manage."

Amelia rolled her eyes. "Kelsie doesn't need extravagance. She'll be content with wherever you both end up."

"Regardless, I want to give her something better than the bare minimum."

...

Kelsie was lucky to have Ethan, Amelia thought, as she sprinted to class. She was sure they'd meet up after school to discuss their good fortune. Amelia ached from knowing she couldn't do the same with Malcolm.

That evening after supper, she dug her written letter to Malcolm out of her desk drawer and stuck it in an envelope. Her hand shook as she wrote out his address, and tears pooled in her eyes. She only wiped them when they started running down her cheeks. With the letter addressed and sealed, she flung it on her bed, sat beside it and cried with her face cupped in her hands.

Her mom stood on the threshold of Amelia's door and stick her head in. "What's wrong, sweetheart?"

"It's not fair," Amelia sniffed. "Everyone else has their Courtship papers, and I haven't heard."

Her mom came and sat next to her, placing an arm around Amelia's torso. Amelia leaned into her mom's side, and her mom wrapped her other arm around her. "I know this isn't going to help, but it's only been four days. There are a lot of applicants in the City, and not everyone can get news at once. You need to be patient."

Amelia swiped more tears with the back of her hand. "Maybe it would've been better if we hadn't applied. Then we'd know we could date again in a few months."

"Do you think Malcolm wanted to wait?"

He didn't. Amelia knew it in the way his face brightened when she'd agreed to his proposal. Malcolm had been willing to risk never seeing her again for a chance at getting married. "No."

"Whether you get a rejection letter or not, going after the one you love is always better than not."

"Even if we can never see each other again?"

"It wouldn't be fair to either of you to date a few months every year. There's no future in that."

Her mom was right. That didn't make it easier for her to sleep that night or go through another day with no news. It was a Saturday, removing school as a way to distract her. At least she had the weekly shopping with her mom, though that only lasted a few hours at most.

Amelia got out of bed as late as she could get away with. She heard her parents muffled voices coming from the kitchen, and after a glance at the clock, showing it was mid morning, Amelia rolled out of bed. Her mom must've not been in a rush, so she would've woken Amelia up.

She threw on a t-shirt and jeans, finger-combed her hair and went to find some breakfast. On the kitchen counter was a letter addressed to her from the

Government. Heart pounding in her chest and fingers trembling, Amelia picked it up and tore it open, her rumbling stomach forgotten for the moment.

Amelia dropped the envelope to the ground, unfolded the letter and squealed when she found a card tucked into the letter. *It was here, and she had to find Malcolm.* She flew back into her room for a nicer looking top, flung the one she was wearing to the floor, used an actual brush on her hair and went back into her kitchen.

Her parents entered with wide eyes. "Someone just dropped off your letter," her dad said. "Was it good or bad news?"

Amelia held up her Courtship papers, feeling herself grinning. "I have to go see Malcolm. Sorry for missing shopping, Mom."

Her parents were embracing her before she finished her sentence. "Take your time," her mom said. "I'll bring your dad with me."

"We're both happy for you, sweetheart," her dad said.

"Thanks," Amelia said. She wiggled out of their arms and grabbed an apple for breakfast. It was easy enough to eat on the stairs and the bus.

Amelia felt like she was floating as she went downstairs. She'd believed for so long that she and Malcolm were destined to fail, though deep down she'd always hoped. Now her heart had overtaken her other senses, and nothing would ruin her joy. Not Kylie or even Scarlet.

Her mood dampened a bit when she got outside, and Malcolm's car wasn't parked on the street. Amelia told herself that meant little. He might not have gotten his mail yet. Her showing up at his doorstep would be a welcome surprise.

The bus was crowded, and Amelia snagged one of the last seats, clutching her bag tight. She couldn't risk losing her Courtship papers. Getting replacements would be an expensive inconvenience and ruin her surprise.

The bus took its time crawling north. Everyone on it seemed to want a different stop, causing it to move in spurts with constant interruptions. Amelia sat through it all until her stop. The route from it to Malcolm's house was familiar, from their Rebel Cause meetings, so she let her mind wander to what Malcolm might think as her feet carried her and her heart pounded.

Malcolm was exiting his front door when Amelia stepped onto his street. His hair was glinting, and his skin was glowing in the morning sun, making him look like polished gold. Amelia ran. She couldn't let him get in his car and drive away without seeing her.

"Malcolm!"

He raised his face and smiled. "I was just going to go see you."

Amelia slowed her pace to a walk as she reached his driveway and clasped his hands when she reached him. Butterflies were doing flips in her stomach. "I guess I got my letter first. I've missed you."

Malcolm titled his head down, resting his forehead on hers, holding tight to her hands. His eyes were shining and bright, like glittering emeralds. "This is real, isn't it? We didn't get rejections?"

"It's real." Amelia released one of his hands to reach into her bag and produce her documents. "We're getting married."

Malcolm sucked in his breath, wrapped Amelia in his arms and lifted her off the ground. He kissed her, their lips coming together like desperate magnets. "I love you," he said when he set her down again. "And it's been torture not being able to see you."

Amelia had felt the same, but that torture and despair were a distant memory as she kissed him on his driveway in sight of his parents and neighbours. There was no one who could stop them now. "I love you too."

The Epilogue

Four years later

Amelia reclined on the pillows of her plush bed. She turned her head to the right so she could see Malcolm, his face relaxed in sleep and his hair mussed. That was a rarity these days with a toddler in the room down the hall.

She'd wanted to keep working, but the exertion was too much for her. Malcolm had hired a house cleaner and a chef to come daily while Amelia was pregnant. The house cleaner now came twice a week and the chef only on weekdays at lunch. Malcolm did the laundry, cooked suppers and breakfasts and did most of the grocery shopping, with Amelia pitching in when she felt up to it. That was the compromise she had agreed to. She wasn't helpless, just her pregnancy had zapped her energy, and now she had a rambunctious toddler. Soon Amelia would do her part of the housework, and they could get rid of the house cleaner. In the meantime, it was nice having others to rely on.

Malcolm yawned and stretched his arms over his head. He gave Amelia a sleepy grin, and she propped herself up to kiss him.

"Good morning," she said.

"Good morning to you too," he said.

It was a weekend, and Malcolm didn't need to go into class or his office. He spent his weekday mornings taking university classes and his afternoons working a desk job for a business in their Quarter.

Amelia had finished her last two years of high school and was doing correspondence classes to get a university diploma as she hadn't had the prerequisites to get a full degree. Another reason she liked having a house cleaner and chef was without them there would be no time or energy for her classes. As it was, she did most of her schoolwork while her daughter napped.

"What time are we meeting Ethan and Kelsie?" Malcolm asked as he sat up and smoothed his hair.

Amelia watched him. She thought he was adorable when rumpled from sleep, and their daughter shared his colouring. "Noon."

Malcolm glanced at the clock. "You should've woken me up."

Amelia flung the covers off and got out of bed. "You looked peaceful; I didn't want to."

Malcolm got to his feet, pulled his pajama top off and dropped it into their laundry hamper, letting the morning light shine on his abdomen, which sped up Amelia's heart rate.

"I'll get breakfast," Amelia said. To distract herself from the urge to pull Malcolm back to bed, she stripped off her pajamas, donned a day dress and brushed her hair. An afternoon in the park with Ethan and Kelsie was too casual for her to bother wearing makeup, so she left her face bare. And today was a good day for her in terms of energy. Their daughter had slept through the night, and Amelia felt rested.

"Okay," Malcolm said, having put on his own outfit. He knew not to deter her from doing what she could.

Amelia exited the bedroom and went into their child's room. In the crib, wearing pink and white onesie pajamas, hugging a soft doll, her daughter opened her eyes.

"Mama?"

Amelia went over and lifted her little girl up. "Good morning, sweetie. Are you hungry?"

Her daughter bobbed her blonde head and wrapped her little arms around Amelia's neck. "Hungee."

"Good," Amelia said. "Let's find Daddy so he can get you dressed while Mommy makes breakfast."

"Otay."

Amelia carted her daughter into the hallway and transferred her to Malcolm's arms. She kissed her little girl's forehead and went down into the kitchen. It was much bigger and newer than the one in her parents' apartment. Amelia and Malcolm had taken months to decorate it and set everything up after they'd moved in.

Amelia knew it intimately now and pulled out mixing bowls and frying pans from their places. She mixed the batter and ladled it into a greased pan. Her daughter loved banana pancakes with chocolate pieces sprinkled in, while Amelia and Malcolm ate them without.

She made her daughter's last and was plating them when Malcolm came down the stairs carrying their kid dressed in a pair of blue overalls with a dove grey t-shirt underneath. He'd put her hair into two pigtails, a style that had taken him months to master with no help from the wiggling toddler. He placed her in her highchair, fastened her bib, and she swung her dangling feet.

Malcolm set an envelope at Amelia's table place. "This was by the door," he said with a knowing look.

Amelia grabbed it and slid it into her pocket. If it was what she thought, she didn't need or want to read it in front of their toddler. "Thanks. I'll open it later."

Malcolm nodded as he took his seat and tucked into the pancakes. Breakfast went the way it normally did with her little girl ending up with a messy face and sticky hands. She was great at holding a fork yet awful at using it to get food into her mouth.

Once Amelia and Malcolm washed her face and hands and put shoes on her feet, they grabbed the diaper bag and fastened her into her car seat. Amelia had learned how to drive and had her own car, and toddler car seat. This time they rode in Malcolm's.

Amelia watched their neighbourhood pass by as Malcolm drove to the park. It was a longer trip for Kelsie and Ethan on the bus, but it was their turn to travel farther. Next month, Malcolm and Amelia would drive into Kelsie and Ethan's Apartment District and go to a small café where both kids, Malcolm and Amelia's daughter as well as Ethan and Kelsie's son, would charm the staff.

When they got to the parking lot, Malcolm got their kid, while Amelia unloaded the stroller. The park was busier than it had been when Malcolm had proposed. Couples were strolling along, and some had a kid running along the paths and through the grass. Other people sat on benches. Amelia walked past them all to the grassy clearing where Ethan and Kelsie were sitting on a blanket next to their two-year-old son with Kelsie's curly hair and Ethan's eyes.

Kelsie and Ethan got up, leaving their son licking sandwich crumbs off his fingers. "Hi!" Kelsie said as she approached Amelia and gave a wave. "We got here a little early. Max decided to cooperate with putting his shoes on when he found out we were coming here. He usually fights it."

Kelsie and Ethan were the first of the friend group to have a baby, and everyone had cooed over Max when he was born. Amelia and Malcolm's daughter had come a little over a year later and, once Amelia hadn't felt exhausted every second and her daughter had started crawling, they'd set up a monthly play date.

"We aren't at the terrible twos stage yet," Amelia said as Malcolm set their daughter on the blanket next to Max and sat beside her. "I fear it might be worse for us if the letter I got this morning says what we're hoping for."

Kelsie placed her hand on Amelia's arm. "You haven't read it?"

"It didn't seem appropriate to read at breakfast. Max distracts her enough that I think I can read it here." She also counted on Kelsie' and Ethan's support in case the letter gave unwanted news.

Amelia went with Kelsie to join their husbands on the blanket. The kids were up and toddling through the grass, her daughter trailing Max. The sight brought joy to Amelia. She hoped her daughter would always have friends to lean on, whether they included Max or not. She leaned into Malcolm's side, his arm around her torso.

Amelia tore open her letter and unfolded it in sight of Malcolm. When their daughter turned one, Amelia and Malcolm had gotten a second child permit, which was no secret to their friends. She had worried her friends would've been upset as they couldn't afford such a permit themselves, but they'd been supportive, even Dina and Jack who so far remained childless.

Her hands shook as she held the letter and scanned it. Malcolm must've been calmer than her, as she was still struggling to focus on the words when she caught him smiling at her. "Are you ready for this?"

Amelia teared up when she spotted the line on the letter displaying her pregnancy test result as positive. She was going to have another baby. "Yes, I think so."

"Congrats, you two," Ethan said.

Kelsie bobbed her head. "The kid's going to be lucky. You make great parents."

Amelia and Malcolm thanked their friends. Amelia turned to watch her little girl, running on her short legs after Max. Amelia and Malcolm had to find a way to break the news that she would soon be a big sister. Would a toddler understand?

When the kids tired out, Malcolm and Ethan scooped them up and carried them back. Amelia got the stroller ready, and her daughter fell asleep as soon as Malcolm settled her in it. Amelia and Malcolm said goodbye to Kelsie and Ethan and wheeled their kid back to the car.

"Do you think she'll like having a sibling?" Amelia asked when they were in the car and on their way home.

"I don't know," Malcolm said. "I hope so."

Amelia did too. She wanted her family to be happy and feel loved. Later, after her daughter woke from her nap, Amelia would explain the change that was coming. For now, she rested her hand on her stomach and let herself relish in the joy this news brought. She and Malcolm had no personal experience with siblings, but, like everything, they would figure it out together.

Coming soon: a short story collection in the POVs of supporting characters from The Liberator, The Vanquisher and Causes and Courtships.

Acknowledgements

Thank you to:

My friends Ana Harris and Steven Isaacs. Your continued support and friendship are priceless.

My dog Hunter. You brighten my days with your adorable face and unconditional love.

Gus, my special bunny, who I'll love and miss always. You were the greatest, sweetest, most gentle and easy-going bunny I could've asked for.

Lena Yang, my cover designer. As always, you did a fantastic job on the cover.

And you, the reader, for taking a chance on my work. You give me a reason to keep publishing.